DESCENDING
THIRDS

A Novel

By
NICOLE CONN

ISBN: 978-1-970157-70-3

Story Merchant Books
400 S. Burnside Avenue #11B
Los Angeles, CA 90036
www.storymerchantbooks.com

This is a work of fiction. Names, characters, businesses, places, events and
incidents are either the products of the author's imagination or used in
a fictitious manner. Any resemblance to actual persons, living or dead,
or actual events is purely coincidental.

Front Cover Design By: Nadia Afzal
Book Interior and E-book Design by Amit Dey (amitdey2528@gmail.com)

*For Mommo, who gave me the gift
of classical music,
For Gabrielle, whose birth
sparked the muse
For Nicholas, whose passion for
classical music inspires me every day.*

"Music is the art to which all other arts aspire"

Walter Pater—19th Century essayist

ALEXANDRA – 1965

*P*laying piano is a dangerous life.

Alexandra knew this truth as intimately as she knew herself. As she gazed out the wintry glass of the airplane window on her way to Portland, Oregon, Arthur Rubenstein echoed in her mind: *It must be lived dangerously. Take chances, take what comes… Plunge, give yourself entirely to your art and to your audiences… and if you don't lose five pounds and ten drops of blood, you haven't played a concert.*

The irony wasn't lost on her. Here she was, flying towards the most pivotal moment of her career—the International Ketterling Competition—feeling as though she had far more to lose than blood or weight. Her entire future hung in the balance, suspended in the air, like this plane, ready to soar or plummet based on the whims of a few discerning judges.

Two months ago, when the telegram arrived, she paced the grand entrance of her family's impeccable Queen Anne Colonial. Her lean, elegant fingers had trembled so perversely the missive slipped to the floor. Slowly she bent to her knees. It took every bit of will for her to focus on the crisp Western Union CAPS: Alexandra Von Triessen had, indeed, been selected as one of the top forty contestants to compete in the most coveted aspiration of every classical pianist: the International Ketterling Competition.

How could she know it would become her life's defining moment?

Had she a crystal ball she might have saved them all from needless suffering. But on that extraordinary spring day, of her twenty-fifth year, as Paul McCartney's voice lingered over *Yesterday* from the radio,

1

Alexandra twirled her lush French braid in exaltation. She allowed herself to feel the sheer triumph of making the cut, followed by a satisfied gloating at telling Claire.

Claire, her mother, was a pragmatist from a long line of pragmatists and would be certain to point out that while Alexandra may have made the first round of this internationally prestigious competition, "let's have no illusions of you winning. What we need for you to do is place in the top three." Claire was always at the ready to bring Alexandra back down to a beleaguered earth.

Peering into the blameless sky she contemplated human limitation, perfection, and the expectation that you couldn't allow the former to catch you for a moment as you endlessly chased the latter. Running in circles. Always ending up with yourself. She wished she could be more like others who seemed so intrepid, thriving off their opposition, confident their nerves wouldn't best them, but she just wasn't a natural competitor. In fact, it was her Achilles heel. In competition, you were relentlessly put into situations created to uncover every shred of flawed humanity because, after all, the jurors were there simply to find fault.

Did you have what it took to tour? Could you speak intelligently for interviews? Endure the stress of travel, learn to play with different orchestras, temperamental conductors, last minute changes? Alexandra spent most of her time worrying about all the things that could go wrong, instead of just concentrating on the music. Because a million little snags could kill a good performance: sweaty fingers slipping at the keys, the laggard action in the battered, over-used pianos at these contests, jurists interrupting in the middle of play, demanding this piece, now that, and the worst of all horrors, a blackout.

Who would think, upon seeing these mild-mannered artists who appeared timid and distracted, who smoked too many cigarettes and drank gallons of coffee, also possessed an all-consuming desire to win? It was the bane of her mother's existence that Alexandra was so ill-suited for battle. All Alexandra cared about was performing a piece in a way that mirrored her soul, where every note flowed effortlessly, and the world faded away, leaving only the music pulsing within her and her within it. When she reached that pinnacle, only then did the warrior inside her awaken.

The past few years, she had barely survived the flurried circuit of competitions and, in doing so, had learned what almost stopped her from playing altogether. The world of music, and singularly classical music, was as political and distasteful, as the plunging of daggers into the backs of colleagues in chrome-colored boardrooms. It was as violent, as physically demanding, as any athletic challenge, kill-or-be-killed sudden death match.

With musicians, competition merely sounded prettier.

Alexandra arrived mid-afternoon to a perpetually grey Oregon day and hailed a cab in the drenching rain. As she made her way to Lewis and Clark, nestled in the lush and verdant acreage not far from the heart of the city, she only wished the weather wasn't so bleak. She knew from acquaintances who attended the bellwether college that the climate was something you simply tolerated to study at the prominent institution. It certainly wasn't Juilliard but its reputation as one of the serious schools for music in the Northwest was impeccable.

The rain stopped just as she arrived on campus. She filled her lungs with the clear air and walked through the manicured grounds to the front office. She noted other contestants, some vaguely familiar, while the others were clearly students native to this campus—earthy hippie jangles, frizzy hair, and heavy wools in shades of blue, purple, and lavender. Was she completely out of place with her latest Jean Louis light blue tailored-jacket and a knee-length skirt? She pursed her lips into a superior smirk, not unlike Claire, and stopped in her tracks.

She whisked her braid aside, flinging thoughts of her mother behind her as she waited for the people milling in front of her to disperse, delayed by a man who was flirting with the pretty young volunteer trying to keep order at the Check In tables.

Ah, yes, that deep espresso accent belonged to Russo Gastino. Alexandra had competed and flirted with the infamous Italian playboy at the Leeds Competition several months back, where she had suffered a fatal memory lapse. She had turned to the judges and shrugged helplessly, as if she'd had a lobotomy right in the middle of her performance. Confusion was soon overtaken by paralysis. She shivered as much from the memory as from the nippy damp air. Draping the silk scarf about her shoulders she realized he had spotted her.

"*Bellissima*," Russo beckoned with his glamorous accent, which Alexandra knew he thickened like sweet cream at every opportunity. She smiled primly as he air-kissed both cheeks, then stood back sizing her up and down. "You need to take," he teased, "a little nap, no, *bella*?"

Alexandra cleared her throat, trying to sever nerves from her response. "Yes. Just one of those days, I guess."

"*Per niente.* Don't let it worry your pretty, little head." Russo, ever the gentleman, offered with condescending grace. "It cannot happen twice in a row."

How thoughtful of him.

When they called her name she registered, received her informational packet, and directions to a small single room in the east dorm. She was informed that the opening reception was to begin at the Rose Garden at six sharp. Nodding, she made a hasty retreat from the growing crowd, the buzzing energy, the intensity of group neurosis that had only just begun.

Her room was a dingy cubicle reminiscent of her old tiny Academy dormer. She dumped her suitcases crammed with sheet music just inside the door, then flopped onto the rickety single bed and let out a long sigh she had been holding since she had first stepped onto the plane at JFK.

Her body felt like a dead weight free-floating in anxiety. *Just make it through the first week.* She would be happy with that

"Competition is not for the faint of heart," Alexandra's mother, Claire von Triessen, proclaimed when Alexandra shared the telegram. A blue blood from the English side of her DNA, she had once been a strikingly handsome woman, but over the years, Claire's delicate features had morphed into brittle, icy lines. She raised a skeptical eyebrow, even though it was clear that she was quite pleased.

"I suggest you call your teachers and get started. We both know you've gotten quite rusty," Claire said with a bemused smirk of her trademark Revlon *Blazing Roses* lipstick.

Alexandra had been one of a handful of the few young women in her class at the Royal Academy in London. The cockier her male counterparts became, the more Alexandra withdrew into nerve-vetting sabotage, frequently mistaken as Kim Novak aloofness. While Claire had driven Alexandra to this very pinnacle, Alexandra knew her mother didn't possess more than a shred of faith in her daughter's talents. Did Alexandra herself *really* believe she had the talent to make it to the finals? No. But it didn't mean she wouldn't put every shred of her heart and soul into the attempt. Not for her, but as an homage to this art that fed her like nothing else.

But let's be clear. Winning the Ketterling *made* you, allowing a musician to leap over years of angst and *might-have-beens.* The winner garnered a healthy check, and two fully managed seasons crammed with 250 concert bookings while playing with the finest orchestras around the world, all buoyed by the kind of press that created minor sensations. To win, to be handed the Gold Cup by Leonard Bernstein in a sleek James Bond suit and have the world see you in shimmery black and white on Zeniths everywhere around the world—it was the ultimate fantasy of every young pianist.

"Good afternoon, dear colleagues! Welcome to the Ketterling!"

Ketterling was even taller than she had imagined, his slender build only accentuated by his freakish height. For several decades now, Georg Ketterling was at the top of the most gifted and talented artists in her small universe, achieving world-wide fame by winning almost every competition from 1943 through 1952. Seeing him perform on TV was one thing, but to meet him was a lifetime's dream. He was considered an anomaly in the world of music—kind, gentle, and warm, especially to the women in this male-dominated milieu. As he put up his long arms the crowd stilled.

"I'm sure you're all as happy as you are terrified to be here." Ketterling grinned knowingly. "While you are the best and the brightest, this competition is here to weed out the exceptional from the merely talented, the genius from the simply great."

The 1965 Ketterling competition, was held over a nail-biting, three-week period, featuring the most gifted and talented pianists of its day. Unlike many international musical contests, the International Ketterling was held but once every four years, a schedule that upped the ante, the risks, and the devastation. Judges traveled from Moscow to Milan, from Portland to St. Petersburg attending concerts, music academies, and recitals, both the highly touted and the eccentrically obscure, to handpick these distinctly special contestants. From rigid structuralists to the latest in Avant Garde performers, pianists were put under glass, scrutinized and analyzed, until performances became nothing but numbers on a grid, sublime compositions a language of technique and timing. These strict jurists held the careers and fortunes of the contestants in limbo until the announcement of forty placements was posted by international wire.

This was the part of Alexandra's life she detested, the necessary evil. Why couldn't it just be about music? *Why all the need for stacking one up against the other* she had asked Claire one day, early in her journey.

"You're so hopelessly naïve when it comes to the world of music, Alexandra."

Naïve? Too idealistic? Yes, perhaps she had been, in the beginning. Now, she accepted the grimy underside of this business. To do what she loved, she had to embrace what she detested.

"Right. We don't know one another yet," Ketterling declared. "But when we move into the next week, and the week after, each of you will play your heart and souls out and then, we will all become the most intimate of friends."

Everyone glanced around, sizing up their competition, but with a gentle understanding that they would, indeed, come to know one another more deeply than many of their friends, or even family.

"Don't be afraid of the drive to achieve. Art. Commerce." Ketterling put up his hands as if weighing the scales, the words resonating deeply for Alexandra as this dichotomy was her greatest struggle. "These are inextricably wed, however painful that may be." He flashed his effervescent smile.

"Please, people, if you learn anything at all here: Don't be a cliché stuck in that early career conundrum: How can one possibly maintain their artistic integrity while surviving this hellish business? This is real life, and you choose your attitude toward it."

"Now then." A representative from Lewis & Clark stepped forward, holding up a replica of the coveted golden trophy. Inside the prize cup, folded slips of paper lay waiting. With a composed air, Ketterling closed his eyes and extended his slender hand, fingers delicately swirling through the chits before plucking one from the bunch. "Uri Sokolov. You will have the honor of performing first!"

Ketterling continued to read out the names of the attendees, handing them a piece of paper with the order of their play when they came forward.

Alexandra glanced around to see the reactions from the other pianists. Was she hiding her anxiety as well as they seemed to be hiding theirs? Scrutinizing her competition, she was suddenly aware that she was also being observed by the intensely unwavering eyes of a man standing straight across from her.

He stood beneath the fluttering "Welcome to the International Ketterling Competition" banner, the northwest winds tussling his thick unruly hair. She quickly averted her glance, but when she looked up again, his eyes were still directly linked to her own. He smiled, which drew her eyes to his lips... full. Ripe.

She hadn't caught his name as he sauntered over to choose his placement. "Thirteen!" he said and bowed humorously. Incandescent blue eyes peered into her own as he refolded his paper and returned to his place under the sign.

Alexandra was one of the last names called. She walked up and gingerly pulled her assignment. Twenty-two. A deep sigh of relief. Right in the middle. If you had the misfortune of being at the front you set the standard. By the end, the judges were tired and had already picked their favorite. It was a perfect placement. When she looked up, there he was again, making his way toward her.

"Alexandra!!"

The voice came from behind her. Startled, she turned and there, to her great delight was Chandra.

Chandra Zhang had been a student at the Scottish branch of the Royal Academy and first met Alexandra during a chamber contest hosted by the Academy in London. When they discovered they were among the few Americans in Europe and part of the rare handful of women in their field, they eagerly sought out every bit of information about each other through the grapevine.

They became instant friends, drawn together not only as a defense against the tight-knit British nationalism but bound by their exotic reputations, as distinctly different as two women could be. They made a stunning and intriguing duet; Chandra's petite and wiry body belied the cliché of a shrinking Asian lily. Tough, dedicated, and driven, she matched swaggering dilettantes with her cynical barbs and was as fond of outperforming contestants as she was drinking them under the table.

With her aloof single-mindedness and classical beauty, Alexandra dashed about with her omnipresent moat of sheet music. She became known as the "untouchable." Chandra cut through Alexandra's defenses within moments of meeting her and discovered that Alexandra was almost pathologically shy. So, it became Chandra's *raison d'être* to bring Alexandra out of her shell, and soon after the chamber contests, she transferred from Glasgow to join Alexandra at the London Academy. They became inseparable and were at one time even rumored to be lovers.

Their theme song became "Night & Day." Alexandra was always clad in conservative Christian Dior, Doris Day skirts, her hair meticulously French braided or tucked into gentle chignons, while Chandra was the first of a new breed; a rabid feminist involved with one of the countless subversive underground movements, sporting ever more wildly bohemian "get ups." She was a kooky and outlandish Shirley MacLaine to Alexandra's Grace Kelly cool, her side of their room plastered with Dean Martin, James Dean, and Elvis Presley, Alexandra's with tasteful prints of Monet, Cassatt, and Renoir.

Chandra was a brilliant technician and won many of the Technical Merit Cups from the conservatory. Alexandra stood in awe of Chandra's structure, timing, and sequence, just as Chandra envied Alexandra's innate ability to connect with the music on an emotional level, so complex and intense at times it scared Chandra. They paired themselves in duets whenever they could to complement each other's shortcomings.

With Chandra, Alexandra finally found someone she could be completely and splendidly foolish with. Having both been tethered to the hemorrhaging umbilical cord of their restrained and over-controlling parents—in Alexandra's case her mother and Chandra's her father—they became with each other what they had never been allowed to be before: Children. Wednesday afternoons after their Baroque History class, they'd play darts in their favorite pub and get snookered on "black beer," giggling and gossiping, releasing their tensions to the smoke-filled tavern for the afternoon.

On weekends they adventured to increasingly more obscure and fascinating haunts in the city. There was only one criterion: these little treasures—the hidden London that locals knew and kept securely away from classless tourists—could have nothing to do with music.

Sunday afternoons they gorged themselves on truly terrible American cinema: *The Creature from the Black Lagoon, Plan 9 From Outer Space,* and the absurdly bad Hitchcock film, *Stage Fright.* The cheesier the better, howling at the ludicrous plots. Governed by schedule, practice, and discipline, they dedicated themselves to hedonistic anarchy in their free time, which always ended in obscene fits of laughter. And late at night, they would lie awake snuggled safely in their flower-speckled cotton gowns, their pale dark whispers fading into dreams for tomorrow.

"I am naturally promiscuous," Chandra would often proclaim, "as an antidote to becoming my parents."

"You? Promiscuous?" Alexandra retorted.

"Shagging—what a delicious term—is the only way I can get through this place," Chandra said as she painted her toenails, preparing for one of her ceaselessly anonymous dates. Alexandra remained virginally pure. Not because she wanted to be, but because she could find no one with whom *shagging* seemed the least bit appealing.

"You really need to loosen the chastity belt." Chandra encouraged Alexandra without mercy to pursue Giles Pemberton. "He's a fading Brit—think of it as your patriotic duty to restore him to his legendary notoriety."

Giles Pemberton, their aging and openly alcoholic professor of theory, was indeed a renowned womanizer whose pursuits were the target of endless gossip.

"It's like shagging Richard Burton, Albert Finney, and Alan Bates all rolled up into one sumptuous package!" Chandra exclaimed.

Alexandra would fend off Chandra's ridiculously unsubtle machinations, but it only made her more persistent.

"Look. All you do is go in on Sunday afternoon, he's always there, half in his cups. Child's play." Chandra puffed her lips into a churlish grin, then, walking up to Alexandra and staring at her as they both looked in the mirror, she added, "I mean can you blame him? Have you seen his hideous wife?"

"Who made him marry her?"

Chandra snorted, rifling through Alexandra's wardrobe. "Demure is the key. That slinky cocktail dress you wore to the last recital—"

"Right, I just happen to be all gussied up at three in the afternoon?"

"You let him know you've got a date, silly. That's the bait. His challenge is to get you to break it. 'Sir Pemberton,'" Chandra said, affecting a sultry upper-class English accent. "'Look, old man, I'm having a bit of a spot with this theory thing. Pray, dear disheveled, slack-jawed but virile professor, fancy helping a lass out?'" Chandra's hands circled her waist, then snaked up over her chest and slithered through her hair.

"Yes, that would be demure alright," Alexandra mocked.

Chandra put out her hands as if she were the very definition.

"And by the way, was that supposed to be an English accent? Sounds like Jane Wyman in *Stage Fright*, trying even harder than usual."

"Ohhh, lousy viscous!" Chandra considered enthusiastically. "Yeah, I like that on you."

"Right, then, shall we get on with it?" Giles asked her after several shots of whiskey.

Alexandra stood in his office, not in her black gown of seduction, but in a soft cashmere sweater and her sexiest pencil skirt. They walked to his apartment where he undressed and stood expectantly as if he were used to being a pound of flesh, and later smirked at her empty victory with an expression on his face that said, *now, did you really expect anything different?*

Seducing him hadn't been in the least difficult, and unlike anything she had ever read in books or seen in the movies—no echoing violins, no poetic wooing. It certainly didn't include laying numbly on his sofa, its nubby coarse wool gouging couch burns into her back.

"How was it?" Chandra waited with high expectations.

"Painful. Painful in every way."

"I hear you, but…" Chandra spoke encouragingly, "you can educate almost any man that's got half a brain. Don't ever let them think you're enjoying it too much, though—their heads swell as fast as their dicks." Alexandra had stopped blushing at Chandra's crude delivery. She found it quite refreshing. But she also suspected that Chandra was suspect of every man because of her father.

Sunday after Sunday she would return. They rarely talked. He never asked her one personal question. Giles seemed distantly aware that Alexandra was beneath him as he pummeled forcefully against the backdrop of wet afternoons that turned into chilly evenings. As she walked back to the dorm, she would always promise herself it was the last time. For about a semester, Alexandra desperately tried to convince herself that she was in love with Giles, until Chandra pointed out he was, "a not-the-least-bit subtle Freudian attempt to get back at your mother." She had pushed Alexandra to sleep with him, but she'd never anticipated it being more than a one-time thing.

It was true. Giles was the Anti-Claire. He was everything her mother wasn't, with her tidied expectations and serene distaste for the vulgar. And while that was almost enough of a payoff, she wondered at her very lack of feeling for Giles. Perhaps she *was* cold and frigid. Yet another reason to only rely on her music, not humans.

"Let it down, will you?" Giles tugged at Alexandra's hair one late afternoon. She maneuvered herself unsteadily off the sofa, stood up, and began to rebutton her blouse.

"You're like something you pick up at a rare market—a fragile trinket." He lit his pipe, took a puff, and spoke as he exhaled. "That needs to be stuck behind a glass cabinet to admire from a safe distance."

"Do you always talk like you're writing a bad play?"

He picked at a fleck of tobacco on his lip, took another puff. "Yes… you might imagine what it feels like to touch, but never quite get to enjoy the experience."

She had spent the last hour listening to this rubbish. "You know nothing about me."

"I suppose I don't." He shrugged. "But since you haven't given me the vaguest idea that a human heart exists beneath your scrumptious tits—"

She finished dressing and flexed her shoulders to release the tension in her neck. She saw his eyes follow the curve of her jaw and her skin prickled in irritation.

"Have I been a bit of sop for you then?" Giles asked as he poured himself another scotch with his pants still undone. He swallowed his drink and stated with gentle exasperation: "See what all this free love and women's liberation gets you?"

"I haven't been burning *my* bras."

"No matter. Just look at it this way: I'm the greatest object lesson in the obviously predictable you'll probably ever know—so learn from it, darling."

She ended it with Giles that day. But the exchange clung to her for weeks. What did he mean? How was she supposed to take those words? But before she knew it summer was around the corner, and she would be free. Sort of. Freedom meant returning to her mother.

Leaving school also meant leaving Chandra. They kept in fierce contact through the summers, writing voluminous letters, which inevitably dwindled to the occasional article paper-clipped to a buck slip: "Love you — miss you! When can we ever get together?" Alexandra had all but lost touch after Chandra graduated a year before her.

When Chandra spotted Alexandra across the crowded campus of Lewis and Clark, she ran to her as if to her savior. "Oh, God, am I glad to see you." She flung her arms around Alexandra like one would a life preserver.

Alexandra embraced her friend, thrilled that Chandra was there, excited by the opportunity for them both. When they finally calmed down from the surprise, she noted Chandra's jittery hypertension. "Hey, relax, Chandra. Look we made the last forty."

"Yes. I know. My father's carefully choosing my weapons as we speak." She grinned, but there was no humor in it.

Alexandra squeezed Chandra's hand in understanding. Far too many nights, she'd heard the litany of terror Chandra suffered at the hands of her father. Chandra performed the part of the hawkish Mr. Zhang as a comedy routine at first, but as their friendship had grown more serious, Chandra's tales exposed the raw pain and terror her father imposed upon her: his insane extremism as he would bark out timing in his broken English in the cramped apartment above her father's fish market in New York's China Town. The fumes from the city heat mingling with the pungent brine wound its way to her senses, making Chandra dizzy and nauseous. He ordered her to play again and again, keeping her up so late one night to perfect a final movement that she literally fainted from exhaustion before her performance. He repeatedly thwacked her knuckles with a ruler, leaving behind feather-wisp scars, and when she came in second at a contest, she should have easily won he screamed. "Second place – No! No good for Zhang. Second not what is desire. First Place! I expect nothing less."

"I don't think I've ever seen my father smile. Ever! Even when I've *won* recitals." Chandra had shared with Alexandra after they had gotten stoned with some of the other students and talked late into the night. "Never the slightest acknowledgement of anything I've accomplished. Music holds no joy for him, it's simply a means to an end…a way to master Western success by utilizing Eastern fortitude and discipline." Alexandra had crawled into her friend's bed that night and held her close until she fell asleep.

Alexandra pushed aside the old memories. "Oh, Chandra… does he really have to be here?"

"Naturally, to poison you all of course." Chandra's laugh was forced.

Alexandra embraced her friend again, thrilled that she wasn't alone.

"Come along *ol' mate*. I think a few stiff ones are in order!"

Chandra looped her arm into Alexandra's and began to lead her down one of the shrub-lined paths. As she followed, Alexandra turned around one last time and surreptitiously looked around for the man with the dark hair, but he had vanished.

Each day the contestants were divided into various groups to play either assigned pieces from the repertoire, introduced to new compositions, or to withstand a series of playoffs, while others booked in practice time. After the first three days, the contestants performed a chamber recital with the famed Salieri Quartet from France, emphasizing the importance of classical music as a team sport, even while they were competing with one another.

Playing with these talented musicians after just two hours of rehearsal felt like a recipe for failure, especially when one was accustomed to spending weeks or even months perfecting a piece with an ensemble. Like the Olympics, the four-year time span created an atmosphere of crushing anxiety to be absolutely perfect, only better than absolutely perfect!

At the end of each day, Alexandra and Chandra rushed to meet one another at a little hole-in-the-wall brewery right off the Lewis & Clark campus. Unwinding, they regaled one another with their misadventures of the day and habitually reassessed the other contestants, most of whom they'd done battle with at the European competitions, and others whom they knew by reputation or rumor mill.

"God we've only been here five days and it's a been a millennium." Chandra moaned, then asked, "What do you think?"

"Oh, Lord, I don't know." Alexandra shook her head and focused on folding the napkin into ever smaller squares. "Just glad we made the first cut, I suppose."

Chandra absently tore at her beer label, rolling the soggy paper between her fingers. "Did you hear about Hampton? He apparently doubled his meds."

Alexandra nodded. She hadn't bought the story either. She had run into the lanky Californian, his pock-marked skin and waxy grey eyes darting as if he was pumped on amphetamines. "Your father may not have so many of us to 'off' at the end of the day."

"Straight up? This isn't the competition. The real thing starts after this circus is over. Did you hear the sigh of relief from Kirkov when they released him? Poor guy didn't even get to make it to the first cut."

After a stream of performances on demand, and rigorous drills through various judges, the first cut had reduced the field to twenty-five at the end of that day's concours. "I mean how did Kirkov even get here in the first place? He's such a troll."

"Chandra," Alexandra admonished. Peter Kirkov's nervous ticks were legendary, and he categorically belonged to the best heard-but-not-seen musicians.

"He's definitely a beneficiary of the screened auditions." Chandra sniffed.

"That was low, Chandra."

"Christ! I don't know why I get like this." But they both did. Her father. This contest. The battle of nerves simply brought out the less appealing side of them all.

"Come on! You really think once a troll like Kirkov slips past those nose-in-the-air screeners they're going to choose someone as," she lowered her voice, "utterly *fugly* as Peter to bring in those phenomenal ticket sales?"

"Of course not. But it does level the playing field."

"No. You know what levels the playing field? A bad fish platter. A crappy night's sleep. Coming down with the flu. Or all the above? You can play scales until the cows come home, churn out Chopin Etudes all your damn life. But the moment you go out to perform in competition, you have no idea what will contribute to that specific performance. Is it an exalted culmination of all the blood, sweat, and tears, thousands of hours of practice and preparation? Or that you just got the curse and brain fog pushes you ever so slightly off your game, just takes the edge off enough that you've lost your brilliance?"

Alexandra put her beer down. "You're right. I guess it all boils down to… Fate."

"Fate?"

"Honestly." Alexandra sighed and glanced around her. "I'm not altogether convinced fate, for all its bold promise, is in our best interest. Do we control it, or is it destiny's obligation to dangle before us situations where it's impossible to save us from our baser instincts?"

"Shit, Alex! That's too heavy for me to contemplate. But now that you mention it, have you really put this whole competition into any frame of reality? I mean, do I even want to win? Can you imagine, me traveling with my father all over the world, him living in my shadow for two years?

Chandra raised her Olympia beer bottle to a bartender, indicating another round, but Alexandra put up a hand, instead fished in her purse, and retrieved a pack of cigarettes.

"When did *you* take up smoking?" Chandra asked.

"If you can't beat 'em…" Alexandra indicated the room full of smoking pianists. She lifted her braid, shook it back, and lit her cigarette. "It does calm the nerves."

"Is Ketterling what you expected?"

Alexandra didn't answer. The man she had seen that first day, with that cock-sure grin and those full red lips, had strolled into the pub amongst a group of gangly introverts, misfit pianists, who flocked about him as he told an easy joke. They all laughed.

She leaned to Chandra. "Who is *he*?"

"You mean to tell me you haven't heard of Sebastian D'Antonio?" Chandra leaned close. "He makes Russo look like child's play. He's a comer. The ultimate charmer."

Yes. A Renaissance man, a romantic reborn, Alexandra mused. Much more on the order of a lady's man than the other uptight and eccentric musicians who awkwardly shuffled around, bereft of social graces. His panache seemed sorely out of place.

"Is he any good?" Alexandra asked. She now remembered off-handed references to his name.

"They say he's quite good." But Chandra's tone wasn't referring to his music. "He's sort of a Liszt meets Byron; don't you think?"

Alexandra grinned, a little more intrigued than she wanted to be.

"Very handsome. They say he plays like him, the virtuoso's virtuoso."

"Colossal flash, hmmm?" Alexandra knew the type, style over substance.

"And you know what else they say about Liszt." Chandra appraised Sebastian. "He was in constant heat for the spotlight."

"Yes, but is this, what was his name?"

"D'Antonio–"
"Is he, you know, a contender?"
"I guess we'll find out."

"It would be a mistake to think that the
practice of my art has become easy for me."

Wolfgang Amadeus Mozart

The first name called to walk up on stage was Chandra.

On day ten they announced the final cut. Only eight of the original forty musicians would compete over the last week in the final two parts of the competition. Chandra's father didn't blink, nor did he clap with the others. She was followed by two Russians, an Italian well known for his instruction at the Tchaikovsky Conservatory, Sebastian D'Antonio, the brilliant and favored Czech, Sokolov, and two unknowns. The last finalist was announced: Alexandra Von Triessen.

She barely felt her legs as she joined the rest of them. She had never expected to make it this far, but the moment she stepped on the stage the cold blast of challenge awakened her like nothing else! Alexandra's mouth went dry, her body tremored, her heart quaked in her chest. This *was* war.

Almost immediately she began to analyze the other accomplished musicians and finally view them as her opponents. She had survived enough contests to understand the competitive drive, but it was here, fighting for the grand Ketterling, that Alexandra finally understood the lust for combat. As they exited the stage that night, her eyes caught a stoic glimmer from the Italian, the superior arch of Sokolov's brow, and with each descending step, she walked with a new conviction. *Maybe... just maybe.*

The next morning, she woke to see an envelope had been slipped beneath her door. It was a message from Claire: "Surprised to hear of your latest accomplishment. If you think you can win, we can be there for the finale. We send our regards, Mother."

Surprised? Absolutely. Both were. But her mother, as always, couldn't restrain herself. Instead of simply offering congratulations, she couldn't resist the urge to interfere. Alexandra had been crystal clear: she didn't want her parents, especially Claire, anywhere near Oregon for the competition. Yet, the mere thought of her mother's disappointment—unable to claim the spotlight or bask in her daughter's achievements as if they were her own—ignited in Alexandra a sudden, fierce determination to prove her worth on her terms. She wanted to win, not just for herself, but to show her mother she didn't need her. So, she sent a simple response: "Thank you, Mother. I think it's best if we wait and see how I do."

Keeping Claire away was every bit as important as choosing the right piano.

Like a shot of Vodka, a dazzling clarity coursed its way through her mind and body as she tried the various pianos all propped on moving dollies upon the stage. The finalists had each been assigned an hour in which to make their choice in the empty theatre. She closed her eyes and began to consider them in earnest. Which weapon would best broker her claim to victory?

Alexandra wrestled obsessively over which concerto would showcase her strengths. Rachmaninoff's *Concerto No. 2 in C Minor* had been her first choice with its lyrical and melancholic passion but her mother's jeering glance during her last performance had shattered her confidence. Though she adored the piece, she knew it didn't highlight her technical prowess. Instead, she leaned toward Prokofiev's *Concerto No. 3 in C Major*—a demanding, quirky favorite that could compensate for her technical shortcomings if executed perfectly. She had practiced relentlessly, until the notes haunted her, and her fingers flew over the keys like a machine. But just that morning, Chandra informed her that Sokolov had also chosen Prokofiev's *Third*. How could she possibly outshine a man whose virtuosity was of Lisztian proportions? That left only Schumann's *Piano Concerto in A minor*—a rhapsodic, crowd-pleasing concerto that played to her best qualities. With Schumann, she was confident she could secure third place. Practical, just as Claire had taught her. But if competition weren't a factor, she knew exactly what her heart would choose: Rachmaninoff's *Second*.

As she obsessed compulsively over her options, she sat down, felt the cool white keys of the Steinway, savoring several minutes of the

Rachmaninoff, soon lost in the sweeping first movement. She made herself stop, walked to the next piano, and did the same, only this time attacked Schumann's opening. No. Action was too loose, a dangerous pitfall for which a pianist had to reconstruct fingering. The third, the action was too tight. It would exhaust her by the third movement, but at least she could rely on the keys. She began to feel like Goldilocks as she passed up the next piano.

"Oh, the agony of it all." A voice in the dark said, startling her.

"Pardon me?" Alexandra stared into the void.

"You seemed so certain of yourself on stage the other night." His voice was deep, sonorous. And then she saw him. Sebastian D'Antonio sat alone, beyond the tenth row of seats. "But now, you've gone from one piano to another ruminating over all the possible nuances, the distinctively different shadings each of them will offer."

Alexandra grinned. It was true.

"Just remember what Ketterling said." Sebastian smiled back. "Make sure you have 'total confidence in your instrument.'" Sebastian walked the length of the aisles toward the stage.

"I think I left total confidence somewhere over the Midwest." Alexandra felt a brief tremor through her stomach as he climbed the stairs onto the stage.

"Sebastian D'Antonio." Sebastian offered his hand. Instead of taking it she picked up her sheet music and went to the next piano.

"Sebastian with two A's. Just like—"

"Yes, I know who you are."

Alexandra sat at the next piano while Sebastian leaned against one opposite her. "What's wrong with this one?" He patted the open lid. "You have something against the benefactor's piano?"

"I'm sorry, Mr. D'Antonio, but I'd really like to concentrate here."

"It's okay. I already know which piano I'm using." His voice was alluringly egotistical.

"I suppose it's that one?" She indicated the sponsor's piano by which he was standing.

"Yes. I believe it's good form to win for the promoter."

"How politic of you." Alexandra dismissed him with a withering glance. She folded her sheet music, shoved it in her purse, and walked off stage. She signed the form with her choice of piano and faltered as she wrote down Schumann's *A Minor* as her concerto selection. She took the stairs at the back of the auditorium and exited outside.

Within minutes he was next to her, walking beside her in silence. She kept her head forward.

"I'm sorry. I guess I was a bit of a jerk back there."

"A certain possibility."

"Just sort of comes out of me when I'm around a gorgeous woman."

She turned to him then, noting his thick dark hair, rich voice, and ridiculously handsome features.

"Speaking of stunning views," he kept his eyes on her but referred to the plush tree-filled campus. "It's beautiful here, don't you think?"

"Yes," she mused. "A clever camouflage."

"Camouflage?"

"To what's really taking place. Mortal combat belies the serene setting."

"Someone has to win." Sebastian laughed, then pulled a cigarette from his shirt pocket and offered her one. "Please tell me you're not one of those who think these competitions kill the artist in us all."

"Let's call it a necessary evil."

"But an absolutely wonderful form of motivation."

"I don't know…This might just be a setup for the least confident to perish, leaving the golden ring for one of you *golden* boys."

"She stated with just a whisper of anxiety." He grinned as he lowered his voice.

"Can we drop this?"

"Sure." He lit his cigarette. "Don't worry. I won't tell anyone you chose the Steinway."

She assessed him. He was awfully handsome. "As did you."

He conceded with a flash of his perfect white teeth and a tilt of his head.

She stopped walking a moment and considered him. "I've seen you play three times now and I have a bit of advice if you're open to hearing it."

Sebastian raised his hands in a "by all means" gesture for her to continue.

"You're good."

He smiled. Flirtatiously.

"So do yourself a favor and stop being such a big shot." Her tone deflated his swagger. "Speed is only good if it can get you there in one piece. You rush ahead as if you can't wait to get off the stage. The Steinway will slow you down. Give you more control."

"Control… hmmm." He paused as if to consider. "Is control important for you then?"

"The lighter the touch," Alexandra began earnestly, then realized she had stepped right into it. She held up a hand. "Never mind."

"No, please do go on," he baited her, a glint of amusement in his eyes.

Alexandra shook her head, pursed her lips as if deep in thought. "You know what I love about musicians?"

He awaited eagerly.

"Their humility." She nimbly fished a cigarette from his pocket. "Which is only equaled by their insecurities."

She walked away, feeling his eyes follow her. She was thankful she'd managed to avoid him up to this point. She hated to admit that she wished she'd spent just a bit more time with him, now that the competition was ending. He was irritating, but oh so provocative.

But she had a fast and firm rule, no consorting with the enemy during competitions.

That night she lay on the bed, staring at the ceiling again, melding the crackling plaster into memories like floating clouds. She lit a cigarette, the glare of the match the only light in the room. The echo of her mother's voice stiffened her body as she thought back to the beginning; a childhood that had been painted by her mother, a canvas of stormy red battles, cool dark blues of restrained affection, and bleak grays of resignation.

She had spent her entire life observing this woman, yet Claire remained an enigma. What drove her mother, Alexandra would never understand. The only certainty was Claire's militant routine, executed with almost surgical precision: awake at five-thirty a.m., hair and makeup flawless, a thin slice of toast, black coffee, then the day's endless parade of shopping, phone calls, lunch engagements. By five-thirty p.m., it was time for the Manhattans, followed by dinner at seven sharp. On the rare evenings without a show, a gala, or some society event to attend, Claire would sit quietly, sipping a nightcap as she flipped through *Vanity Fair* or *Harper's*. When her husband was home—which wasn't often—a vague, detached goodnight would follow, as they retreated to separate bedrooms. A life so perfectly curated, yet so distant and cold.

Richard Von Triessen was born into one of New Rochelle's largest shipping dynasties. He spent most of his time away for work. His sheer lack of presence or curiosity about his wife and daughter was in direct opposition to Claire's incessant need to mold the universe to her will. How she ever came to be conceived was a mystery too horrifying for Alexandra to contemplate.

For as long as she could remember she felt the smallest infractions with the vibrational intensity of a tuning fork. She grew up constantly monitoring the tension in a room, the heat generated by her mother's undercurrent of bitter, passive-aggressive anger, wed to the oppression of Claire's endless drive. When Alexandra was punished or spoken to harshly, her heart would be crushed, desolate beyond proportion. Her hypersensitivity was a great trial for her parents. Presumably because they had never intended to have a child in the first place.

Perhaps as she lay in fetal limbo, she had absorbed this very lack of desire for her, tainted with a sense of inadequacy that would insinuate itself into the rest of her life. Richard and Claire had debated abortion. But, in the end, it was simply too distasteful to Claire who assumed the role of 'mommy' rigorously attacking it as she had all her social obligations—with vigor and competitive earnest—channeling all her energy into the world of childrearing its chief commodity, Alexandra's beauty and talent.

Whether or not Claire loved her daughter never really occurred to her. You were obligated to do what was right by your progeny; you taught them scrupulously, made sure they were armed with the necessary arsenal to succeed in whatever arena they pursued. Forget all the smarmy affection she saw with other mothers and their daughters. All the snuggling in the world wasn't going to achieve success. It was certainly a perk that Alexandra was bright and exceptionally beautiful. Claire was endlessly delighted when perfect strangers stopped her to comment on her daughter's thick auburn hair, high cheekbones, and elegant patrician features. Even at a young age people used the terms "stunning," "timeless beauty." Yes, Claire had decided, her daughter was somewhat of a *visual sensation*. Even if Alexandra was possibly *touched—something off*—with her extreme "spells."

Alexandra's emotionalism was something she simply had no control over. The prickling excitability shot up through her stomach, spread through her chest like brandy-coated warmth, and tingled down her arms to the tips of her fingers. She couldn't hold this nameless force within the confines of her skin—it demanded release. And so emitted from her throat a high-pitched keening, the release so sublime she felt compelled to shriek. The tension in the house always teetered between simmer and full boil, and when it became too much, Alexandra would throw her head back and let her voice surge forth, a wild and uninhibited bellow giving her sweet relief.

"I will not tolerate this excessive display of…of emotional epilepsy!" Her father's beet red face and narrow angry eyes were branded in Alexandra's head. "You best get this under control, Claire. This behavior will not be permitted!"

And then one morning as Alexandra began filtering the palpable tension between her mother and father she began humming. As it turned out,

Alexandra possessed perfect pitch. Claire was pleasantly surprised. She pulled out all her records, sat Alexandra on a hardback chair before the Magnavox stereo, and played Doris Day, The Andrew Sisters, her favorite Frank Sinatra. Claire's eyes brimmed with excitement as Alexandra mimicked each song right back at her. When Alexandra sang along with Shirley Bassey to "What Now My Love," matching the savvy inflection and mining the depths of the lyrics, it gave Claire chills. Clearly, Alexandra was fated for opera, and she, of course, would fill the role of diva backstage mother.

Claire promptly enrolled Alexandra in a private preparatory academy for girls, but at eight Alexandra suffered acute appendicitis. While she was intubated during emergency surgery, the hard plastic tube tore into the bands at her larynx. Long after she recovered, she still sang with passion, but the scarring forever strained her vocal cords, eclipsing any career she may have had. Without the release of singing Alexandra became depressed, and her father, worried she might revert to her previous behavior, returned home one day with a huge truck following his Cadillac.

And out rolled a glorious mahogany Steinway.

From the moment she saw the burnished majestic piano Alexandra thought it might be the single most beautiful thing in the world.

Claire was ecstatic. After directing the placement of their new Steinway piano for maximum visual impact, she breezed past her daughter Alexandra, who was sitting on the couch. In an uncharacteristically cheerful mood, Claire patted Alexandra's head before heading to a seldom-used closet. From it, she retrieved faded red John Thompson piano primers— first scripture and foundational texts for young music students nationwide. Without delay, Claire sat Alexandra at the piano bench and began teaching her the basics.

Alexandra wasn't as at ease with the piano as she had been with singing. Singing allowed her to simply open her heart and release whatever emotions were churning within, offering instant satisfaction. The piano, however, demanded more from her. Her slender but strong fingers lacked the instinctive grace, and every note required painstaking effort, as she labored to master the technical precision of scales. Yet, despite the struggle, she was utterly mesmerized by the piano; its full, deep and textured richness far outweighed her own voice. The moment she heard its tone, shape, and resonance, she fell in love.

Within weeks Claire enrolled Alexandra in a class with a neighborhood teacher who taught from her home and was reputed to bring out the best in troubled, but talented, students.

Mrs. Hoven was a small but fierce Hausfrau, who looked less like a piano teacher than a friendly German grandmother, who offered fresh stollen and hot cocoa first and asked questions later. She made Alexandra laugh with the funny pronunciations in her soft accent. But when they sat at the piano, Mrs. Hoven's thin lips tightened, her arched nostrils flared and the sounds that came from her Baldwin were commanding and formidable. Alexandra thought Mrs. Hoven was the most incredible human on the planet, infusing her with enthusiasm and curiosity to explore each new piece. She was the happiest she had ever been.

"I've entered her into a recital contest at the conservatory," Claire informed Mrs. Hoven one day after Alexandra's class.

"Oh, nein... she is not ready, Mrs. Von Triessen."

"Nonetheless, she'll get her first taste of stacking herself up against others, which, if I'm not mistaken makes all the difference between having a successful career." Claire sniffed and smiled beneficently. "Or being a teacher. Come along, Alexandra."

True to her word, Claire dragged a very anxious Alexandra to her first competition.

Age nine. Alexandra had been inordinately thirsty and to calm her nerves and deflect the grueling tedium, she hastily drank Dixie cup after Dixie cup of sugary grape Kool-Aid. Shifting uncomfortably on the hard folding chair, she watched the other children; nervous, unsteady waifs struggling to recall their notes. Their faces twisted into anxious frowns as they searched for their parents in the audience. Alexandra noticed the pleased glint of satisfaction in her mother's eyes, a flicker of pride each time another child stumbled.

Up last, Alexandra was given ample time to vacillate between wanting to throw up and a growing awareness of the gnawing pressure at her bladder. Three times she tried to whisper to her mother that she wasn't feeling well, but Claire shushed her, gently tapping Alexandra's knees to keep her from fidgeting.

When her name was called, Alexandra sat frozen on the spot.

"You're up, dear." Claire turned to her daughter.

Again, her name was called but Alexandra remained rooted to her chair.

"Don't let your nerves get to you. You're fine." Her mother looked annoyed rather than sympathetic. But Alexandra wouldn't budge. "You get up right this instant. You're embarrassing Mommy."

Still, Alexandra couldn't move.

"Alexandra!" Claire yanked her daughter off the chair, then gasped.

A wet puddle remained behind. Snickers floated around her followed by giggles and hushed tones of falsely sympathetic murmuring from the other mothers.

"Alexandra!" Her name was an epithet in her mother's mouth. "How could you?"

The disgust-laden accusation sliced through Alexandra's body, and in a primal instinct to save herself, she ran from the room, out of the school's theater, straight through a large clover field that bordered the neighboring woods until she ran out of breath and collapsed into a lump. Without fail, she would relive this horror-filled memory at the start of every competition.

A year into her lessons Alexandra arrived early at Mrs. Hoven's one day. As she slowly walked down the hall, the most intoxicating and captivating music caressed her impressionable ears. Upon entering the study, she saw the bird-like woman crunched over the keys, appearing every bit as if the piece was playing her.

"What is that?" Alexandra asked when she had finished.

"*Clair de Lune.*"

"It gave me shivers here," Alexandra said, pointing to the back of her neck.

"Ja, I git dem here." Mrs. Hoven patted her forearms. "Every time I play it."

In that instant, the true concept of desire crystallized within Alexandra. She craved this musical excellence and hungered to perform the melody, bending over the piano like her teacher, capturing the wild animal and breaking it, just as Mrs. Hoven had.

"When can I play like that?"

"Alexandra, you must understand something, ja? Anyone can sit at piano and execute the notes. But not everyone has the… *was ist es, die Seele—oder das Gefuehl*—the soul, the feeling, for the music. You cannot practice enough hours to buy the soul of music. It is a gift and part of your being."

Alexandra knew she was hearing something very important but wasn't entirely sure she comprehended the message.

"Ven you study long und hard. You practice. Then practice more. Then practice noch mehr. Dann, mein Liebchen, dann you can play it, ja?"

Alexandra met the terms with great willingness. She spent every afternoon perfecting the songs that rapidly turned into two and three pages, each sprinkled with more of the egg-shaped circles strung together as if they were a flock of birds flying in formation. More tic-tac-toe signs and the loopy backward b's, and further stretching of arms to reach to the clinkedy keys at the top and thundering booms at the bottom.

Alexandra attacked the simplistic pieces with the same swaying movement that she had observed in Mrs. Hoven, even if they were just the childish melodies of *The Fairy Chord*, *A Little Waltz*, and *The Spanish Fiesta*. Soon the music naturally bent her, drew her in, caressing her fingertips with a new sensation, a reluctant sadness when she came to the end of a song. She felt a sense of loyalty to the piece as it had given her yet another venue in which to feel.

Alexandra became voracious, soon skipping over nascent John Thompson, eagerly diving into the more sophisticated and difficult Burgmüller, Heller, and Clementi, preparing for her journey into the repertoire. She quickly became Mrs. Hoven's most dedicated and promising student. It was an outlet, it was catharsis, it was a complete reprieve from her mother.

"Sit," Mrs. Hoven said one day when Alexandra arrived for her lesson.

Alexandra sat, waiting expectantly. Mrs. Hoven opened the first page of sheet music and set it before her student.

"*Clair de Lune*"

Alexandra began tentatively playing Debussy's most famous piece when Mrs. Hoven abruptly stopped her. "No… not for me. Play for you, *mein Liebchen.*"

Alexandra stopped, closed her eyes a moment, clearing her head of any clutter. Then, she played as instructed, delving deeply inside herself. When the last note left the air, Alexandra turned to Mrs. Hoven and saw her flushed with pride. She put a hand on Alexandra's shoulder and led her into the kitchen.

"Don't vorry about anything," she said over tea and spicy Zucherkuchen. "Don't vorry about the problems, neh? Only one thing must keep you straight on course. Dein Herz." Mrs. Hoven simply put a hand to her chest. "Your heart." Then she took Alexandra's hand and whispered, "Your heartbeat is your metronome."

Alexandra took Mrs. Hoven's mantra deadly serious. She had read *The Fountain Head* and *Atlas Shrugged* when she was twelve, forging herself into a Dagny Taggert character, infusing her work with absolute purity. Ayn Rand was just a part of Alexandra's dive into full-blown adolescence. Every ounce of feeling was devoted to her music so that she was deliciously transported into Chopin's poetic melancholy and Beethoven's fiery expressionism. As puberty arrived, she was swept into ever higher levels of angst and torment. She played endlessly in the dark, tears streaming down her cheeks as the music consumed her. Claire finally called her husband, away on business in Hamburg, and demanded that he return home immediately for a family meeting.

They sat Alexandra before them to tell her they were concerned. To be more precise, they accused her of contriving her melodramatic behavior to provoke them. It simply wasn't right that she sat there, playing in the dark every night, crying over very somber music. They made it clear this behavior would not be tolerated.

"It's too predictable, Alexandra. Playing at the churlish teen who's convinced her deep dark thoughts are real. You have nothing to be depressed about." Claire sat with her hands clasped properly in her lap. "You have been given every advantage."

"I'm not depressed," Alexandra snapped. "Being at the piano provides the most uplifting moments of my day." Alexandra had officially entered the hellish realm of seventeen, and everything had seemed insurmountable. Clearly, no one understood her, and there was no escape but music.

"Then you should be overjoyed to hear that we've applied for a scholarship to the Royal Academy in England," Richard informed her.

"You what?"

"Yes," Claire said, "we've already sent your audition tape and resume. I thought you would be pleased."

"But I thought I was going to the school in Boston?"

"Your therapist indicates to me that you're 'begging' for attention, that we need to take your music seriously, because it's important to you. And since you've managed to keep up your grades, even with all your ridiculous antics, we think you can get in."

"And do I have anything to say about this?"

"Of course you do," Claire answered with an ingratiating smile that said *of course you don't*. "And that would be thank you. It will also give you a chance to travel overseas. See Europe, and get you ... finished."

She still didn't know what 'finished' actually meant, but as much as she wanted away from her mother, she hadn't imagined being shipped across the globe.

"One more thing; I've set up twice weekly sessions with Madame Kiretsky. If anything will scare you into technical brilliance before you leave for school, it's that old hag."

Madame Kiretsky terrified Alexandra. She wasn't anything like Mrs. Hoven. The razor-lipped crone was so skinny it appeared as if her bones were wrapped in crepe paper.

Well into her seventies, the quintessential Russian instructor had become known as the infamous "Russian Roulette" because no one ever knew which Kiretsky they were going to get: the stern woman whose attention to detail enthralled conductors, or the over-blown diva who would scream at the flute section and walk off stage. Alexandra tiptoed on jumbo eggshells as she studied with the tough and austere Vladimira Kiretsky.

Even when Alexandra went to the Royal Academy, every summer she returned home, she practiced as though she hadn't left. Day after sticky humid day Alexandra sat at the keyboard as Madame Kiretsky, paced, barking commands, never once touching the piano as she instructed Alexandra to repeat a passage over—as many as seventy times—until she had hit each note exactly right. She insisted on scales, three hours a day, followed by whatever piece they were perfecting at the time, playing without pause save a brisk lunch break.

Indiscriminately, Kiretsky would snap a number from the air, expecting Alexandra to pick up that bar of music and play until she shrieked, "What is this I hear?!" Snapping, "This is certainly not Prokofiev's music! Have you become a composer now?" After her fourth summer of belittling and scathing remarks, Alexandra could endure it no longer.

"Then you play it. Show me."

"No."

"Please, Madame Kiretsky, if I am beyond all redemption, please just show me how it is done."

"I told you when you start. I. Do. Not. Play."

"Then I don't see how you expect to teach me to play."

When Alexandra gathered her music and headed toward the door the old lady shrieked. "Stop!"

Alexandra turned. Then heard the choked whisper, "Come here. Now."

She apprehensively returned to the older woman, more than a little afraid. The last thing she expected was for the teacher of every famed European virtuoso to collapse in defeat, but in the convex shoulders, Alexandra glimpsed a melting of armor. The deep-pitted eyes gathered a veneer of lament as the lips disappeared into resentment. "I no longer play, because I no longer play perfect."

The breath slowly exhaled from the old woman and, as it did, Alexandra felt her shoulders slump in fatigue. A rush of futility overwhelmed her as she realized what would encompass the rest of her life. The bar of excellence would be set, only to be moved out of reach. She now joined the legions of every other pianist on earth facing the same unachievable goal: The quest for perfection.

And that is exactly how she spent her years under rigid supervision at the Royal Academy, wading through the complex curriculum, the punishing and so often humiliating "stripping down of self" to get to the music. Practice, theory, harmonic counterpoint, chamber music, piano literature, recitals, more practice. Her chief instructor was a small but stout Hungarian who delighted in humiliation and told her from the beginning, "You will have no ego. You are nothing but a pair of hands, which, incidentally, get no preferential treatment because they are attached to a pair of breasts."

Yes, there were moments, profound moments, when she felt what she produced was true. Pure. The best of what *she* could do. But how did it stack up against all the other musicians who labored eight, ten, fourteen hours a day? Would she ever be able to call herself a musician, a pianist, without turning revealing shades of pink? She spent most of her hours castigating herself for imperfect performances and fighting for more time in the practice rooms.

She felt small and broken after she graduated, even with high honors and awards in interpretation and presentation for she knew what all the students had come to understand: A precious few of them were bound for fame and glory, but the majority would maintain their play only to show off at dinner parties, end up as lounge acts, or more likely transition to teaching so yet more musicians could flood the extremely narrow playing field. She had endured the stiff upper lip, non-emotional approach to the divine arts, where emphasis was placed on the science of music, the logic of construction, the ascendancy of form only to feel she was repeatedly drawn to the task of throwing out the chief reason she was there: Her passion.

But it was in the dangerous halls of academia that she learned about survival. Constantly on guard, she navigated through the heated blood-lust lurking in the air, the narrowed eyes of assessment, the buzz filling the halls with gossip, and the overcharged defensiveness. Each student and professor were there to do one thing and one thing only, to make her a true performer; hone her strengths, detail with exacting precision her limitations, liabilities, weaknesses. There was no room for imposters. And with those suppressed emotions and feelings aching to escape, it was in England where Alexandra learned to cut herself off at the neck, finessing the skill of detachment.

It was this very skill she most needed now; that cool and unfeeling dis-engagement as she played for the Ketterling. She tried to clear her head as she lay in the smooth dark. Forget the man with the beautiful eyes, Sebastian. Even Chandra, her closest friend had to be viewed through the lens of opposition. Sokolov, definitely her greatest foe, had flirted with her in his clumsy Russian when they ran into each other while refilling their coffee thermoses.

He'd laughed about whether there was enough caffeine in the world to get through "this conquest," and Alexandra wondered if it was his bad English or if the word had been intentional. They were all just…people. Was it necessary to make them out the enemy to be bested? *You're so close, Alexandra, don't you even consider going soft now.* All their voices blended in her head as she drifted to sleep and into the recurring dream that had plagued her forever: Hazy inchoate images as she sits at the piano in a room filled with thousands of people. Her fingers are on the keys, but when she looks down at them, they are made of dust, so when she plays a note, silence ensues, the swirl of hazy particles dance about her. She looks down to see her knobby knees. She has forgotten her skirt. And her underwear. A judge appears decked in courtroom garb, his powdered periwig suspiciously similar to her own mother's New Rochelle bouffant. A condescending preamble follows. "I'm sure you are acquainted with the dress code for competitions, Miss Von Triessen. You simply cannot attend them naked."

Alexandra woke with a start. That damn dream.

"Naked, but not beaten," Alexandra whispered as she curled into her pillow and doggedly began to form notes backward to Rach's Second, an exercise that worked, no matter how far backward into the piece she had to go before her breathing softened and she fell into blissful unconsciousness.

"Prizes are badges of mediocrity."

Charles Ives

"It is imperative you always have at least two, and I recommend three or even four, concerti at a heartbeat's notice. You never know what might happen, if a conductor falls ill, if part of an orchestra is grounded and backup is sent, you need to be able to have a repertoire that will satisfy any contingency!" Herr Fenzig, the notoriously temperamental conductor, motioned his baton from above the heads of the finalists to the eighty-piece orchestra. "Now, we will talk about the synergy between you, myself, and these fine people, who will follow you and depend on you. If they like you, they just might cover your mistakes and make you sound better than you are."

Alexandra fiddled with a paisley umbrella, still wet from a Portland downpour as she joined the other finalists. She watched as each of them got up in turn and took their place at the piano, so the conductor could run them through drills, pointing out dangerous pitfalls, rhythm mistakes, and mistiming cues.

The Italian was the first to play with the orchestra. Fenzig wound him through perilous territory to the oft-repeated errors of the solo pianist who loses their way with an orchestra. Even with the heat of competition, Alexandra was drawn to each of the finalists, and knew the personal obstacles they faced, as she was intimately familiar with all the selections being played.

When Sokolov teased the spirited clarion call of Prokofiev's, *Piano Concerto No. 3 in C Major,* she knew in an instant she would have been slaughtered if she had gone up against him. Sokolov was a typical virtuoso, possessing a laser concentration that did not brook failure. The *NY Times* Sunday's Entertainment section suggested, "He is certainly the odds-on favorite. The question remains whether the volatile Molino from Italy will place second to the technically superb Chandra Zhang. However, this music lover will hazard a long shot on a relative unknown: New Englander Alexandra Von Triessen."

Naturally, Alexandra was flattered by this mention, and knew it should have elevated her fight, but she battled with the nagging compassion that always overtook her as she watched other pianists play. Sokolov's brilliance was undeniable, but he was blessedly difficult to watch. His tortured grimaces, his head flopping as if ensnared by seizures, fingers stomping at the keys like a bull in mid-flight. He laid his heart bare as sweat dripped onto the ivory from his furrowed brow.

Musicians were such a fascinating and complex breed. They were capable of every contortion the body can sustain at the piano, armed with shy smiles that turned to appeals, as they bowed to a crowd, a self-awareness of their otherness, yet so willing to share their deepest emotions. What Ketterling had said was true. These people *knew* one another most intimately. She wanted to help Sokolov dress better, cut his hair, teach him rudimentary social graces. Alexandra had to stop herself: It was ludicrous, this ardent charity when she needed to best him.

Herr Fenzig called her name, and she walked to the piano. Alexandra took her seat, closed her eyes, and swept the strict French braid from her shoulder with a delicate flip of the wrist. She began Schumann's *A Minor*. Her nerves felt strung through her body, as if her fingers had been thrust into an electrical socket; but within moments her breathing calmed and her trembling fingers played with ever-growing confidence through the first and second movement.

Fenzig flung his baton, and as the joyous third movement careened toward its triumphant conclusion, the piano—still parked on its dolly—shifted slightly. Consumed by Schumann's rhythmic vigor, Alexandra squinched forward on the seat, her arms stretching farther and farther to reach the keys. And as she struggled to keep up with the piano, her body could no longer bridge the widening distance.

Ka—thwump.

A deadening silence filled the auditorium as the musicians stopped on a perfect beat, followed by an audible gasp of surprise. The other contestants released a mutual sigh of relief from the front row of the stage. Horrific, yes. But thank God it wasn't them.

The conductor jumped from his podium, rushed to her side, and helped to lift her up.

"Miss Von Triessen, are you alright?" Fenzig asked in clipped English.

"Yes… yes, I think I am." She got up, brushed herself off with the most grace she could muster. "I'm sorry. I guess I was sitting a little too far away."

"Nonsense. It's the infernal dollies." Fenzig snapped at a stagehand. "Get someone in here to remove these damn dollies!"

As Alexandra looked around, she saw pity and smug satisfaction. When her eyes met Sebastian's, he smiled sympathetically. Alexandra knew that was the moment they all wrote her off. What they couldn't know was it was precisely this unlikely event that shook the final nerves from her.

"I heard your run-through was quite a *ride.*" Chandra grinned over her beer at Alexandra.

"Oh, yes. My finest *movement.*" Alexandra rolled her eyes, still reliving the humiliation.

"I hate to say it, and no disrespect, but damn I would have liked to have seen that!"

"Where were you?" Alexandra asked as they sat in their smoke-filled drinkery, several newspapers lying between them.

"Having my one-on-one with Ketterling."

Chandra quickly tore at one of the newspapers. The local press had described them as "the token women," lending credence to the tired whispers and sly innuendo as to how any woman made it to the final stages in any competition. God forbid they might have talent.

"Don't let it get to you," Chandra said, rubbing her fingernail obsessively against her thumb. This nervous tick finally drew blood at the sides of her cuticles.

"Hey, are you okay?"

"If I hear this stupid song one more time." Chandra mimicked the endless stuttering as she sang along with the Hullabaloos' *I'm Gonna Love You Too*—apparently a local favorite as they heard the song every time they met there, blaring from the jukebox. "I mean, have some class! They're the antithesis of the Beatles!"

Alexandra's grin turned from gay to sympathetic as Chandra continued picking at her thumb.

"Come on." Alexandra sipped her beer. "What's going on?"

"I need to get laid."

"Chandra—"

Chandra glanced around, dropped the cynicism, and turned to Alexandra, her dark eyes weary with vigilance and pain.

"Your father," Alexandra stated factually.

"He's… he's just gone nuts. I don't know what it is about *this* competition—"

Alexandra arched an eyebrow.

"Yeah, okay, it's the big one. But he's become possessed. It's like if I don't win this competition, he's going to commit *Hari Kari* on both of us—or maybe the judges."

"Hey." Alexandra leaned to her friend sympathetically.

"I can't do this. I can't live like this, Alex. He's making me crazy."

Alexandra shook her head. Why couldn't her father just lay off?

Chandra started ripping at her cuticles again. Alexandra leaned over and molded her hands above Chandra's, guiding them to stillness. "Just stop hurting yourself. Your father's doing enough of that for the both of you." Alexandra's voice was warm with encouragement. "Forget him right now. This is about you, Chandra. Your dreams and what you want."

Alexandra thought about her mother's ability to destroy her confidence and how grateful she was Claire was nowhere near her. No wonder Chandra was buckling, her oval eyes filled with anxiety and fear.

"Is it? Is this what I want?"

The following morning Alexandra dashed into the coffee room to fill her thermos before her next practice session. As she turned, she barreled into a man's back spraying her cashmere sweater in fine-flecked brown.

"Damnit!" she sputtered.

"Are you burned?"

Alexandra glanced at her ruined sweater, which had saved her from that affliction. "No... I'm fine, I'm..." She realized it was Sebastian.

"I'm so sorry."

"I'm fine!" she snapped.

"Look, I can take that to a dry cleaner. If you want to change—

"Please. Stop."

"You've got to let me pay for it at least."

"What part of I'm fine is lost on you?"

But when she looked at him, his forehead burrowed in a delicate frown, his ocean-blue eyes appealed to her own.

"Look," she conceded. "It's all good."

"I just... I guess we're all just that close—" his fingers measured very little daylight "—aren't we?"

"I suppose we are."

"Are you..."

Another silence followed.

"...Terrified?"

"Damn straight I am," Alexandra did not have time for subterfuge.

"I love your honesty."

"Aren't you?"

"Yes, Alexandra," He took her hand, released her thermos, and wiped it clean with his handkerchief. "I'm scared shitless. But not because of the competition."

She swiftly glanced at him. Clearly, he had all the time in the world to flirt.

"If you had a wit of clarity, you'd realize Sokolov is going to oust us all!"

She grabbed the thermos back from him and briskly made her way out of the coffee room, but as she walked away, she could feel those exquisite blue eyes follow her into the shadows.

The rapping in her dream segued into reality. She twisted so that she could see the clock. 4:15 a.m. The knocking persisted.

She dragged herself to the door of the cramped dorm room. "Who's there?"

"It's Chandra." A man's voice rumbled through the door. Urgent.

She pressed her ear to the door. "What?"

"It's Chandra." Louder now. She opened the door.

Sebastian stood before her, his clothes askew. His eyes were frantic, if bloodshot.

"What? What do you want?"

"It's Chandra… she's having some sort of… of melt down. Please come with me."

Alexandra shook her head, grabbed her robe, and pulled on some boots.

Sebastian took her hand as he led her to a car, then drove a few blocks to an apartment. She glanced at him; keenly aware she wasn't dressed. He could be driving her off to the woods to strangle her for all she knew. But he stopped suddenly, killed the motor.

She followed him up the back stairs and into a high loft, nicely furnished with a huge Grand in the middle of the living room. Chandra, huddled against the base, was grasping onto the leg as if she had been cast out to sea.

"What happened?" Alexandra didn't look at Sebastian, and slowly approached her friend.

"A few of us were having drinks, you know, trying to lose the nerves, and then on our way back… she went berserk." Sebastian's coat was draped over Chandra's shoulders.

"For Christ's sake, D'Antonio!" Alexandra turned to him. "You knew how on edge she was. Did you really need to take her out and get her loaded? Or is everything up for grabs now? All's fair—"

"I didn't know she was… was going to—"

"Shut up."

Alexandra knelt in front of her. "Chandra… Chandra?" But Chandra only rocked back and forth as if enduring the blast of a cold wind. Alexandra gently brushed the tears away and her touch brought Chandra back.

"I can't. I can't do it." Chandra continued swaying.

"You can," Sebastian said. "You're one of the best in this silly contest."

Alexandra whipped around to him, shut him up with a glare, then turned back to Chandra. "Talk to me."

"My… my father spends every last dime he makes scaling fish so—" Chandra's voice was eerily flat, disassociated— "so that I can become… become his famous Asian prodigy. He's in that audience every day, and when I see his face—his eyes…" Chandra stripped Sebastian's jacket and her sweater aside, revealing her chest, splotched with red sores, her fingernails, cracked and bleeding. "I haven't slept since I got here. Every night after dinner my father handicaps the other contestants. He plugs theories into mathematical formulas he's created to tell me every day I'm losing a percentage point here, a percentage point there!" And then she began to crack. "I feel like I'm up for arbitrage, for Christ's sakes. Oh, and in case you think you're immune he tells me how to take advantage of all your many weaknesses."

Sebastian and Alex glanced at one another, wondering how he'd sized them up.

"We all have weaknesses," Alexandra spoke in a soothing tone. "This contest is designed to bring them out, to see if we have what it takes to tour and not fall apart."

"I don't. I don't want to tour. I just want to play."

"Then play, god damnit," Alexandra ordered sharply. Sebastian raised an eyebrow. "You've made it to the final round, Chandra. Only one last night. One last night. Just bear it, okay? Bear it, if for no other reason than to prove to him that you *can* win."

Something in Chandra responded to the fervor in Alexandra's words.

"Shove it down his goddamn throat," Alexandra continued, lifting Chandra by the arm. "Come on. You're coming back with me. I'm giving you a shot of brandy and you're going to get some sleep."

Chandra stood, then seemed to realize what a mess she looked, excused herself, and went to the ladies' room.

Sebastian shook his head, seeming genuinely disturbed. "I didn't know she was this on the edge. Really, Alexandra."

Alexandra walked to the window, turned around, and took in Sebastian's lodgings. "Nice pad."

"Friends of the family," Sebastian answered apologetically.

Alexandra fidgeted, sighed, then shook her head. "I'm sorry I went off on you like that."

"I guess it's getting to all of us a bit."

"You?" Alexandra looked directly at him. "I don't see a whit of nerves on you."

Sebastian shrugged humbly. "I'm just not a nervy kind of guy. And, really, if I'd known how fragile Chandra was…"

"I know. It's not your fault. Truce."

"Does that mean I can make it up to you?" He arched an elegant brow.

Alexandra looked at him a long moment, followed by a slow inviting smile. "Well… not until *after* I've knocked you from your perch."

"What I want to hear is that an artist has taken the music, absorbed, assimilated it, digested it and then brings it forth as his own and then he speaks the music to me."

Juror, Van Cliburn International Contest

"And now we've entered the final phase of the competition," Ketterling informed the packed audience. "Each contestant will play a concerto of their choosing, performed with Heinrich Fenzig's internationally renowned Heidelberg Orchestra."

Behind the proscenium curtains, Alexandra desperately searched for Chandra. Her performance was up following Sebastian, who was next, trying to appear calm and assured as he paced behind her. He stopped a moment as if to relieve his anxiety.

"Any sign?"

Alexandra shook her head.

"I hope you find her. Look, I'm up next, and I'd like to ask a favor."

Preoccupied, Alexandra turned to him and was shocked to see in his eyes the first sign of real need, his vulnerability, and the terror she knew all too well.

She heard the final notes of Sokolov's dashing finale and was faintly cognizant, in the part of her that was racing through the battlefield with a sniper at her heels, that it wasn't his best performance. She drew her attention back to Sebastian's sapphire eyes void of their cavalier glint.

"Can you… will you wish me luck?"

"You?" she teased, but then felt his raw exposure as his eyes pierced her own.

She placed her fingertips on his cheek, then with gentle emphasis, kissed his bottom lip.

He took her hand, surprised, but delighted, then exhaled with full force as he heard his name announced. "That would be me."

"Good luck, Sebastian."

As Sebastian walked out to the audience Alexandra heard the tight control in Mr. Zhang's voice behind her as he propelled Chandra by her right arm. His terse tone didn't require interpretation. They hadn't come all this way for her to turn away in disgrace. Alexandra couldn't bear to see Chandra so completely eclipsed. She walked over to lend a hand.

"Don't touch." Zhang's accent was dense and harsh. He moved his daughter as if she had no will and would certainly drop into a melted puddle if he weren't there. Alexandra couldn't conceive how Chandra would pull it together to perform. She moved like a zombie, her eyes blank, her expression vacant. Alexandra glanced at her hands and saw the rings of blood around her fingernails. She tried once more to approach them, but Zhang whirled Chandra from her and led her to a private corner.

She could hear Sebastian now, and the gothic pronouncement of Liszt's *Piano Concerto No. 1 in E-flat Major*. She had stayed away from watching the performances, but now she wanted to see Sebastian play. She found a place behind the stage where she could just peek through. This piece was written for him, she thought, with its triumphant and swaggering flair. He played fluidly. Masterfully. He was as at home with the delicate yearning of the second movement as he was the show-stopping, hand-flailing finale. He had developed a relationship with the orchestra she hadn't previously noted, and his intensity grabbed the audience right out of their seats.

She felt the smooth angle of Sebastian's cheek, the press of her lips upon his, and knew that she had given in to the enemy, knew she had given Sebastian strength to perform, with scarcely a thought that she would be following him. In the moment she saw Sebastian rise before his adoring audience, clasping his right hand to his heart with the brilliance of tears in his eyes, she let go of winning the competition. She felt her heart melt to this man, and winning simply didn't matter as much as this new sensation welling inside her.

Between Sebastian's first and second curtain call, when Herr Fenzig walked back to take a drink, Alexandra addressed the conductor. This feeling, so full in her chest, had broken her need to win, giving her the courage to do what she wanted. Now it was about her passion, not the competition. She informed Herr Fenzig that she would be playing Rachmaninoff's *Second Concerto* after all. He frowned a bit vexed, then shrugged. "Certainly! As you wish."

Silence.

She waited in that timeless moment as she sat before hundreds, breath held in anticipation, the pulsing of her heart reminding her of Mrs. Hoven's admonition to use *your heartbeat as your metronome*. Lifting her hands, she calmly placed them upon the ivory keys she knew as well as her own fingers.

She began.

She eased into the introduction's quiet desperation, gave voice to the solace of the very notes Rachmaninoff had written to climb out of the abyss of depression.

Alexandra felt the lead weight that had oppressed her from the moment of her arrival, break open and fall away. Gone was the shadow of her mother. Forgotten were the mechanics that ruled her every waking moment. The desperate nerves erased. In those first bars of extraordinarily haunted isolation, the competition disappeared. She played entirely from her heart, blissfully oblivious to the fifteen hundred people in the audience and the clunky *Lost in Space* television cameras. Best of all she was completely oblivious to critical judges noting every missed technical point. Nothing was as imperative as this piece, which more than any other, spoke to the essence of who she truly was, conveyed the sweeping love affair she had with this vast creature called music, which offered her the most exquisite joy, darkest heartache, richest and fullest array of feeling that no other experience had equaled. And when it was over she heard a new sound, a great swelling, a roar that sounded as if a storm had taken over. Slowly she turned and saw the audience standing, cheering in jubilation at her performance.

She knew in that moment she had won.

CONRAD - 1965

"Music was invented to confirm human loneliness."

Lawrence Durrell, British author

Conrad was in Mexico when he heard Sebastian play. Cabo San Lucas. He had spent the last week studying with an eccentric serialist composer who had briefly been a student of the grand Avante Gardist himself, John Cage. When he wasn't at the piano, Conrad walked the white sandy beaches, listening to the rhythm and patterns of the ocean, feeling the sedentary pull of the earth at her axis. He spent hours basking in the sun, playing rondos of sand, silty grains sifting through his fingertips. He would lay back and let the elements wash over him, in concert as one organism. It was the same everywhere he went. The music of the earth lived in him, playing forever and endlessly.

When he came home that evening, he was reminded of the Ketterling competition. He had received a telegram informing him that Sebastian was a finalist. While he didn't directly invite him to the event, he repeatedly mentioned this competition was what they'd both been waiting for all their lives, and it would be a shame if Sebastian couldn't share it with him. Conrad tracked down a short-wave radio and tuned in to hear the final performances.

Conrad smoked a cigarette thoughtfully as he listened to Sebastian play. His brother had done well. He nodded, pleased as the applause abated and the next contestant was introduced. Conrad reached to turn off the radio but paused when he heard the first powerful notes of the Rachmaninoff. He sat back down. He had never heard such expressive poignancy in the opening.

As Conrad listened to the sweeping certainty of the final movement, what had seemed garishly overdramatic in the hands of lesser performers, or overly sentimental in recycled film scores, became an exquisite dialogue of questions and answers—the ultimate expression of understanding one's soul. He felt the music injected into him over the airwaves, and marveled at the utter rawness, the absolute nakedness, the courage in such a performance. Purity. Not once did he move through the entire piece save the single tear that dropped beside his foot.

Champagne glasses raised. Salutes. Festivities, tears, and congratulations.

Sebastian walked to Alexandra's table, where she sat with several of the other contestants and their families. His tux was awry, his shirt unbuttoned as he recklessly swilled his champagne. He looked down and realized his glass was empty. "Oh, hell. I was just going to toast lost souls and losers everywhere."

"Don't be a spoilsport." Alexandra lit a cigarette, took a cool puff. "You too won a recording contract and tidy little sum."

"Yes, but to the victor." He challenged her, wanting to pick a fight. "Go the spoils."

"'We go to gain a little patch of ground, That hath in it no profit but the name.'"

"Is Shakespeare supposed to heal my wounded ego?"

Alexandra's eyes held an amused expression, half puzzled, half seductive.

Sebastian ground out his cigarette in a crystal ashtray. "You may have won the trophy, my dear, but I won what was important tonight."

Alexandra raised her brow. "And what might that be?"

Sebastian straightened his tuxedo, then leaned close to Alexandra, his tone serious. "Your heart."

He bowed, and walked unsteadily away.

Alexandra watched him go. She took another long puff of her cigarette. He said what he needed to say. Now it was in her court. She considered the evening's events for a moment, took a careful sip of her champagne, and decided in that moment to make him a wonderful memory.

Conrad couldn't get the music out of his head. It played on and on, running its loop, accompanying him on his tour in the bus that drove through the dusty roads of northern Mexico. Mexico, where he eagerly sank into the lazy beat of a Latin rumba, the press of hot bodies, the cloying smell of sweat and salt. Where music was a strum-plucked exposition of hearts on sleeves, a lyrical romance with life.

Conrad's body tingled. He had joined the Tarahumara pilgrimage for a taste of "god's flesh." Delicious peyote-teased hallucinations summoned the souls of the men and women before him, swirling out as deep indigo notes, their bodies undulating as they chanted invocations, praying for corn, rain, and bountiful harvest. It was the belief of these people that all actions possess musical meaning and Conrad immersed himself in ceremony, unveiling, morphing…now an eagle, soaring high above the raging bonfire, where the music of the earth erupted in a symphony of colors. The moon's pearly white sang a chorus of angels, the steely magenta sky released lush violins, and the blazing stars a pizzicato waltz.

His body hurtled backward in time to the moment sound was first produced; the creaking groan of the earth birthing herself, spilling into a torrent of ocean waters to the clatter of bones in dank caves, the lyre graced by flowing robes, medieval chants that blistered contrapuntal fugues on Bach's harpsichord. Mozart, Beethoven, Chopin, Debussy— he heard it all, every note of music ever played, every shift in form, its evolution spinning about him in delirious ecstasy, reaching deep into his senses, laying claim to his soul.

When he woke, he was alone, near the emberless fire pit. His skin hurt to the touch his nerves cut raw by the sensations of the previous night. He walked slowly down the hill, wobbly and weak, to find the bus that traveled out to these hills but once a day. He climbed onto the too-warm, too-fragrant clatter trap and barely noticed the passing scenery. In the back of his mind, the notes from the radio performance buzzed in his ears. He wanted to know what had led to the execution of that brilliant piece, on that specific evening? What had the performer unlocked within herself in that moment that she had become one with the music? Had she had such an experience as he, felt the notes become her body?

He couldn't erase the performance from his mind, for it defied a tenant he had long held as an irrefutable truth: that recorded play could never live up to the vital and unpredictable charm of live performance. If twelve takes of a given measure were all quantitatively different, which then did they set down for immortality? How did man achieve balance between what music was in its most perfect present moment, and what it became afterward?

"But what about the enjoyment of the listener?" Sebastian had scoffed at Conrad's early idealism. "Surely you don't expect the entire world to go without music because of your tedious philosophy?"

"It's called live performance. Remember? The middle class used to live by it."

"In case you hadn't heard, that's in the hands of record companies now, and I don't think they're doing a half-bad job. We have much more music available to us than ever before."

Now, having heard the contestant's performance the other night, he considered that Sebastian might have a point. He would like to hear that one piece, rendered precisely in that way, over and over again, as he now played it in his head. It unsettled him. Never before had he given a thought to his moral certitude toward music as a constantly shifting animal. But he didn't want that piece to shift. It was perfect, exactly the way it had been. He sighed, lay back, and let the passing hills and trees become a backdrop for the music, reliving it once again in his mind.

*"When there is a snowstorm, the flakes seem to dance
and drift from the woodwinds and the sound holes of the
violin; when the sun is high, all instruments shine with an
almost fiery glare; when there is water, the waves ripple and
dance audibly through the orchestra … The sound is cool
and glassy when he describes a calm winter night with a
glitteringly starlit sky. He was a great master of orchestral
sound painting."*

Sergei Rachmaninoff —
on Rimsky-Korsakov's orchestration.

When playing with an orchestra, few instruments speak with less forgiveness than the piano. Its precision is its joy and its agony. When the pianist is asked to track the movements and signals of the conductor and merge seamlessly with the eighty or ninety-odd musicians that comprise the orchestra, the weight of the burden to deliver music with clarity and panache lies within the solo performance of the pianist, as if the orchestra didn't exist.

A character and personality were assigned to each musician so that when Alexandra spoke with a cellist, she heard the sturdy warmth and austere confidence of the instrument, not the person. It was the smoky sensuality of the oboe or the eager portent of the clarinet with which she conversed, not its player. The sweeping soul of the strings, and the mysterious woodwinds with their ancient wooing, all lent additional flourishes to her ever-maturing range of emotion and inspired within Alexandra a spectrum of infinite possibilities and feelings.

This unique attachment bound her to these musicians, who looked forward to her arrival during rehearsal. It was clear they were the sole recipients of her warm and genuine, if somewhat eccentric, loyalty. She sensed herself as the nucleus of the malleable organism, this ragtag band of devoted artists, reveling in each creation. Her sense of frustration with the state of music had all but disappeared, and because she spent ninety percent of her time on tour, she had very little interaction with her mother. She was the happiest she had ever been in her life.

"It's not enough to perform your best at the Ketterling," said a judge from the competition who came backstage after one of her performances early into her tour. "It's how you play once you're out amongst the people, every night, sometimes five cities in a week."

Alexandra, the critics concluded, not only played her best every night but indeed, pushed herself to remarkable limits. It wasn't because she felt the compulsive drive she had seen in so many other musicians clawing their way to the top. She was in joy. She counted her blessings daily; she wasn't only playing the music she loved, but working with kindred spirits, those who only had the music's best interest collectively.

Within a year she had firmly established her name as one of the rising young pianists at the precipice of a promising career. Although it wasn't difficult for her to grasp the merits of the press, she nonetheless began to gain a reputation for being aloof, unapproachable by a few cynical reporters whose flirtations and advances she had quickly rejected. The furthest they ever went on the printed page, however, was "reticent," or "the restrained Miss Von Triessen seems to put all her ardent energy into her performance, scarcely leaving any for her eager fans." All but the most rigid of structuralists were "deeply moved" or "highly affected" by her performances.

Sebastian, too, as the glamorous second-place runner-up to the Ketterling, was beginning to cause a love affair with the box office: "With his flashy good looks and tender communion with the fairer of the sex, no matter how purple his Chopin, his popularity is unquestionable." His personable approach, his warm interplay with the tightly packed rows of glittering chiffon and endless tuxedoes made him a hit with "the people and season ticket holders." His signature hand upon heart and his willingness to sign autographs and mill around in Q & A sessions long after the klieg lights had dimmed, drew him as a favorite among the masses. The critics were far less kind in their reviews, however, which tended to range from "mediocre" to "should stick to flashing his pearly whites and leave the real keys to professionals."

The Ketterling Foundation couldn't have been more thrilled with its finalists. Sebastian, with his rakish charm and sensual romanticism, played famously to the old guard stuffed in their sequined evening gowns and sparked the imagination of the youngest deb. Coupled with their first prize winner, the beautiful, if somewhat somber, Alexandra, they were quite smug regarding publicity. It also didn't hurt that the two seemed to have "a fondness for each other," according to the press.

Moving into the second year of the two-year contract the Foundation took advantage of its handsome couple and began to put them on the same billing whenever it was geographically feasible. Though Sebastian usually had a groupie on his arm, and Alexandra was intently focused on the constantly shifting pieces she was expected to master, neither left any of these rare meetings without thinking of the other for several days afterward. Alexandra, thirty thousand feet up in the sky, might suddenly conjure Sebastian's earthy grin and, in turn, smile herself. Sebastian would find himself contrasting his date's eyes with the deep-set penetration of Alexandra's hazel-green, this blonde's anemic locks with the epicurean auburn of Alexandra's full plaited hair. He often wondered what it looked like when she set it free.

So, they were not caught completely off guard when they finally ran into each other at *Notes from Above*, right in the heart of NYC, an upscale coffee house that catered to the classical musician, as well as a revolving door cast of straggling writers, poets, and painters.

Sebastian spotted her the moment he walked through the door with a group of friends. She sat at the far end of the café, deeply immersed in sheet music. She sighed, closed her eyes, and leaned back, lost in her private reverie, unaware of the clatter of dishes and chatter of patrons. He stood for a moment observing her; lips gently tensed, strong chin edged forward, the curvature of her long slender neck beautifully exposed. And then, as if coming out of a dream, she opened those insanely gorgeous eyes and saw him.

She watched as he excused himself from the group, gently removing a sullen beauty's hand from his forearm to approach her.

"Hi."

"Hi." Her voice was soft and low.

"Aren't you supposed to be in London?"

"Next week."

"But—"

"I came home early."

Sebastian avoided looking at his companion, who was watching them closely. "Oh...homesick, are we?" he asked. "Poor lamb. I knew it would only be a matter of time before the rigor of travel, riches, and fame got to you."

"I'm sure you've been beside yourself with worry." Alexandra glanced at the woman he had come in with. "Or at least, beside someone."

His face lit in a touché grin, his eyes holding her gaze a moment too long. She reached for a cigarette, which he lit.

"You've been well?"

He shrugged.

"And the tour?"

Sebastian cleared his throat. "Maybe you've been gone too long to know I'm not exactly a favorite with the critics."

"But you are with the fans." Alexandra's lips curled into a grin around her cigarette.

Sebastian seemed unable to tell if her remark was a subtle insult or not. "Anyway, I have a theory about critics."

"What's that?" He waited, encouraged.

"No matter where a critic picks his grapes, they turn sour." She blew out a puff of smoke and he liked the way her lips moved.

"Oh... so that's why it's so hard to swallow."

Alexandra put her cigarettes in her purse.

He shoved his hands in his pockets and, chewed his bottom lip a moment. "I've been thinking...well, considering lately about whether

I want to continue touring. Thought maybe about moving into composition."

"Oh?"

"Yeah. My agents have limited offers, but it requires far more travel, and now my Ketterling tour's pretty well finished I'd like to stay home. Settle, you know?"

Alexandra began putting her sheet music into an elegant briefcase as Sebastian continued. "I thought I'd come up with something to prove the critics wrong."

"I wouldn't give them a second thought if I were you. Do what makes you happy."

Their eyes held a moment, then she glanced away.

"Hey… whatever happened to Chandra?"

"She's one of the reasons I'm in town." Alexandra's voice lowered as she completed stacking her sheet music together. "She was hospitalized."

"I'm sorry. Is she—"

"She's had a rough patch." Alexandra laid a bill on the table. "I think it's hard for someone with her talent to not be working."

"And no pity for the others you've left behind?"

Alexandra put on her jacket and stood, then pegged Sebastian square in the eye. "Any time you want to stop this ridiculous game, you know how to find me."

CONRAD & SEBASTIAN — NEW YORK, 1944

"Child prodigies, instinct in music from babyhood, develop a certain kind of aural and digital response, and before they arrive at their teens, they already are masters of technique. They have imbibed the literature from the cradle, have become secure craftsmen, can do anything they want to do as easily as breathing."

Harold C. Schonberg,
"The Lives of Great Composers"

Every Christmas holiday, for as long as anyone could remember, Antonia D'Antonio, Sebastian's mother, had visited the Bedford Church of St. Benedict's and its orphanage armed with several bags her butler, "Sir Walter" (so named because he bore a striking resemblance to Walter Pidgeon) would haul into the day lounge. Each year, the nuns, led by Sister Marta, while grateful for her generosity, would quietly lament that Antonia's lavish gifts—porcelain dolls, leather-bound books, and silk undergarments—were so extravagant that the orphans had no idea how to appreciate them.

"It's not good for the children to want what they cannot have."

"Nonsense." Antonia waved her off, as she did every year. "It is the best motivation in the world to want what one cannot have." And every year, despite the good sisters' appeals, she continued to bring expensive trinkets at Christmas and grand Easter baskets each spring toppling with chocolate-covered eggs and ermine bunnies.

Antonia felt the uncommon chill as bitter winds swept through the halls of the church in the small upstate New York berg. She should have worn something warmer. The weather hadn't cooperated with her latest fashion statement. Antonia was known to be a trendsetter, and once set, she would boldly move on to her next couture adventure. Tall and striking, she could easily be mistaken for Rosalind Russell, although she considered herself quite a bit more regal and sensual. "Ros is great, but she doesn't radiate a shred of sex appeal." Further, Antonia appeared easily ten years younger than her age, boasting this advantage as having lived without encumbrance, giving each and every moment its due, but most assuredly as a result of her exquisite lineage. She currently wore the latest Nina Ricci, from her last visit to Paris, and touted the "New Look" before anyone in her ever-burgeoning circle knew about it. Now, the damp snuck up her neck, the thin cropped jacket no barrier to the winter wind. She wrapped her stole tighter about her then stopped. She frowned upon hearing the robust tones echoing their way through the isolated halls of the church.

"What is that intriguing cacophony?" she asked Sister Marta.

"It's the piano, from the day chapel."

Antonia handed her bag of gifts to the sister and wandered down the hall, the clip of her shoes the only other sound, save the extraordinary, ahh, now she placed it, Prokofiev. She had had the great fortune to see the iconoclastic Russian the last time he toured America and had found his controversial music quite divine. Now, as she rounded the corner she saw a newt of a child, possibly just shy of five, his tiny legs dangling from the piano bench, hair ruffled as if he'd just gotten up from bed.

"Boy. You… boy!"

But on he continued and as she walked closer, she saw that he was in a trance-like state, his eyes glazed over, his little mouth set in a firm line. She put long slender fingers to the keys to capture the child's attention.

Startled, he looked at her with large, soulful eyes, a frown gathering on his forehead.

"Do you know who I am, dear boy?"

The ragtag creature considered her a moment. "Yes, you are the 'outlandish bohemian.'"

Antonia laughed at the delicious candor of the child who had clearly overheard this deft description from the nuns.

"Then you must know that this 'outlandish bohemian' is handing out gifts?"

"Yes."

"Would you like one?"

"I don't care for any, thank you," the boy said softly.

"Don't *care for* any? You have no need for a new toy?"

"I like to play in here when it's quiet."

"Everyone likes nice things. Come along. I want to show you some very nice things."

The boy, Conrad, eyed her suspiciously, assessing her grand stature, and the elegance of her dress. She knew he saw something utterly different than that which he was used to, surrounded as he was by drab nuns always in a state of religious fervor. As she cupped his chin, the boy's defenses melted under her warm affection. He took Antonia's hand and walked right out of the orphanage with her.

A brief but unconvincing struggle ensued between Antonia and the sisters. But if there was one thing Antonia had a talent for, it was getting what she wanted.

"This is most unusual. He will not be used to your life. Your..." The nun didn't know how to kindly refer to Antonia's infamous lifestyle and the salacious gossip her behavior had engendered.

"Mrs. D'Antonio, Conrad is... he's a special case. His mother left him many nights, alone without anyone to watch over him while she, pursued a senseless career," she explained, then added with extreme disdain, "One of those entertainer sorts. What kind of mother leaves a child alone while she sings all night."

As the nun sighed in desperation Antonia's interest was further piqued. "I often think it is the more desperate the beginning that rewards a greater end."

The nun shook her head dismissively. "I don't know about such notions for I see many of these children given the love of God end up in terrible situations."

"One cannot live by God alone. Certainly, he put us all down here for a reason."

"Mrs. D'Antonio, I'm not going to debate theology or psychology with you. This boy is peculiar. He's adopted a strange, rather odd manner and his obsession with the piano has left us bewildered. There have been nights we were half out of our wits trying to find him, only to discover him asleep under the piano, in the raw no less. Our good Doctor Williams suggests his kind of early abandonment often turns to mental illness. He's well-mannered and I don't mean to be uncharitable, but the boy is not remotely interested in anyone. He will require a strong hand. Need to see a psychiatrist. Most importantly he will need strict rules—"

"Don't you think what he needs is care?" Antonia interrupted. "A little pampering? Do you believe breaking his already fragile psyche is going to help this child?"

"Fragile isn't a term I'd apply to this youth."

"This boy is special. Your lives are sheltered here, Sister, and that is fine for the others you so kindly keep in your care. But he needs sun and light—an open canvas where his talent can expand. If left here he would surely shrivel up and die."

"I pray you are not suggesting he has been ill-treated?"

"I think stifling talent is the vilest form of abuse." Antonia rose. "My attorneys will see you in the morning to begin the process."

Shortly after the new year, Conrad was brought to the daunting D'Antonio estate. Antonia discovered the true depths of the young boy's talent and hired the same private eye she used to check into the backgrounds of many of the eclectic visitors to her estate. She had to know where he came from. Perhaps Conrad too, like her own family, possessed great musical lineage, arduously pursued through the maze of ganglia-like connections to the divine Bach himself!

After several months the detective found an attractive, slender blonde, slight like her son, with the same exquisite blue eyes. She was a jazz singer with three black backup tenors who performed in a rundown entertainment hall. When Antonia confronted the young woman, she refused to claim, with any conviction, that Conrad was her son, nor would she provide any other information about his heritage. She hesitated only momentarily when Antonia offered her a packet with a generous sum of money and papers to sign. The young woman took the money defiantly, and then closed her eyes for a full moment, sighed deeply, and signed the documents. As Antonia was about to leave, the woman put a hand to her forearm and said simply, "He wasn't made for being here. For this." The woman spread her hands at a loss.

"I will take the very best care of him." Antonia nodded in reassurance and from that moment, no one ever questioned again that Antonia was Conrad's mother.

Conrad adapted to Antonia's free-flowing, unconventional lifestyle quite easily. Behind the exclusive walls of the D'Antonio estate, Avante Garde was the norm. The more exotic, the better. Of the many artists, writers, and poets whom Antonia drew to her like a Patron Saint Pied Piper, only one rule existed, one code of ethics to which she demanded strict adherence, and that was to "follow the heart's desire."

Antonia's greatest focus had always been her only son, Sebastian. She had conceived him very late in life and had such a delicate pregnancy, that when he was born healthy and "crooning love songs" (as she referred to his crying) Sebastian immediately became her one true love. He was a D'Antonio through and through, and so it terrified her friends to see that she had brought home this rag-muffin from the orphanage, this slender and quiet child whose eyes bore directly into their souls until they uncomfortably ruffled his hair to break the spell. Later, they would gossip among themselves that Conrad was "a strange one," a "genius savant," with the way he cocked his head slightly, rolling his eyes back when hearing a piece of music, only to sit at the piano minutes later and outperform in spades whoever had just played it. With his angelic blonde, white hair, he was an unsettling creature, and everyone was certain an epic case of sibling rivalry was lurking right around the corner.

So it was with sharp eyes that Antonia's menagerie waited for the inevitable sparks of jealousy, the unavoidable friction that must occur as Conrad was brought into the fold. But Conrad idolized the darkly beautiful Sebastian, the older, stronger eight-year-old, whose poetic beauty had already inspired several portraits from the painters in Antonia's entourage.

Constantly touched and fussed over, Sebastian had long grown weary of the attention, praise, and platitudes from Antonia's set. Although Antonia's universe always struck Sebastian as one big treasure trove, he had spent his entire life cooped up with adults, intense and crazy artists who bored him with their lengthy soliloquies about art and their impassioned philosophical debates. So, when he first laid eyes upon the blonde waif his mother brought home Christmas Eve, he was exhilarated to finally have someone, at last, with whom to engage.

The first time Sebastian heard Conrad play the piano his stomach twisted with a painful balancing of emotions. His delight at Conrad's supernatural talent only just eclipsed his envy and fear. But with Conrad's untouched soul, and the essence of purity about the strange little creature, Sebastian was infused with a kind of hope he hadn't yet experienced, even though it threatened him in the same breath.

Up to this point, Sebastian had been Antonia's favorite project. From the moment Antonia had first held her newborn, the tender aroma drifting off talcum powder skin, his silky body melding with her own, she knew he was destined for greatness. Antonia had proudly claimed his illegitimacy as "a secret she must keep to her grave," lest she shock the world.

Rumors abounded, but those closest to her doubted Antonia even knew which of her many grand flames might have sired this progeny.

Sebastian hadn't only been a gorgeous little infant, but a quick one too. Antonia lavished praise upon her treasured cherub whose every stage of growth was chronicled by portraits, photos, and even impressionistic paintings that lined the walls of the D'Antonio manor. He began crawling at five months, walking at nine, and by the time he was four years old, he sat at the piano, plunking out interesting note configurations. Antonia immediately seized upon Sebastian's random interest as a sign that he would one day become a great pianist. She didn't bother to investigate other talents he might have.

"Whatever for?" she would say when asked. "Sebastian is a distant but direct descendant of the exalted JS Bach, himself!" She immediately hired a teacher and Sebastian's career was launched.

By the time he was eight, Sebastian had mired through the scale inspiring *Well Tempered Klavier* and Chopin's *Preludes*. His teachers were extremely well paid and they, in turn, all assured Antonia that "Sebastian had the gift." Antonia would beam each time she heard such pronouncements. Beckoning him with a bejeweled hand, she would walk Sebastian through the French doors that opened to a large pool and show-case gardens to present to him the "exquisite glory of all that nature and the gods had to offer."

Towering shrubs shielded the privacy of Antonia's grand 9,000 square foot mansion, which she called *Maison de la Passion;* an epic estate, an idyllic playground of exotic imported plants, a vista of shapes and chroma that awed the artists who spent endless hours trying to capture the exquisitely haunted gardens.

Imported mythological statues strategically graced the grounds. A robust Bleeding Heart flanked the marble arms of Eros, its aching stems drooping red and white heart-shaped flowers for the God of Love. As one traveled the endless maze of cobbled footpaths, one might stumble upon Prometheus, Aphrodite, and naturally Apollo, God of Music. Or if reading by the Chinese lanterns under a star-filled night, glimpse an imagined wink from Venus ensconced near the Asian alcove, where Japanese ivy blazed scarlet in the fall.

Antonia touted her horticultural fantasy as "that of Hesperides combined with the dogged spirit of the country garden, for one should not tame the growth of any marvel of nature."

Sebastian loved the ritual late afternoon strolls through Antonia's botanical menagerie, as she proffered obscure facts about new arrivals. "They called these gigantic tubers Hottentot's bread because they were eaten during times of famine," she might explain.

Or when Sebastian giggled at a large paw-like growth and said, "It looks like its foot's swollen," Antonia laughed right along with him.

"Like the poor fellow sat in the bathtub too long, eh?" she winked, and Sebastian laughed all the harder. "This is known as *elephantipes*. She took care in precise annunciation. "And where do you suppose it gets its name?"

Sebastian frowned a moment. "A elephant?"

"*An* elephant. Bravo, darling." Antonia took his hand and drew him along the ever-winding paths. "Names are important. You'll understand that more as you grow older. That's why I called you Sebastian instead of Ralph."

"What's wrong with Ralph?"

"The same thing that's wrong with Roger, John, and Fred." She said the names as though they were sour on her tongue. "They're uncommonly common. Sebastian is special."

Sebastian's favorite parts of the garden were the dark edges that bordered the thick evergreens; mysterious skin-prickling adventures where dragons lived at the heart of the forest. Sebastian alone must conquer the evil warlock who had cursed them so that good could reign over the land once again.

"What a delicious imagination you have," Antonia said as she leaned over Sebastian, who gazed in fascination at the sundews, their fuzzy tentacles and red top a glistening sticky seducer of gnats and mosquitoes. They had stopped for several days to check the progress of a mucus-smeared midge that had slowly succumbed to the tentacles.

"Guess he's had it but good!" Sebastian exclaimed in awe.

"I'm sure this poor insect thought he was merely stopping for respite. And now it's sweetly wrapped in death's caress. One must be cautious when enticed by the succulent, by the appearance of one thing when it may turn out to be quite another."

"Someday I'm going to put this in one of my stories."

"Yes, dear." Antonia's voice was uncharacteristically void of encouragement.

"Did you like the last one I wrote, Mother? Uncle Max thought it was super and said I was on my way to becoming a 'thorough,' whatever that means."

"I believe he was citing Thoreau." Antonia sniffed. "And it's wonderful for you to have your stories, sweetheart, but you must never forget your true calling."

Sebastian glanced at his mother and appeared to pout. "But… what if that's not my calling?"

"Don't be ridiculous, Sebastian. Music is most definitely your destiny."

"It's just I don't want to make a mistake and become something I'm not supposed to be. Don't you always say the only important thing is to follow the 'heart's desire?'"

"Yes, my dear. And your heart's desire is most certainly the piano. It runs in your blood. Why, darling, it's in your very DNA."

Sebastian returned his gaze to the dying bug. The sun began to slant over the dogwood trees as Antonia continued discussing his future. He watched her profile in the darkening blue, entranced by the soothing tones of her voice, her sculpted fingers tracing a half-moon upon his cheek as she bent to kiss him on the forehead.

She pointed a finger toward the lifeless insect. "As you can see, such momentary lapses in judgment can alter the course of one's fate forever."

𝄞

After she adopted Conrad, Antonia cleared the center of the grounds for direct sunlight and erected a monument to Hermes, patron of music, surrounded by fifteen of the rarest breeds of her favorite of all flowers, the rose. And the following spring when Sebastian was ten, and Conrad seven, she whisked her "young muses" off to Greece where she purchased a marble statue of Anteros.

Sebastian fell in love with all things Greek Mythology, steeped himself in Aristotle's *Poetics*, Sophocles' *Oedipus Rex*, and devoured *Antigone*. Conrad, on the other hand, spent hours watching glorious Santorini sunsets as he wrote music.

Several weeks after their return, she created a special arbor for the Hermes statue next to the brother of Eros, God of mutual love. The superstitious took this as a sign of foreboding.

"Antonia, the brothers were considered opponents in mythological lore. Why tempt the fates?"

"My dears, haven't you realized yet that we're in the process of creating our own mythology?"

As the boys grew older, Antonia knocked out a wall in the library to accommodate two opposing Steinway Grands so Sebastian and Conrad could play duets together. She would often sit in the corner, eyes closed in utter contentment when she heard the two distinct personalities joining in "musical exaltation." She reveled in it and urged them on from her favorite alcove just between the house and the pool, reluctant for the music to cease.

Although Sebastian was outmatched, his age, larger hands, and sheer determination leveled the playing field. Each heightened the other's gift, honed their instincts, induced a competitive edge that wasn't born of gladiators in the ring, but of the highest purpose of accomplishment.

"It's rather strange and wonderful," noted one of Antonia's current consorts, sipping a Manhattan poolside.

"What's that?" Antonia asked.

"The way they play. They compete, but not like men."

"Darling, they're boys."

"Boys turn into men."

> *"It is a wise tune that knows its own father,*
> *and I like my music to be the legitimate offspring of*
> *respectable parents."*
>
> Samuel Butler (1835—1902),
> English author.

"This family is swollen with musical genius," Antonia declared to a motley group of artists after dinner one night. "My my, haven't I told you all why the boys are so talented?"

Sebastian and Conrad jostled each other as Antonia began to tell her favorite story to a horde of new and eager listeners. "Because, my dears, their great-great-great grandfather was an direct descendant of the unequaled and divine Bach himself. Did you know that?"

The current legion of Antonia fans would gasp in awe as the boys would shake their heads, raise eyebrows.

"So you've proclaimed," Conrad said.

"About a million times, Mother! Oh, do please tell us the story again." Sebastian groaned as Antonia warmed to her performance. The boys play-acted the parts, both rushing about like wild beasts or Conrad jumping to the piano to melodramatically accompany her unfolding story.

"...and as you know, the prodigious and exceedingly prolific Johann fathered twenty children. By some reports as many as twenty-three. He was redressed by the authorities for consorting with an unknown maiden in the organ loft..." Antonia always baited her listeners at this moment, taking a long and emphatic draw from her rhinestone-studded cigarette holder. "And even if they determined for propriety's sake—or biography's sake—that the maiden to whom they referred was Maria, his first wife, well, we cannot know the whole and entire story, can we?"

At this point Antonia would take a slow, deliberate sip of her drink, savoring the anticipation, teeing up the next dramatic moments: "Why," she'd begin, her voice dripping with mystery, "they're not even sure the body they uncovered during the new construction at the Church of St.

John is truly Bach's. Buried in an oak coffin. So were twelve others." She'd wave a hand with a dismissive flourish. "So… I went ahead and hired a master genealogist, a true sleuth of bloodlines. And he discovered that my great-great-great-grandfather, Franco Ricci D'Antonio, was indeed born from that very same inestimable genius." Her voice dropped, tinged with sorrow and scandal. "Unfortunately, like many in those days, he was also born a bastard son, his mother dying in childbirth, leaving her dark secret to a priest who took the boy in and raised him as his own. It was only on that priest's deathbed that he finally confessed: Franco Ricci, and by extension, my family, could trace our lineage, indisputably, to Bach himself."

Antonia would pause, relishing the gasps, the reverential sighs, the awe-struck silence. Once she had them spellbound again, she'd lower her voice, leaning in and proceed in a terribly dramatic voice: "And on the day I was born, it is said that Franco Ricci, at the venerable age of ninety-eight, was so absolutely delirious with my birth that he finished the last in a series of concerti which he proudly entitled, *For Antonia,* and with the last note traced upon the brittle paper, he keeled right over with a smile on his face, passing the torch of genius to the next generation." Antonia shut her eyes, quivering in minor ecstasy, and then beamed at her audience as if she had just imparted the eighth wonder of the world.

It was rare, but occasionally a guest would challenge Antonia to produce evidence of her stated claim, but she merely motioned with her flowing sleeve toward either Conrad or Sebastian at the piano. "I should think that's all the proof you need."

As the boys grew older, Antonia was gratified to see them help each other to become better. Sebastian, who was quite simply good at anything he tried, taught Conrad to ride, hunt, play tennis, and one memorable summer while they were home from boarding school, exposed him to a stylized version of the "Flight of the Bumble Bee."

"'The Bumble Bee Boogie,'" Antonia said sharply one afternoon, "may be the high point in some unemployed lampooner's career but will not be in my boys' repertoire."

Sebastian encouraged the first illicit movements toward rebellion and as soon as Antonia left the house, raced Conrad to the library where they hastened the syncopation of the boogie to furious speeds, outpacing one another until they could go no faster and fell into a heap of giggles.

Conrad returned the favor by showing Sebastian simple techniques at the piano. Even with his large hands, Sebastian faltered repeatedly over difficult fingering, so Conrad instructed artful alternatives that not only made the passages easier but increased his range with fluent elegance. And when Sebastian struggled with timing Conrad suggested, "Use your left hand as sort of a metronome. That will keep your right hand in tempo."

"How'd you get so smart, genius?" Sebastian teased him good-naturedly. "*You* must be the one related to Bach!"

When Sebastian turned twelve, Antonia and Conrad drove him to his new boarding school, a private musical preparatory where Conrad would join him when he came of age. On the drive home, Antonia was caught off guard when she realized that Conrad was crying. His pain was so un-childlike; Conrad's silent tears stained his cheeks as he stoically peered out the window.

"Darling boy." Antonia cradled him to her side. "We're going to do something special to help distract us from missing our dear Sebastian. Yes, we have such an adventure ahead of us."

Because of her extreme wealth and her seats upon many of the musical societies, those who might have snickered, or gossiped wildly behind her back, were very clear Antonia was inordinately powerful in the world of art. True, she had no talent of her own, save to appreciate talent. At best, she sang opera with strangled vocal cords, sketched inferior landscapes, or massacred violin cantatas for bored but generous guests. Her own achievements dwelled in mediocrity, but it didn't matter. "I am rich, and I have money," she was fond of saying, and her generous spirit was the lynchpin to keeping her soirees financed and happy. Antonia had many "projects" and was eager to assist a struggling artist if she deemed they had a modicum of ability. And if she sensed there was greatness, there were no lengths to which she wouldn't travel.

"I believe an artist's surest destruction is to isolate from the world and forget that there are other things besides their art," Antonia said.

They had just come from a session at 30th Street Recording Studios, also known as "The Church," in Manhattan, listening to one of Antonia's protégés record the dense meditations of Bach's *Goldberg Variations*. Afterward, Antonia took Conrad to one of her favorite "Top-Offs" as she called all her after-dinner drinkeries. Antonia ordered Beluga caviar and two shots of Pepper vodka at the trendy hangout. She poured Conrad a small bit of vodka cut with a large dollop of water and then leaned to him. "We won't allow you to turn out like other child prodigies."

"Prodigies?" Conrad asked, for he had heard the word applied to him time and again.

"Mozart, for instance." Antonia sniffed with melancholic disdain. "An over-pampered, bug-eyed boor who never had a dime to his name. Unfortunately, genius is imperative for the great, but it can be so bloody unbecoming. Look at Beethoven, who composed—" she wrinkled her nose "—beside overflowing chamber pots. No, no, no. I won't have that." She grinned at Conrad and then became serious. "Indulging in the heedless excess of the self-obsessed or remaining stunted in your emotional growth is not required to become a brilliant and successful musician." Antonia waved a filtered cigarette over his head. "And it isn't about balance. Pah! It's perfectly appropriate for you to be utterly absorbed with your music, but don't forget there is another world outside the melodies in your head. A world of people, places, and things you will from time to time want to taste and take delight in. Don't cut yourself off from that world, for it is the universe of the living with all its delicious and very flawed humanity that will make your music spring alive."

"What is my world, Antonia?" Conrad asked quietly. As much as he loved spending time with her, Conrad often interpreted Antonia's words as contradictory, and he was already devoted to and obsessed with his music.

"Why, it's with your brother, Sebastian, and me, sweetheart." She put her hand over his.

Conrad stared at Antonia's hands, soft as velvet, with her bracelets and many rings secured about fine veined fingers, then turned it over and traced the lines in the palm.

"But, Antonia, where do I come from?"

"The orphanage, dear one."

"No. Before that."

"Did you know it was Bach who said the sole aim and reason for music is 'none else but the glory of God and the recreation of the mind?'"

Conrad frowned. That wasn't an answer. "Who's God?"

"God is you." She held him close, kissed his forehead. "You, my child, are divine. But you mustn't tell anyone. They shall be frightened by what they don't understand. That is the difference between you and Sebastian. He is talented." Antonia took a long draw off her cigarette. "But, my dear, he is extraordinarily mortal."

Conrad practiced in the mornings and was tutored in the afternoons in math, literature, and history for his eventual enrollment in Sebastian's prep school. Several evenings a week he and Antonia would travel into the city to attend opera, foreign films, theatre, and occasionally a salon of literary and artistic individuals for whom Antonia would have Conrad perform. It was what the world had been like for Sebastian before Conrad came along, and now, with Sebastian gone, it was Conrad's turn to keep Antonia amused. It was during such an evening that Max Ehrenshoffer, Antonia's longtime friend and a professor of composition at Juilliard, first heard Conrad play. He had been on a lengthy sabbatical and hadn't yet met "the wunderkind" referred to in many a correspondence.

As usual, Max arrived winded because he had dined to excess and drank a few too many Gewürztraminers with fellow colleagues. Rotund, balding, and on the quaint side of surly, Max arrived that evening and handed the ever-shadowy Sir Walter his derby as he followed him into the over-crowded parlor. He stopped and closed his eyes as he heard Liszt's commanding "Mephisto Waltz." The frenzied glissando plucked the hairs from his neck, and it was only when he bumped his way through the mass of bodies, just as the music peaked in a shattering crescendo, that Max saw a young boy melded to the piano using a foot pedal.

"It's one thing for Liszt to have pulled off his own music," Max said in his gruff Teutonic accent, "but for a boy in britches to achieve such utter brilliance…" His voice had broken with reverence as he cornered Antonia. "You must let me teach this child, Antonia."

"As you wish." Antonia smiled, as that is what she intended all along.

Several days later, Antonia invited Max to the house and when he arrived, she led him to the library, where he paused, listening outside the door as Conrad's fingers flew over the keys in thirds, sixths and just as nimbly jumped into major 7ths. The boy already thought far beyond formal structure, Max realized, and was quite comfortable expanding the levels of atonality.

"Conrad, this is my dear old friend, Professor Max, remember? From the other night. He would like to hear you play," Antonia explained after entering the library where Conrad was busy practicing. "I will let you two gentlemen at it, and we will have lunch poolside in an hour."

Max's mouth went dry. He was nervous, expectant. He wanted to hear Conrad almost as much as he feared it. Had he witnessed a virtuoso the other night, or had he simply imagined it? And if he hadn't, and this boy was as remarkable as he believed, then what? He tried to calm himself.

"What would you like to hear?" asked Conrad.

"Why don't you share with me your favorite Mozart."

Conrad began with Tchaikovsky's "Nutcracker" and for a moment Max thought he had misunderstood him, but then he began to tease the piquant melody into a minuet, segued into Chopin for a brief interlude, climbed a scale to enter Mozart's *Eine Kleine Nacht Musik* and then counterpointed it with Bachian panache, switching back and forth between the two, illustrating the influences one had upon the other. Max was astounded. This child was making the statement that to hear one composer, one hears the composers who proceed and follow him, the influence and derivative—a testimony of musical history. And then he presented an altogether new piece of music, a sweeping Rachmaninoffian escapade which sent chills up Max's spine.

Eyes closed; Conrad's muscular tiny jaws clamped in a state of fervent grace. He gently swayed with his own creation. It struck Max that he was a child possessed. When Conrad finished, he waited a long moment and then opened his eyes and refocused as if he had just returned from a journey and was pleased to see he had alighted in the same room from which he left.

"What was that you were playing?" Max asked.

"I call it Antonia's Passion."

"It's yours then? Your composition?"

"I rather think of it as Antonia's," Conrad remarked, jumping from his bench. "Are you ready for lunch?"

*"I listen to the birds singing. I marvel at the manifestations
of rhythm in its million different forms in the world of light,
color and shapes, and my music remains young through contact with the eternally young rhythm of Nature."*

Leoš Janácek

When Sebastian returned home for the summer the two boys spent as
much time as they could away from the piano, continuing their explo-
ration into the neighboring forests. When they ran into the barriers of
barbed wire fence, they returned the next day with wire cutters. Their forays took them farther and farther from home, and soon they began packing enough food for the entire day.

They were ravenous by dinner and Antonia had to slow them down,
informing them more than once that, "the difference between beast and
man is not only the thumb, but the ability to use a salad fork."

There were few evenings when the three of them dined alone. Most
nights, the usual suspects sat elegantly dressed and smartly quipped at the
long dining room table. There were insignificant regulars, and of course,
one or two new protégés added into the mix. Max was often present and
invariably asked the boys to play. Having taught thousands of students
over more than forty years of living and breathing music, he was amazed
that two such talented musicians resided under the same roof. It was clear
to him, however, that while Sebastian had a sense of style he had rarely
seen in one so young, his chief talent lay in his ability to mimic.

"He's a quick learner, that boy of yours, Antonia."

"And Conrad?"

"He has no need to learn. He possesses the music as it possesses him."

Antonia's eyes narrowed at this remark. "Have I mentioned to you,
Max, that we are direct descendants of Johann Sebastian Bach?"

"Dear Antonia." Max lowered his voice. "You know how much a
scholar such as me would love to entertain the notion that Sebastian is
indeed related to the *Meister,* but a man of knowledge requires evidence."

"Oh, Max, you're being a poo-bear! I've told you my great-great-great grandfather wrote brilliant masterpieces that were ahead of his time, but that no one was willing to publish them."

"Then share them with the rest of us?"

"It's buried somewhere up in the attic, isn't it, my sweet?" She winked at Conrad, who was listening while he sat at her feet, toying with the exquisite malachite metronome Antonia had discovered in Greece, the metal reed clicking back and forth between a miniature agate Apollo and Dionysus. Tick tock. Tick tock.

"Yes. Antonia showed it to us," Conrad said, "didn't you?" And Antonia laughed at Conrad's complicity.

Max realized he was being teased. "Now why would you make up such a story?"

"It's not a story. You heard Conrad for yourself. We are of gifted blood in this family." As if she'd completely forgotten that Conrad was adopted. She stretched out a slender arm. "Sebastian, come and kiss Mama and off to bed, the both of you."

After eight long months in the musical preparatory dedicated to nothing but rules and regulations, Sebastian longed for the freedom to roam the forest and skip stones against a lake, climb a tree, or race Conrad to the edge of the huge canyon they had discovered his first week back from school. He adored Antonia and didn't want to anger her, but there were times when her obsession with the piano, and his future married to it, rankled him.

Antonia watched her dark-headed beauty saunter off with Conrad. He had begun to test their golden rule, skipping morning practices, she noticed, sleeping in later and later. Scurrying off with Conrad and secreting him away as long as he dared, so that as the days passed, he sat at the piano for fewer and fewer hours. She let it go only because she knew he studied hard at boarding school, and Conrad had little need for practice.

Every day Sebastian would nab Conrad so they might unearth all the exotic mysteries that lay deep in this forest beyond Antonia's fortress, a magical land of damp leaves and dank air, where they had captured evil villains, protected damsels in distress or slayed fire-spewing Minotaurs to save their kingdom. Fighting all those monsters worked up a powerful appetite, so they stuffed themselves on fresh blackberries, lolling about in a plush stretch of clover near the lake, and in the stillness of humid afternoons, they shared lazy secrets, ambitious dreams, inventing the world, inventing themselves.

Sebastian would take out his notebook and jot notes for his next story. Or he would read them aloud to Conrad who begged him every time to hear more. "It's like being right inside an adventure, Sebastian, like the movies!"

"Yeah?" Sebastian would crow, feeling pride. He would lean against a mossy rock and sigh, for it was these moments he absolutely loved more than any. And found the nagging thoughts return: Why must he practice so often? Why all the endless hours of discipline? What if he had no desire to play? Why couldn't his talent to spin a "helluva yarn" as Antonia's latest "gentleman friend" had observed be just as acceptable? Why not leave the mastering of this fine instrument for the one who had all the potential: Conrad?

He would come upon his strange younger brother positioned at the tip of the pool or transfixed in Antonia's Garden, eyes closed, gently moving, leaning back and forth, his hands errant with movement as if conducting his own private symphony. Sebastian studied him closely, wondering what it was he was doing, but also knowing that it was something special and private, something he couldn't be a part of.

"Conrad, I told you it's time for lunch," Sebastian snapped one day after he had clocked Conrad gently swaying by the pool for nearly an hour.

Conrad opened his eyes, blinking in confusion.

"What in the hell were you doing?" Sebastian demanded.

"Feeling it," Conrad said.

"What?"

"The tone… the vibrations."

"What tones are you talking about?" Sebastian found himself becoming increasingly confused and angered by Conrad's differentness, as they got older. But Conrad merely looked through him.

"The music."

"What in Christ are you talking about?"

"The music in the earth..." Conrad's huge eyes were filled with genuine awe. "Can't you hear it too?"

Sebastian shook his head. "Jesus! What malarkey. One of those poet-philosophers fill your head with that pompous rot? You know they're all full of shit."

Conrad's eyes filled with tears. Sebastian leaned down, put his ear to the earth. "Know what I hear?" His eyes grew large with eager surprise. "Applause."

But when he stood, Conrad wasn't laughing with him.

"Never mind." Sebastian kicked a twig by his foot. "Go ahead, Connie." He felt a quick stab of regret. "You go ahead and listen to it..." His voice was soft as he ruffled Conrad's hair, "...whatever it is, little genius."

A few weeks before Sebastian was to return to school the boys discovered a new boundary to their kingdom they called "the great abyss." They frequently stood at the edge of the craggy cliffs in companionable silence staring into the deep and vast expanse that overlooked the canyon, both absorbing the absolute enormity of their lives and how infinitesimally small they were in it.

In those quieter moments, Sebastian sensed, more than he knew, that he didn't command the same gifts for music so evident in Conrad's performance. Although he nurtured a certain style and élan, a flair for showmanship with his gargantuan hands that had extraordinary reach, his virtuosity didn't come easy. It was difficult to entertain jealousy because his younger brother clearly believed Sebastian walked on water, and loved him for being able to swing across the lake on a rope, for his ability to span the huge kidney-shaped pool in half the time Conrad could make it, for showing him how to spear a nightcrawler on a hook and cast it to where it was most likely to catch a fish. Sebastian knew Conrad loved him for more than what he had to offer musically; he loved him with unmatched purity. He could harbor no genuine resentment toward his brother.

Conrad felt at home in the deep of the forest or the edge of the canyon, hearing all the sounds seep up from the ground. Shutting his eyes, he would release the rest of the world from his mind and listen: The general hum reverberating from the surrounding landscape became instruments warming up, moving from chaos to a gentle distillation of melody. Yes, he heard the first whisper of a motif. The wind swelled in plaintive accompaniment, and now the crescendo of a hawk segued into the next movement. The timpani scuttle of an animal accentuated a recurring theme until every flicker of vibration turned into a symphony of nature, the source of music as real as if it belonged to a ninety-six-piece orchestra. Conrad became a spirit possessed by the terrene melody as it infused within him, becoming part of him. In that moment Conrad understood Antonia's words. He was with God. What else could it be, this absolute purity, this unequaled sensation thudding through his veins—

"Conrad!" Sebastian screamed.

A hairline crack opened beneath Conrad's feet. Sebastian saw the shale, splinter, scattering loose pellets into the void. As he lost his footing Conrad felt the collapse of the earth below him into the deep ravine.

Sebastian leapt with surprising agility as he lurched for Conrad, snapping a hand about Conrad's wrist, sickening at the sound of Conrad's body as it thwacked against the side of the cliff. Sebastian heard the cracking of his skull, saw his forehead rupture, a cinematic trail of blood painting his cheek. Sebastian held on for dear life and with more strength than he knew, pulled Conrad's battered body up from the cliff.

Conrad's gasping and choking were only interrupted by Sebastian's insistent mantra, "you'll be okay, Connie… hold on, Connie, we're almost home." In fact, they had at least an hour's stretch, and Conrad flopped over Sebastian's muscular body like a sack of flour. Each step was harder than the last. Sebastian's shoulders ached as if he'd swum miles, but the fear of Conrad's blood now cold and sticky against his jaw propelled him forward. Conrad's agonized cries finally exhausted into stillness.

When Sebastian entered through the open French doors, caked in mud, sweat, and blood, the lifeless Conrad over his shoulders, Antonia turned a ghastly pale. She grabbed Conrad and calmly instructed Sebastian to open the garage door. They slid into Antonia's sleek Spider Alfa Romeo, Conrad limp and cold upon Sebastian's lap as Antonia sped recklessly through the countryside to the hospital.

Hours later, after Antonia heard Sebastian's stuttering defense, his hands still frozen, his eyes red with tears, Antonia knew she wanted to die if Conrad was going to. She held Sebastian close. She stroked his head and distracted him with stories, a bravura reprisal of her old life when she had misguidedly trained to be an opera singer, of the nights when her throat became so raw she could no longer make sound. "That was sacrifice. Sometimes one must sacrifice, darling." Antonia forewarned, knowing the loss of Conrad would somehow make the parade of their lives cease to make sense. "Don't misunderstand. Sacrifice has gotten an ill-deserved rap. It is not necessarily a bad thing."

When the doctor finally came to them, his shadowed expression awakened her worst fears. "He's in a coma. We are running more tests and doing all that we can, but Mrs. D'Antonio, I'm afraid the only thing we can do is wait."

For the next three nights and three days, Antonia and Sebastian lived in Conrad's room, his round face pale, his long lashes enhancing the darkened circles beneath his eyes. Sebastian held Conrad's hand, examined the skin, shape and tendons, as if in studying them he could somehow understand more of Conrad's essence. He had failed Conrad as his protector and, while punishing himself, he tried to quell the flicker of hope that ravaged his stomach. If Conrad died, perhaps some of his brilliance would ebb its way into his soul, his own gifts wouldn't appear so lacking. He bit hard into his bottom lip, hating himself for such selfishness, that such a thought could enter his mind when all he wanted was for Conrad's eyes to open. He wept at his grief and collusion.

At first, Antonia's words were a distant chatter but as he focused on his mother pacing beside Conrad's bed, a mythical halo blazed about her in the early morning light. An optical illusion? Sebastian's mind was fragile with exhaustion and grief, but as he watched her lips making words, stretching over a wide chasm, she once again told the story of their esteemed family's lineage. How tragic that they couldn't have met this great descendant, but how extraordinary to know his magic lived on in them all. How pain was part and parcel of an artist's life and the only thing one could do was to use that pain to better one's art.

As Antonia continued with her ardent soliloquy, her words began to filter in and through him, their potency resonating as gospel truth. The more he listened the more he believed. While Conrad's life hung in the balance it was the only thing he could hold onto, and it was here that the family legends and myths took seed and were transformed from the pithy flights of Antonia's fancy to a powerful and sacred legacy.

On the third day, when Antonia said, "And you and Conrad shall be great pianists, world famous. That is your purpose in life."

Conrad's eyes opened. Neither Sebastian nor Antonia aware that he was watching them talk.

"Yes, we will play for you, Antonia," Conrad responded weakly, but with utter conviction. Antonia and Sebastian moved with cautious urgency to his side. Apprehensive with relief, they each took a hand, fearful he might slip away again.

From that point on, an unbreakable bond formed between Conrad and Sebastian, and the covenant between the two of them to Antonia was impregnable: Their world was created solely for the three of them and their music. It didn't matter how many outsiders might flow in and out over the years, this triad was the core of their existence. Antonia loved her boys without end or exception. Sebastian rose to the challenge as Conrad's protector and Conrad challenged Sebastian to elevate his standards. The fourth plane of this tautly constructed tetrahedron was music. It gave their union shape, meaning, and motive, and their symbiosis created the solid matter that was their world.

> *"To do easily what is difficult for others is the mark of talent.*
> *To do what is impossible for talent is the mark of genius."*

Henri—Frédéric Amiel (1821—81)

Sebastian grew into the densely muscular form of the father he'd never known, with a full-blooded Italian sensibility controlled by his quick intellect. He was shamefully handsome, and not unaware of his assets. Sebastian drew people in with his multifarious gifts; wit, generous charm, exquisitely kissable lips that broke into a killer smile, accompanied by the humor in searing blue eyes. And "The locks of Heathcliff," Antonia always quipped as she ran her long, slender fingers through his thick, unruly, dark romance-novel hair. He was always surrounded by people, regardless of the venue. Magnetic. He was eagerly sought after by students and was just as easily appreciated by his teachers, who found themselves wondering if their belief in his talent wasn't somewhat persuaded by his genial flair.

Conrad, on the other hand, seemed utterly divorced from any sense of style or social mores. From the moment Conrad entered the pristine halls of the prep school, the military row of beds and the austere walls filled him with anxious memories of the orphanage. He didn't possess the easy diplomacy of his brother, nor did he care to exercise restraint with his opinions. He was, in fact, quick to point out a professor's mistakes in timing and phrasing. It wasn't a cockiness born of presumption. Comments drawing attention to a professor's errors were made in earnest, without a hint of guile.

When he suggested to one teacher that he was inordinately attached to the traditions of Romantic and Classical structure and therefore ill-equipped to analyze his compositions, the rebuke was so gently direct that it caused more hard feelings than if he had been arrogant. Amongst themselves, the faculty couldn't quite pin down what it was that frustrated them so, because in truth Conrad was often right. It wasn't that he was full of conceit or superiority, either. His comments weren't made for impact. He never resorted to histrionic theatrics as so many others. His insistence was substantially more irritating because it was quiet and certain, and because he never questioned his stance on a matter they concluded, finally, that his was a "socially regressed state." Yes, he was "a social misfit."

Without Sebastian's constant interference, the argument could be made that Conrad would have quickly faltered and failed to thrive. As it was, Conrad sequestered in his room, where he wrote endless sketches. But the more the staff was willing to write Conrad off, the more determined Sebastian became to make Conrad sociable. He spent many an afternoon pulling Conrad out of his room or hunting him down during one of his isolated walks while the rest of the boys were boasting about girls and talking about Sophia Loren's "rack."

Conrad's lanky body grew faster than he could control it, and while he was incredibly strong with his wiry musculature, he had no use for sports.

"What the hell is wrong with you, Con? I've seen you throw a football almost as far as me. Why don't you put your heart into it?"

Conrad merely glanced up at his brother. "It's a waste of time for me, Sebastian. But you enjoy it, so I'll come to watch your games. How's that?"

Over time, Conrad's unique personality, which had originally held Sebastian captive, now caused him considerable embarrassment. He grew weary of jumping to Conrad's defense, trying to explain his bizarre quirks, arguing with him about what was appropriate and what was better left unsaid.

Antonia noticed the delicate thread of tension between them, a snappish defensiveness that only relaxed as the summer unfolded and they fell into old patterns, easy familiarity. Antonia tried not to be disturbed by the opposing trajectories her two young princes were traveling toward at the speed of light. She masked her anxieties by calmly attending to their needs. She instructed Tula, the German cook, to make their favorite foods. Sir Walter attended their every comfort. She bought them new clothes to fit their growing forms. Just when she thought Sebastian and Conrad had returned to their unbreakable bond, tempers would flare, and a ridiculous argument would erupt.

"Next year you better stop with all idiosyncrasies, okay?" Sebastian, lying by the pool, flicked water toward Conrad. "Do you understand? This is my last year. I'm not going to always be there to go out on a limb every damn time you decide to make a point of something. And why do you have to do it, anyway? If they're wrong, they're wrong. Don't make them feel their ineptitude."

"But they're doing the music a disservice."

"Connie, damnit! They're a bunch of old fops on tenure. They've been teaching the same damn theory, composition, and interpretation for the last century. Humor them."

"Like you do?"

"I know when I'm right. I know when I'm wrong. The difference between the two is a quick smile and a wink."

Conrad got up, disgusted.

"And cut your hair. You look like a vagrant." Sebastian's voice echoed after him.

Antonia frowned as Conrad removed himself into the house. Sebastian glanced uneasily her way. "Really, Mother, does he have to be such a goddamn eccentric?"

"He has to be who he is darling, just as you must." She gently ruffled Sebastian's hair, then got up and followed Conrad into the house. She found him in the library tinkering upon his piano.

"Come with me," Antonia whispered as she took his hand and led him into the gardens. For some time, they walked in silence and Conrad found himself relaxing in the exotic beauty, these paths as much a tonic for him as they were for Antonia.

"Darling, you look as if you carry a great burden upon your shoulders. Whatever is the matter?" she asked while pulling a pesky bug from a leaf.

"Sebastian thinks I need to say I'm wrong when I'm not."

"Sweetheart, that's because Sebastian does not want people to think you're difficult or off-center."

"But I'm not interested in being in the center."

"Yes, darling," Antonia declared, "we're all quite clear on that."

"Do you want me to try harder?" The only person Conrad never wanted to disappoint was Antonia. "I will, Antonia. I promise I'll make more of an effort."

Antonia continued down the path to an arbor shaded by a huge row of grape vines. "Why do you suppose I've planted these exquisite celandine poppies around this arbor?"

Conrad shrugged.

"Because they require very little sunlight. They live on their own inner strength." She led him farther on, then stood before a showcase of delicate miniature roses, trellised all about Icarus with melted wings. "And these exquisite creatures require sun. Sun shining bright and fiercely upon them."

She watched Conrad's lucid gray eyes take in the allegory and then walked him to the gazebo that housed opposing marble statuettes of Apollo and Dionysus. She sat and patted the space next to her.

"It was Apollo with his kithara—" Antonia gently flicked away Conrad's bangs so that she might see his eyes "—that created simplicity and clarity. And over there you have Dionysus who preferred the reed-blown woodwinds full of sensual abandon and earthy emotionalism. From the beginning of time, it appears the real has opposed the intuitive, the intellect countered the imagination. It represents the two extremes of aesthetic."

Conrad frowned as he glanced from Dionysus to Apollo. "Yes, you two are different," Antonia said as if reading his mind. "Vastly different. But that does not mean there isn't room for a meeting of the minds."

Conrad jammed his hands into his pockets. "I don't know if that's possible anymore."

"You know I have spent many years creating this garden. Not just this—" she waved her hands at the vast expanse of shrubbery and statuettes "—but with all the things I do, the people I bring here. These influences are for a purpose. To have you both exposed to a hotbed of talent, to beauty, to all the things that an artist needs to feed his soul. I want the seed of purpose and aesthetic planted so thoroughly that when you go out on your own you will suck the nutrients you require from the world to grow into the men that you shall become. After you leave our little greenhouse, it will be up to you to acquire the things you need to make yourselves whole."

Conrad absorbed this. "But all I want to do is my music."

"Naturally. But there will come a time when you want to love, though I trust that will be far less of a need for you than Sebastian. Just remember dear, the more light he gets, the better he grows."

By the time the boys were both attending the Juilliard School of Music, their distinctions attached themselves to their bodies as ornaments to a Christmas tree. Sebastian grew a fashionable goatee, his deep-set eyes became a richer blue, his rebellious crop his crowning glory. He wore tailored suits, tweeds, rich-colored vests, and snappy shoes, dressing for success; his free and easy laughter, his delicate charm, his generosity all twinkling allure.

Conrad's attraction came from his lack of artifice. It was his bareness that drew people in, his absolute disregard of the physical. His slender form eventually filled into a lean musculature. He cut his hair so that it fell softly at his neckline, exposing his chiseled jawline and intensely soulful eyes. He moved about with quiet grace. His hands were born for a sculptor's stand, so sensuous and slender they became the object of many a private fantasy long after lights had dimmed.

Even with their contrasting personages, the two young men were never considered separately but always thought of as a pair. If a young woman became attracted to Sebastian, his swarthy eyes teasing her, she would inevitably think of Conrad, and wonder what ardor lay in his silent strength. Or if drawn to Conrad's gentle presence, they might suddenly blush to imagine Sebastian's full lips nearing to kiss them. Antonia once remarked her sons represented the two elements of man, intellect and animal, and one experienced a yearning to know both. The D'Antonio brothers. The composers. "*Les frères créateurs.*"

Sebastian's instant popularity was no different at Juilliard than it was anywhere else. He had a reputation as that rare breed—a musician who wasn't only talented, but handsome and personable in the bargain. While Sebastian held court late into the night with his many admirers, Conrad labored long, solitary hours creating orchestrations, stark and original, so unlike the intensely theatrical compositions of his brother.

Max Ehrenshoffer, who now taught them in a professional capacity had grown quite fond of both, had been intrigued to see how they would mature once they escaped Antonia's Garden of Eden, which he believed to be a parasitic cesspool of talentless egos, all of whom took advantage of Antonia's beneficence.

"*Mein Gott*, Antonia," Max would bluster in his thick accent, "why do you waste so much time and money on these no-good drifters?"

"Because I want Sebastian and Conrad exposed to the world of art."

"But these are just a bunch of sycophants."

She glanced at Max with an amused expression. "Precisely."

The following summer, Antonia quite suddenly realized her two boys, had indeed, transformed into men. Sebastian now sported a robust five o'clock shadow. She delighted in the savagery of his intoxicating grin as it picked up the glow from the Chinese lanterns, drinking cocktails in the evening. As they lay at the pool, she could see the stretch of sinewy muscles as Conrad's lean body flung taut off the diving board. Sebastian's deep brown accentuated his white teeth, and his blue eyes Antonia sighed "are the color of a cerulean sea." Conrad's rich honey-blonde hair, stained by the summer sun, became a halo around his perpetually thoughtful face. She gazed at them admiringly, repeating her constant refrain to guests, "Conrad's my beauty, slender and fair; Sebastian my beast, with raven-black hair."

Nightly parties filled the marble hallways with gossip, politics, and theatrics. It was an education of pomp and personality, of rapier-edged repartee, of meaningless diatribes on the meaning of art, of words spread around to feel their weight, paid by the pound. For Sebastian it was as if slipping into a hot bath, invigorating, stimulating; he felt relaxed and the wiser afterward. Endless debates of art versus man, art for art's sake, what did an artist owe to the world, became nothing more than mental masturbation for Conrad. He would often stop the rhetoric with a succinct response that stunned his listener dead in their tracks. But mostly he begged off early, while Sebastian greeted many a morning with bloodshot eyes and stubbly cheeks, growling charmingly when Antonia asked if he had had a good time.

Practice remained the only serious regime of the household, and no matter how few hours' sleep Sebastian had, he managed to settle himself at their newly acquired Bösendorfer piano, its immaculately polished spruce gleaming in the afternoon sun. "With nine extra keys, you should be able to compose infinitely more music!" Antonia teased. "Liszt believed the Bösendorfer was the only instrument able to withstand the power of his play. How fitting that it should be your weapon of choice!"

Antonia's favorite moments were walking through her gardens while hearing the echoes of her offspring deeply immersed in practice; Sebastian remained forever devoted to the Classical and Early Romantic composers with an affinity for Beethoven, Chopin, Schumann, Mozart, and of course his doppelganger, Liszt. He exhibited little intellectual curiosity in expanding beyond the most popular and standard of the repertoire. The post-modern movement made him uneasy with its wild disregard for structure and discordant bent. His reticence revealed itself in his early compositions, uninspired knockoffs of his favorite masters.

Conversely, Conrad ran through every conceivable musician from the early Renaissance and Medieval composers straight through to the experimental works of Schoenberg and Cage. Cage had caused quite the controversy in the universe of music with his "4'33".

Sebastian said, "So he gave us four minutes and thirty-three seconds of nothing. If you ask me, nothing more than silence and a poke in the eye."

Conrad defended Cage's innovation. "But his intention was for you to hear beyond the silence, to take in the ambient sounds of one's environment."

"Sure, Connie, whatever you say." Sebastian shook his head, but he felt a bit inferior. He didn't understand how Conrad had the ability to hear the music in Cage's composition, just as he hadn't heard the music of the earth when they were children. He didn't share his brother's fascination with all the experimentation, nor with progressive pioneers.

And while Conrad could appreciate the new movement in music, he didn't do so without maintaining a constant attachment to, and fixation with, Bach. He tasted every piece of music available to him, savoring the familiar sweetness, as well as the bitter discord, devouring composer after composer, until he felt he had "distilled their original intention."

"But whatever do you mean by that?" Sebastian snapped.

"The more exposed I am to a composer, the more I understand where he began, and how everything grew out of—"

"Extracting their DNA, are you?"

"If I can find the kernel, I know that composer."

"Sure, Con… sure." Sebastian slapped him on the back. "They're just men, like you and me." But the grin disappeared as Conrad returned to the piano. He knew all too well that, despite sharing and forever being bound by their unwavering devotion to Antonia, he and Conrad had grown into vastly different men.

"So, life fades and withers behind us,
and of our sacred and vanished past,
only one thing remains immortal — our music"

Jean Paul

Antonia strolled through the paths of her garden, and quite suddenly couldn't remember where she was. Invariably she found herself in the middle of something, somewhere, unable to retrace steps. She blamed it on the lonely winters; less and less seemed to be filling her time. Now that Sebastian had graduated with some acclaim he would often stay at The Algonquin in the city, where he met with agents, managers, but mostly old classmates he'd party with. Conrad was preparing for his third year of Julliard. Without her "jewels," the world was less inclined to glitter, her proteges were less and less appealing and rarely inspiring. Even her grand gardens she found lacking. And time was playing tricks on her; the short days dallied, endlessly long, while the summers' long days went by in a flash. Why, the boys had barely been home, and so often returned to the city for recitals, meetings, and dates, although she found very little evidence of anyone sticking. But how she missed them. *Now, where the hell were her rose clippers?*

Conrad and Sebastian too had noticed Antonia's increasing distraction. She would trail off in the middle of sentences, and several times Conrad found her sitting in her favorite alcove, as immovable as her marble gods, well after it had gotten dark. He would gather her up, her skin chilled, and wrap his blazer around her shoulders, leading her back to the house. But in other moments she returned to her steadfast enthusiasm for her projects, regaling both over cocktails about a brilliant new painter, or try to tempt them to view the exceptional orchids now blooming in the hot house.

Tall shadows followed Antonia, Conrad, and Sebastian one fall evening as they ambled through the gardens. Antonia continually stopped and sighed, tenderly observing all the plants and trees, the statues she had lovingly hand-picked.

"Oh, my lovely, lovely garden," she mused and then, as if talking to herself, "who shall take care of it?"

"What do you mean, who will take care of it?" Sebastian prodded.

"'Tis the last rose of summer.'" Antonia leaned down to smell the fading rose bush, all the blooms closed in the evening chill. "'Left blooming alone; All her lovely companions are faded and gone.'"

"That was lovely, mother." Sebastian kissed her cheek, and they strolled on. "Thomas Moore is excellent company."

"Well, I must have someone to entertain me while you two are gone."

"And what of your *protégés?*"

"I'm sick of them. I'm sick of all of it," Antonia snapped sharply. "It's nothing more than laundry detergent, don't you see?"

"What?" Sebastian asked glancing at Conrad.

"Nothing more than a commodity with no care for the art." Antonia's voice was full of disdain.

"Is it then?" Conrad's voice was calm, as he nodded imperceptibly toward Sebastian. It appeared Antonia was experiencing one of her tangential shifts and the two were trying to follow her train of thought.

"Really, Mother, you're sounding rather morbid tonight," Sebastian gently teased Antonia.

"Well, you two must certainly know half the idiots in this country think Stravinsky is a brand of Vodka!"

Suddenly Antonia lost her balance. Conrad quickly took an elbow and steadied her gait. She grabbed his arm, and looked up at him with a weary desperation in her eyes. "Oh, Conrad. Don't ever let them destroy you because they don't understand your talent."

Conrad brushed the hair from her face. "How 'bout we head in for a nightcap, then? It's getting chilly."

Antonia turned to them both, and looked at them, quizzically. "Don't I seem the picture of health and vitality?"

"You, Mother, seem absolutely delicious." Sebastian picked her up and whirled her about. "A rose is a rose, or so the saying goes, and you, mother dear, are a rose for any year."

Antonia began laughing and Sebastian joined her, and they laughed until they couldn't stop. Conrad loved that Sebastian had such a talent to make Antonia happy, especially in these past months.

"Come on." Sebastian put her down. "I'm going to perish if I don't have a Manhattan."

"Yes," Antonia said. "Why don't you go make us a batch? Excruciatingly dry. And I'll be up shortly. I just want to sit here until the sun sets."

They turned to her with doubtful faces.

"Bloody Christ." Antonia threw her hands up. "Go on. Go on."

Conrad and Sebastian walked to the house. But after a half hour, when Antonia hadn't returned and Sebastian was deep in conversation on the phone, Conrad decided to fetch her. He lit a cigarette and walked through the darkening paths when he saw her sitting in her favorite alcove in much the same position they had left her earlier.

"If you want a cocktail, you better hurry. Sebastian's already two drinks up on you."

She didn't respond and as he approached her in the dusky shadows, he could see she was attempting to make words, but nothing was coming out.

"Antonia? What is it?"

But her lips distorted, as she lifted a hand to Conrad, a terrorized plea in her eyes, for the words she couldn't utter.

Conrad swept her up, half running with her trembling body in his arms, screaming for Sebastian, who flew down the stairs, saw his mother flailing awkwardly in Conrad's arms.

"Oh, Jesus, NO!" Sebastian ran to them, putting his hands to Antonia's face. "Mother, speak to me!"

But she couldn't speak, though her eyes spoke her terror.

"God, no… Please, Mother—" Sebastian looked frantic as Conrad tried to steer them both to the couch.

"Help me get her down," Conrad panted.

They lay her stiff body on the couch, but she began jerking as if she were having a seizure. Conrad picked up the phone, and tersely ordered an ambulance.

"Come on, Mother, we're here," Sebastian said, "we're right here. We're not going anywhere." He cradled Antonia's head in his lap, and looked at his brother as the horror of Conrad's childhood accident washed over him with startling clarity. "It's just the three of us. Like always. Remember what you said when Connie got sick? 'Can't have it. Can't bust up our little trio.'" Sebastian's large hand gently caressed her cheek. "We'll even get on, right, Connie? No more bickering."

Conrad stood there, helpless, his voice barely audible. "No more bickering."

Conrad paced anxiously through the corridors, up and down the hallways, then finally approached Sebastian, who sat repeatedly rubbing the furrows in his brow. He offered him a cigarette.

"Tell me she's going to be okay, Connie."

Conrad nodded with the certainty that Sebastian counted on. The certainty that had that very morning infuriated him.

Their need for this woman bound them together, the foundation of their lives threatened. If something were to happen to Antonia, it would leave them motherless, and with no one to appease their growing differences.

The prognosis was indeterminate. Her seizure had all the symptoms of a stroke, but her behavior challenged the diagnosis. The second day she was in the hospital she returned to her old self, spouting cultural challenges to the day nurse until they released her, and she left, informing the doctor, "I don't know how you can expect anyone to survive in the antiseptic isolation of this prison. Put some paintings on the wall, for God's sake."

Sebastian and Conrad looked at one another in heady relief. Life resumed its natural shape, and they left with their foundation intact.

The boys were leery of leaving until Antonia appeared to be the picture of health and ensured them both, "I'm not going to entertain any such folly as depraved as death!"

Sebastian returned to one of Antonia's city properties and Conrad to Juilliard. In their youthful optimism, they believed everything would be perfectly normal. But with each visit, it became painfully clear Antonia's health was rapidly declining. They became much more attentive to her needs, coming home every weekend, and attempting to understand the vast requirements of the estate. One late afternoon, Conrad sat in the darkened living room with Sebastian.

"She's so pale and drawn," Conrad whispered.

"She looks so... so old." It was a statement of disbelief. Sebastian shook himself free of the image and rose to stretch. He surveyed the library, his eyes lingering on his brother, then he wandered outdoors for distraction.

Sir Walter slowly escorted Antonia into the room, then re-emerged with tea. He fastidiously adjusted the tea service as Conrad joined her. When Sir Walter cast aside the heavy drapes to reveal the sun throwing angular shadows, they could see Sebastian cleaning leaves from the pool.

Conrad poured Antonia chamomile in her favorite teacup and watched her as she tried with great difficulty to lift it to her mouth. His throat tightened with sick futility as he watched his mother, now barely recognizable as the vital woman she once was, devastated by illness, frail and thin, her hair in an elegant turban, a blanket loosely gathered by her knees.

"Sit, Conrad." Antonia's voice was a whisper. "Sit with me a moment."

She patted the settee and Conrad edged onto the corner as he pulled the blanket to cover her better. He sat with her in silence for some time, until she moved brittle hands over his own.

"Your hands are a piece of art, Conrad, strong and beautiful. But most importantly, the tools of God."

For a long moment, she was silent, and he felt her grasp weaken. Conrad wondered if she had dozed off, then realized her eyes were focused on Sebastian as he aimlessly pushed the dying leaves from one side of the pool to the other.

"It's sad for him... he doesn't know."

Conrad heard a strange note of unfamiliar resignation in Antonia's voice. He frowned.

"I have one regret. I never allowed Sebastian to do the one thing he truly wanted."

"What are you talking about?"

"His stories…" She smiled bitterly. "I was selfish." Her voice cracked and she took a long moment before she added, "And I'm going to be selfish again when I ask you to promise me, Conrad." Urgency made her voice stronger. "Promise me."

"Anything."

Antonia turned to him, and he was shocked by the harsh finality in her eyes.

"Promise me that you will help him make beautiful music and that he will never know the truth about himself. About his talent. He must always believe in himself. If he doesn't… he won't thrive."

Conrad glanced at Sebastian, his fine and handsome brother, then back to Antonia.

"I promise."

NEW YORK, 1968

"Great music must always come from the heart. Music should always be first emotional and only after that intellectual."

Maurice Ravel

It was late afternoon as Alexandra strolled out of Armory's music supply store in the heart of Manhattan, her arms laden with new sheet music. She walked briskly, taking in the God of Hermes majestically enveloped in subway steam atop Grand Central Station.

She dashed as quickly as possible to *Notes From Above* where Peter, a friend was holding a work-shopping recital featuring Chopin's most poignant and evocative Preludes, and Nocturnes. Crowded with people and smoke, she tiptoed in, not wanting to distract.

She took a deep breath and settled herself so she could concentrate on the exquisite artistry not only of her colleague, but Chopin who remained a favorite novel; familiar, oft returned, a best friend.

She closed her eyes and listened to the exquisite *Nocturne No.15 in F Minor,* the haunting, silky climb of notes as they turned on themselves.

"Ouch!" She exclaimed as someone jostled into her while trying to squeeze past. She opened her eyes, barely registering the man attempting to escape the crowd. "So sorry! Excuse me," gruffly uttered as he made his way out the door.

She almost didn't recognize him, his head hung low, but it must be.

She followed his path out.

"Sebastian?"

When he turned it took him a moment to collect his bearings. "Alexandra..." He smiled vaguely.

They stood in silence a moment. She noted a difference about him, a diffidence uncharacteristic of his self-assured swagger. The fullness in his face made her think he had gained weight, but his body appeared the same. His eyes were red. Clearly, he had been as affected by the music as she had been.

"You, okay?"

"Bad night."

"Oh. Hungover, are we?" she baited then saw he was struggling.

"Bad nights. Bad time, I guess you could say."

"Sorry to hear that." She stopped teasing.

He seemed lost.

"Are you still with Ketterling?" Alexandra asked.

"Yes and no. They extended my contract, and I have one more performance and a recording to fulfill... but I've taken a leave after that."

"But why?" Everyone knew that stopping in the middle of a tour could kill a fledging artist's career.

"I think my brother was right," he responded as if she knew what he was referring to. "One can only do so much with the repertoire. If you've heard one mediocre retelling of a master's notes, one should certainly have the good taste and breeding not to subject audiences to another."

"Are we feeling sorry for ourselves?"

He attempted a sarcastic smirk, but she saw all the cockiness fade away. Naked. Fragile.

He cleared his throat, unsuccessfully. Choked a bit as he turned from her.

"Sebastian, are you all right?" Alexandra checked her watch. "Look, I'm terribly sorry, but I have to be somewhere."

His eyes rimmed with tears. He sniffed defensively

Alexandra whispered. "Please tell me what's going on?"

She watched him as he seemed suddenly shy, deflecting her gaze as he quickly dabbed his eyes. "My mother. My dear, sweet mother. How she loved that piece... the Nocturne."

"I didn't know."

"Damn, was she extraordinary. So endearingly eccentric."

"I'm sorry."

"You know how you hear from people who've lost someone that they never know when the spigot will suddenly—" He glanced down the street, flecking another tear from his unshaven face, trying to collect himself.

"I'm so sorry, Sebastian. I had no idea."

"Really, it's ridiculous. It's been awhile now. It just happens to be her birthday today. She's the one who introduced me to *Notes*. Somehow, I still can't quite get used to it."

Alexandra glanced at her watch.

"How rude of me. Please. I don't want to keep you."

"I don't think I should leave you."

"Really, I'm fine."

"Is there someone I can call?" Alexandra wondered if she knew any of his friends. Sebastian was always surrounded by people. "You mentioned a brother?"

Alexandra peered into Sebastian's eyes and saw his pain, a vulnerability that made her suddenly feel deeply sorry for him. "My mother's throwing a terribly boring dinner party and it's probably the last thing in the world you'd like to do or even need to do, but at least you won't be alone."

"I'm loathsome company."

"Loathsome's perfect." She smiled with encouragement. "But if I know you, you'll have *her* eating right out of your hand within minutes."

They stood in silence. One weighing the options, the other weighing the cost.

"Truth is, Mothers do happen to like me." Sebastian exhaled, shrugging casually to revert to his former self.

"Don't get too far ahead of yourself. You haven't met mine." She juggled the packages in her arms so she could scribble down the address and noticed that the cuffs of his trousers were wrinkled too. She passed him the slip of paper. "Here you go. Dinner's at seven. And I won't blame you a bit if you beg off!"

Claire Von Triessen's lips melded into the same studied smile she reserved for all celebratory occasions. It was a special Sunday dinner with several well-appointed guests; Amongst the twelve participants was a news reporter from the Village to ensure mention, along with their marginally useful neighbors, Fritz and Mimi, and Mr. Irwin, the new curator of Bedford's Historical Musical Society.

Claire had become a board member of the Society shortly after Alexandra had won the Ketterling and had appointed herself the chairwoman for the annual fund-raising dinner. Alexandra watched with a mixture of irony and irritation as Claire spared no expense in using her daughter's fame to anoint herself Queen of the Arts & Philanthropic Wonderfulness.

"Maybe you should finish up your face before our guests arrive." Claire's deft innuendo wasn't lost on Alexandra, as her mother was clearly aware she had already finished preparing for their guests. But to relieve herself of Claire's demoralizing appraisal, she escaped up the stairs.

As Claire watched her daughter walk away, the smile slipped from her face. She had never truly expected her daughter to rise to fame, always doubting she had the resilience for such a ruthless world. Yet, despite her reservations, Claire couldn't help but feel a sense of satisfaction at her own ascent within the social sphere where she so effortlessly reigned.

It was only when she rigorously removed her makeup that she could wash away the strain of affectation. As she smoothed back the ever-deepening creases around her eyes, only then did she allow herself to feel the growing resentment she felt for her daughter. Had she not created the gold platter of opportunity for Alexandra that she herself had never been offered? The grudging jealousy singed like heartburn.

When the doorbell rang after her guests were seated in the drawing room with their respective martinis and Manhattans, Claire couldn't hazard a guess as to who would interrupt the Sunday cocktail hour. She excused herself and walked into the foyer as one of the kitchen staff opened the door. She knew the man but at first, couldn't place him.

Ahhh, yes, it was Sebastian D'Antonio. He'd aged and something more since the night of the contest, yet he remained inordinately attractive as he appeared in the framed eight-by-ten photo by the piano—Alexandra, victorious at the Ketterling, with Sebastian and Chandra flanking her sides.

"Mrs. Von Triessen?" he offered warmly.

"Mr. D'Antonio, isn't it?" She put out a gracious hand. "Isn't this an honor? A surprise, to be sure."

Alexandra was just coming down the stairwell and upon hearing the smooth voice, felt her hand tremble at the railing.

"My daughter failed to inform me that she had invited a guest."

"I'm sorry mother." Alexandra made her way down. "My mistake."

"I do so hope you will join us." Claire began to add up the benefits of having this devilishly handsome runner-up at her dinner table.

"I don't want to impose."

"No imposition at all," Claire's voice regained its purr. "I'll have staff set an extra plate." She waved the waiter toward the kitchen. "Alexandra, can you take Mr. D'Antonio's coat and join us for drinks?"

Alexandra waited until her mother had left, then slowly walked up before him, and studied him a long moment with curious eyes.

He gazed at her. He couldn't quite understand why Alexandra's beauty always took him by surprise. Sebastian was no stranger to the glamorous and exotic, but for some reason, Alexandra's allure was different. He was always caught off guard by the intensity of those electric green eyes half-mast with feigned disinterest, the seductive clef in her chin, the refined features, her elegant neck.

She led Sebastian into the dining room where Claire was already ushering her guests. As Sebastian sat and began talking to one and then another, she observed him carefully. He had returned to his suave and self-confident manner, but having seen the pain earlier, she now knew that another Sebastian existed, much like the anxious and insecure musician the night of the Ketterling finale. It was that man she wanted to know. She noted that she was finding no displeasure whatsoever as she watched him regale her mother's guests with his careless bon vivant charm. Just risqué enough for the bluebloods to enjoy themselves without feeling they'd crossed any boundaries of their impeccable breeding. Just as she had suspected, by the main course Sebastian had every one of them eating out of his hand. Especially Claire. His calculations weren't mean-spirited. He simply enjoyed people enjoying themselves and liking him.

"So, Mr. D'Antonio," Claire started.

"No. You must call me Sebastian." Which, of course, made Claire blush and pleased her vanity.

"Sebastian, are your tours over?"

"Almost. I have one last concert at Carnegie next week along with a recording and then I will have finished out my obligations with Ketterling."

"Why, you make it sound as if it's torture." Claire laughed.

"It may well be … for the audience."

"Now you're being too modest," the curator said.

"They've kept Alexandra so busy," Claire said, her chin tilted almost defiantly.

"As it should be. She was the winner."

"I'm sure you are every bit as talented, Sebastian," Claire said with evident non—modesty. "You know these things are so often political."

"Your daughter's winning had nothing to do with politics, I assure you."

"What are you working on now?" Alexandra was eager to turn the subject.

"Actually, I've decided to move on to composition."

"How ambitious," Claire exclaimed.

Alexandra cocked a brow his way. She put a finger to her temple, which she commonly did in moments of study. Sebastian just didn't seem the type at all to write music.

"And how is that going?" Fritz's wife Mimi asked.

"Quite frankly, it's going terribly."

Alexandra heard the desperation beneath his wry humor.

"Hitting the stone wall?" Fritz asked.

"So much so I considered taking out insurance." They all laughed.

"Don't be so hard on yourself. Sometimes it takes just that one glimmer. A moment where you see something and then it becomes instantly clear what you should be working on," the curator kindly offered.

"Yes," Sebastian answered looking directly at Alexandra. "I've been waiting for that to happen."

"All it takes is persistence. My wife and I argue about this all the time," Richard interjected, so as not to be excluded from the conversation. He put both hands in front of him palms up, weighing the scales of attributes. "Talent/persistence. Talent/hard work. Talent/commitment."

"Seems your daughter got the best of both of you." Sebastian nodded graciously to both Claire and Richard.

"You didn't tell us he was so charming, Alexandra." Claire's pronouncement was laced with the question on everyone's minds; how charming did Alexandra find him?

"Yes, well, I knew he'd get around to telling you himself." Alexandra gave nothing away, but her smile was infectious, and he joined her, and they all began laughing.

Claire insisted on seeing Sebastian's performance at Carnegie and purchased tickets not only for the family but also invited Mr. Irwin, the new curator, to tag along so she could boast at her next bridge party about the outing. The last thing in the world Alexandra wanted to do was sit with her mother while listening to any kind of music. Particularly when it was someone she shared both ambiguous and strong feelings for. She was tense throughout the day and by the time they arrived at one of the true legendary halls of musical history, she had a teeming headache.

She stood idly by, vaguely aware that she was drinking a bit too much champagne to dull the throbbing at her temples. Amid the throngs crowding the foyer, she noticed an unusually large number of much younger women, all unmistakably there to swoon over Sebastian's performance. There was a twittering excitement in the hall. And it wasn't because these women were thrilled they were about to hear the transformative works of Liszt and Prokofiev. No, it reminded Alexandra of the feverish adoration she had sensed from a crowd awaiting The Beatles who happened to be playing at a conjoining venue with her earlier in the year.

"Your friend is quite popular!" Claire remarked as she handed Alexandra a program. "I don't know that I've ever seen people so enthralled by Liszt."

Alexandra didn't respond as she took the program and used it as a fan. She just wanted to get this over with. But as she sat there, waiting for Sebastian's performance to begin, she felt the same drill of nerves for him she had fought the night of the competition, only more so. She glanced at her mother, who was watching her carefully and felt her stomach heave. Something about Claire... and Sebastian... she couldn't put her finger on it.

As Sebastian stood on stage the audience roared in good-natured appreciation. And true to form, Sebastian played with the flair fitting this theatrical arena. But she couldn't enjoy the performance. Not because of the headache, but because she was nagged by something that eluded her and made her increasingly tense.

Something about Sebastian reminded her of her mother.

After the performance, Sebastian invited Alexandra, her parents, and their group, along with several of his acquaintances, to join him for drinks at Smithey's, a well-known hangout amongst the classical music crowd.

Sebastian bowed modestly at the applause upon his entrance. He played the perfect host to the motley group of people who had no connection to one another save the experience they had just shared. As the evening progressed, Claire and Alexandra's father left with a tipsy Mr. Irwin in tow.

"Finally." Sebastian sat next to Alexandra, who had kept to herself most of the evening and now wished she had left with her parents. "Well?"

"It was… lovely, Sebastian." Alexandra lied. While the majority of his screaming fans had no clue what they had heard, Alexandra and Sebastian both knew it fell short. He was capable of so much more.

"Alexandra," he scolded.

"Given the circumstances," she muttered quietly

"That bad, eh?"

"I didn't say that, Sebastian."

"It's okay. We both know I wasn't prepared. Truth is, I didn't give a shit. I just wanted to get it over with." Sebastian lit a cigarette. "Thing is, once I was up there and saw the crowd, I was mad as hell with myself for pissing away this opportunity. I love playing for people. I… shit. I screwed it up, but good."

Alexandra found Sebastian's honesty compelling. She put a hand on his. Sebastian glanced at Alexandra but looked away again quickly.

"Give it time, Sebastian."

"I think I've given it all the time I can afford." He mashed his cigarette against a bread plate. "Look, I'm leaving for a few weeks tomorrow. May I call you when I get back?"

Alexandra nodded silently.

Sebastian looked at her then in earnest, leaned as if to kiss her, but simply put his lips to her ear.

"Miss me."

Two months later, Sebastian showed up at the house unexpectedly. Alexandra was deeply immersed in John Updike's *Couples*, tucked neatly between her lap and the covers of *Life* magazine, in the backyard near Claire's prize roses. The moment she heard his rich, languorous voice, her throat tightened, her heart suddenly making its presence known. She pretended to be caught up in the novel all the while listening as Claire pried with sly innuendos. Sebastian lobbed back intriguingly vague retorts until Claire, her voice smooth as silk, offered, "How does a Manhattan sound, Sebastian?"

"Fabulous idea!" Sebastian winked.

Claire smiled back flirtatiously, and Alexandra felt nauseous as she watched her mother's unctuous maneuverings.

"Come on!" Alexandra grabbed Sebastian's hand the moment Claire returned to the house.

They made a mad dash to the perfectly trimmed hedges of prize roses in every hue. They laughed as they slowed their gate, both grateful but slightly awkward now that they were free. Alexandra gave Sebastian a polite tour of the silvery cinquefoil on the left, and then her favorite "Brandywine Petals" on the right. The sun was lulling its way to the horizon, bathing the impeccably pruned gardens in an amber glow.

"Extraordinary!" Sebastian nodded his head as he feigned interest.

"Okay. Enough about the family Rosacea..."

They walked a few more steps in silence.

"So, what have you been up to?

"Not much."

"No, really Sebastian—"

"Again, not a hell of a lot!" Sebastian muttered. "No matter how long I sit at the damn thing. Nothing."

"What does your teacher say?"

He shrugged.

"You are still taking lessons?"

He shook his head. "What's the point in playing well, if you have nothing to perform?"

"What an odd thing to say."

"It's true, isn't it?"

"Practice is law, number one and number two, the point is to get to the heart of it." She pulled her exquisite French braid along her collarbone. "To make yourself better. In any event, to at least *think* you're getting better."

"I guess I've been procrastinating." He stopped and turned to her. "It seems no matter what I try, it doesn't work. I mix things up, practice, play, search." He threw up his hands. "I've tried every trick in the book."

"Perhaps too many tricks?" Alexandra mused.

"I don't know. Is there such a thing?"

They could hear Claire's voice as she searched for them. Sebastian quickly pulled Alexandra beyond the dense hedge and out of sight.

"Trust me. We can't hide from her forever."

"No?" Sebastian peered into Alexandra's eyes "How do you know me so well?"

She considered a moment, the first notes of desire stirring in her. "Honestly, we're not very different."

"What do you mean by that?"

Alexandra started walking farther away from the house. "For one, we're both quite good, when we work at it. For another, it's not like it comes naturally for either one of us."

"Let's give us a bit more credit than that."

"I'd rather call it as I see it. We've both got the drive and are simply too terrified not to suit up in our Sunday best. We're going to make it no matter what gets in our way. We rise to the occasion and we're arrogant enough not to fold during competition." She paused to pick at a gnarled petal curling in decay.

"Okay, I'll settle for second place, but nothing is quite as good as winning." His eyes pierced hers. Teasing. Challenging.

"Seriously, Sebastian. You still haven't figured out why we won?" she asked.

Sebastian's eyes turned serious. Suddenly what she thought was very important to him.

"We're the perfect poster children for the impossible-to-fund world of serious music," Alexandra stated dryly.

"We won because we deserved it," Sebastian defended.

"Come on, Sebastian. Sokolov was head and tails above us all. But he's a complete gnome—hardly presentable on a marquis. And poor Hampton's beyond brilliant but he medicated himself out of the competition. Even Molino—catching the flu? I don't think so. He simply couldn't take it the pressure."

Sebastian's eyes clouded as a part of him empathized with the terror that had driven Hampton to such self-destruction.

"Like Chandra," Sebastian murmured.

"Chandra's a better technician than both of us put together. Her father made her choke."

"That's just it. You can't choke during a concert."

"I know Chandra. She never choked before in her life. Playing for people who were listening to *her*, not her commander-driven father's idea of music. Don't you see?"

"No. I don't."

Alexandra sighed in frustration as if she were dealing with a young child who didn't grasp the self-evident.

"We're impostors." She tossed a shriveled petal to the ground.

Sebastian studied Alexandra, his eyes reaching into hers for a long moment, a question framing the inevitable. He gently pushed Alexandra against the shrub. She tried to stave him off, but he leaned to her slowly, ever closer until she could barely breathe. And then his lips were brushing her own, gently, tenderly, then nibbling their way down her neck, as arousal began to overtake her.

"And what about this?"

"Sebastian, my mother—" She pushed back, breathing heavily

"Am I an impostor now?" He bent to kiss her again, this time his eyes heavy with desire.

Suddenly she found her arms around his neck, pulling his hot breath into her, eager to feel his full lips against her own, hungry for his tongue.

He kissed her deeply. Thoroughly.

"You know why I couldn't work this summer?" he asked between ragged breaths. "Because of you..."

"Because of me." She mocked but allowed him to continue kissing her neck and collarbone, his lips trailing a new hunger through every part of her.

"...wrote sloppy phrases because you eluded me," he playfully whispered while his warm hands covered the length of her back.

"Seriously... doubting that." Alexandra was barely able to form words.

His hands slid under the soft cotton to the rounded flesh of her buttocks. "You break my concentration..." His lips venturing hotly toward her breast. "I need you."

She felt the wet heat of his lips as they pressed against the material of her blouse; the teasing, aching of her nipples pressed against him as she arched for his mouth, grasping his head, pushing him into her.

"Is this not real enough? Am I an impostor now?"

Alexandra bit at his neck, her lips, desperate to meet his desire for her... hers for him.

He kissed her so with such hunger she became lightheaded. "Alexandra... I need you."

They looked rather like a renaissance painting, she thought, as she studied their reflections in the massive floor to ceiling mirror in Sebastian's bedroom. It was two days later. They had broken free of her mother, speeding madly to Sebastian's large estate, kissing, bodies entwined, clothes scraped aside as they barely made it up the stairs, the anticipation electric and primal. They fell to the bed, limbs entwined, pulling, tearing at one another, their bodies meshed in one heaving ravenous embrace. Dawn, sunlight, sunset, time evaporated as they devoured each other. Now, voluptuous purple grapes rested upon the smooth skin of her stomach, lit by the tainted morning blue.

Sebastian plucked one of the grapes and rolled it tenderly over her rib cage and between her breasts, then pushed it forward with his lips as he brought it over the length of her neck up to her mouth, crushing it with his teeth, the cool juice dribbling down her cheek.

He lay back, exhausted from their lovemaking, and reached for a cigarette, but she leaned over him and threw the cigarette to the floor. Pushing the grapes aside she stretched her body over the length of his, her hands pushing his arms above his head, nuzzling his hair, reveling in the odor of sex sweat. She nibbled at his belly button, up and down his sides, lingering over the taut muscles in his stomach, her long soft hair draped over his heated flesh. He was hard by the time she moved down the trail of coarse hair, her tongue gently flicking the tip of his erection, tender pinkened hardness that she took fully in her mouth, sweet and gentle suckling until all he could do was give in to her ministrations. She continued to fondle him, the strokes so slow he knew he would come each time, and each time she held him off just long enough until she finally slid onto him, so wet, so warm and so ready that he shuddered helplessly, moaning as she moved against him until her shudders matched his own and she fell upon him.

He lay motionless, falling into black slumber, neither a twitch nor muscle moving between them save the rhythm of their breathing hearts.

As Alexandra joined him in sleep her last conscious thought was that she mattered. Sebastian had reached for her. Sebastian needed *her*.

She had to return to the flat she kept in Manhattan for clothes.

"I do have a life somewhere beyond the walls of this fortress, Sebastian." She had teased him when he tried to persuade her to stay. He'd insisted Walter could go get her things, but she had countered she would be back in a few hours. She needed to tidy up her absence with her parents, answer mail, pay bills.

Alone, he was forced to think about himself. His future. His career.

"There's nothing as dead as yesterday's performance." Sebastian stood, relieving himself at the toilet, dwelling on this stingy aphorism, and began to feel queasy.

Ordinarily, he prevented just this kind of self-reflection by keeping people around him, whether he liked them or not. Like his mother, he plucked up fledgling companions along his route and brought them to the crumbling estate. Being by himself wasn't yet a skill he had mastered. When he sat in his cavernous demesne alone, he could feel Antonia's every touch and imprint, and it made him miss her desperately.

And Connie. He missed him too.

Without distractions, thoughts edged up around him, making him pithy with self-recrimination. He missed the hectic, hurly-burly pace of Juilliard, the race for a free practice room, the vacuum of timelessness at the piano. He hadn't found Juilliard's ostentation overwhelming. Rather, he had reveled in it, preparing for his debut into the world of the performer.

He didn't love coming in second to a woman. But Alexandra was truly talented. He had mastered the role of second-place dilettante, though, and had enjoyed every moment of it. Even the work. He enjoyed the labor and practice because the judges had validated him. They had chosen him, after all, as one of the preeminent artists of the day. If they believed in him, he certainly could. How could Alexandra be so jaded? They... *he* was not an imposter. He had loved playing for the fans who adored him, approaching obsequiously, molesting his space, touching him as if they had a right to him for the price of a ticket. It had inspired and galvanized him.

As his Ketterling tour was coming to a finish, he had haphazardly worked on pulling his New York debut together, which had received mixed reviews at best. He had filled the audience with his many friends and fans, but their applause couldn't detract from the *Times* review.

"Dramatic? Certainly. Electrifying, to be sure. Didn't his epileptic body English convince you?" or Esquire's "On the whole, a delightful bit of entertainment by an untenably pretty chap whose virtuoso concertizing would best be show-cased with Mr. Arthur Fiedler and the Pops." Cutting words, devised to punish, to excoriate the heart of an artist.

He fixed himself another drink, then sat at the Bösendorfer in the middle of the living room, and placed his massive hands on the keys. Rotely, he played Beethoven's *Appassionata*, a lethargy in his movements. He needed something to propel him forward. Something to give him an edge, to set him apart from the hordes of talented musicians pursuing rapidly at his heels. Just yesterday he had read of a young new talent taking the circuit by storm. Being gifted at eighteen was infinitely more interesting than being gifted at thirty.

In a couple of months, it would be four years since the competition, and he would be thirty-one in July. He walked to a mirror and studied the reflection closely, running a finger over his heavy shadow, around the bridge of his nose, his lush brows. He could see the whisper of paper-fine creases at the forehead, the whites of the eye, imperceptibly duller, a pale yellow despair. Teeth stains a little more noticeable from coffee and cigarettes, his twin vices. He didn't count alcohol. He could drink as much as he wanted and never suffer a hangover. Vague shadows of deterioration might be visible if one closely examined. But who looked that closely? The people he surrounded himself with certainly didn't.

If the critics had been kinder, he would have been able to enjoy another full year of adulation and travel. He detested the whim with which they could destroy, even when he knew his charm would only last so long. As his third gin and tonic laced his fears of obsolescence, anger stirred toward Antonia. She had manipulated him into a career he had never wanted in the first place. He had wanted to be a writer. To create new landscapes. To live out fantastical dreams. *Damn Antonia.* Tears threatened. He could never stay mad at his mother for more than the briefest of moments. But now that he was here, and she was gone, what next?

He was uneasily certain the gifts he had weren't enough to maintain a high-level career as a performer. It left him only one option. Composing. His most natural inclination had been to tell stories, to spin his imagination onto paper. How much different could it be to turn what he believed was a more organic gift into writing music? Sure, it didn't come to him naturally like it did to Connie. Nothing came to him like it did to Connie. But he could hear the traces of a melody.

Yes, he could hear the music, the clanging, discordant howling, but could he find form to give the clamoring shape? Did he have the discipline or technique? He bolstered himself with the belief that although Connie was more talented, Sebastian had far more drive to succeed. That's what got him here in the first place. The drive to please Antonia and his instructors. To play music people *wanted* to hear. Compelled to win them over. Yes, he had gotten quite far without Connie's talent. And where was Connie? Traveling all over the god-forsaken planet like he was an ancient Bedouin, for Christ's sake.

Sebastian paced in front of the piano and looked idly at the pool, making a mental note to call maintenance to prepare it for the summer. The gardens were frighteningly overgrown. Ancient fumes of decay began to drift about the grounds. Antonia had attended to these things, and he had let them run to seed, but he excused his inertia because of the expenses. The trust had trickled to an extremely modest income and now with his Ketterling contract completed, he wasn't sure how he would keep his mother's beloved home intact. God, how he missed her.

He sat and cried. Long, anguished sobs. He was lost and so uncertain of what to do, where to go next. Without Antonia, the structure of school, or the Ketterling tour, he was terrified that he wouldn't have the inspiration to create any sort of path for himself. He needed ... he needed someone to anchor him.

"This house is far too large for one person." Alexandra lay next to Sebastian on yet another elaborate four-poster bed that looked out to the west side of the gardens.

"It wasn't large enough when my mother was alive." Sebastian unfurled a cigarette from a mangled pack of Marlboros from the bedside table. "She had so many people wandering through here it was Grand Central station meets *Notes From Above*." Sebastian lit the cigarette and then regaled Alexandra with Antonia's eccentricities and his unorthodox childhood for the next hour.

"But what happened to your father?"

"It depends on who you ask."

"What do you mean?"

"According to Antonia, it was a terribly important secret, but the last I heard he was a tormented sculptor."

"Is that where you get your brooding angst from?"

"It certainly wasn't from Antonia. I don't think I ever saw that woman depressed about a single thing." Sebastian exhaled. "Maybe that's what living in a fantasy does for you."

"What makes it a fantasy? Maybe it was real for her."

"So, just because you make it real, it is?"

Alexandra sat up. "I don't know. I didn't think you were real at first. And now look at us."

"What do you mean?"

"You know the dashing artiste mixed with musical genius. And—" she paused wickedly "—you're not in the least bit bad to look at."

"You can thank my mother for that!"

"Yes, she was a stunning woman." Alexandra had taken in the many photos and paintings adorning the walls.

They were silent for a while, lost in their thoughts.

"So, what happened to him?" she asked.

"No one seems to know. But one day Antonia got a telegram and proceeded to topple several brandies. Apparently, he had just up and died. 'Aneurysm,' she said. But when I went to Italy a few years ago I did some digging, and from what I could tell with my terribly broken Italian, his aneurysm was caused by a bullet through the head."

"He was murdered?" Alexandra lay down to face him.

"Suicide," Sebastian said quietly. He turned to her, deep sadness in his eyes, but he covered it with a wink. "How can someone possibly let go of life when it's so…" He kissed her intensely. "Ripe with potential." She kissed him back and then snuggled into his arms.

"Was it just you and your mother roaming about this Vatican?"

"And Connie."

"Who's she?" She arched a brow.

"Conrad. My brother."

"Oh, the long-lost brother."

Sebastian got up and walked to the window, while Alexandra admired his fine shape, thick and muscular. He had filled into manhood since she had met him four years ago, and she suspected his was the kind of physique that would trend to dense and thickened weight as the years passed unless he ate well and exercised.

"Well, where is this mysterious brother of yours?"

"I wish the hell I knew."

CONRAD, 1969

"In my music, I'm trying to play the truth of what I am.
The reason it's difficult is because I'm changing all the time."

Charles Mingus

Music. He hears music. No... maybe it's only another illusion. He lies on the threadbare cot, haunted by a series of terrifying images of the orphanage. He sees the other children, the poor unwanted, their faces twisted into Edward Munchian cries of despair.

Suddenly he is running in a thick maze of fog through the gardens, trying to find Sebastian. Staggering over wild ferns, shadows at every corner, he catches a glimpse of him just beyond Antonia's alcove. Yes, he sees the edge of his shoulder, but the moment he reaches out to touch him, Sebastian turns to stone, joining the panoply of Antonia's statues, a garden full of grotesque Sebastian profiles.

Conrad awoke, drenched from fever. It was only when he could feel his heart gutted from his center and the reality that Antonia was indeed dead, that he knew he was lucid. He rolled over on the narrow cot in the canvas tent as the past washed over him, and suddenly felt suffocated by the leaden stamp of Antonia's absence. Even after all this time, he still wore her loss like an anvil upon his heart.

Acute consciousness woke him to the ever-present reality. It was no dream that Sebastian was thousands of miles away, that Conrad had, in fact, picked up and walked right out of their lives.

He drank tepid water, a salve to the blisters at his lips as he fought the last of the fever, the result of a nasty virus he caught several days before boarding the bus in Nairobi. Rattling and knocking about endlessly on the unpaved roads, his emptied stomach a thrashing storm as he slumped, drenched in sticky sweat, until they finally made it to the camp at the Masai plateau, in the middle of a flat savanna.

All through his travels, as he trekked by foot and clatter-trap bus through Asia, India, Afghanistan, into Egypt, and across Algeria, he had been captivated by the will and testament of musical form, humbled by its vast complexities.

Now, a desert and a lifetime away Conrad could feel a chill run up his spine, through his dampened shirt, a cramping twist in his chest. The familiar ache from the time before Antonia and Sebastian, lonely hours crying out from a half-busted crate his mother had buffered with Salvation Army blankets. Crying out to no one, for his mother wasn't there.

As a child, he had often awoken at night in the orphanage, in the long narrow hall where the children slept like lined-up shoes, hands curled beneath his chin, to see his mother leaning over him, her Veronica Lake hair falling softly at her shoulders. But in the early morning pale, when he rubbed his eyes, he saw only the murky outlines of the sacred Jesus in the painting on the wall and cold wrapped its tentacles around his small, shivering body. She hadn't visited him at all. It had been a dream.

Even then he heard the music. He'd tiptoed down the shadowy tunnel of a hall to find Sister Charlotte, the buoyant doe-eyed sister who attacked the organ with gusto for all services. Tagging along behind her sweeping habit he'd stolen sacred moments in the early morning hours before the business of God officially commenced, to privately listen to Sister Charlotte as she indulged in Debussy, Brahms, and her latest obsession with the controversial Prokofiev. It was in the haunting vibrato of the booming pipe organ that Conrad heard the muted alto of his mother's voice as she had sung to him in the afternoons, the aching husk of her crooning, the rising and falling tremolos of disillusionment and pain. Sister Charlotte encouraged Conrad's quiet enthusiasm as he sat listening, first in a pew, then beside her, and finally, underneath her, his hands on the majestic instrument, its vibrations filling him. Healing him.

One morning, after months of such clandestine meetings, Conrad's brows came together in consternation.

"Could I sing the piano?" he asked with quiet solemnity.

When he repeated Prokofiev's First Concerto with absolute perfection, Sister Charlotte immediately ran to tell Sister Marta that they had been sent a miracle. That Conrad was most assuredly a sacred gift from Cecily, patron saint of music. When Sister Marta reluctantly joined them in the day room, Conrad had already begun experimenting with an inverted fractalization of the music, and it sounded every bit like any other five-year-old banging away at the keys. "Yes, quite the miracle," Sister Marta muttered dismissively. But Sister Charlotte knew she had a bona fide prodigy on her hands and spent every available moment teaching Conrad what she knew.

He had adored the overweight and nurturing Sister. When she nestled him in her huge arms, swaddling him in the serge wool, he felt safe. She'd given him his first sense of security. But it was from Antonia's exuberant style and lavish praise that Conrad felt loved, beyond reason or condition. Because Antonia understood that Conrad required a life altogether different than most people. He spent hours sitting with her in her gardens listening to her lilting voice as she explained the world to him. And when she bent to him, cupped his cheek in her smooth palms, and peered into his eyes with a smile, Conrad knew Antonia saw *him*. All of him. And now Antonia was gone.

The night Antonia's lawyer finished reading the will after her death, Conrad had stood rigidly at the glass doors while Sebastian absently wandered through the tender melancholy of Bach's *Siciliano* at the higher octaves of the piano. Neither had slept since Antonia died, and their eyes were mirrored images of inconsolable grief. Their solace was in the music they played for her, for one another, in honor of all that she had given them, her aesthetic, beauty, and grace.

"...and Mrs. D'Antonio has seen to it that you are both provided for, at least throughout the rest of your schooling." The attorney read with practiced condolence. "I see here you graduated from Juilliard a few years ago, Sebastian, and Conrad has yet another year to go." Here the attorney stopped and cleared his throat. "Unfortunately, Antonia's extravagance has cut into what was once substantial wealth, and Juilliard is quite expensive. Don't worry, Conrad. You will be able to complete your schooling, but it has reduced the allowance she set for both of you. Her holdings are quite diminished from what they once were, but the trust will provide for the upkeep of the, uhm, gardens —" again he cleared his throat casting about for the proper verbiage "—the valet/butler and a cook. However, it won't last much longer than five years, at which point I would advise selling the estate. The upkeep on the grounds alone—"

"Dear God, this is our home!" Sebastian broke in. "You act as if we don't plan to make a cent. We haven't been tinkering with the piano all these years merely to delight the debs. Conrad and I are both on our way to promising careers in the extraordinarily lucrative world of classical music."

Sebastian's scathing sarcasm was lost on the attorney, who closed his briefcase. "Very well. If there is anything I can do, or you wish assistance with any of the accounts, please call my office."

Conrad quietly ushered the lawyer out the door. When he returned, he found Sebastian rifling worriedly through the books. Their eyes met in concern.

"Looks like she stopped paying attention to the market." Sebastian sighed.

"I guess *we* should have paid a bit more attention to help her." Conrad's voice trailed off as he pulled another ledger from the pile and flipped through it. They spent the rest of the evening determining which of the staff would remain and settled on Walter and Tula.

"I think we should let the gardens resume their natural growth. Did you have any idea how much Antonia had spent on the hothouse?"

Conrad shook his head no.

"Extraordinary. But then, she won't be here to enjoy it, and it's simply too extravagant. What do you think?"

"It's up to you."

"Just like her, no?" He looked at his brother. This was the last of his family. He cleared his throat, and sighed. "To spare no expense on her appetites. All her little projects and protégés."

"Antonia lived for the beauty of art." A tender smile lit Conrad's face in memory.

Sebastian glanced at his younger brother, sensing a barrier resurrecting itself around his pain. "What do you think, Con?"

He was quiet a moment then shrugged. "Please don't sell anything."

"That's not an option." Sebastian's voice sharpened.

"I don't intend to return to Juilliard." Conrad looked directly at Sebastian.

"What!"

"It isn't for me."

"What the hell are you talking about? You must finish, Conrad. For Mother."

"It just doesn't suit me."

"You can't be serious!" Sebastian shook his head.

"I am."

"God damnit, Conrad. I get that you're different, but how could you ever walk away when you know that's all Antonia has wanted for us?"

A long moment passed. Sebastian looked at Conrad, so much a part of him, yet such a stranger. "Don't do this for my sake. I'll figure out a way to make ends meet."

"It *is* for *my* sake, Sebastian, and I've made up my mind."

When their eyes met, they both saw the inevitable. If either had held on to the fading expectation that they would move forward through life together, they knew now, in that instant, they would have to go their separate ways.

"Run away, Connie… just go and fucking run!"

Later that night, Conrad found Sebastian sitting in Antonia's favorite alcove, his head in his hands, a torrent erupting from his shuddering body, trembling so badly he could barely manage to take the cigarette Conrad had offered. As Sebastian's anguished sobs filled the evening air, Conrad gently cupped a palm to his neck.

"What ... what am I going to do, Con?" Sebastian wept like a young child. A gust of wind eased dying leaves about their feet. Conrad had no answers.

The next morning, Conrad sat at the marble table overlooking the pool. He appraised the gardens as he drank his coffee and felt Antonia's presence still lingering about him. A part of him despaired at leaving this home, the smells and essence of the familiar, at being away from Sebastian, especially with Antonia gone. But the stronger part ached to be far away, unattached and unencumbered, the state to which he was most disposed when in pain.

Sebastian joined him, unshaven, still in his bathrobe. Suddenly he was moved to touch Conrad. He leaned over to pat him on his shoulder, but feeling exposed, pulled cigarettes from his brother's shirt pocket instead.

"So, what are you going to do, Con?"

"Travel."

"You're going to trash it all, then? What about your education? How will you go on with your music?" Sebastian's voice was strained with incredulity.

"There's more than one way to learn. Besides, I think you know better than anyone, I'm not cut out for that kind of education."

"I suppose," Sebastian replied. They sat for a time in silence then Sebastian said softly, "Just keep in touch so I know where to send your checks, right?"

Conrad nodded.

"I can see you now, out on some sand-swept dune, isolated from humanity, just the way you like it."

"I don't dislike people, Sebastian." Conrad's voice was low.

"But you have so little use for us." Sebastian was glib, but the hurt was at the surface, as were the old tensions. Sebastian took a long and rather desperate pull off his cigarette, then frowned as he felt tears threatening. "Right, old boy. What would you like of mother's things?"

Conrad glanced at his brother, could see his evident agony, and admired the part of Sebastian that cast the disturbing aside, that made short shrift of the unpleasant. "I don't want anything." He smiled to take the sting out of it.

"Don't be absurd."

"I'm not. I came with nothing. I'll leave with nothing."

Music. He heard it again.

He had fallen asleep, and when he woke it was late in the night, pitch black save the obscure glow of distant fires through the flap of his tent. He could just make out Mussorgsky's *A Night on Bald Mountain* with its chattering witches, perverse violins, and trombones mocking the spirits. He chuckled; how appropriate to have this music burning in his ears.

He tried to get up. Collapsed. He was too weak to move. But he had to find the music.

He rose unsteadily. Trying to maintain balance, he slowly followed the notes to the northern end of the camp, to a large tarp shack that stood sheltered by a single acacia tree. He wandered in and spotted an old Victrola, and beside it lay a towering man with shaggy hair and an unkempt beard yet dressed in fine clothes that exuded an unmistakable air of wealth and refinement.

"Is it the American chap, then?" the man said without turning.

Conrad tried to place the accent, guessed at Scandinavian tempered by boarding school English. "Yes. I heard your music."

"It always snares Westerners into the lair." The man lifted his enormous body from the cot. "I'm Lars. Heard you were traveling through."

"Yes."

"A composer, they tell me."

"Yes."

"I've been waiting for our paths to cross. I knew in time they would."

Conrad held out his hand and they shook.

"And are you here studying? Or searching?"

"A bit of both."

"Running from? Or running to?"

Conrad shrugged.

"But you're here for a purpose."

"Yes. I believe I am."

"Then you must join me for the Olngesherr."

"What's that?"

"To describe it wouldn't do it justice. When we head to the next kraal in a week's time, you shall see." Lars walked to a cooler and pulled out a canteen wrapped in canvas. He poured two glasses of an amber brew, and handed one to Conrad. "Honey beer. Not my English lager, dear chap, but not too bad either."

After they drank several glasses, Lars told Conrad that he had been a marginally reputable violinist in several chamber quartets at the beginning of his career.

"Then I got lazy and doped up and became a jazz violinist." He quaffed back the brew. "I'm much more passionate about the idea of music than the doing of it. The bane of my existence. I am happiest when it washes over me, but I don't care much to play it."

Lars' eyes were kind and Conrad felt instantly at ease with the older man. He continued to serve beer and talk in his dapper accent, filling the course of the evening with wild adventures of the African outback.

"Originally, I came here to write a book: The recurring pulse and contradictions governed by the number twelve, the most critical number in African music. You see, I'm also rather a math whiz, and I had intended to reveal the deep profundities of such algorithmic music. But after a year of living with these gentle, pastoral people, I no longer wanted to analyze or dissect them. I just wanted to be with them." He had resigned himself to stay in Africa, and buffered by his monthly trust check, supplied whatever goods and medicines made the lives of his wives' tribes easier.

Conrad glanced around Lars' camp shack and stopped at a large framed black and white still of Lars, sporting a younger version of himself next to a slain lion with a group of Masai.

"My good luck charm. I caught that fat cat on my first hunt." Lars' eyes gleamed with an ancient victory. "Put up a helluva fight."

"How long have you been here?" Conrad asked.

"Fifteen years." Lars sighed. "Christ, it goes fast. I began travelling with the Masai, rising each morning to breathe in the rich African air, scratch my belly and live like a fart in the wind."

Conrad chuckled.

"I know what you're thinking—you all lean and hungry—but I learned something a long time ago. I can fight to make things happen or I can sit back and enjoy what comes. All I require is more than sufficiently provided for by my wives and my shipments of music and books. Sure, I still like the sniff of adventure, but I've become reliably sedentary."

Lars then asked Conrad to catch him up. "How 'bout some news now, my good friend? What have I missed?"

Conrad shared with him global highlights, man's best achievements—landing on the moon, Concord's first flight, and man's darkest travesties, the Manson murders. "Oh, and if you are a sporting man, Willie Mays was picked for the All Stars and the second player to hit 600 homeruns. And, oh yeah, there's something called a *mouse* being introduced for computers."

"A mouse? Indeed." Lars chuckled. "Do we go forwards or backwards with our forward thinking?"

"A bit of a wash?" Conrad said.

One of his wives brought in two plates filled with goat meat and maize and handed Conrad a mug of hot tea with the familiar smoky flavor omnipresent in the drinks they had served him as he recovered from his illness.

"Interesting palette, no?" Lars asked as if reading his mind.

"Makes me feel somewhat primal," Conrad answered, and Lars laughed.

"Yes, that would be the blood in it." Lars studied the younger traveler. "Let's dig in, shall we? What is it you're in search of, young man?"

At dawn, a cow was brought into the center of a huge circle of tribesmen. All day long a blistering heat spun lazy circles of vultures smelling the kill. Kudo horns trumpeted preparations for the ceremony until well after sundown. At last, the full moon shone over the campsite as hundreds of Masai prepared for the ritual ceremony.

"They pick an unblemished cow with no markings," Lars illuminated as a slow, husking chant emanated from the tribesmen. Dressed in togas of decorated hides, they jumped from side to side in their ritual dance, a frenetic leaping of sinewy legs as they circled and then closed in on the beast. An arc of blood spurted out in torrents from a spear thrust into the cow's neck, painting the frenzied warriors who captured the sacrificial blood in mud-thrown bowls. The chief sprinkled dusty chalk into them which Lars explained was "magic powder."

"These Masai warriors now become elders," Lars said as each of the men sunk to their knees and drank of the potent offering, then they passed the bowls to the older warriors.

Conrad stared at the congealing potion of blood, milk, and honey beer, then glanced at Lars, whose eyes held the amusement of a father watching his son pass the indelible mark into manhood.

"The hunt is over." Lars handed the bowl to Conrad. "It is now time to let the wisdom and knowledge they have gained rule their destiny."

Conrad drank the sharp sweetness, the fetid stink of the kill filling his nostrils. As they collectively passed from one threshold to the next, the warrior's chanting became a guttural beat that worked inside him. This was his passage, too. The last of the cow's blood passed his lips and a sense of purpose surged through his veins.

Perhaps it was the mysticism now coursing through him, but he felt a powerful shift taking shape in his work. He yearned to integrate all that he had learned on his travels, from the disciplined structures of the past to the daring spirit of history's trailblazers. Equally intrigued by today's bold, progressive mavericks, his vision was clear: Conrad's quest, now, was to fuse the music that had once touched the depths of the human soul with the pulse of the future, crafting a sound that would serenade man's heart and ignite the imagination.

ALEXANDRA & SEBASTIAN 1969

*"It is the stretched soul that makes music, and souls are
stretched by the pull of opposites—opposite bents, tastes,
yearnings, loyalties. Where there is no polarity—where
energies flow smoothly in one direction— here will be much
doing but no music."*

Jean Genet (1910—86)
French playwright, novelist

She woke to Sebastian standing by the window in the same posture
he assumed quite often, smoking a cigarette, restless, a caged animal
pacing. What vexed him so?

She tiptoed behind him, the erratic energy pulsing from his skin. She
took his cigarette with one hand and with the other smoothed the lines at
his forehead. He moaned sweetly, as if given the perfect elixir.

Taking his hand, she walked him down the stairwell into the living
room. She sat at the piano, introducing Chopin's evocative *Nocturne in C
Minor, Op 48 No.1.* The way she felt him, felt the desperation inside him,
made her choose that specific piece. He slumped beside her as if giving
into the mood clawing from inside his skin. The music seeped through
them both until he put his hand over hers, silenced it.

"It can't be so bad," Alexandra said.

He got up, dug at one of his many packs of cigarettes, lit up. "Yes, Alexandra, I'm afraid it is."

In the past three weeks, travelling from the city flat she'd rented once the Ketterling tours began, she'd zip back to the D'Antonio estate on the weekends and noticed a distinct trend. Their first hours together would be filled with inescapable hunger for each other and once sated, a downward spiral of depression ensued. Sebastian tried to remain charming and attentive, but she knew he suffered great frustration and loneliness. She would wrap her arms around him, trying to soothe him. Gentle kisses led to exquisite lovemaking, or a walk in Antonia's gardens while he recounted childhood stories; or, as in this moment, where she attempted to bring Sebastian back to his music through her own.

One morning Alexandra picked up the remnants of her clothing, walked to the bathroom and saw the aftermath of their three days and nights of lovemaking, little food, too much wine. Sebastian liked to drink more than anyone she knew and seemed unaffected by the endless cocktail hour.

She went to find him to tell him they needed to put some guardrails up, but when she found him, staring out at the pool, he looked bereft.

"I've lost it," he said quietly.

"No, you haven't." She rushed at him as much for herself as him. The fear that one might suddenly lose their ability, like a creative aneurysm, was a terror that consumed them both. "You haven't lost it… you've just lost your compass temporarily."

He snorted derisively. "My compass, eh?"

"Sebastian."

"Alex. I can't." Sebastian didn't want to make the words official. Nor did she. She merely swallowed them up in a kiss and put a hand to the man in him that did work, that functioned masterfully, so that Sebastian could feel whole, strong, and well again.

Sebastian lay next to Alexandra who slept beside him, regarding her exquisite throat, arched ever slightly as her head rested away from him. He studied her strong profile in the dimly lit room. The simplicity of her beauty touched him in a way that made his throat constrict, threatening tears.

When Alexandra had walked through the door hours earlier, it was as if he hadn't eaten in three days. He needed to consume her, but he couldn't touch her, kiss her, feel her soft skin enough. The more she opened him up, the closer he felt to the tender bruise of heartache he thought he had put behind him after Antonia's death. These intense emotions baffled him. He was not one to lose his head in affairs of the heart.

Alexandra had only been gone a week for a special Ketterling engagement in Los Angeles, but it had felt inexorably longer. She had asked him to join her but tagging at her coattails didn't appeal. Instead, he had fussed about, taking long walks in the garden and spending an inordinate amount of time in the pool, his muscles growing strong, his body stealth brown. Yes, he had felt sorry for himself, drowning himself in gin and tonics, then entertained an old flame. He rationalized infidelity because she was an ex and was of no emotional consequence. Besides, he was almost too drunk to perform.

When Alexandra returned from her trip and he held her in his arms, the burden of guilt made clear to him that she had propelled him beyond his momentary forays with new and old paramours. When he was with her, clinging to her soft skin, smelling her perfume, there was a state of grace and peace he had only encountered with Antonia.

He first experienced it when he came upon her in the living room one afternoon. She was leaning over the piano, the sunlight illuminating her flawless perfection; the waves of thick brown hair, lavishly cascading from her loosened braid, her elegant neck, thick brows over those extraordinary eyes; intensity married to vulnerability—but only at certain moments. She kept herself as carefully guarded as he did himself. That's how she knew him, and he knew her.

Stripped raw he lay open, vulnerable. With her, he could shed his musculature, reveal his inadequacies.

He had known from the start if he were to get involved with her, she would be important, and now the needling observation that she was becoming something akin to a lifeline began to unsettle him. He had never relied on anyone other than Antonia and Conrad. He wasn't sure he wanted someone else to whom he belonged. Needed this much. But the more he was around Alexandra, the less he could deny it.

Watching her perform was as agonizing as it was necessary. It gave him sustenance. Her poignant interpretations fed him, nurtured him, and delighted a part of him which, at all other times, felt dead. He loved her expression, her insight into the music, the way it took her over, consumed her. He desperately wanted to play as she did and recognized, one morning as he scrutinized her, the same feeling he used to have when he spied on Conrad. As though if he examined either of them long enough, that indefinable element that eluded him would make itself known.

Now, he slowly pulled his arm from under the pillow, careful not to disturb her. He got up and threw on a loose pair of jeans. He glanced at her once more as he tiptoed out, lit a cigarette, and began to walk down the long marble hallway, wandering through the house in the muted early morning hours.

As the sun rose, Sebastian continued to pace restlessly, stopping at this statue, Antonia had purchased in Greece, or staring at a photo of himself, Conrad, and Antonia at a roadside café in Tuscany.

He had been having problems sleeping. It wasn't just that his career was becoming a disappointment. He had long ago stopped looking at Antonia's brokerage statements and couldn't bring himself to analyze the reduced earnings, the sorry state of his financial circumstances for which he had no remedy. The only time he fell into a deep slumber was by the pool in the afternoons after he exhausted himself with a long swim.

Out of the corner of his eye, he could just distinguish the bronze chain dangling from the attic stairwell. They had moved most of Antonia's things upstairs into the attic before Conrad left, and it saddened him to think of her joys of beauty, her collections, her statuettes, and exotic artifacts, languishing up there in a blanket of dust and mildew. Antonia's presence was so strong he couldn't stop himself from walking to the chain, pulling down the hanging stairs, and clambering up the planks.

Even for early summer, the attic felt humid, cloaked with the sharp mustiness that harbors aged memories. He sighed as he took in the maze of history. Weaving through the boxes, he was barely able to distinguish one thing from another in the dark. He found the frayed cord to the single bulb that lit the room in a pale forty-watt flicker. He rifled through old estate ledgers then began sorting through musty papers, and anemic photos.

Ah, yes, this one taken when Sir Walter had driven the boys to meet Antonia at the airport home from one of her "Fabventures" as she referred to her travels. The hue and chroma were bleached by passing years, but Sebastian remembered it like yesterday, had laughed at her Ava Gardner stance in brimming hat and scarf, could still feel the rim of it, as she had plopped it upon his head and called him the "Sultan of Charm."

Antonia had always arrived with five times the luggage she had left with, new trunks filled with unusual treasures. As he gazed into another photo, he remembered Antonia unpacking the new miniature bust of Handel, her slender fingers stroking it with reverence, citing his *Messiah* as "one of those rare moments when God became man and man became God. Did you know, dear boys," Antonia declared, "that when he wrote his divine masterpiece, he spent twenty-four days, without food, sleep, or any other human comforts, and that the very pages were wet from God's tears?" The boys had looked dutifully impressed.

Sebastian flipped over an old painting from one of her protégés. And then he stopped. He leaned over a box and pulled out the contents, slowly examining the papers and files inside.

He spent a long time simply staring into the dimness of his past, wanting answers for a future he couldn't yet fathom.

"Antonia," he pleaded, "Tell me… show me." She would know how to direct him, place him firmly back on path. Holding her remnants made him feel closer to her until he saw her sheet music and began to weep. Sebastian slipped to his knees, crying, and praying in the same breath. He knew Antonia was with him, and between her and Alexandra, he prayed he might find his way again.

Alexandra woke abruptly to find Sebastian gone. She had been staying with him the last week and a half before returning to the final leg of her tour, their days an aimless, structureless improvisation. Making love, eating, strolling through Antonia's ever-wildering gardens, sharing stories, swimming, basking lazily in the sun, and drinking wine. Too seldom, she ran through one of her concerti to keep her fingers limber.

Alexandra shivered when she got out of bed. It was late morning, but the sun hadn't yet warmed what she teasingly referred to as the "fortress no earthly mortal shall enter." She threw on the cambric shirt Sebastian had stripped off hours earlier and began wandering around the house trying to find him. She passed a door, now ajar, that she had never seen open. She walked into the library, delighted to see the two opposing pianos and marveling at the high ceilings. The light here was abundant and serene, unlike most of the house, which was cast in gothic shadows. She was immediately struck by the huge portrait of a graceful woman with entrancing eyes: Sebastian's mother. And Sebastian was absolutely her son. He had inherited her dark beauty and full lower lip. She found such features earmarks of mischief and seduction. Antonia's patrician nose and high cheekbones kept her from looking too earthy, unlike Sebastian, whose very essence sprang from rooted sensuality.

She left the beautiful library and as she moved farther down the great long hall, she saw the attic stairwell hanging down. She climbed the planking slowly, and when her head cleared the attic floor she adjusted to the dim light, just making out Sebastian's silhouette as he moved through the cluttered debris.

"What are you doing?"

He was jolted from his reverie. "I'm sorry. Didn't mean to leave you, but you were sleeping so peacefully, and I didn't want to wake you." As she joined him, he scuffed a bare arm to his face, quickly wiping away the last of his tears. "I've been busy cleaning up some of my mother's stuff."

"Sebastian, what is it?"

"She has so much junk. I mean, I don't know what to keep." Sebastian shrugged as though it weren't a big deal. "And Connie's no help at all, off God knows where. Shit... What do you think I should do with all this?"

"Sebastian." Alexandra's tone was tender as she kneeled beside him. "What's going on?"

"I... I know this sounds silly, but when I'm up here... I feel closer to her."

"If I were into psychobabble, I'd suggest you cleaning the attic of all this *stuff* paves your subconscious clear." She put a loving hand to his calf. "So, you can prepare your life's masterpiece, she mused poetic," Alexandra teased then suggested graciously, "And I don't think it's silly at all. Missing her is honoring her."

"That's what Max says."

"Max?"

"Yes. Dear Max. You'll meet him soon enough. A relic. He was our professor and Freudian father, since we're musing allegorical."

Alexandra leaned to him and took his free hand, kissing his fingers. "I just want you to be able to work, Sebastian. Nothing will hurt you more than not working."

Sebastian withdrew his hand, and pulled out pages and pages of sheet music. He began humming to the notes. "My mother's operas."

"She sang?"

"Terribly." His eyes welled for a moment. "What I wouldn't do to hear one of her dreadful cantatas... the damn woman was tone deaf."

"But she must have had some talent to be so successful." Alexandra gestured to the house and the grounds.

"'The austerely eccentric and legendary beauty, Antonia D'Antonio,'" Sebastian read from a newspaper clipping he had picked up. "If that's a name that doesn't lead to excess, I don't know what does!" But then Sebastian stopped smiling and said quietly. "No, darling, she had no talent."

"Then where did you get yours?"

"Don't you know?" Sebastian laughed now with a tear running down his cheek. "I'm an indirect descendant of Bach."

"Pardon me?" Alexandra glanced at him, baffled.

"Never mind." He wiped his face, tears now mixing with sweat in the insufferably hot attic. "Darling, go jump in the pool. I'll join you in a bit."

Alexandra kissed his forehead and stepped back.

Sebastian continued humming the opera. Alexandra turned before she went down the stairs and felt a catch in her throat as she watched him commune with his mother. She prayed it might alleviate the pain of her loss, and shift him to a direction of hope. *The longer he dwelled*, but she banned the thought from her mind.

After she had a strong cup of coffee, poached eggs, and toast, Alexandra dove into the pool, clear, deep, and cool, washing off the sex and sweat of the night before, then lay on one of the deck chairs. She had dozed off.

When she suddenly heard his laughter, it was hours later, long and loud, a gale of humor floating from the attic window over the pool and through the trees. He ran through the door and with a banshee scream, flung himself into the pool. When he surfaced, he swam towards her, an evil glint in his eyes. He picked her up and tossed her back into the water with him, then dove below and with the smooth plane of water between his hand and her skin caressed her with cool liquid strokes that began the aching hunger all over again. When he came up for air he kissed her breasts, and then her neck. His tongue found hers, and she could feel his growing erection as he picked her up half out of the water. As he entered her, he began chuckling, not lewdly, but like a man who has just discovered the joke of life and needs to celebrate it with that which made life worthwhile.

CONRAD 1969

*"[music]...is entirely independent of the phenomenal world,
ignores it altogether, could to a certain extent exist if there
was no world at all, which cannot be said of the other arts.
[Music,] is the copy of the will itself...That is why the effect
of music is so much more powerful and penetrating than that
of the other arts, for they speak only of shadows, but music
speaks for the thing itself."*

Schopenhauer — German Philosopher

A bracing sea spray cut into Conrad and Lars' faces as they stood at the head of a freighter bound for Greece. Lars glanced at Conrad. Since he had discovered the true level of Conrad's talents, Lars's growing affection for the young man had turned into a deep affinity and a paternal sense of protection. It wasn't that he just enjoyed Conrad's gentle disposition, his avid love of music, and quick intelligence. He suspected this lad was gifted in a way he had never experienced.

Peering over his shoulder one day, Lars had caught sight of one of Conrad's musical sketches. He studied the composition for a very long time.

"I'm impressed," he told Conrad later that night as they sat under a sky filled with ardent stars. "And believe me, I don't impress easily."

Lars was all too happy to invite himself to join Conrad's grand quest, a musical adventure not to be missed.

From Greece they took another boat to Sicily, their pace of travel easy and relaxed. Every day they discovered something new. Quickly, Conrad realized Lars was a true musical scholar, a virtual fount of anecdotes, information, and little-known esoterica.

After a few glasses of brandy, he'd pull out his pipe and discourse about the one passion in life that got away from him, often blurting out complete non-sequiturs. "Did you know Dvorak was obsessed with trains? Yeah, knew all their schedules by heart." Or one early morning as Conrad rested a tired head in his hand, Lars noted jovially, "Tchaikovsky was so terrified his head was going to fall off while performing, that he kept it propped up with his left hand to make sure it didn't."

As obsessed as he was with his musicological trivia, Lars was as endlessly transfixed by the female tourists, and it was quite common after they had spent a day out touring for Lars to finish his wine and sloppily tuck in his shirt after dinner with, "Think I'll just see what the natives are up to ol' boy." Conrad wouldn't see him until late the following morning.

As they continued their journey by bus, train, and backpack all through southern Europe, Conrad would play at any piano they happened upon; in a restaurant, a bar, coffee houses—all essential transfusions for Conrad. They found one of the many Beethoven exhibits and stood transfixed at the composer's death mask. A shiver ran up Conrad's neck as he peered at the plaster cast of the ultimate romantic with his petulant will and strength of determination.

After, they lay by the Danube riverbanks, letting the sun stream over them as they lazily finished wurst and pommes frites, washed down by pilsners.

At that moment a group of USC Californian long-legged blondes passed by. Lars conducted a careful surveillance, while Conrad seemed deeply lost in his thoughts.

"My god, don't you have any interest in pussy?"

Conrad glanced their way with disinterest.

"Shit, boy." Lars shattered his reverie. "You've been mongreling among the dead too long."

Lars stood, tipped his hat, and followed the bait, leaving Conrad to his thoughts.

𝄞

Conrad wandered the streets until it got quite late. He found a small Ratskeller where he ordered a Bauern omelet and Bröetchen. Afterward, while sipping a glass of brandy, he felt the pull of someone several tables from him. When he turned, he met the gaze of an older woman whose beckoning glance was direct and inviting. He twirled his glass, glanced away, but when his gaze returned to her, she hadn't flinched. Her intentions were clear.

He stood up and walked to her table, sat beside her. Tall, angular, and upright; her grey-tinged blond chignon showed signs of wear. It appeared she had been sitting for some time with several empty espresso cups as well as two snifters of cognac. In her eyes and affect, she appeared both confident and impeccably pedigreed, but a bitterness settled in the lines around her mouth. Resignation.

Neither spoke a word. She continued to look directly into his eyes as they both finished their drinks. Her ring finger grazed the top of his hand.

"You work with your hands," she said in French.

He nodded.

Again, they remained silent as he paid the bill, and she led him wordlessly to her hotel room.

Once in the room, she turned to him, slowly slid a hand to his neck, and pulled his lips just short of her own, then yanked him to her, hungrily kissing him, he kissing her back.

She led him to the bed, slowly undressed him, her confident hands smooth over his skin. They made love like two animals, fond and playful with each other. Their needs were easily satisfied and afterward, they burrowed close to each other for warmth as they smoked cigarettes and drank cognac.

She was from Paris, visiting Cologne for the weekend, a professor of literature who had left her husband and children, as she did every six months for a couple of days to remember that she was "still a woman."

"Musicians have always fascinated me," she said as they lay in the dimming room. "... how they come up with, how you say? *Les histoires?*"

"It is not so different from words on a page," Conrad said quietly. "We use notes for words, chords as paragraphs, recurring motifs become our themes."

"Anais Nin says, 'a writer writes to live life twice.' Is it the same for a composer?"

"Yes." Conrad laughed. "That is the remarkable advantage of the artist."

"So... do you live again when you play your music?"

Conrad considered the question. "Honestly... I live more."

Sebastian sat naked at the piano, still slightly damp from an afternoon swim, as he structured a poignant melody, playing the lower keys as a counterpoint to an interesting measure in the higher octaves, switching phrases until a lyrical harmony presented itself. The music that came from his hands was as expressive as Beethoven, as romantic as Chopin. As pure as Bach. Yet laced with contemporary phrasings and sequences.

He glanced at Alexandra, who had walked in from the kitchen with iced tea, baiting her. "Do you know what this is?"

"No, but it's beautiful, Sebastian."

"It's you, Alexandra." Sebastian continued to play and as he did Alexandra saw in him a new vigor, as if in their union he had found himself. Her heart filled with ever-deepening affection for him. If giving herself to him created such beauty, then she would happily lay herself open for him.

When he finished, he walked to the window and sighed. "That is what I'll work on while you're away on tour."

She moved up behind him, the heat of his body inches from hers. "It's quite extraordinary. I'm so happy you ..."

"No." He turned to her, took her face in his hands. "It's *you*. You gave this to me. Gave me the courage to..." He searched for the right words. "To own me ... to own what has been struggling so long to get out."

"Darling, this is all *you*."

"No," Sebastian repeated with seriousness. "It isn't, Alexandra. All these months you've stood by me when I was struggling when there were absolutely no guarantees. I don't think I will ever be able to thank you enough."

"You're being entirely too humble. Not to mention too hard on yourself."

They embraced and then moved to the couch and held each other.

"I'm kind of terrified," Sebastian said quietly.

"Don't be." Alexandra smiled at him. "Sebastian, you're on your way back."

Sebastian's eyes pierced her own. "'On my way back.' Yes, I guess that's a perfect way to put it."

Alexandra brushed her long thick hair, which she had taken down at Sebastian's request last night, smiling as she remembered it getting in the way as they had made love. She braided with swift facility as if she were practicing scales. Glancing at her image in the mirror, she noticed the palish blue under her eyes. Tired. Unlike Sebastian, excess didn't come easily for her. She quickly cast a bit of rouge over her cheeks for color and let it go at that. Presentable, she walked into the living room.

Sebastian sat at the grand working on the same piece he had been sketching the day before. A large, framed photo of Antonia sat at the serving table that already held a half-empty pot of coffee and an ashtray full of stubs.

"Have you been at this all morning?"

He nodded. She picked up the photo.

"Is she where you got your love of music?"

"She is where I got my love of beauty," he said, standing. He grabbed Alexandra as if to make the point.

"It appears you're back to work." She smiled invitingly.

He laughed and kissed her deeply again, then returned to the piano bench. "Yes, I am. And now, if you'll excuse me."

"And what about me?"

"You're more than welcome to sit there and stare at me in utter adulation."

"Sounds electrifying. But I've got to get back to the city. I'm leaving tomorrow morning."

Sebastian didn't hear her. He was already immersed. "Wonderful, darling."

She watched him with tender affection. It was astonishing that in the short space of time they had been together, he had let her in, had allowed her to plumb his depths to expose the real Sebastian, a man whose ambitious drive was hampered by conflicted uncertainty. Wasn't that the artist's way, she thought ruefully. Remarkably, she had been able to help him out of the slump of depression that had blocked his creativity. It cultivated a wistful adoration for his ability to be human and filled her with an unusual sense of accomplishment.

Buoyed by these new feelings Alexandra's latest Ketterling tour of West Coast cities was considered a uniform success. From Seattle and San Francisco, south to LA and San Diego, Alexandra never dropped a note except for those written to Sebastian by postcard; framing the city's skyline and on the back: 'Darling, I miss you more than you can know... Always, A.'

Formerly cynical critics now raved that she "has grown into the pianist we have been waiting for. Full of vigor, intensity, a wellspring of emotion, but with a new maturity to control the subtlest of expression. Miss Von Triessen was born to play Chopin." These reviews, coupled with a new management company hot on her heels, inched Alexandra's career ever closer to the small list at the top of established working musicians. Conductors were calling, requesting repeat performances— the single most crucial aspect of a performer's life. Alexandra's career was well on its way.

Conrad and Lars traveled to Thuringer, where they retraced Bach's life's works as he moved from one organist's post to another. In Leipzig, they came upon the Thomaskirche, where Bach had been cantor. The instrument, meticulously refitted and refurbished, was one of the original pipe organs Bach played in the early 1700s. Lars persuaded the musical director to allow Conrad to give it a try. "But this is not common." The director tsked. "Not common at all."

"Ahh, but God's work is not common," Lars insisted, pulling out a wad of cash. "I just bet a large donation to the church would prevail upon the director to see the importance of bending little rules."

"Yes, well." The director bowed modestly as he accepted Lars' donation. "God's work is certainly the most important of all."

Conrad sat at the bench, placed his long fingers at the hallowed keys, negotiated the creaking stops, and began one of Bach's most famous, *Toccata and Fugue in D Minor*. As the vibrations of the pipes filled the church, a searing pain cut through him. He felt the sting in his eyes as he was overcome with the history of the church, his own history, and his first true cognitive connection to music. The sun glowed radiantly through stained-glassed portals and Conrad could hear the polychoral sweep of ancient voices as visitors stood frozen in place, the majestic tones and layered harmony of the organ transporting them all to a time past. Dense, hushed silence filled the church when he finished.

"Thank you, Lars." Conrad's voice still quivered with awe later as they sat finishing dinner at an outside café. "That was an experience I will never forget."

"The first time I heard Bach…" Lars shivered. "It shattered me. I… I cried like a baby." Lars paused for a sip of wine to collect himself. "His music made me ache. Made me feel melody as colors… sound as textures."

"I know exactly how you feel." Conrad put a hand on Lars' arm, who wore his heart on his sleeve, and was slightly tipsy now after several bottles of wine.

"He was the greatest composer of all time," Lars pronounced emphatically.

"Mozart is candy. Beethoven, a robust cup of coffee. Debussy, a nice toke of weed." Lars winked. "But Bach, ahhhh, he was divine. Autodidactic, Conrad, like yourself."

Lars poured more wine with a Cheshire grin then slapped the table.

"My God, Conrad, I know you said to wait, but damnit, I just couldn't resist. I helped myself to your Saharan Overture last night and I…" Lars faltered a moment, trying to find the right words, then blurted out. "It goddamn snakes in and yanks you by the gut!"

"Thank you—"

"God damnit, Conrad, I'm not blowing smoke up your ass. I'm asking you, what the hell you want to do with all this talent of yours?"

Conrad's jaw tightened as he heard all the music in his head. "Like I said, I want to bring the music that lives in me… I want to bring it back, Lars. I want to reclaim it." Conrad continued, slightly self-conscious at the presumption of his words. "Music."

Lars nodded as if sensing the huge possibility. "Yes… and?"

Conrad smiled self-deprecatingly. "I know it sounds like the worst kind of tripe, but music that touches the listener again—but not in the old ways."

"Exactly!" Lars agreed. "'Not in the old ways.'"

They both contemplated his words in silence.

"The difference between you and me," Lars said, "is that you can't help your talent… and mine couldn't help me."

"Lars… it's not the talent. You're happy doing what you do. I'm only truly alive when I'm playing."

Lars toked his pipe a moment. "Christ, lad, you better get busy. Have you listened to music today? It's pitiful. Lamentable. I detest Avante-Gardists. Anyone can plunk boorish keys, splash paint and eggs all over a piano and call it something morbid like *three eggs in shellshock*. Without form all you have is anarchy."

"Don't subscribe to art as an ever-changing medium?" Conrad observed wryly.

"Absolutely, but not in that direction! No one's interested in working for anything." Lars growled as he held up his glass. "What happened to losing oneself to the spiritual depths?"

"I thought you were a practicing agnostic."

"Only in the morning. In the long African evenings, when I play my Victrola and sit with my Merlot and my pipe I believe in greatness. A power and grace that elevates the puniness that is man." Lars sighed, then spoke evenly, "Greatness is an absolute imperative. Humanity depends on it."

They both sat for several moments, sensing a shift in their journeys.

"The problem in facing one's greatness—" Lars stared at Conrad, his gaze penetrating "—is that it takes a great deal of courage."

"An artist is only an ordinary man with a greater
potentiality—same stuff, same make up, only more force.
And the strong driving force usually finds his weak spot,
and he goes cranked, or goes under."

D. H. Lawrence (1885—1930)
British author

Sebastian worked all summer long, starting his days at the Bösendorfer from the first moments that he would wake, stumbling from the couch, a sheet thrown over his naked body. In the humid East Coast air, he didn't bother with clothes. He would set a towel on the bench, sit and begin. He remembered a writer friend describing the abject despair of the empty page, that the writer would type a string of letters that made no sense, simply to reacquaint his mind with the act of writing. But Sebastian no longer had to resort to such collusion. He had all of it there. Waiting to come alive, one note after the next and the next.

His hands trembled when he first began but now, they were sure and graceful, filled with the kind of power that caused elation, and with each measure building on the next, he created a melodic domain in which he was master. There were moments when the beauty of the composition overwhelmed him and he would stop, paralyzed by the enormity of his task.

But this was his destiny. He knew it. Knew it to his very core as he focused for endless hours. When his body began cramping, he would stretch as if it were a sacred ritual, the delicious unwinding, followed by a sensual arousal and a dive into the pool. The crashing impact of liquid on his body made him feel stronger, more certain and he would swim for an hour, two on days where he felt he had made significant headway, so excited and terrified by his achievement that he could find no other way to expel the energy.

Exhausted, he would pull his body from the water to lie in the sun, idly smoking, his dark skin melting into bronze. Aroused from the combination of exhilaration, warmth, and the wet chill on his skin, he would take himself in hand, the same hand that had spent the morning stroking the keys, and come easily, his guttural explosion of pleasure filling the silent air. Cigarette stubbed out, he would roll into the pool to swim off his seed and return to the piano.

He usually ate around four in the afternoon. As much as he regretted doing so, he had let Walter go some months back to save money, so it was only he and Tula. He instructed her to cook light meals of chicken or fish and a salad. He wanted to stay hungry and lean. As soon as he was finished with his meal he would return to his creation and continue in the same vein, the room filling with smoke, the viscid summer air clinging to everything it touched.

Day in and out, Sebastian followed this routine until the first part of October when he sat at the bench, late in the afternoon, and let out an enraptured sigh. He straightened his back muscles, exhausted from his labors. He pulled in a deep breath, aware of the potent musk of his own smell. The last three days he had worked in frenzied inspiration, un-showered, unshaven, barely sleeping, surrounded by untouched food, half-filled coffee cups, and maligned cigarettes. He had made Tula leave so he could be alone as he neared the end. It was too important. Too sacred. Too unbelievable what he had done.

Finished.

He ran through the open doors and screamed in ecstatic abandon as he dove into the freezing pool and swam until his arms could no longer propel him forward. When he finally pulled himself from the cleansing waters, the sun had set, but he was thrilled by the invigorating chill. He rushed inside, jumped into the shower, and quickly dressed, returning to a civilization he yearned for once again.

He drove into the city and visited a dance club he used to frequent, where bored music students and aimless Juilliard grads hung out. He wanted to share this night, this moment with Alexandra, but when he called her hotel, she was gone. In her absence, he picked up a fawning debutante, whom he later bedded in her palatial apartment, his eyes closed and heart distant. When they were finished, he mumbled meaningless words and excuses he vaguely recalled from the days before Alexandra. He spent the night wandering the streets, trying to walk off his newborn guilt. His heart cried for her. Some things he couldn't fake, and pretending she was beneath him was one of them.

Alexandra finished her tour in mid-October, spent, but happily so. With her fourth Ketterling contract, she had booked more than two hundred performances and many of those had spurred on other venues.

"Alexandra, I don't know how you do it." Her favorite conductor shook his head. "Even performers I know who have been tested and on the circuit for years would be drained after what you've just done. Yet, you seem as tireless as a child on Christmas morning."

"Maybe that's because that's how I feel."

Tours required the stamina of a marathon runner. It wasn't the playing in three or four different cities within a week, nor the exhausting travel, or even the quirky inconveniences of bad room service and terrible coffee that were most taxing. It was the adjustment to new concert halls, the acoustics, adapting to different orchestras, and different conductors who ran the gamut; the egomaniacal auteur to the dashing commercial-riven star, requiring precise calibrations. It took all-encompassing concentration to remember the music, to be inside the piece, to devote oneself to it when there were so many tugging at her skirt hems; her publicist arranging interviews, plucking her away at any given moment for photo ops, her agent packing her schedule, her manager dragging her to parties to meet all *the* people she "absolutely needed to know."

When her plane landed at Kennedy, she was running haggard, a bit defenseless, and barely recognized Sebastian, so lean and tanned, until he flashed his perfect smile at her from the waiting crowd.

"You look like some swarthy pirate on the cover of one of those wretched books!"

"'Tis a pirate you're after!" He scooped her in his arms, kissing her fully, thoroughly, and arousing her to the point of embarrassment in front of the baggage claim wheel. Alexandra was so tired she didn't care what the other passengers thought.

"I guess you missed me then?"

"You have no idea." Sebastian laughed as he sped back to the estate, his thick hair unruly in the wind. His hand grabbed hers and he kissed her palm. He *is* a modern pirate, she thought, feeling like one of those absurd women in romance novels who subverts her soul to her captor because she simply cannot deny his primal sexuality. Maybe those books weren't fantasy. Maybe the choked-up world of stillness and inner calm were. With Sebastian, she felt completely alive.

When they arrived at the estate, Sebastian dropped her bags at the entrance, slammed the large door shut with his foot. He kissed her hungrily, leaning her up against the back of the door, and by the time he maneuvered her to the couch, she was half-undressed, and he was inside her. His aggression took her off guard, but there was a wild excitement in it too. She clasped him to her, even when the lapsed moments of finesse danced at the edge of her mind, a moment where he might have asked how she was, offered a tender kiss before his passion overtook them. But Sebastian seemed so filled with need that Alexandra wrapped her arms tightly around him as he came, screaming her name as if she were the only thing that mattered. In the end, she felt vindicated, reassured that this man needed her as she needed him.

Alexandra was truly speechless. She sat on the floor, gazing at Sebastian's profile, sweat dripping from him as he wound to the finale of his third movement. Much as he had teased before she'd gone on tour, she did sit 'staring at him in utter adulation,' tears lining her cheeks.

The delight in her eyes matched his.

"I had no idea." Her voice was small next to the shattering experience of Sebastian's new concerti. They were the most innovative compositions she had ever heard, with an emotional depth and uncanny maturity that surprised her. It wasn't just because she was in love with him. Long before she ever slept with him, she had objectively assessed Sebastian. At that time, she promised herself if they were ever to become involved, she wouldn't allow herself to attach more talent to him than she knew he possessed. And she hadn't. But now, this music was something altogether on a different plane. Composition was clearly where Sebastian's real talent lay. No wonder he was frustrated and unhappy before. He wasn't doing what he was born to do. Write music.

"So?" He looked like a young boy waiting for praise.

"Darling, it's brilliant. But you know that, don't you?"

"I think I do."

"It is every bit as unbelievable as you think it is."

"I needed someone else to tell me. I needed you to tell me it is what I think it is." Sebastian sighed with contented exhaustion, then reconsidered her with puzzled amazement. "It is... isn't it?"

"Yes!" Alexandra embraced him. "Yes, yes, and yes!" She nibbled kisses all over his neck and cheeks. He laughed. And she joined him in reckless abandon at this new piece of him they both knew would change their lives forever.

Conrad sat at the piano as he played before an unending vista of beauty. From the upper berth of his flat, he could see the red tile rooftops of Venice swept by a mist of clouds. This was the last leg of their trip together, and they had settled for a week in the rented palazzo which housed a decent piano so that Conrad could play for Lars all the music that had been germinating within him from his travels.

Every morning Conrad would sit ritualistically observing activity in the square below. The mart opening, a colorful array of vegetables and fruits being plopped against one another, rough brooms sweeping cobblestones while ice swooshed from a bucket to prepare for the thud of sea bass and cod smacked upon it—all melodies of the street mingling together.

Throughout the morning and the rest of the day, Conrad would play. Hour after hour Lars would listen to Conrad work at his compositions, reflecting that Conrad's music was an exquisite homage to the classical and romantic eras, yet he had broken out of the confines of their structure and predictability. Melodically rich and haunting, textural, and chromatic, its restraint expressed something altogether new. While it held promise of the post-modern world, Conrad's music tempered the need to be discordant for discordant's sake. He had somehow managed to express all levels of the soul—the elated, the tragically flawed, and savagely tortured—in thrill-inducing splendor.

Late in the afternoon, Lars would make a rich and bitter espresso which he downed without a flinch, grinning as he watched Conrad's mouth twist every time the murky liquid passed his lips.

In the evenings they watched the sunset, then would take a stroll to a taverna for drinks and dinner where they would discuss, debate, and analyze Conrad's work. No stone was left unturned, no note unheeded.

"Your melodies transport the listener. They travel with you until they are *inside* the peyote-teased hallucinations, an indigo sunset, they feel the blood run down your cheeks in tribal ritual. Do you know how difficult it is to capture those evocations?"

Conrad grudgingly accepted the compliments. He wasn't comfortable with praise.

"And the melodies… haunting, salty, bare-assed raw." Lars sighed. "It works."

"I've always wondered what defines melody—the real essence of melodic progression." Conrad took an elegant puff of his cigarette. "It's so abstract on one hand, so difficult at times to define, yet so ubiquitous and immediate. Is melody the most important element of music? Or rhythm and structure?"

Lars rubbed his chin. "Baahhh! I say one should not make bread without flour *and* eggs, as both are necessary for the best culinary outcome."

Lars would make suggestions and Conrad would ask questions, for he trusted Lars as he trusted no one about music since Max.

"That last piece, the fourth bar in the second movement… it's somewhat reminiscent of Rachmaninoff."

"Yes." Conrad's voice turned quiet. "It's somewhat of an homage to him and a performer I once heard play his second concerto."

Lars raised his eyebrows. "Ahhh, Rach's hands could reach anything. He, my good man, was a master. Even if he was screwed over by the critics."

"Critics," Conrad mused with sarcasm. "I don't think I've ever really read any of them… who the hell are they?"

"Well, my dear fellow, they're the exalted chaps who tell us what to think!" Lars sipped his drink and lit a cigar. "Personally, I've always felt a bit sorry for critics. To me, they seem like people who once had a passion and were not able to achieve anything with it, for lack of ambition, talent, what have you, so they decided to force their opinions upon everyone in sight."

"To what end?"

"To many a fine musician's end." Lars grunted. "Look at poor Tchaikovsky, such a silly ninny… a lavish little poet. Women shot themselves in his day after hearing one of his performances…okay, well that's a bit hyperbolic… but his music was so emotional, apparently, the rest of their lives were pointless after such an experience. Critics, on the other hand, said to hear his music was to smell rotting brandy, that it 'stunk in the ear.'"

Conrad cocked his head, surprised at the vehemence of the description as Lars poured the last of the wine into their goblets.

"I believe you have the kind of talent to become a master, Conrad."

"I'm not interested in being a master, Lars. I just want to create the music that I hear."

"That's your challenge, Conrad." Lars beckoned him forward. "You must breathe life into it. And finally, kind sir, you must share this most important gift with the masses, for not to would be a sin."

"But my music has never spoken to… to —" and Conrad only then formulated this as a possible weakness "—the lay person."

"The lay person is humanity, Conrad. Do you intend to keep all of mankind from your work?"

Again, a long silence filled the air.

"What makes something *musical?*" Lars leaned forward, peering into Conrad's eyes. "Think about what music really is. Nothing more than sounds of pitch strung together. It spans all that we know, every culture, every fiber of humanity, yet it is unlike any other phenomena we experience. What is it about minor keys on the piano or a wailing violin, that tugs so fiercely at one's heart that they are compelled to weep over notes, which in and of themselves mean nothing? Everyone hears something different, yet there's a consensus on how it makes us feel."

Conrad said quietly. "Considering the listener and whether they can relate to my music has never been a motivating factor."

Lars puffed on his pipe. "It won't be an easy road for you, Conrad. There will be those who scoff at the lushness of your sound and say you are trying to do too many things. They won't understand at first. But you must give them time and," he added gravely, "you too, must give yourself the time to understand people."

Conrad frowned, mulling over Lars' words.

"Trust me, lad, the time will come when the inside of you will want to share this gift. It will make you whole, Conrad. Until then..." Lars let the words sift into the night as he sipped the last of cabernet. "It's all rather beautifully pointless."

Over the next few months, Sebastian spent polishing his four concerti, hoping to enlist a manager and to find a producer interested in recording them. Alexandra spent most of her time in the city working on her fourth record at the studio. On the weekends she commuted to the country and met Sebastian for late Friday dinners.

They chatted excitedly about their futures in between lovemaking and sitting at the grand, both admiring and advising the other, both struck by the perfection of their lives. They were just as the Ketterling Institute had suggested, an unbeatable combination. With their intensely charismatic personalities, shiny good looks, and talent, they would be the talked-of couple in the classical world.

There were no more words of impostors or insecurities. Sebastian knew that people gossiped behind his back, still cast him in the role of runner-up to his lover, but it didn't matter anymore. They would think differently when they heard his music.

"Do you know Max offered to help me find a teaching job?" Sebastian asked one night as they sat by a roaring fire drinking hot toddies.

"He didn't!" Alexandra couldn't conceal her shock. "What did you say?"

"I told him packing it up to slowly evaporate at some obscure university was not exactly the career path I had in mind."

"Have you played your music for him?"

"I did today. You should have seen the look on the old fart's face." Sebastian's eyes were filled with an almost evil glint of vindication and then softened as he turned thoughtful. "I'm sorry, I guess I shouldn't be so smug. But he almost dropped his infernal glasses. I know he thought I was scarcely more than a playboy at school, but he's like an old uncle that I... I'd like to make proud. He told me it was time I got back on stage."

"Yes. It is." Alexandra's voice was soft. "There's nothing worse than having it all locked up inside you."

"And you, darling, are my key." He winked.

She could feel the excitement emanating from his chest. "It's just... how does it get any better than being on stage? For me, performance is man's greatest high. So, maybe it's not the most fashionable thing to say—not terribly chic, you know, to want to please the audience instead of yourself. But sharing it is what gives *me* inspiration," he sipped his drink. "There's this silence when you know they're truly listening, when you know you've got them: There's a sharpness to it—like a crisp sunny day—a blinding clarity. I love all of it: the dreadful rush of nerves, the tingling at the back of my neck, the finger-biting apprehension—it's all excruciating. And delicious." He kissed her tenderly, then remarked with fierce intensity. "There's almost nothing that I wouldn't do to perform."

"Music is spiritual. The music business is not."

Van Morrison
Irish rock musician

Sebastian had finally managed a hearing with Monetizzare Classics, the management company to which all ambitious musicians aspired. The day he was to audition his concerti for them, Alexandra drove them into the city with him. She waited for him at *Notes From Above,* while sharing coffee with Chandra to fill her anxious time.

When he rushed in, his hair wind-blown and wild, eyes the icy blue that always shocked and delighted, Alexandra knew it had gone more than well.

"Darling!" Chandra watched as he grabbed her into his arms, enveloping her in a vacuum of contagious enthusiasm. "They loved it. They goddamn swooned over it!"

He leaned over and pecked Chandra exuberantly on the cheek.

"Come on, let's go someplace we can really celebrate."

Sebastian led both women, his adoring Alexandra on one arm, the less enchanted Chandra on the other, uptown to Sardi's. As they slid into a leather banquette Sebastian grinned at the caricature-lined walls. This is where he wanted to be; among the celebrated and infamous. "Your finest Perrier Jouët!"

"Extravagant." Alexandra grinned as she looked into his eyes, awash with a fierce brightness. She kissed him, soaking in his delirium, so happy for him she could barely contain her excitement.

Chandra cleared her throat. She was about to say something but was interrupted by the waiter who happily presented the elegant bottle of bubbly and poured. Chandra downed her first glass in a single gulp.

"When the producers heard me play the concerti today, you know what they said? They said, 'We're going to push you as the second coming.'"

Alexandra considered him with a lascivious grin. "More like the Antichrist."

"The second coming of Bach, darling. They're going to play up my great grandfather's lineage. They're mad for it—think it's a brilliant way to intrigue the masses. They want to do a huge promotional campaign with it! Let me tell you, these guys are the kings of marketing."

"Does the name Max Reger ring a bell?" Chandra asked, slapping down her empty champagne glass like an exclamation mark.

An awkward silence ensued.

"He spearheaded the Back to Bach movement at the turn of the century. His most notable accomplishment is that he now reigns on most critics' list of the top ten worst composers of all time."

"I hardly think that's fair," Alexandra defended Sebastian. "Reger's raison d'être was to write Bachian music. That's not what Sebastian's is…it's—"

"Chandra's entitled to her opinion." Sebastian refilled Chandra's glass. "The fact of the matter is, it didn't work with Reger because his music was pointless. Mine isn't."

"I'm sorry. I didn't mean to… " But Chandra let it float off. "Do either of you have a cigarette?"

"Darling." Sebastian immediately produced a cigarette for Chandra, lit it for her, but only addressed Alexandra. "It's incredible. Really. They plan to spare no expense. And I hope you'll be happy about this, but they want to do a couple of doubleheaders with us as well—"

"Oh, the *Intermezzo* of it all." Chandra's attempt at humor couldn't cover her thinly disguised resentment. "Tell me, Sebastian, wherever did you get your inspiration?"

Sebastian raised his flute glass to Alexandra, a welling of genuine emotion in his eyes. "Look no further."

"I've always pegged you more as a Tchaikovsky or Chopin knock-off—you know, someone who would indulge themselves in *their* deep angst because they hadn't any of it themselves."

Chandra's comments shocked Alexandra. She had been increasingly aware of Chandra's aversion to Sebastian, but she had never known her to be ungracious.

"Ah, but there's so much more to me than meets the eye." Sebastian wasn't in the least bothered by Chandra, whom he considered weak and, therefore, inferior. Not the weakness he possessed, but the kind that would make Chandra unable to survive. Sebastian would always survive. This instinct he now wore as a mantle of distinction.

"Maybe you've had enough," Alexandra suggested.

"Let her get plastered." Sebastian's good humor was laced with impatience. "We can be generous with success."

"See, Alex, he wants to share his good fortune. Don't be stingy. After all, its life span is only slightly longer than melting ice-cream." Chandra smirked.

Sebastian topped off their glasses. "Here's something which even you, Chandra will toast." He turned to Alexandra. "To my inspiration and my strength."

"Hear, hear," Chandra answered and drained her glass. Several minutes later she belched. "I've had too much to drink. Call me a cab." She slurred at a passing waiter and got up unsteadily. "Success. Fame. Money. They are of little value. May you learn to fail, Sebastian. Only then can you understand the benefits of depravity." She bowed and walked tipsily from the table.

They both watched until she had left the front entrance.

She kissed his right cheek. "You didn't deserve that. No one should have rained on your good fortune today."

"Forget it." Sebastian shook his head but something about Chandra's words bothered him.

"She's never gotten over what happened at the contest."

"What do you mean, never gotten over?" Sebastian snapped at her.

"Darling, calm down. I just meant it's been a rough go. After she lost and was hospitalized, her father cut her off. Disowned her. Thank God she's just landed a wonderful teaching position. I feel for her, but I don't like what's happening to her. And it certainly doesn't give her the right to lash out at you—"

"You know what?" Sebastian's tone was generous. "The truth is she is extremely talented. But Alex, she's not like you and I. We... we have something else. We connect. People want to hear us play. We have that certain..."

"*Je ne sais quoi?*" Alexandra's eyebrow shot up self-effacingly.

"Precisely."

Alexandra didn't want to stifle his enthusiasm, but Chandra had a point. "Sebastian, are you sure?"

"About what?"

"Well," she faltered, "it will beg comparisons, and there aren't many who've been able to stand up to Bach. He is, after all, somewhat the musical standard."

"Darling, that's the point."

A fragile thought nagged at her for a moment, but she let it pass. She wasn't going to let her own fear of the critics ruin anything for him. She merely leaned closer and nuzzled his ear, kissed his neck. "I'm so happy for you."

"This won't harm us in any way?" Sebastian asked, his eyes serious.

"What on earth are you talking about?

Sebastian seemed a bit confused and took another sip of champagne while he measured his words. "Alex. What is it about me that you love?"

"Well, Sebastian, I could say that you're a wonderful man, utterly charming—even with your consummate ego—that you rival James Bond as a lover, or that I'm mad for your brilliance... but none of those are the reasons."

"Not my brazen good looks then, eh?"

Alexandra lifted her chin slightly and looked directly into his eyes. "It's because we are cut from the same cloth. And, because you need me."

Three nights before Sebastian's concerti debut, he had an attack of killer nerves. Nerves the likes of which he had never experienced. To the point where he needed several shots of brandy to steady the tremor in his hands, and then a dangerous amount of pain killers for a migraine that shut him up for hours in pitch dark with several rounds of ice packs.

Alexandra wanted him to call off the concert. Maybe something else was terribly wrong. Maybe the headaches were a prelude to an aneurysm. Maybe Sebastian was getting sick. But when the first sneak critique came out on his recording hailing "Sensation D'Antonio—Classical Music will never be the same!" Sebastian's headache suddenly disappeared, and he was a new man. He was all smiles and good jokes, the old Sebastian that Alexandra had fallen in love with, not the man of brooding depression and nasty irritability of the past forty-eight hours.

Carnegie Hall was packed to standing room only. Extra security had already been added and the tour hadn't even begun. By the end of the second movement of the "Immortal Romance Concerto," reporters were jamming out of the doorway to hail the second coming as an understatement.

At the rear of the auditorium, a man stood watching the rapt audience in a sort of astonished bewilderment.

His eyes narrowed, jaw triggered, as he momentarily found it difficult to breathe, listening to this music, this music Sebastian was playing, watching his brother do what he was so clearly born to do: Perform.

Conrad closed his eyes, taking in the dazzling scope, the superlative melody, and as Sebastian built to a crescendo, the muscles in Conrad's hands tensed, feeling Sebastian's hands as they climbed octave after crescendoing octave.

His eyes flashed open, a sharp stab of resentment washing over him followed by a bewildering sense of disbelief. So, this is what had happened while he had been gone. His brother was on his way to making himself famous.

When Sebastian finished his last note, a split second of silence hovered in the air. His rapt audience jumped up in unison followed by a thundering ovation.

Conrad was snapped out of his reverie from the roar of applause, and he looked up to see Sebastian, his eyes filled with glory. They clamored for Sebastian over and over as if they were rock groupies, not sophisticated socialites out for an evening with their season tickets.

Sebastian bowed and bowed again, clasping his right hand to his heart, the gesture that had so moved Alexandra the night she fell in love with him. On this night it made her love him even more, for she knew how hard he had worked to pick himself back up and make this music for these people, for the world he had just given such an extraordinary gift.

An ironic smile tugged at the corner of Conrad's mouth as the audience walked past him until Conrad stood alone, immobile, staring at the empty stage.

Max Ehrenshoffer walked to the backstage door knowing it would be packed to the gills with well-wishers, new best friends, producers, agents—all wanting a piece of this new sensation. But Max wasn't taken in by the frenetic buzz of praise and wild tribute. He was too much of an old hand at this game to be overwhelmed by much. The music, yes, to be sure, was truly remarkable, but the gift for him this evening was that it came from his old student Sebastian.

"It's unheralded," remarked one of Sebastian's managers.

"We'll stage the European Concert in the spring," the others eagerly agreed.

"You know his appearance fee just doubled," added his agent with a grin.

"I've never seen anything like it. It probably was just like when Bach first hit the scene in Europe—my God, it's astounding," said another, who merely mimicked what he had read in the *Times* review.

Clearly, these people had no idea of musical history. Bach hadn't been received in his time as a pop icon. While highly regarded by those in the musical universe, for the general public he was merely a paid organist. But Max knew history was irrelevant to these people. They would make it all up to fit whatever perception they needed to create Sebastian in Bach's image.

Suddenly, Max caught sight of a vision that momentarily tore him from the events of the evening; a tall, slender woman her arms bare, long, graceful, and muscular in a way that made strength sexy, that made a man wish to be thirty years younger. She was the finest, most regal woman he had seen in ages, a bold statement of control wed to beauty.

"Allow me to introduce myself." Max proffered a beefy hand to Alexandra.

"But of course, you're Max." She took his hand warmly as he bowed, old-fashioned and yet somehow appropriate. His heavy accent almost made him a caricature, but a kindness and warmth in his eyes made him very real.

"Sebastian's told me so much about you," Alexandra exclaimed.

"Oh, then he told you what a monster I was?" Max suggested. "How I made him practice so long, so hard, no time for women, dance, and wine?"

"Somehow I think he broke the rules."

"Yes… Sebastian is a rule breaker." Max frowned a moment, adjusted his coke-bottle spectacles. "Perhaps you were what it took to make him focus?"

"Yes, now there's only *one* woman in his life." She graciously accepted the compliment.

Max pulled her to the side, trying to create some privacy. "Tell me, how did he... well, how…" He took off his glasses to wipe them against his vest. "See here. I consider myself a good teacher. Some might even call me great, but not even my skills could... could …"

"Couldn't make up for all my bad habits?" Sebastian butted in. "Don't be so damn modest. You were the best teacher a person could have, but I must be honest, it was Alexandra who made me see the world differently. She made me feel my music."

Max arched a brow, readjusted his glasses, and took a long look at Alexandra. Indeed, she could spark the fire within any man. He smiled at them both, individually and at their union.

"Did she help you … did she help you create this then?"

A pregnant pause. She put her arm through his to save the moment. "You *are* a task master, aren't you? This is all Sebastian."

"Oh... dear boy, Sebastian, I... forgive me. I... it's just—"

"You didn't think I had it in me. Don't feel bad. I didn't think I had it in me, either. It's quite remarkable what the love of one good woman and the memory of another can do for a man."

"To the Four Seasons!" Charles Monetizzare of Monetizzare Classics nabbed Sebastian by the arm. He was an imposing man with penetrating eyes and the kind of wealth that overwhelmed most people. His athletic build had yielded to the frame of one who enjoyed the good life. He only associated with the wealthy and successful, and to have Monetizzare endorse you in the musical world was better than having God in your pocket. He put a paternal arm about Sebastian. "Come on everyone. We have a good deal of celebrating to do."

The cheers and clamoring continued as everyone followed Monetizzare, Sebastian hand-in-hand with Alexandra.

Only Max stood alone, frowning as the foyer emptied, once again, trying to figure the matter out. "*Verdamt.* Achhh!"

"Better late than never," said a voice from behind him.

"Eh?" He turned but couldn't believe it. "Dear lord, boy. It's you!" Max sputtered, his eyes welling with tears. He covered his sentimentality by grabbing Conrad in a gruff but hearty embrace.

"Mein Gott, it's so good to see you, son." Max patted Conrad's shoulders to make sure he was really there.

"It's ... I'm glad to have returned in time for the festivities."

"Let's find Sebastian! He'll be so happy you're home."

"No. I'll go by tomorrow. This is his night. Let's let him focus on that."

"Remarkable achievement?"

"'Better condemned to greatness,'" Conrad grinned ruefully, "'than lost to mediocrity.'"

"Can you believe our boy had it in him?"

"Can I believe it?" Conrad chewed at his bottom lip a moment. "Yes. I suppose I can."

> *"Counterpoint is the technique of contrasting and expanding two lines of melody to create a harmonic union while retaining individual expression. The first theme is called the subject. The second the answer. If a third voice enters it is known as the countersubject and moves with complex precision as it counters the theme, enhancing the melody as it marries the two. To make counterpoint work successfully one must be exceptionally talented as the polyphony must promote two opposing purposes yet serve one another harmonically."*

Professor Max Ehrenshoffer,
Inter-relational Dynamics as it
Applies to Composition

It took a long moment before Conrad was able to walk through the grounds. Antonia washed over him, triggering a deep yearning. The pain he had tried and failed to escape by racing around the world grew even more unbearable. He studied the estate, letting the memories shroud him like an aura. He took a deep breath and opened the gate.

As he strolled along one of the less trod paths of Antonia's Garden, he noted that the untethered growth, which had always been by careful design, had become a massive, intertwining of foliage fused with willful neglect. He smiled sadly when he remembered all the many times Antonia bent to pull an intrusive weed, orchestrating gardeners and landscapers to create her botanical masterpiece, her 'growing art.'

Conrad moved quietly along the edge of the house and entered through the opened French doors where he spotted Sebastian, sitting in a bathrobe, playing the piano with tired elation.

Conrad tiptoed up behind him and tapped a high note.

Sebastian turned, heart in throat, and when he saw that it was his brother, he jumped up and grasped Conrad into his arms.

"Connie!" Sebastian held Conrad close. He had missed him more than he had known was possible and allowed himself the thrill of seeing him before all the competitive implications could take over. "God damnit, Connie, you know how to give a guy a scare."

He gazed at his brother, holding Conrad by the shoulders, looking him over. In his younger brother's eyes, he saw new wisdom, the shadow of his travels, and something else. Sadness, disappointment. "So. Don Quixote returns."

"Yes, I'm back." Conrad moved out of his brother's hold.

"Did you sail the seven seas? Climb the highest mountains? Find man's darkest secrets?" Sebastian knew he was rambling, as he tried to feel his brother out. He was the same, yet so changed and it frightened him. "Don't you know everything a man needs to know is in here?" He thumped his chest.

"Let's just say I found no matter where a man runs, he can't escape himself... or his past."

"Shit, Connie... I don't know if I can get so profound without some coffee." Sebastian frowned, then chuckled a bit nervously. "Jesus! It's good to have you home. Come on. Let's have our smokes out on the terrace, like old times."

Sebastian wheeled the coffee service out and they sat at the same table they had always sat at, in the same chairs, and for a moment, it did, indeed, feel like five years hadn't passed since they had seen one another.

As Conrad watched Sebastian pour their coffee, he saw that his brother had finally grown into his skin, filled out his muscles. His sorrow at losing Antonia was buffered by a new strength, a poised confidence.

Sebastian pulled a pack of cigarettes from his robe pocket, and offered one to Conrad.

"Well!" Sebastian lit his own and then Conrad's cigarette. "You do know how to make an entrance. How the hell long have you been in town?"

"I came in yesterday."

"Yesterday." Sebastian pulled deeply at his cigarette. "Hell, if I had known that I would have had you—"

"I was there."

Sebastian's hand froze in midair, almost dropping his cigarette. Flicking away ashes, he turned to Conrad, adrenaline pulsing through his entire body. He was facing judge and jury, apprehension spreading through his limbs. He wanted to reach out to Conrad, to grab him, to say, "look what I've done!" but he couldn't get past the irony of Conrad's timing. Had it been calculated? The arrival of his brilliant brother, just as he was beginning to have his moment in the sun. And yet he wanted Conrad here, wanted to feel his envy, his pride, his belief in him.

"Yes, it was quite a performance, Sebastian." He smiled, then got up and walked to the pool. Sebastian followed him.

For a moment they gazed at their undulating reflections in the water below them.

"Oh, shit, Connie. I know it's not your cup of tea … I know that you're into all that progressive stuff."

Even in the shifting image, Sebastian could see his brother battling with his own emotions. Conrad must envy him. Maybe now he could see more of who Sebastian was, how he had underestimated his will.

"For Christ's sake, are you trying to torture me, Connie?" Sebastian's voice was brittle. "Tell me you liked it just a little."

Conrad sighed. "It's remarkable, Sebastian. Surprisingly remarkable."

A calm washed over Sebastian, followed by ebullience. "Oh shit! Oh, holy shit, Connie! You had me going there." Sebastian whirled Conrad about, holding on to him, almost weak from relief. "I wanted you—you of all people—to love it."

"You..." Conrad grabbed Sebastian's face, pulling him close, near tears, staring at him as if seeing him for the first time. "Sebastian..." A long moment wavered between them, a moment of truth.

"It's what Antonia always wanted," Sebastian's voice choked.

"Yes." Conrad grasped him, faltering a moment, then shaking his head in the affirmative. "Yes … you have given her the gift she always wanted."

Alexandra walked through the densely grown thicket from the gated entrance to the D'Antonio estate, lingering to smell the faint scent of blooming gardenia, when she heard the melody. The music sounded familiar but was quite different from Sebastian's other compositions; a jagged, haunting lyricism, disturbing yet compelling in its beauty.

As she neared the house and the music grew louder, she stopped for a private moment, basking in its strangely intoxicating melody, the music digging beneath her skin. It was clean. Untouched. She had never heard anything like it before. Sebastian must have been working on this new piece for some time now. It was quite complex and accomplished. She wondered why he hadn't shared it with her and as she stepped into the room she asked, "Darling, have you been holding out on me?"

As her eyes adjusted to the absence of sun, she made out a man she had never seen. His frame was lean and muscular, hair the color of golden ash wood, its shiny abundance falling about his clenched jaw as he swayed with the music. An aquiline nose suggested the statue of David. Much finer features than Sebastian's. But what she really noticed were his eyes as he looked up and caught her own. Steely blue-gray—almost luminescent.

As he continued to play, he held her gaze with a gentle hint of a question, until she began to feel a bit foolish. She felt she ought to know him, and then knew of course, that she did. His photos lined the walls alongside Sebastian's. Here was the missing half.

"Conrad?"

"Alexandra?" His smile softened the stern and focused set of his face, and he was suddenly more approachable. When she moved forward to shake his hand, she noticed his muscular but slender fingers. Contrary to romantic myth, most pianists possessed pulpy palms and overlarge fingers, on the whole quite unattractive hands, but Conrad's were lean, sculpted, artistic. The touch of his skin took her off guard, and she moved away from him toward the open doors.

"He's ... he's missed you. Terribly."

Conrad got up from the piano. "I didn't know I'd be gone so long."

He walked toward her and inclined his head to the patio where a pitcher of iced tea was sitting. He poured her a glass and handed it to her.

"Sebastian says you've been all over the world." She stopped. Sebastian also described him as the 'mad nomad in search of his soul.' But when she saw his eyes light with memories, he didn't seem in the least lost.

"Where is Sebastian?" She cast uneasily about her, feeling off-kilter.

"In the den on the phone with his agent. Or publicist. I'm not sure which. They're creating some terribly complex media blitz to revive the soul of Bach."

"Sounds like you don't approve."

"Bach's soul is already alive and well." A grin teased Conrad's mouth. "Why not simply build Sebastian? Make it his story?"

"I think they're just trying to frame his music for the public..." She shrugged, finding the well-worn explanation suddenly lacking.

"Not afraid some people will find it presumptuous? Not to mention pretentious."

"I'm sure they know what they're doing." A sharp edge laced her tone, but she wasn't entirely sure why.

"Yes. I'm sure they do." He simply looked at her then with those eyes, so clear and undiluted that Alexandra found herself discomforted by their intensity.

"I can't tell if you're on his side or not," she said defensively.

"Is it about sides, then?"

"No. It's just...well, everyone seems to be absolutely crazy for his music. Except those closest to him—I don't know—seem to somehow find his success... untenable. And I think you're all just jealous," she finished.

Conrad nabbed a cigarette and while lighting it never took his eyes from her, openly assessing her. "Perhaps we are."

"There you are, darling." Sebastian walked out on the patio, gave Alexandra a quick peck on her cheek, then turned to Conrad, and placed a hand on his shoulder as if presenting an honored scholar. "Alexandra, this is my long-lost brother and compadre, Conrad."

"Yes. We've met."

Sebastian stared out the corner window of Anthony Monetizzare's high-rise suite, watching the sun set against the powerful skyline of New York City.

"My boy, there you are. Sorry to keep you waiting." Monetizzare whisked in.

"No problem," Sebastian said.

"I have the most exceptional news."

Sebastian waited, eager.

"Your record went platinum this morning. How do you like that?"

Sebastian whooped and threw a victory fist into the air. He grabbed Monetizzare in a bear hug and lifted the large man a foot from the floor. Monetizzare was from the old school where men rarely hugged, but Sebastian knew he wasn't only putting Monetizzare Classics back in the running for prestige and awards after a long dry spell but was going to make them all a hell of a lot of money. "That's tremendous. Oh, Jesus, that's unbelievable."

"Yes…" Still suspended, Monetizzare waited for Sebastian to slip him back to earth. "We're all so proud of you, Sebastian."

"I've got to call Alexandra."

"By all means." He pointed to his phone.

Sebastian dialed with the grin of the exalted, but the phone rang unanswered. "Oh well. I suppose it will have to wait for the Rainbow Room tonight."

"Make it late. We've booked you on Carson."

"You're serious?"

"Yes, my good man. And we've got to get to the studio in 20 minutes."

"Marvelous."

"Are you ready for this, Sebastian? You're about to take off to the moon."

Sebastian's smile only grew larger. "I've never been more ready."

That evening Sebastian took Alexandra and Conrad with him to the Rainbow Room, with a small party that soon swelled to more than thirty people, from Monetizzare's staff to Sebastian's agent, press people, and a media consultant, all of whom were discussing the elaborate and encompassing strategy for the various "Bach Lives" campaigns. They already had a wide slice of the tried-and-true followers of classical music. But now an entirely new demographic was available, young women from sixteen to twenty-four who had no previous attachment to the repertoire, all drooling over Sebastian, swooning dramatically at his concerts, loving the rebel in his dark rakishness, much as they loved Elvis or James Dean. Sebastian was the perfect Brontean hero for the early seventies. No carryover from the tie-dyed, bell-bottomed, fringe invested 60's hippie revolution for Sebastian—with the notable exception of his hair, which he wore down to his shoulders. Alexandra loved the beautiful wavy fullness that reminded her of her swarthy pirate and for his audience conjured the wild and untamed artist. With his turtlenecks and peacoat he cut a dashing figure, just bordering on the free-love movement for the new converts—yet kempt appropriately enough for his conservative fans.

His "look" was meticulously designed to sell Sebastian's roguish charm in the "Bach to School" campaign and was so enormously successful that the major studios were clamoring for him, outbidding each other for the exclusive use of his concerti for scores, no matter how inappropriate the film. In fact, his agent was negotiating for a science fiction epic, for which, of course, the concerto would have to be re-arranged; "You know, slap on a percussion track, tease the strings for suspense, then we'll cut a version with lyrics for the end crawl." There was even talk of doing a biopic on Bach and commissioning Sebastian to write the score.

While all of Sebastian's managers and handlers talked business well into the night, Alexandra watched Sebastian bask in the multi-faceted role of composer cum movie star celebrity and business maven, knowing instinctively this transformation was the beginning of a snowball that would never roll backward. As much as she tried to enjoy the excitement and genuine enthusiasm these people directed toward him, she couldn't help but find the commercial direction the campaign was pursuing a little distasteful. And, she had to admit to herself, she agreed with Conrad's fear that it was a bit much.

But she gave Sebastian a lot of credit. From the beginning of the onslaught, he attempted to keep her abreast of every single detail and new development, but she recognized before he did that it was simply impossible. As the weeks had spun out of control, she watched him trying to contain the ever-burgeoning growth of his talent as a commodity. He never lost sight of her, even if their time together was dramatically reduced. Like tonight, where he constantly returned to her seat, checking in with her to help them both maintain a sense of equilibrium, stopping to whisper in her ear or place a warm hand against her bare shoulder.

When she found herself watching Conrad he seemed gently amused by the evening's events. He found her gaze easily, and she could sense his concern for Sebastian, but also for her, as if he were gauging her response, lending support while he continued to converse heatedly with Max or one of the other musicians. He rarely spoke to Sebastian's handlers, or even to Sebastian himself, although she caught one bizarre exchange pass between them about Sebastian's rumored lineage to Bach, but it was more in what wasn't stated than what was that she couldn't decipher; nor she suspected could anyone else. Yet, when she turned to Max, she saw he understood their private discourse and when the old man's eyes met hers, they held a sadness she couldn't fathom.

Several days after the party, Alexandra rounded the corner of the garden path and spotted Conrad, standing absolutely still, eyes closed, mesmerized as if in a trance. She studied him a long moment. His physique was not unlike the statues that littered the garden, fine and beautiful, but not of this earth, out of place. She didn't wish to disturb him, but as she tiptoed backward her foot snapped a piece of gravel.

"Alexandra?" His voice came from far away, eyes still closed.

"Yes. I'm sorry, I—"

He opened his eyes and studied her unapologetically.

"I should get—"

"You know, you're nothing at all as I imagined."

She couldn't help but show her surprise, but he continued to observe her without flinching until she turned away slightly to deflect his gaze. "I'm not sure what you mean by that."

"The fact that you won the Ketterling and Sebastian didn't let that stand in the way of… of your relationship is a compliment to you both. It's good to know that Sebastian's gone and grown up."

"I think people who underestimate Sebastian don't understand him. But that can't be the case with you, since I'm sure you know him better than most."

"If you had known Sebastian all your life, you might be pleasantly surprised, not only at his accomplishment but with the company he keeps."

"As compliments go, I'd call that backhanded."

"I didn't mean to offend. I'm happy for him."

She allowed her defenses to settle and gave a slight nod.

"I'll walk you back to the house," he said.

For several moments they said nothing, but as she became aware of him by her side, she felt the need for conversation.

"Sebastian tells me you up and left Juilliard and then disappeared."

He nodded.

"Why did you quit?

"I'm not made for arbitrary curriculums. And I was a terrible student."

"I can't imagine that's possible, having heard you play yesterday."

"Oh, believe it is very possible." Conrad stopped and offered her a cigarette. She declined as he lit one up.

She observed Conrad; the soft shadow that formed at his cheekbones as he gently inhaled, followed by a suspended state of grace as he held the smoke in, then exhaled. She couldn't recall ever seeing anyone quite enjoy a cigarette this thoroughly, as if smoking was an activity of purity, of pleasure—so unlike Sebastian, whose quick desperate hits were born of annoying need.

She was aware she was staring, but you could tell a lot about a person watching them attend to their habits, and she wanted to know more about this man she had so often wondered about, but about whom Sebastian rarely shared any information.

"Were you a student there?"

It took a moment for Alexandra to remember what they were talking about. "No. No, I studied at the Royal Academy in London."

"Hmmm... how did you find that?"

"An extreme dichotomy," she said quietly.

"How's that?"

"I wanted to be as far away from my mother as I could possibly get, which worked out wonderfully," she began, then faltered. "But I went there like most musicians, full of naive and silly dreams."

"It's difficult, isn't it?" Conrad's eyes were bright with encouragement and compassion. "When we think everyone shares our view on music, that every single student requires a different form of instruction, only to discover one size must fit all. Were you disappointed?"

"My story isn't at all original. I, along with every other female student, dreamed I was going to be the next Martha Argerich. When she had won the Geneva and Busoni competitions back-to-back at sixteen, I was mad for her! I mean, really, how much more awe-inspiring could someone be to a young girl starting out? Seems my professors had other ideas." Her voice quivered as she thought back. She cleared her throat and tossed off cavalierly, "You know, tear it all down to the distilled musical blocks—"

"But when rebuilding, they forgot the passion."

"Yes," she answered, quietly.

He grinned sympathetically. "There's a reason they're called conservatories and academies."

"I needed those blocks, but a little encouragement goes a long way."

"Is that what you give Sebastian?" He exhaled and turned to her, catching her eyes. She felt baited.

"I make sure to give him whatever he needs."

The night before Sebastian flew to London for the first leg of his tour, his manager hosted the last of the dinner parties to see him off as well as to take advantage of 'every angle of press ever considered,' Alexandra teased Sebastian one night on their way to yet another event. This night they were flanked only by the most powerful and intimate of his *people*. Aaron, his manager, to his right, then Alexandra, Monetizzare to the left, his publicist, and then farther down the table sat Max, Chandra, and Conrad.

Sebastian and his "crew" were constantly figuring out new demographics to target and Alexandra had grown weary of the endless "Bach-isms." She found herself straying to Conrad's hearty discussion about his "misadventures" while traveling around the world, his anecdotes endlessly amusing.

"...but it was the second time that Lars took me out, that I fully understood the thrill of an expedition." She couldn't help but find his stories more entertaining than the redundant details of Sebastian's tour and campaign blitz.

"Go on then, tell them what happened. And don't be modest." Max laughed eagerly. Alexandra saw the kind of warmth bestowed by a father for his son on Conrad. She could tell he took great joy in these stories, riveted by the specter of Conrad stalking lions with Lars.

Max wasn't the only one suspended by Conrad's charms.

"Do tell." Chandra purred as she draped a hand over Conrad's forearm. "Savagery can be so alluring."

"Chandra," Alexandra snapped, acutely aware of Chandra's intentions. "Can you pass me the cream,"

"You're absolutely right," Conrad agreed. "Savagery can hold a great deal of beauty."

"Well, we're all waiting with bated breath." Chandra ignored Alexandra.

Conrad spoke quietly but with an intensity that drew them all in. "We had been on the trail for three days, in the blistering heat, but I hardly noticed it I was so in awe of the plains of the Savanna, a thundering of zebra half a mile away waltzing through the tundra. Everywhere you turn, you see vistas of raw endless beauty." Conrad paused a moment in reverie. "We found a small pack of lion cubs, the female presumably foraging for dinner, so we knew the lion must be nearby. When she returned with a limp gazelle hanging from her jowls, we caught movement in the tall bush. When the lion came into our sights… he was impressively large."

"You sound like Clark Gable in *Mogambo*" Chandra teased. "Was there a Grace Kelly by your side?" Chandra had been drinking heavily, her words a bit tattered around the edges. "Seriously, what could be more romantic than a game hunter catching his prey to lay before his love, the conquering hero."

"No cinematic theatrics, I assure you." Alexandra was embarrassed but Conrad continued pleasantly, unfazed by Chandra's groping. "It was as simple as life in the wilds.

"Kill or be killed," Chandra mused loudly. "Just like all of us."

A moment passed where everyone stopped speaking altogether. Sebastian glanced at his brother from across the room and then returned his attention to Monetizzare.

"Go on," Max encouraged.

"The lion left, but the lioness picked up our scent. She stared us down. We both had our guns primed, aiming at her. I didn't want to kill her, but she began to charge us. Lars yelled that he had her in his sights, so I waited, but as he went to aim, he stumbled backward, and I had to shoot. I aimed for a clean kill. The lion was only fifty feet from us. But when I went to pull the trigger, the action jammed. I didn't even think. I leapt for Lars' gun, picked it up, and aimed somewhere in the general direction of the racing beast, pulled the trigger blind from the dust and just caught her rear flank. She yelped in pain and rage and fell." Conrad stopped a moment. Alexandra could see how much he regretted the end. "I finished her off as quickly as possible."

"We're simply grateful to the hunting gods that you lived to tell the tale." Chandra leaned closer to Conrad. "But what I want to hear is what you're not telling us. What happened to the mighty hunter, with a kill under his belt? You must have celebrated. You said Lars had plenty of wives. Perhaps he had one he could spare—"

"I'm not a man in the business of taking what isn't mine."

"Savage and moral. What a delightful combination."

Alexandra couldn't do anything to stop Chandra from pestering Conrad. But when Chandra began to dig into Conrad's love life, Alexandra let her explore unimpeded. Though gracious and conversational, Conrad was a complete enigma. He delivered no tidy pieces of evidence, no reverential sighs when he said this name or that. Alexandra found it equally plausible for Conrad to have courted his travels with unending trysts, or with the celibacy of a monk.

Chandra drank more wine and Sebastian glanced at Alexandra sharply as if to say, *I told you so.* Chandra had been invited at Alexandra's insistence even though Sebastian had forewarned that she would "simply end up in her cups, and while I don't give a damn, I'd rather not have her around my people."

"*Your* people?" Alexandra snapped jumping to Chandra's defense. She had hoped that being around the musical elite would reinvolve Chandra in her career. But Sebastian had been right.

Chandra guzzled one glass of champagne after another to "insulate myself from people who are only involved in music as a means to designer labels and penthouse mortgages."

She was too tipsy to argue with, but Alexandra also felt the keen schism between the musical purists and the commercial sharks. She kept an eye on Sebastian as he listened intently to numbers, sales, and projections, more business and commerce over cognac. She fully expected to hear it was time for port and cigars in the study. But only for those who had the potential for great revenue streams.

Later, when she had returned from the ladies' room, she saw Monetizzare and Aaron off speaking with colleagues. Max had taken one of their seats and seemed to be facing down Sebastian in earnest discourse. She walked to Sebastian's chair and put a hand on his shoulder. Conrad leaned against the wall next to them, looking paradoxically relaxed and interested.

"Does it bother you in the least their arrangement of your music? Orchestrally speaking?" Max puffed as he wiped his glasses vigorously.

"Ever the professor, eh?" Sebastian forced a grin.

"It doesn't seem, I don't know, quite *you* somehow."

"What do you mean, not me?" Sebastian demanded.

"I know you, Sebastian. You would never have had the strings accompany you in the end of the second movement. You would have wanted it all for the solo. It's not a crime to want to shine. And in this specific instance, it allows the solo piano to tell the pain of the story with the simplest poignancy."

"To tell you the truth, I thought it made it more moving." Sebastian's tone inferred that Max's pedagogy was now all but irrelevant. "Should have thought of it myself."

"You didn't find that it threatened the integrity of the phrasing? It is the most exquisite passage—"

"And the most difficult. It's the one place I can stumble," Sebastian snapped, then covered with a chuckle. "This way, the strings will cover me."

"Bahhh." Max growled. "Why write it if you cannot play it? It flattens the intention. One loses the meaning..."

"I won't have nearly the practice time on tour that I have at home," Sebastian replied testily.

Alexandra and Conrad exchanged glances.

"Come on, Max. This is a party, not a lecture hall," Conrad intervened.

"I'll think about what you said." Sebastian tried to be magnanimous, but his voice was tense.

"It's Sebastian's music to do with as he pleases." Conrad closed the subject.

"Thanks, old man." Sebastian cocked a brow. "I appreciate your giving me license."

Alexandra watched, intrigued, as Conrad lifted his glass to Sebastian. "To Antonia, and the fulfillment of dreams."

Aaron put on his coat, and several other guests appeared to make overtures at leaving. Alexandra put an arm around Sebastian's neck from behind and whispered into his ear. "Are we ever going home?"

"Darling. Did you hear?" he responded, ignoring her question.

"What?"

"They've booked all of Europe and the UK venues have sold out already. It's—"

"Magnificent." But her voice was tired. "Sebastian, I'm so proud of you."

He turned to her. "Are you, darling?"

"Sweetheart, no one knows better than I how hard you've worked."

Alexandra's voice was filled with emotion, and Conrad watched as his brother basked in the bright glare of her love.

"I'm going to miss you so much," Sebastian whispered to Alexandra. "I wish you could go with me."

She nodded, a sad resignation on her face. "I'm so far behind on my own work."

Sebastian glanced around the table and tightened his arm around her. "It's happening, Alex. It's truly happening."

She leaned over and kissed him gently on the lips.

Expressionless, Conrad regarded Alexandra as Sebastian scooped her into his lap, his arms loosely circled about her waist, and Max watched Conrad observe the ways in which the two young lovers interacted. He wadded up his linen and tossed it to the table.

"Lovebirds." Max glanced at his watch. "I'm afraid this curtain call is over."

Sebastian couldn't sleep from the excitement of leaving the following morning, even after having made love to Alexandra, which usually always relaxed him. After he heard her even breathing, he got up, careful not to wake her. He closed his bedroom door and could hear the echo of music from downstairs. In the dark, he followed the exotic melody down the stairs into the living room.

He stealthily crept to the arched entry to see Conrad bathed in moonlight, bent over the piano, playing his intensely vital and haunting "Saharan Overture." Adrenaline seared his stomach, nerves prickled up through his spine, as the captivating notes thrust Sebastian into a panic. He was witness to the chilling reality that no matter what fame he was garnering, his brother's talent would always outweigh his own.

In the pale cast of the moon, Sebastian couldn't help but remember the conversation that always came to mind when he felt anxiety, when the reality of his world caught up to what had been mere dreams. That evening, he was probably the most famous classical musician in the United States, and soon, potentially, all over the world. And yet, Alexandra's long-ago words echoed in his mind. *We're imposters, you and I...* He felt the heat of the words at his brow. As he watched his brother play, he wondered if he would ever know how Conrad felt about his music. He was quite certain the concept of being an imposter never once gave him pause.

Memorial holiday travelers streamed through the JFK airport along with the rest of Sebastian's entourage and the media as they took photos and asked final questions before Sebastian was about to board. Sebastian raised his hands, and his manager finally moved everyone to the side. "That's all folks. Mr. D'Antonio thanks you for your time."

Sebastian drew Conrad and Alexandra to the side. "So, Connie, keep an eye on my Alex, will you?"

Conrad nodded.

"Alex…" His voice faltered. "I—"

She put a finger to his lips. Conrad walked from the boarding gate to give them privacy. Sebastian bent to kiss her, and they embraced, fully, intimately. "I'm with you… just know that I'm with you…" she said, her lips pressed to his neck.

A final call blared from the loudspeaker for Sebastian's flight. Right before he left the terminal, he turned, spotted Alexandra, and characteristically put his hand to his heart. She waved, blew him a last kiss, and then he disappeared.

Monetizzare had a car waiting for Conrad and Alexandra to return them to the D'Antonio estate. They sat on opposite sides, Alexandra staring out the window. Neither of them spoke. A few tears slid down her cheeks. Conrad retrieved a handkerchief from his jacket pocket and handed it to her.

"He'll be fine. Sebastian's remarkably good at taking care of himself."

Alexandra dried her tears and said, without the least bit of comfort, "Yes, I know."

"Music is the art of thinking with sounds."

Juels Combarieu (1859—1916)

She watched Conrad's slow, lazy strokes as he made his way across the pool. She realized, suddenly, that from inside, shielded by the drapes, her actions were that of a covert spy. She felt compelled to study him, as if by doing so she would understand the shift of tension since his arrival. Intrigue hung in the air. Secrets had been hidden away in this estate, or possibly buried with Antonia. Maybe the secrets were hidden deeply beneath both Sebastian and Conrad's consciousness, but something, some essential dynamic, had surfaced between the two brothers and she planned to unearth the mystery.

She observed his lean body as he lay on the diving board, letting the sun dapple dry his fine muscles, his taut stomach still breathing rapidly from the swim. A hint of a smile caressed his jawline. *He's content.* She had no earthly clue what it took to find such peace. Even with her successes and her remarkable relationship with Sebastian, Alexandra didn't feel at peace. It wasn't that she was unhappy. She was... unsettled.

She had been at her place in the city until Claire informed her some of their family was coming into town and needed the space. She had happily agreed to stay at Sebastian's instead of returning to her mother's, but now she wondered if that had been the wisest decision. She needed to get to work, and here she was harboring these absurd fantasies of clandestine secrets and hidden agendas. She removed herself from the window and walked to the piano to polish up the piece she was supposed to have recorded a month ago.

It had been difficult to be Sebastian's lover for the past few months. It hadn't only cut into her practice time but into her recording time, as well. How could it not? The house had been filled with his *people* for weeks as they prepared for the European tour, and there were many interviews for which Alexandra had been requested as a sidebar.

A certain part of her enjoyed the accolades and attention and, to be practical, she knew it would only benefit her own career. But it didn't matter one whit if all these wonderful things happened, and she couldn't back it up with work. And not just any work, but work that shone, that bettered the last piece she had mastered. Though clearly not a technician, she was perpetually consumed with improving her technique. It required absolute solitude and concentrated focus. She had to live with the piece, make it her own by performing it in so many variations of feeling, so specific and with such nuance, that only the most trained ear would detect the differences. Only then could she incorporate her final choices in a public performance, whether that was at the recording studio or in a recital at Carnegie. Now that the last of Sebastian's stragglers had finally left, maybe she could get back to work.

But her hands moved over the keys with laconic indifference as she thought about seeing him off at the airport, without a moment of privacy to tell him how much she loved him. Something she hadn't been able to do the night before he left, either.

They had come in so late, and she had felt an urgency to make love, knowing they wouldn't see one another for the next few months, probably longer. Undressing in his room, she had walked to him and put her hands on his back, moving against the surface of his skin, up and above his shoulders over the fine mass of hair at his chest, softly caressing the tips of his nipples. She heard the sharp intake of breath and was stunned when she heard, "Connie."

"What?"

"Wait a minute." Sebastian pulled away to open the bedroom door and came back in and whispered to her. "Conrad isn't in his bedroom."

"So?"

"I…" He glanced at her sheepishly. "I just don't feel, you know comfortable. I don't want him to hear us."

"Then don't growl like the king of the mountain," Alexandra suggested a bit sharply.

"I'm sorry. Alex, oh darling, come here." As he wrapped her in his arms, she could feel his erection growing beside her. "I'm being a stupid fool. Come on then."

He took her to the bed and entered her quickly, thrusting mechanically, coming in a few minutes, muffling his ardor into a pillow, and then putting his fingers inside her and working her steadily as his other hand covered her mouth when she came.

"You're not paying attention."

A tiny drop of water plopped upon F sharp.

Conrad stood right behind her. She felt the avalanche of a blush suffuse her skin as he leaned over, placed his thumb and pinky at an octave interval, and reconstructed a different phrasing of what she had just lazily performed.

"I was—"

"Your mind is somewhere else leaving your poor hands neglected," Conrad teased her gently.

"Just thinking about Sebastian. Guess I lost my concentration."

"I've heard you when you're really inside the music." Conrad walked in front of her then, his blue eyes looking directly into her.

She looked at him quizzically.

"I heard both of you on a wireless in Mexico during the Ketterling. Your performance was... exquisite." His low, tempered voice was so quiet she could barely hear the words, yet they were charged with emotion. She wasn't used to this strange, quiet kindness, and felt a level of simpatico with him she hadn't expected.

"But?"

"Nothing you don't already know. Technically—a bit thin. But you chose that. I can tell by the way you disregarded only the most conservative rules."

"I don't do well with someone from a hundred years ago telling me how I should feel."

"Precisely. I don't think any composer writes music to dictate how it must be played, only to request a performer remain true to his feelings when playing it."

She smiled, but his eyes didn't waver and as she turned, cleared her throat.

"Do you mind?"

"Mind?" Alexandra asked, puzzled.

"Would you play it for me?"

Alexandra's stomach churned. It wasn't as if Rachmaninoff's Second wasn't the very centerpiece of most of her performances. But suddenly it felt as if she'd rather play for thousands than this one man.

"Please?"

She closed her eyes.

She went back. Back to the night of the Ketterling finals, reliving the delicious swirl of feelings that first stirred within her for Sebastian as she replayed moments from the second movement. She tried to match them, but the music moved her differently now. Her passion was different, a slightly strained and melancholic impression as the melody floated about them. She let her hands drop from the keys.

"You're missing him."

"It's just not the same in the house when he's gone."

"Nor when I'm here." It wasn't a question, but she almost heard him asking her permission.

"Conrad, look, I'm the interloper here. I told Sebastian I could stay with my parents until he returns."

"Nonsense."

"This is *your* home."

"I don't think of it that way." Conrad moved to the side table and picked up the framed photo of Antonia Sebastian always kept close to him while working. "I've always thought of it as Antonia's, and naturally now that she's gone, as Sebastian's."

"But you grew up here."

"Yes. Sometimes I felt like I had walked in on a private conversation. Like they would have been perfectly content without me."

"I rather doubt that. From everything Sebastian has said they both adored you."

"Yes… we made an interesting trio." The subject was closed. He walked to the windows and stood looking out, and again she saw the contrast in the two who had grown up as brothers. Sebastian always appeared to be a caged animal, pacing to get out, whereas Conrad seemed to let the outer world seep in, in small, precise doses.

"You know you're far more talented than Sebastian," he stated flatly.

"Please don't say things like that—"

"You misunderstand again. I was going to tell you how much I admire your loving him, helping him become the man he was always meant to be."

"Why is it when I hear your words, they say one thing, but I feel as if you mean another?"

"You must believe me. I am genuinely happy Sebastian has you."

"No one *has* me."

Conrad turned to her. "Are you going to meet up with him soon?"

Alexandra looked directly at him. His words were clear but what he was asking was: *are we to be here together, then?*

"No," she answered.

A smile flickered in his eyes. "Then perhaps I'll see you later for dinner."

He turned and walked back out to the pool, and she could feel the crash of his body as he dove into the water.

Two nights later, as Alexandra sat at her dressing table unbraiding her hair, she heard the music. Conrad's music. Like Sebastian, she was struck by the potency of his composition. It was fresh and new, exciting, adventurous. Maybe even a little arrogant in its unconventionality. Conrad clearly felt and interpreted his music in an altogether unique manner, even in the way he fused elements of classical structure to his own take on postmodern impressionism.

She aimlessly picked up her brush, ran it through her hair, teased by the melody seeping through her limbs. An unusual *mal du siècle*, created a riveting poignancy that wound inside her and made her feel restless and disquieted.

She quickly re-braided her hair, checked her makeup in the mirror, then walked to the bedroom door. Stopped. She opened the door but turned and walked back to the bed. She lay down and listened.

His music continued late into the night, and she didn't stop listening until the last note dissipated into stillness, but when she got up the next morning, she felt not in the least bit tired. He didn't seem tired either, when she found him by the pool where he sat with black coffee, sketching several phrases on blank sheet music.

"May I?" Her voice was soft. She didn't mean to interrupt him, and he invited her with a welcoming smile. As she sat, she noticed that he had arranged for Tula to lay two of everything. He poured her coffee, a gallant gesture, she thought, then offered her a cigarette, which he lit.

They sat in easy silence for some time. Alexandra's eyes traveled from the pool, shimmering in early morning sunlight, to the gardens, and finally, she let them rest on Conrad as he worked. Again, his focus was singular and private, but not exclusive, as if he easily embraced the world around him and integrated it right into the notes. She didn't find the furrowed brow she had so often observed at Sebastian's forehead, whose work seemed to cause him as much frustration as furor. When Sebastian was at a session, Alexandra tread lightly, fearful he might blow up at any point, with a "For Christ's sakes, what the hell is this?" or "Darling, I'm just hanging by a thread here, do you suppose you could give me some privacy?" It wasn't as if Alexandra hadn't been busy with her own work. She often spent hours up in the library rehearsing while he worked downstairs. Well, not much lately, but she had always been good at staying out of his way. Conversely, Conrad appeared he would have no trouble working in the middle of Grand Central Station.

"Your music, Conrad," she started and suddenly became shy. "It's quite... disarming."

He turned to her.

"It … it fascinates me." Alexandra continued uncomfortably, feeling as though she sounded like a student gushing to her professor. "There's a familiarity to it … yet it's so fresh. You haven't fallen into the trap so many modern composers do, you know, dissonance for dissonance's sake." She wasn't sure she was expressing what she meant.

Conrad smiled graciously.

"Your music is so refreshing. A sort of Debussy meets Prokofiev, with a dash of Rachmaninoff thrown in. You don't seem to be afraid at all to play with a sort of lush expressionism, the kind of music that just hasn't been around for ages, yet it's not corny… not saccharine, because you've set it in such contemporary shadings and rhythms." She stopped quite suddenly. "Okay, now I'm embarrassed. Have I gushed enough?"

"Don't be. That was sweet."

Sweet? Now she was humiliated. As if she didn't have the depth to understand his music. She fussed with her coffee and toast as if she was finishing and preparing to leave. He returned to his pages as if they hadn't had any conversation at all.

"It just comes to you, doesn't it?"

He didn't look at her as he continued working. "Like breathing."

Later that night, Alexandra returned from the city after dinner with Chandra. The house appeared empty. It was hot so she walked out to the patio to sit in the cooler air, and some moments later heard Conrad's footsteps.

"Mind if I join you?"

"Not at all."

He nabbed two cigarettes, lit them both, and handed one to Alexandra who immediately pictured Bette Davis's arching eyebrows as she glanced up with melodramatic flair in *Now, Voyager,* and couldn't help but grin.

"What?" he asked.

"Nothing… nothing." But she began laughing.

"It's not polite to laugh at someone without letting them in on the joke."

"Okay. You just reminded me of the German actor in that Bette Davis movie who lights her cigarette every time they steal silent moments together. It's supposed to be a not-so-subtle innuendo that they're having sex."

His chuckled. "Corny, eh?"

"No. It's nice."

They sat for some time enjoying their cigarettes. She felt an easy comfort for the first time since her ridiculous conversation with him earlier that morning. But when he turned to her and she saw his eyes, she was quite suddenly aware that he was a handsome man, and she was a solitary woman on a dimly lit patio.

"I guess I'll head to bed." Alexandra rose. "Good night."

"Do you play tennis?"

"Yes, but not well."

"At the courts tomorrow, after practice?"

"Sure."

"Good night, Alexandra."

"You're very good," Conrad noted as they walked off the courts.

Alexandra wiped her arms with a towel.

"You're being very kind. Thirsty?" Alexandra asked. "I could go for some iced tea."

"Tula's out for the day."

"I'll make it."

"Oh no you won't." Conrad reached for her hand. "Come with me."

Alexandra felt shy suddenly but took his hand as he pulled her up a small ledge to one of Antonia's beautifully adorned paths that had been impeccably trimmed now that Sebastian had plenty of money rolling in. The path bordered a steep incline to the only hill on the property.

Once on the trail, he let go of her hand, but she still felt the heat of his palm. He strolled toward a gently gushing stream of fresh spring water and cupped his hands to fill them for her.

She eagerly sipped. "Wow, that's the best water I've ever tasted."

"Nature's iced tea!" Conrad nodded eagerly, refilled his cupped hands, and drank some more. She filled up her own hands, offered them to him, then at the last moment splashed him instead.

"Oh, that's the way you want to play this?" He whisked his hand into the stream and splashed her back.

More swashes of water at each other until they began giggling, then laughing, then unable to stop laughing, bending into one another until she lost her balance.

He swept her close.

They froze.

She smelled his intriguing cologne mixed with sweat.

She didn't remove herself but then he gently pushed her aside. "I need to get back to it."

"Yeah. Me too."

He walked ahead and down the path. She wasn't sure if she should join him, so followed behind, suddenly heady, anxious, and confused.

They had both showered and retired to their separate workspaces. Alexandra realized she had repeated the same passage now three times. She found herself losing her concentration, flashing back to the tanned, muscular Conrad with his blonder than blond hair as he maneuvered gracefully about the tennis court.

She was up in the library and could hear him playing in the living room below. Shaking her head, she attacked an extremely challenging scale, admonishing herself with staccato precision lest her mind kept wandering. She paused.

Silence.

He must be taking a break.

Alexandra cleared her throat and rose from her piano bench.

She wandered down the hall, looking for traces of him, and finally found him playing chess by himself outside, drinking iced tea.

Not turning to her he said, "I made a particularly good batch."

"I'll be the judge of that."

She winked at him, then immediately blushed, turning from him to pour her tea. *What the hell was she doing?*

"You play chess?"

"I do." Still with her back to him.

"Great. I'm getting tired of beating myself."

She laughed, then sat across from him as he set the board with ornately carved pieces of wood and marble animals of Africa; the Queen and King—Lioness & Lion, Knights were cheetahs, the pawns monkeys. Crafted of Koto Cherry Wood, additional etchings of African lore bordered its elaborate edges.

"This is beautiful."

"A gift from Lars."

"The gentleman you were talking about at Sebastian's party."

"No gentleman, believe me. Yes, he was my travelling companion from Africa throughout Europe." He put out a hand for her to take the first move. They played in silence for a half-hour, until he suddenly stood.

"Cigarettes." Patting himself down, Conrad found them in his shirt pocket. "Ahh."

He lit one for each of them and grinned along with her at the earlier reference.

"You're good at this as well."

"Doubtful that I'm giving you a real run for your money."

"You are." He grinned, then added, "Competitive."

"It was only once in the ring, that she smelled blood." Alexandra teased. "Just didn't want to embarrass myself. I'm definitely rusty so thank you for going easy on me."

"You're holding your own."

A long moment of silence.

"All the performance competition I suppose."

"But now it's just you and your audience."

"Yes, I know. But I still feel like I'm in the heat of the race, only now the competition is not to lose my career."

"You're too good to feel that way." Conrad cocked his head. "Tell me about performing. Tell me how Alexandra lives inside a performance."

She turned to him and thought a moment. No matter how many times she had been asked this question she felt the leaden anxiety that pushed against her ribcage the moment she walked on stage. "You mean after I've swallowed the water buffalo?"

Conrad laughed.

"I get the nerves so bad, I—"

"No, I didn't mean the periphery. I mean when you're *in* the performance," Conrad gently redirected her.

"I feel..." She paused trying to find the perfect word. "Weightless. The closest thing to sublime I can imagine." She took a sip of her tea. "Are you familiar with the ego disillusionment phase of a *trip*?"

"You mean when you're *flying*? *'Go ask Alice when she's ten feet tall,'*" he warbled.

"*When the men on the chessboard, get up and tell you where to go,'*" she joined him in *White Rabbit*, pointing at their remaining pieces on the board.

"*And you've just had some kind of mushroom,*" Conrad crooned.

"*And your mind is moving low, Go ask Alice, I think she'll know,*" they finished together.

"I'm surprised."

"That I can carry a tune?"

"No. We definitely butchered that. I'm kind of shocked that you knew the lyrics."

Their eyes caught. She was having so much fun. Of all the people one would consider serious, it would be Conrad. But what seemed truer was that he loved to enjoy himself. Or maybe it was that he simply enjoyed each experience as he lived it.

"Anyway, not that I've taken many trips, but it's that kind of an evaporation of boundaries, where outside becomes inside and… you become the music."

He nodded appreciatively thinking back to his thorough peyote explorations.

"I just heard that." Alexandra laughed. "Not to sound pompous as hell. But I've had equally horrific experiences. You know, slips, hearing something in the audience. Once, during a warmup performance, a woman sneezed so hard I lost my concentration. Completely! The audience gasped. I simply shrugged and said 'Gesundheit,' and the entire audience burst out laughing."

"Ouch."

"Yes, I could barely finish the movement!"

He grinned sympathetically which turned into a warm, infectious smile.

"Nothing more humbling than human error." She patted loose strands back into her braid. "When I practice everything's up for analysis, interpretation, I'm constantly fine-tuning. There isn't anything I take on faith. But when I perform—if I let a whisper of doubt enter my mind—I'm lost."

Conrad offered her another cigarette. She declined, but asked, "What about you?"

"With me, it's just the simple putting of hands on keys." Conrad lit his cigarette. "That's why I left Juilliard. No one seemed interested in the music. It was all about hungry desperate composers blindly following the post-modern movement. No one seemed to have the first clue of what they really wanted."

They glanced at one another, eyes holding a second too long. "I'd like one after all." Alexandra fussed with his pack of cigarettes.

"There used to be this running joke at school." Conrad lit her cigarette. "Ingredients for winning a composition competition: Take a couple of random instruments. Write an utterly incomprehensible score."

Alexandra nodded her head, enjoying Conrad's achingly deadpan delivery. "Stir for an indeterminate time—as long as that time is longer than anyone can endure—whip into athematic froth. Dash of Dada to taste. Voila; Post Modern soufflé."

"Oh yes, the self-seriousness of it all." She laughed.

"Seriously writing scores no one can read," he countered

"Pounding the piano with a flute while a soprano sings under it," she lobbied back

"Twelve radios all tuned to random stations while water echoes in conch shells." He cited John Cage.

"Hands down the worst." She shivered. "Dissecting a piano with butcher knives!"

They both laughed.

"Breaking light bulbs on tin panes has, for some time, escaped me as a musical form," Alexandra declared sardonically. "Innovation without inspiration leaves me cold. It's the height of narcissism to engage in Avante Garde pyrogenics created for an audience of three."

"You know, you *are* allowed to throw out the baby with the bathwater." He winked at her. Alexandra smirked and Conrad's poker face broke into a grin.

Alexandra shook her head, laughing, and said grimly, "It's such a shame that the lay person has no real concept of composition in our world. All they know is the conservatory-trained repertoire."

"The irony is—" Conrad closed his eyes, turned his head slightly, listening to the sounds around them "—that it's all right here."

He opened his eyes and looked at her. "Music lives everywhere. The legato lapping of water in the pool, the rhythmic canon of tennis balls, back and forth, swoop, thud, swoop, thud. Hear this gentle breeze winding itself to a crescendo as leaves snare-drum against the branches? The pizzicato plucking of Tula's coffee maker—all this friction, this movement, creates natural sounds. And each is followed by the reverberations and overtones of those that we *don't* hear…" His hands motioned in fixed movements above him. "It's all around us for the taking, but all these tortured artists keep banging themselves over the head to break through new barriers, to find the *new* music—the next evolutionary cycle—when it's already here."

Alexandra watched Conrad, as intrigued by his words as the tendons in his forearms as he gestured almost like a conductor, graceful and sure, the flash in his blue-grey eyes as he spoke of his passion.

"Oh, Lord. Now I sound like a pompous madman!" He laughed at himself.

He offered his hand. "Let's walk." It wasn't a question. When she put her hand in his, she felt the involuntary tug wrenching her stomach. She immediately removed it, fussed with her braid.

They strolled through Antonia's gardens for quite some time in easy silence until they approached the alcove with Dionysus at one end and Apollo at the other.

"I did understand what you were saying, Conrad, earlier." Alexandra stroked a rose petal. "And it makes me understand your process now. You've got it, but it's also got you. Almost as if you're at its mercy."

Conrad stopped. Alexandra understood Conrad's relation to his music as no one ever had, aside from Lars. "The notes and melody chattering in my head follow me wherever I go." Conrad drew from his cigarette. "And until I answer them, create form for them, nothing gives me peace."

"I know it isn't quite the same, because I'm not creating," Alexandra said thoughtfully. "But it's what happens for me when I'm held captive by a new piece. It's all around me. It creates the tone of my waking moments. I feel it in my sleep… it occupies my skin."

"Yes. Everything becomes music for me." His eyes pierced her own. "Even the poignant bel canto of your perfume."

He wasn't being coy, but she suddenly felt shy and moved ahead of him. A long silence ensued. She placed a hand on Apollo and turned to him.

"So, I'm sure you and Sebastian have been compared to our mythic Greeks here."

"All too often." Conrad rolled his eyes.

"Since Sebastian is most certainly the romantic, that would make you the intellectual."

"And don't you think we intellectuals feel as deeply as the emotional romantics?"

"Isn't that the whole Apollo vs. Dionysus argument? Nietzsche's two opposing philosophies of the artistic aesthetic?"

"I think chaos and order have been given a bad rap. One isn't necessarily always in conflict with the other."

"Does that explain your bond to Sebastian?" Alexandra asked.

"No. It explains yours."

"Truly fertile Music, the only kind that will move us,
that we shall truly appreciate, will be a Music conducive to
Dream, which banishes all reason and analysis.
One must not wish first to understand and then to feel.
Art does not tolerate Reason."

Albert Camus (1913—60)
French-Algerian philosopher, author.

Alexandra found the days with Conrad settling into a comfortable routine. Reversing her practice regime with Sebastian, Alexandra spent most of her time at the Bösendorfer while Conrad practiced upstairs in the library, oftentimes isolated up there for days at a time. Alexandra watched Tula take up sandwiches and coffee, as Conrad appeared to have no notion the world lived by schedules pertaining to civilization such as lunch, cocktail hour, etc. He was always surprised when Alexandra mentioned it was time for dinner. He was often absent during her solitary meals, and she found herself not only lonely for Sebastian, but also missing her conversations with Conrad.

For a week, she saw little of him. He was always cordial when they passed one another in the halls, or when they ran into one another over coffee, but he was quite clearly focused and consumed with his work. Finally, one day when Alexandra pulled out of the garage in Sebastian's shiny Jaguar convertible, Conrad dashed out and ran to the car. "Mind if I catch a ride?"

"Sure, but dare you leave the dungeon?" she teased. "I thought you cave-dwellers shriveled up and blew away when exposed to direct sunlight."

"It is awfully bright out here." He put on sunglasses and jumped into the car.

As she drove, she glanced at Conrad, his silky hair blowing in the wind. She found herself drawn to the square of his jawline, wondered what it would be like to brush her palm upon that precise measure of skin that stretched from his cheekbone to his chin. With the aristocratic curve of his nose, it struck her again how dissimilar he was to Sebastian; refined and untouchable. He turned to her then as if aware that she was studying him and lifted his sunglasses, his demeanor serious.

"Do you know where Armory's musical supply is?"

She laughed at the simplicity of his question. "Sure."

They agreed to meet at Washington Square Park at five o'clock, which gave them several hours to attend to their own errands. When Alexandra arrived, it was just past five. She heard the incessant thud of dance beat drums blaring out from loudspeakers as she approached. It appeared to be a block party of sorts. Alexandra put her hand to her eyes, searching for Conrad amongst the ever-growing crowd.

She glanced from an aging Hungarian housewife, who sat on a park bench lightly tapping overwrought loafers, to an obese college student adorned in tie-dye moving with the grace of a gazelle as she danced without inhibition. Just as Alexandra thought she spotted Conrad, a slender man whipped by her, obscuring her vision as he dashed to the tie-dyed girl, and began dancing with her.

Conrad felt the vibrations at the center of his body as he wandered through the crowd trying to find Alexandra. A skinny white youth, gangly and awkward, jerked spasmodically to the beat. Not so different than the Masai, Conrad mused. Several yards from him, two Asian toddlers bounced together, the strain of their bent postures more suggestive of full diapers than of dancing as they giggled with joy. He spotted Alexandra, but she didn't see him, and as he walked slowly through the crowd his eyes never left her.

Alexandra allowed the beat to pulsate from the ground, enter her body, ease her muscles into the tempo, much the same as the hundreds of people drawn to the new and seductive reggae music that had just hit the States. A muscular black man and white woman moved together in an open display of sexuality, while an aging Hispanic cowboy rolled a cigarette with gnarled fingers, his faded boots tapping time.

Suddenly Alexandra felt him, knew Conrad's eyes were on her. They bore into the heat of her back, but she didn't turn as she began dancing for him. The tempo turned slow and repetitive. She improvised a gently swaying pas seul, tenderly alluring for its minimalist sensualism. As she performed for him, they became the center of this nucleus, an undulation of humanity opening to the recurring tempo, both figuratively and literally. People from all walks of life were pulled to this small patch of green, all peacefully and happily listening to a single common denominator, the one thing that unified them. Music.

When the music stopped, she turned to him. He stood behind her, sunglasses propped upon his head, a glint of appreciation in his eyes, his mouth curled into a smile of gratitude and eager curiosity.

"I don't want to head back, yet." Alexandra groaned as they returned to the car. Suddenly the idea of being cooped up at the estate irked her.

Conrad put out his hand. "Keys."

Alexandra considered for a moment, then dropped them into his hand.

He drove them to the Brooklyn Heights promenade and parked the car. No words passed between them as they walked amongst the nineteenth-century row houses and brownstones, the backdrop to the vista of the city to the west. As the sun fell the buildings were bathed in a brilliant hue of peach, the sky turning a rich indigo. And as the city lights began to flicker on, Alexandra intuited a slender thread of change in Conrad's mood, a minor preoccupation.

"Something wrong?" she ventured.

"Hmmm?"

"Is anything the matter?"

"No," he said but was still distant. "No."

"Would you like to go back? I mean, do you need to get back to your work?"

He turned to her then, and asked with a directness that disarmed her, "Would you have dinner with me?"

Alexandra instinctively reached for her braid, smoothed it over her collar bone. "Yes... I'd like that."

They walked a half mile to the River Café and were seated at a table with a view of the cityscape, now sparkling stars in a concrete universe. Alexandra noticed halfway through their meal, other couples dining, leaning close to one another, tipping wine glasses together, touching forearms, and whispering into one another's ears. She felt conspicuously out of place.

"I'm sorry, should we have not come here?" Conrad asked, sensing her discomfort.

"No. Not at all." Alexandra paused, then tried once more. "I... I don't mean to pry, but it seems you're preoccupied by something."

"It's... I've just been ... feeling out of sorts lately. With my work."

"What do you mean?"

"While I was at it this morning, for some reason I began thinking about something Stravinsky once said: that 'music is powerless to express anything,' that it's nothing more than a series of abstract mathematical sounds. When you consider what we were speaking about the other day, it sort of makes one wonder how, as a composer, he found any meaning to his life?"

It was the first note of doubt she had heard from Conrad. She looked at him quizzically and said lightly, "Science and emotion rarely make good bedfellows. I prefer Charles Ives, who said 'music does not represent life. It is life.' Besides, if music means nothing, how do you explain that plants exposed to Bach and Handel have been known to grow taller and bend toward the music, while those subjected to loud obnoxious sound die within weeks?"

"Okay... all things being equal, how can one possibly determine if what one's written will expand the listener's capacity for joy, rather than drive them away, like your poor wilted plants?"

"I wasn't aware that mattered to you?"

"No… I mean not until…" Conrad shook his head, clearly frustrated. "I guess I've hit a bit of a… a fork in the road if you will. I'm just not used to it… uncertainty." She heard the vulnerability in his tempered voice. "For so long I heard it one way and now I'm starting to hear it another, and I'm not sure what's causing the shift. Or what it means."

"You mean a different interpretation?"

"More than that." He held her gaze. "Not just the interpretation, but my whole understanding of the process. Maybe Lars was right," Conrad mused more to himself than Alexandra. "I've kept myself from humanity for too long."

Alexandra cleared her throat happy the waiter had come to take their plates. They sat quietly for a long, tension-laden moment, Alexandra purposefully watching the other diners.

"Brandy?" Conrad asked. Alexandra nodded, happy they weren't returning to Antonia's fortress, where she was beginning to feel isolated, full of Sebastian at every turn, despite his absence. It made her miss him in a different way than she had anticipated. More. And, oftentimes, while in Conrad's company, less.

"Tell me more about Africa, Conrad."

Over the course of several brandies, Conrad shared many of his escapades and adventures, both alone and with Lars. Growing delightfully tipsy, Alexandra loved hearing the many details that helped her to know him better.

"Lord." Conrad sighed wistfully. "There's nothing like it there. Life is so… immediate. Do you know what I mean?"

"I believe so."

"When I left here, it felt like a compulsion. I knew I could never find what I needed to learn if I remained. I thought I had to resolve everything all at once. Where and how did music speak most directly to my soul? As I travelled, I had all the same old arguments with other composers, musicians, virtuosos; A delirious mind-fuck, excuse my language. It seemed so predictable; every artist strives for perfection or brilliance even when they know to reach for it means certain failure."

"The artist's lament. Perfection, however lofty and unattainable, is what drives us."

He looked at her, saw the honesty in her eyes, and lowered his own.

"And... the other reason I left was because of Antonia." His voice lowered. "Without her..."

Alexandra's heart went out to Conrad as she watched him falter.

"It's not as if I ever fit into her world. But she made me feel... connected. I used to embarrass the hell out of Sebastian at school. The eccentric. The misfit. Not only with my work, but out in the world. Was I a Schoenbergian exile? Or a new sort of old-fashioned romantic with my attachment to Bach? But when I traveled as far away from civilization as I could get, out amongst people whose only aim was to live, I knew music wasn't about technique, and form, and timing—it was about blood and guts and flesh—just like this afternoon at the park."

Alexandra listened intently.

"I needed to be inside that in order to understand how to feel... the man in my music."

"What do you mean?"

Conrad visibly shuddered. "While I was away I... I saw things, did things—I would never do today. Yet there, it seemed so natural. A touch of madness..."

"Sort of an occupational hazard," Alexandra said tenderly.

"You think so?"

"Yes. I'm afraid so." She sighed, thinking of the things she'd done and regretted in the pursuit of her dream.

They sat a moment, both lost in their thoughts, feeling a new level of intimacy weave between them.

"When I was a little girl, I felt things so strongly I thought my skin would tear away from me. I was always trying to figure out how to keep up this balancing act of suppressing what my mother considered 'inappropriate tantrums' and the reality of my extreme emotions needing to come out somehow." She was surprised to hear her own words. She hadn't even shared this with Sebastian. But Conrad was so attentive and accessible, she felt safe in continuing.

"When I turned thirteen, I played Schumann's *A Minor*. I was absolutely thrown by it. Riveted. I had to know about him—Schumann—'the man in *his* music,'" she quoted him, enticingly. "I took out every book I could find in the library, only to discover the passion I heard in his music was the very thing that destroyed him. He began hallucinating, visions of demons... he kept hearing the note of A in his head, relentlessly. It terrorized me."

"Go on." Conrad's voice was sympathetic.

"He used to hide out midnight hours to play so he could weep inconsolably from the beauty of the notes. Exactly what I used to do." She stopped a moment, glancing at Conrad to see if she had revealed too much, but all she saw was kindness and warmth. "I was terrified I would end up like him. So, I worked at taking all this energy... this intensity that boils under my skin—" she searched frantically for the right words. "This huge swelling in me that feels as if I'll splinter into a million pieces, and channeled it into my music. Music became my best friend. It took everything I had to give it, and it never judged me. More than anything, I got the reward of being able to feel as intensely as I do." She stopped suddenly.

"And?"

"Nothing."

"No there's something." He stated knowing better.

"I guess the only problem was I put all of myself into playing the piano for so long that I forgot how to give it to anyone else."

"Until you met Sebastian."

An awkward silence ensued until the waiter came at that moment to return Conrad's change.

"All my life people have accused me of being aloof or distant. But to learn how to control everything going on inside me—if I couldn't express it through playing—I simply had to shut it down. Present a façade that must appear... well, cold." She shrugged, feeling defeated with the admission.

Conrad's eyebrows raised almost imperceptibly. "From the first moment I heard you play; I knew you were a woman of incredible warmth."

She allowed herself to look at him for a long moment, then turned away. "Thank you."

He walked into the living room where Alexandra struggled with the phrasing of the intricately yearning Chopin *Nocturne, Opus 55*. He sat beside her and performed it seamlessly.

"I guess I'm not giving it the right accent."

Conrad shrugged. "Can I see that fingering again?" he asked, and she played. "Try using five-four-three-two-three, not three-two-one."

She tried it and it worked better. "If I play it pianissimo in this part I seem to lose the articulation." Dissatisfied, she tried it again.

"He wrote this with love in his heart. You need to bring out the color of love." He sat and played with her at the higher octaves.

She replayed as he had. "Maybe not voice the sharp so much here?"

He played along with her again, and she began to fall into his cadence, mimicking his fingering.

"Should I take a little off the right hand here?" she asked.

"Stop trying so many things and just feel it," Conrad said. "Close your eyes and *feel*."

It worked better but wasn't quite right.

"I still hear the nerves. Relax."

"I'm not nervous."

"Maybe not you … but your hands are. They're trembling. Not effective, even for a tremolo." Conrad winked and then stood up behind her. "You cannot rush pathos. Now, begin with a tranquillo pianissimo—a whispered tenderness—then build slowly to draw one into a crescendo of passion—"

"But—"

"Not because it's marked that way, but because I would like to hear it." She did as she was told, suddenly wanting to please him, to succumb to his gentle Svengalian command. As she finished the diminishing arpeggio, she could hear him singing along with the melody. She began scaling the notes, strengthening the volume into them, attacking the higher octaves with the passion he had requested.

"No, no, no," Conrad said gently, but when she stopped, he touched her shoulder. "No, keep playing."

As she resumed, exploring this new interpretation, she felt something in the center of her back and realized he had begun unplaiting her braid. The intimacy of the gesture unnerved her for a moment.

"May I?" he asked softly.

She nodded. When he had finished her hair fell softly at her back. "There."

She stopped playing. "Why did you do that?"

"It seems strange to hear you playing Chopin with wild abandon while your hair is done up like an old-school Marm." He grinned. "Now, from the top."

She left her hair down purposely that evening, the thick auburn waves shimmering around her shoulders. She was quite conscious that she rarely left her hair down and she did so only for Sebastian, and usually only when they were about to make love. Sebastian never seemed to notice it beyond what pleasure he found when she ran it over the length of his body.

Alexandra had given Tula the night off because she suddenly felt like cooking. She had been drawn to nesting activities since Sebastian had left, as a way to deflect his absence. She investigated the huge kitchen with its enormous stove and rack of chef's pots and pans. For Alexandra, domesticity seldom beckoned, a point which caused her mother grave concern. For, in the quite likely event she couldn't sustain a career in music, how would she manage? "You think I plan on being a sous chef?" Alexandra had retorted.

"There's no need for insolence, Alexandra." Claire had demurred with a sly grin. "But I think you have an inflated view of your skills. You play the piano. What else do you know how to do?" Another reason she avoided her mother as often as possible.

There was very little else Alexandra could or desired to do other than to play, and even now, when she was making money—not as much as her male counterparts but decent and respectable money as a musician—she occasionally imagined a dreary subsistence of slinging hash for a living. For weeks she would practice harder, a punishing drive to ensure she never had to do anything but the only thing she was *able* to do.

Her mother's implication that her only other option was marriage and children left Alexandra speechless. She considered it now as she moved around the kitchen, figuring out what she needed. She laughed at herself as she heard Liszt's overcharged and triumphant *Sonata in B Minor* running through her mind. Hardly a hummable piece, but she put gusto into it, conducting with a wooden spoon as she enjoyed the singularly Zen experience of chopping carrots, broccoli, and mushrooms for a stir-fry. As she put it all into a large wok, she saw how grossly she had miscalculated the portions, carried away with her performance of domesticity.

She heard Conrad walking through the front entrance and dashed out to meet him, a bit breathless, and was disappointed to see he had Chinese take-out in his hands and was heading up to the library.

"Is that your dinner?"

It was clear eating was the furthest thing from his mind.

"I gave Tula the night off." She motioned vaguely at the kitchen.

He frowned and she was afraid he was going to turn her down, though, of course, he had no idea that she had gone to the trouble of cooking. For a moment she felt the plight of womanhood, rejection over the simplest and most inconsequential things.

"Dear Lord, we're not stranded, are we?"

"No. *I've* made dinner."

Conrad held up the take-out bag apologetically.

"No, no. You can't eat that. I've cooked." Alexandra stammered. "And I never cook. I mean never. So, you must eat." And then she felt foolish.

"Duly noted." Conrad grinned.

She smirked, then nabbed the bag from his hands. "That stuff will rot your arteries." She tossed it in the garbage can. "And it seems I've made enough for a small orchestra, so you won't be needing leftovers."

"Not bad." Conrad sighed, pushing his emptied plate to the side. "Maybe a second career in the making?"

"Now that would make my mother terribly happy."

Conrad smiled, his eyes met hers, and held them. She picked up their plates and made her way to the kitchen, needing a moment to breathe. Silverware clattered to the floor. *Damn, get a hold of yourself.* She would beg off with a headache.

When she returned, he had re-filled their glasses with a deep merlot. Alexandra stood, preparing to beg off but instead, she sat. As he gazed out into the night she studied him, his ardent profile, the shadow highlighting the hollowed curve of his cheekbone. *Stop.*

"So," Alexandra shifted to a formal tone, "When did you know you would be a composer?"

"I feel as if I've never known otherwise, but it crystallized for me when I was introduced to Bach. I never tire of his music … three pianos in D Minor, *The Brandenburgs*—"

"The third movement of —"

"— the third Brandenburg," they stated in unison.

"It's one piece of music I love looping—you know when it drones on in your mind over and over again," he stated lovingly.

"Exactly." She sipped her wine, *what the hell.* He made it so easy for her to stay.

"I was supposed to be a famous opera singer." Alexandra giggled.

They were working their way through a second bottle of wine and intimate revelations. "I loved singing. That came to me the second I could open my lips... it was the most natural form of communication."

"That explains the way you play." Conrad leaned back, retrieved a pack of Gauloises and offered one to her. He lit it, the match flaring between them.

"What are these?"

"French cigarettes from Lars. He just sent me this care package."

She took a puff. "They're lovely."

Conrad's eyes caught and held hers, the muscles in Alexandra's stomach constricted; a molten quivering that was altogether too pleasant. She glanced away and cleared her throat. "I want to thank you, for helping me earlier with the piece."

"I think taking the hair down made all the difference."

She felt the keeling in her stomach again. "I couldn't believe it when Sebastian told me your mother was an opera singer."

"Well..." Conrad was about to say something, but instead, he sat back in his seat, took a meditative sip of wine. "I think it turned out for the best, don't you? That you ended up with the piano. Otherwise, the world wouldn't have your exceptional gift, Alexandra."

She blushed.

"And it's clear how passionate you are about Chopin," he added.

"Yes. I'm quite mad for him," she said. "His music never lets me down."

"Yet, for being such a romantic, he never strayed far from a metronome."

"Are we back to the Apollo vs Dionysus debate?" she teased.

"Just pointing out they aren't mutually exclusive."

"I used to be drawn to Chopin because he had such magnificently showy pieces. I'm embarrassed to say, like most, I suffered being quite finger-proud in the beginning." Alexandra shook her head in self-deprecation. "Back in the days when I thought the more and more dramatic it must be. As if that would cover my technical flaws. Now I'm drawn to music that's far more interior, that changes me as I'm changing it."

"Those ever-shifting elements; that's what's so damned mind-blowing about it all."

"Your music is so... so... hauntingly beautiful, Conrad," Alexandra said with such genuine care they were both taken back.

Conrad nodded graciously, then smacked his lips in dissatisfaction. "There's still something I haven't quite got a handle on yet."

"What's that?"

"I can't seem to make myself want to do the business of it all. This notion that I must pimp myself out. Beg for listeners. I don't much care if people respond to my music or not." He held up his cigarette. "A purist until the end."

"But you must find a middle ground. Nothing's perfect, and we all know the music business certainly isn't going to change."

"I'll tell you what's 'perfect.' It's hearing a piece of music that drills to the core of you... that you can't *not* be moved by. I've heard that from other pianists only a few times in my life. And one of those times was hearing you perform the night of the Ketterling."

Alexandra felt the heat climb up her neck. From the wine, the conversation, the compliment so direct and unwavering. She toyed with her wineglass, too tipsy to come up with a gracious response.

Conrad took a long drag from his cigarette. "How can music, with its licensing, packaging, tie-ins, and spliced and diced recordings, ever be considered pure? And look at someone who's had the treatment—"

"Please tell me this isn't about Sebastian—" Alexandra sat back in her chair.

"No. It's about all of us. Some of us are limited. Some of us have no limits whatsoever. One succeeds, whatever that term means. One fails. I simply think that in music, as in life, there is only one point of truth and that is when the music in your head becomes the music in your heart. That's what you commit to playing. Even if it means failure."

"For only to succeed one must fail." Alexandra echoed Chandra's words, which had seemed so jaded and cynical at the time.

His eyes answered her. *Yes.*

She was utterly stimulated by this man. She and Sebastian never spoke of music in this way. They only discussed it as it related to the mechanics of their schedules, or what a concert might mean to their careers. They never entertained music as history, spirituality, or philosophy.

Conrad tamped out his cigarette and turned to her. Their eyes held. Far too long.

Alexandra cleared her throat and rose to make her leave. "Thank you for being my culinary guinea pig."

Alexandra practiced at Sebastian's piano in the library, trying to make up for lost time. She spent the first half of the morning rigorously attacking scales as if they could make up for lack of regimen.

When Conrad played, it never sounded like practice. It was as though he was discovering something new with each note, playfully weaving melodies, refining ideas, lost in the joy of the music. Even when his only audience was the birds perched on the dogwood branches outside, basking in the sunlight dappling into the library, he played with the same effortless passion, as if the performance were a private gift to the world around him.

She was so involved in her circular playing that she didn't notice the gentle touch of Conrad's hands at the piano opposite her.

At first, she was unsure. Was he correcting her technique or guiding her somewhere new? But as he added harmonies to the scales, a sense of playful adventure moved her to follow his pace. When she glanced up, he winked, and they raced together to the top and back down. When he inverted the melody, she matched him. On the third scale, he counterpointed the original harmony but swiftly shifted to a syncopated jazz. She almost couldn't make the transition, but when she did, she laughed. *This was fun!* She then added her own phrasing which he then repeated. In a few short steps he had taught her the game, and now she could follow and lead whenever the impulse took her. Then Conrad resurrected her signature Rachmaninoff. She joined him and they played with each other, challenging and elevating one another. It was as if two voices sang in beautiful concert and unlike anything she had ever experienced; this performance play that expanded and challenged her, ever more inviting and intoxicating. No pretense because you couldn't know what to expect which demanded being in the moment.

Over the next few weeks, when Conrad wasn't working on his music or Alexandra wasn't preparing for her recording, they found themselves, often in the afternoon or after dinner in the evenings, playing exactly as they did that first time together. Sometimes it was deconstructing familiar classics. Other times they explored only sections of a movement, trying all kinds of derivative sequences, as if they were composing music together, which thrilled Alexandra, as it was never an element toward which she felt any inclination. With Conrad leading her, Alexandra felt enough confidence to simply go with her instincts, which turned out to be 'exceptional,' or so Conrad praised but she thought it was more likely that he was such an 'exceptional' teacher. They were constantly in tune with one another's moods and humors, each responding to the slightest nuance in the other's performance.

The notes became their language, fluid and perceptive, often picking up conversations started over morning coffee and continuing through their pianos in the afternoon—until Alexandra was never certain where words had begun, and the music had left off.

The extraordinary thing, she reflected, lying in the dark of night, was the level of intimacy she felt with Conrad. The deepening richness of their communion grew delicately more complex and lent an air of proprietary exclusivity she hadn't even experienced with Sebastian. As she counted the days until Sebastian's return, the anticipation was already tempered by an apprehension that his arrival would destroy this rich and provocative new world that existed between her and Conrad.

She didn't want to give it up.

"Anyone who knew Schubert knows he was of two natures foreign to each other, how powerfully the craving for pleasure dragged his soul down to the slough of moral degradation."

Josef Kenner

Sebastian entered the concert hall with the kind of confidence few men ever attain in their lifetime. He had always wanted to reach this kind of audience, but the outpouring of love and adoration for this newly discovered demi-God in Europe exceeded all expectations, not only those of his handlers but of Sebastian as well. He knew the strength of his rapport from previous concerts, but adulation went beyond simple affinity. He could see it in the tears, the almost fanatical tremors in the handshaking, in the frenzy of goodwill toward him. His music was changing lives, bringing to the people moments of awe wed to unflinching appreciation. It made him feel utterly vindicated and powerful. Yes, excessively powerful.

Power, and its by-products, were not altogether foreign to him, for he had certainly enjoyed an amuse-bouche years earlier with the Ketterling where his popularity gave him a subtle edge over the socially awkward musicians. But this was different, a full-course feast of adoration: delicate appetizers of praise, intoxicating wines of admiration, a heady mix of flavors that became an irresistible aphrodisiac. Even the cultured elite, seasoned by classical tradition, found a fresh voice in Sebastian. He was undeniably the future of music.

At first, Sebastian had taken it in, as Monetizzare had remarked, with good-natured self-possession. Women who lavished him with invitations and innuendoes made him blush with satisfaction. Spindly male students who loitered in hotel lobbies, their sheet music crumbled by innocence and sweaty, nervous palms, begged from him a moment to look over their pages. Composers of stature had their agents call him daily—could they meet for tea that afternoon, a drink at the Ritz? But the requests that made him chill with satisfaction were those from the world-famous conductors requesting his presence with the New York, Tokyo, and London Philhar-monic Orchestras.

Within months, Sebastian grew quite comfortable with his fame. If a need struck him, it was attended to immediately. If he wanted a cappuc-cino, it was thrust steaming into his hand within minutes. When a ciga-rette found his lips, it was lit for him. He was always accompanied by an entourage that seemed to grow with each concert booking. In addition, two assistants catered to his every caprice, the constant question poised at their pert mouths, 'Was there anything else he needed?'

He tried like hell not to be affected by it all. Tried like hell not to become an asshole. And he half-succeeded. But when one is handed one's every whim and desire it is only incumbent upon human nature to desire and whim for more, to stretch the boundaries of good taste and behavior. As he and his staff traveled from hotel to hotel, Sebastian's requests and demands grew into eccentricities. He had to have a spe-cific type of bottled water flown in. At all times a backup carton of the elegant, high-end Sobranies were to be available, because Sebastian not only smoked incessantly but insisted that whomever he dined with also smoke his brand, so they could agree by the end of dinner that it was, indeed, the best cigarette they'd ever smoked. Under no circumstances was he to be disturbed between eight and ten in the mornings when he practiced. His cashmere gloves were to be warmed to a precise tem-perature. He insisted that cheesecake always be available for dessert, yet demanded a place to work out, complaining that all the heavy European foods were beginning to make him sluggish. And even though it was the one thing he promised he wouldn't do, even after his last miserable infidelity, he could no longer deny the assault of seduction he defended himself against nightly.

It was during a moment of magnanimous love for his adoring fans that he invited a fawning redhead to join them for dinner, whom he later took to bed after a huge nose-prickling snifter of Remy Martin's Louis XIII. The next morning, when he noticed his favorite pictures of Alexandra and Antonia in his peripheral vision, he burrowed his thick head beneath the down pillow. He showered vehemently, then practiced with a vengeance, and found this castigation elevated his performance. Guilt produced a demand for a better performance. He certainly owed both the women this penance. When he felt a little stale by the following week, he enticed a chambermaid to bed and rationalized the need for release was allowing him to play better. Rutting into her from behind, the thought occurred to him that this was precisely what his great antecedent had been doing in the organ loft and that it reflected in his own nature a disposition to spread his seed to so many. This link to his progeny made him ram himself into her with studded vigor.

Because he developed the need to exercise this brand of fantasy regularly, he took up with Monetizzare's assistant, Sasha. Blonde and Rubenesque, she wasn't in the least reminiscent of Alexandra. He made sure he was rarely affectionate or even gentle with these women, so he could justify his infidelity not as a betrayal, but as a critical artistic requirement to maintain peak performance, much as he demanded a snifter of brandy for his insomnia, a Sobranie to stave off the nerves, and laudanum for his migraines that had returned.

Missing Alexandra was a constant tender bruising that stretched from the pit of his stomach up through the cavity of his chest. In these moments of sudden melancholy, he would quell the pain with smoking, eating, drinking. He called her every few days, and their conversations made him feel all the stronger as he recounted his glories one by one, embellishing his tales despite the already genuine grandeur of his existence. He loved the way she listened, encouraged, and stroked. It reminded him of when they first started up together, how she had saved him from evaporating, had rescued him from his dismal self before he disappeared altogether. She alone stood by his side, giving him everything.

He loved Alexandra, deeply and profoundly, and was desperate for her to love him back. She was his balance, his tether to reality. As much as she inspired him, when he became a little too self-important, her cool voice would taunt him back to humility: "Sebastian, it can all go away in a second. Enjoy it but with grace." At the beginning of the tour, every-one knew when he had spoken with Alexandra, for he became a kinder, gentler Sebastian. But like a shot of brandy, the ebullience and warmth quickly wore off, and he soon became irritable, tense, and temperamental until the next call.

He rarely mentioned Conrad who he called separately, but seldomly. One night, after he had been drinking and had slept with Sasha, he was moved to ask, "By the way, where is Connie these days?"

"He's here, of course," Alexandra answered.

"He's there? In the room with you?"

"No. He's here in the house. I think he's practicing in the library."

"But what's he up to?" Sebastian needled. "No. Don't tell me. He's pre-paring for one of his nomadic expeditions."

"Actually, he's been working non-stop on his compositions. I want to believe he's working toward a recital."

"My lord, you've got to be kidding. Conrad's finally going to make his debut?"

"I didn't say that. It's just he's been in touch with Max, and I overheard them talking… nothing specific."

"It'll be a cold day in hell before my brother deigns to play for us lesser beings."

"Sebastian!" She couldn't tell if she was more surprised by his sarcasm or her need to defend him. "Your brother's incredibly talented. I thought you'd be happy for him."

"Of course, I am, darling. I suppose better late than never. Anyway, it sounds like you two are getting on."

"Yes. I like your brother—"

"Do you, now?"

"Yes." Then added brusquely, "Very much."

"Ohhh, 'very much,'" Sebastian teased but his voice was laced with edge as well.

"Don't fancy him, do you?"

A pause on the other end of the line.

"Don't be a drag," she said sardonically. "'Fancy him'? You've been around too many Brits. I like your Conrad, Sebastian. And I respect him. He's a fascinating musician and a kind man. That should make you feel good."

"Should it? How good? How good does it make *you* feel, Alexandra?"

"Oh, for God's sake! You're drunk."

She quickly shifted the conversation back to his favorite topic: himself. How had the last concert gone over? How many standing ovations had honored him before he had become the toast of Paris?

"Alex, I'm sorry. I was an absolute shit."

Silence.

"I know you're under a lot of pressure," Alexandra commiserated. "And you know how impossible things are when we're separated by time zones."

"I love you, Babe an' I know I don't deserve you, but Jesus, I miss you." Even beneath the coated tipsiness, she could hear the traces of guilt.

"Sebastian?" Her voice cracked.

"You know I love you, right?" She heard the familiar maudlin that came out when he became inebriated, but something else was going on.

"Yes...?" She waited.

"Damn! I've got to go. They've been holding the table for dinner." She heard him light a cigarette.

"Go then."

"Don't be like that."

"I'm not. Go... and Sebastian?" She whispered, "Be good."

Later, when Sebastian stared out of the window of his hotel, he began digging beneath what Alexandra meant when she said Conrad made her *feel good*. A wrench of jealousy twisted uneasily in his gut, but he quickly reminded himself that women had always preferred him to his brother. Alexandra loved his earthiness. Sebastian needn't worry: Conrad was entirely too *out there* and esoteric for her.

Sebastian was having an affair.

Alexandra said this to herself every few days as she considered the evidence over the past six weeks. His letters began to arrive increasingly further apart. She noticed that he jumped over moments and hesitated at questions during his more scattered and infrequent calls. Those first red flags she put away as being silly and jealous. But a listlessness had begun to infiltrate their connection. At first, she had attributed it to the inadequacies of long-distance communication. It was difficult to be on the same level when one was weary after a long night, the other chipper and ready to start their day. Alexandra knew all too well the hardships of being on tour where everything was relegated to performing, whether on stage, in interviews, meetings, even the dinners afterward—you always had to be 'on.' In marked contrast, she created the pace of her days in the serenity of Sebastian's peaceful home, where she could unwind in privacy by jumping in the pool, taking a long walk in the gardens, or sitting quietly in one of Antonia's arbors.

But the letter she received that morning was strange. She read it in the den before the open French doors by the pool. Stops and starts. Very little cohesion, although he apologized for as much at the end. "Sorry, darling, I'm rather frenetic today, but sending my love nonetheless." In between he had written about his ever-growing successes, but confessed to a letdown to those highs, manifested by intensifying headaches. He had taken to secluding himself away in his darkened hotel room to fight off the migraines, which, he complained, "takes away from my play time."

"You mean practice time."

"No... play time. Away from all this," he snipped. "I've gotta have something to balance out all the work."

A grown man using the term 'play time' struck Alexandra as odd, but then she knew Sebastian was a man of strong appetites, one constantly on the make for new and exciting experiences. She couldn't help but wonder what his "play time" included. She'd seen enough to know Sebastian was constantly exposed to the adoring female fan, the ardent student of music, the grand patroness who had in all her years never been so moved.

Even Alexandra had found the need from fans—their need to touch, to talk to her, to simply be in her presence—a heady intoxicant, but she had never allowed it to mean anything more than it was, a transient, temporary awe; the fan's attachment was based on how they were made to feel, and had nothing to do with her as a person. She also knew Sebastian wasn't capable of such detachment.

She felt the pressure of his index finger upon her shoulder, and then its absence as Conrad removed it. She welcomed the warmth of his companionship. Somehow, she always felt better when he was around.

"From Sebastian?"

"Yes." She quickly folded the letter.

"Everything okay?"

She didn't answer and Conrad didn't push. He walked outside to the edge of the pool and sat. He was in his swimming trunks, his lean body curved, one leg submerged in the water, the other stretched out before him. "You need to call him?"

Alexandra glanced at her watch. "It's midnight there."

"I'm sure he's still up."

"No. I'll wait until tomorrow."

"Come for a swim."

It would take her mind off thinking about Sebastian, and what he might be doing if she were to call him. Alexandra retreated into the house and put on a black one-piece. She ran out of the house and dove into the deep cool of blue.

They swam up and down, not racing, just keeping pace. Then he swam around her and she around him. It wasn't unlike when they played the piano. Like so much with Conrad, an artful beauty graced their union in the pool that was unplanned, unperformed. Simply was.

"Sebastian used to cut through the water like an eel." Conrad laughed. "It didn't matter how hard I tried; I never could catch him."

"Yes, he's a great swimmer," she said, but she was considering all the other activities he was good at.

"I loved watching him in the water. It was something he did so completely gracefully," Conrad said as he helped her out of the pool and offered her a towel.

"No. I'd like to dry in the sun like you and Sebastian always do."

"When we were boys, Antonia told us if we dried ourselves, we were 'depriving the Maker's brilliant vitamin from soaking into our skin.'" Conrad laughed, smoothed his hair back, and raised his face to the sun.

"I wish I'd been able to meet her."

"Antonia," Conrad said with equal parts wistfulness and humor, "was truly unequaled."

"It's clear you both loved her very much."

They shared a thick blanket he spread out for both of them. She laid back, letting the sun begin to dry her body. He stretched out his lanky frame a respectable distance beside her. Alexandra let her eyes slip open, watched their stomachs rise and fall in the same breath, a drop of water coursed down his neck. She compared his healthy tan next to her porcelain white skin and wondered if her paleness was unattractive to him.

"Clearly I haven't had enough of God's vitamin."

"I love the color of your skin," he said after a moment.

"You don't think I'm too pale?"

"No. Your skin is the hue of softness."

"Softness?" She laughed. "Softness is not a color."

"No? Then how can I tell how your skin feels by the color of it?"

Her throat tightened. Her limbs tensed. She glanced at Conrad, but his eyes were closed, his lips slack in peaceful contentment. For a moment she wondered if she should be concerned, then saw Conrad's head tip slightly to the left. He had fallen asleep.

> *"Whenever I attempted to sing of love, it turned to pain.*
> *And again, when I tried to sing of pain, it turned to love."*

Franz Schubert

The lazy glow of light particles danced inside the large stream of sunset, casting muted planes in the library as Conrad and Alexandra shifted from Prokofiev's *Piano Concerto No. 1's* playful and whimsical first movement to the aching, sultry melancholy of the second movement. Alexandra always found this particular piece of music deeply moving and intimate, but it was especially so now, in the glow of the room and the languid warmth of the sun. The questing melody was potent, sensual as it played against a tender familiarity in the final climbing notes, the lilting evocation faded to an unresolved poignancy. Wordlessly they stopped, neither of them wishing to jump into the quirky next movement. Stillness filled the air as the last note echoed and disappeared with the setting sun.

Their eyes held a long moment, thanking each other and communicating in that non-verbal way they had become accustomed to, which meant it was time to take a walk in the gardens, where Conrad, much like Sebastian, regaled her with stories of their past, only through quite different filters. It was fascinating to hear the contrasting views of a specific incident; Sebastian's tendency to embellish and glorify, Conrad's recounting punctuated by nuanced details and an honest sense of who people were coupled with a bemused sense of humor. After their walk they might sit by the pool, share a glass of wine, a cigarette, and vigorously discuss theory, continuing their ongoing debates. Or Conrad would reflect upon his travels, telling her more about Lars and his rebellious antics.

"What do you suppose makes a man toss away his life, his ambitions?" Alexandra asked as they sat in the Hermes gazebo, side by side.

"Who's to say it's tossed? Lars is happier than most men I've known— living with those quiet people, eating exotic foods, and screwing himself mad with his harem." Conrad winked at her.

"But he must have wanted to achieve at some point. He had the ambition to write his book, to become a musician in the first place."

"Or it was expected of him."

"Is that what happened to you?" Alexandra was afraid as the words toppled from her mouth that she had pried too closely. A moment passed while Conrad simply stared at his cigarette.

"I could never have found what... what I was looking for here."

"And what was that?"

"Peace. Direction. Not to sound corny, self-awareness."

"And did you find those things?"

"Yes... I found a lot of it during my travels." He regarded her quickly as he crushed his cigarette beneath his shoe.

"Was it difficult? Leaving?"

"Yes, on some levels. I felt the tug of expectation too keenly and I think it scared me a bit. Had Antonia lived, I would have made different choices."

"Really?"

"Most certainly. I cherished her." As if that explained everything.

"So, you're not the artist who only answers to himself. You're not the absolutist you portray yourself to be—needing no one, and nothing."

"Is that how you see me?" Conrad asked stiffly and Alexandra wished she had re-phrased her words.

"You seem untouched by the world. As if *their* rules don't apply. As if you have something up on us all."

"Not in the least. I simply try to stay..." He searched a moment. "Right within myself."

"You left right after her death." She paused a moment. "I mean, did you stop to consider how it would affect Sebastian?"

"Yes, I did." Conrad wasn't defensive. "I did worry about him at first. Sebastian had relied so much on Antonia, I was afraid at first that he wouldn't cope with the suffering. But I also knew if I didn't go, he would never make it on his own. Sebastian needed to stand on his own two feet, to know he could take care of himself."

"But he took care of you as well."

"Yes." Conrad frowned and then cleared his throat. "He… he saved my life."

"He what?"

"He saved my life. When I was nine."

She looked into him then, saw his nakedness.

"All the more for you to…" She trailed off. "You felt no sense of obligation?"

"I'm always with Sebastian, and he with me. We just have a different way of staying connected." He turned to her then. "Why are you asking me these things?"

"I suppose to know you better."

"Don't you think you know me well enough?"

Not a hint of seduction colored his eyes, but Alexandra felt as if the air had been sucked from her stomach. "I… I…"

Alexandra became inordinately aware of the heat of Conrad's body next to her, the smell of his intoxicating cologne. She studied the hand resting on his leg, and a shudder ran through her. How exquisite his hand is, she thought, not just because it was beautiful, but because of the beauty it brought to the world.

She couldn't help but allow her fingers to brush against his, then stood to get some distance. "I should get back to it."

Alexandra walked up the long gravel path from the gated entrance of the estate to the mailbox. Nothing. She returned feeling an inevitable disappointment. She heard Conrad up in the library and made her way to the piano opposite him. She waited for a pause in his music and then began to drive a discordant melody with anger and intensity until she slammed her hands against the keys, the ugly cacophony tearing into the air. She stood and walked to the window.

Conrad waited a moment. "Was it something I played?"

Alexandra grinned despite herself, then stated with weak nonchalance, "I think Sebastian is having an affair."

Conrad walked to her. He stood next to her for a long moment, then put an arm around her. She briefly resisted, then allowed herself the comfort of laying her face against his chest. She didn't want to cry, but when she felt Conrad's face touch her cheek her throat tightened, wresting tears from her. She quietly wept, dampening his shirt, when she again became aware of his scent, a clean man's smell, faint with sweat, less ardent than Sebastian's, and something else, his cologne, not heavy, a sweet musk and sandalwood freshness.

Alexandra stood in his embrace and knew she had to remove herself, but as she began to, he leaned toward her, his chin grazing her cheek as he moved within an inch of her mouth. Stopped.

They both saw the frumpy gnome-like figure of Max trundling up the pathway through the window at the same time. Conrad took a quick breath, then wordlessly disentangled himself and walked away as Alexandra continued to stare out the window until she finally realized she needed to exhale.

"Our Sebastian has made quite a name for himself." Max refilled his pipe. He and Conrad had spent the last hour catching up.

"Yes." Conrad lit a cigarette. "Hasn't he?"

"Don't you find it the least bit strange, Connie?"

"What?"

"That the one with the talent in the family is sitting here with nothing to show for it."

"Maybe we've all been a little quick with our judgments." Conrad glanced from Alexandra to Max. "I've been told we shouldn't make the mistake of underestimating Sebastian."

"I'm going to get some iced tea. Max?" Alexandra stood abruptly.

"Thank you, Alexandra," he replied and turned back to Conrad. "I'm not… Look. I know the range of his skills intimately. So much so that when I discover that he has written one of the best pieces of work in the last one hundred years I must confess it is quite the paradoxical mystery." He looked stumped. "Tell me. Do you think love has the power to change the inherent talent of a man?"

"You tell me, Max." He considered momentarily, looking thoughtfully toward the kitchen. "I should say a woman like Alexandra could help a man do anything."

The tone in Conrad's voice startled Max as much as his words. Max had never taken Conrad as a sentimentalist. Max looked into Conrad's eyes. They shone with a fierce light: one he'd not seen before.

Alexandra returned and poured their tea before settling back in a chair opposite Conrad.

"My dear Alexandra, how are you?" Max took her hand, ever the gentleman.

"I'm fine, thank you. Have you heard from Sebastian then?"

"Yes, my dear, and he's making a hell of a mark in Europe."

Max watched Conrad glance at Alexandra who smiled weakly. "Yes, he's really tearing it up."

Undercurrents of tension filled the room.

"Wunderbar." Max harrumphed. "I came here personally to tell Conrad of some good news." Max looked expectantly from Alexandra to Conrad.

"Yes?" she finally prompted.

"I have asked Monetizzare to set up a meeting for Conrad with Mark Acorn's label.

"That's wonderful," Alexandra responded.

"How did that come about?" Conrad asked.

"When I spoke with Sebastian last week, he said I could use his name to put it together."

"I don't want to use his name, Max."

"But what can it hurt?" Max removed his glasses.

"I said, I won't use his name."

"Don't be so proud, boy—"

"Pride has nothing to do with it."

Alexandra glanced from Conrad to Max, who had now finished the rote process of buffing his glasses against the tuck of his plaid shirt and resettling them on his face.

"You need to make a living."

"Are you afraid I don't know how to do that, Max?"

"Aaachh! I mean in your field. Someone with your talent should be working in it."

Conrad stood and walked to Max. "Please, Max. I'm grateful. Don't misunderstand me, though. My work is not up for discussion. They're either interested or they're not." And with that, he walked away.

"What is that all about?" Alexandra asked after Conrad had disappeared.

"Conrad refuses to take money from Sebastian—living expenses, you know? And he's going to have to do something with his music sooner or later. He helped me arrange a session with Acorn's studios because they're more, oh, how do you say, cutting edge. Willing to take the chance that a kind of esoterica, as it were, will hit and take off. But Conrad is just too damn stubborn."

"But why should Conrad use Sebastian's name? He doesn't need anyone's help. He's brilliant in his own right."

"Alexandra." Max leaned close to her, as if afraid his words might be overheard. "You like his music, ja?" She nodded. "But you don't find it in the least, I don't know, inaccessible? Not to us, no, not us in the world of music where we all live and know his language is poetry. I mean the person on the street. That is where Sebastian excels. He knows how to excite an audience, how to inspire them, how to make them like it even better than they would if someone else were to play."

"Is that the function of the musician? To make people like the music? Or to be true to how they feel it?" Now she sounded like Conrad.

"Bah! I'm not going to get into a circular argument, Alexandra. I can't keep up with it. But I... I just wish Connie would be a little more..."

"What?"

"Human," he said with exasperation.

Alexandra refilled Max's glass with tea and tried to calm him down. "I don't think Conrad's the kind of man who lets anyone meddle in his life."

"Meddle, schmeddle. I'm trying to help the boy."

"Max, it's okay. I'll talk to him if you'd like."

"Would you?"

"Of course. I don't know that I'll get any further with him, but I'll give it a try."

Now that Max was assuaged, Alexandra thought best how to phrase her next question, since she wasn't quite sure precisely what she was looking for, only that there was so much she wanted to know and understand about Conrad, Sebastian, and, in particular, Antonia.

"I've been learning more of the D'Antonio history—quite the saga—but it seems every time I get too close to certain subjects, Conrad closes down."

"Yes, with the delightful Antonia, there were no ends of stories, possibly fables she would endorse over and over." Max put his hands on his knees. "So, what is it you'd like to know?"

"The other night, for instance, I was talking about the fascinating coincidence that I was supposed to have gone into opera, and here's Sebastian's family, chock full of operatic history, heralded throughout Italy."

"What history might that be?" Max cocked a brow.

"That Sebastian comes from a long line of musical talent." Alexandra frowned when she saw the expression on Max's face. "First, there's his connection to Bach; and that his great-great-great grandfather was also a composer. He also told me all about Antonia's parents, how they met during *The Marriage of Figaro*."

Max chuckled. "Go on."

"How she was the understudy until the lead suffered a terrible accident, and the moment she walked onto the stage Antonia's father realized the silly little aspiring singer he had paid no attention to, was destined to be his wife."

"Stop," Max said gently. "I don't think you, of all people, should suffer the delusion of Antonia's, how shall I put it, creative liberties."

"What are you saying?"

"Alexandra." Max put a hand upon her own. "It is difficult to find any proof of Antonia's great claim to Bach, but let's say for the sake of generosity, we give that to her. The rest of it? Antonia's grandfather was an Italian immigrant who traveled to New York and became a butcher. Eventually, he opened a string of meat packing plants, and the family business grew into quite a success. In due time they were bought out, and that's where Antonia got all her wealth. But her father was a butcher—make no mistake. Antonia's father indeed had one joy and one joy only. He listened to opera every moment he could steal, but never once did he sing. And Antonia's mother was a model for cigarette ads who died from emphysema shortly after she was born."

"But I… I don't understand, why didn't Sebastian tell me?"

"Because these stories are Antonia's myths. She told them so many times I think everyone started believing them a little bit. I think Sebastian tells them now out of a sense of loyalty."

He could see Alexandra struggling with the new information.

"Ach, don't you see? The real stories were drab and meaningless, filled with mere humanity and the mundane business of being on this plane." Max chided as he returned to his familiar defense, cleaning his glasses from his untucked shirt. "Not the stark and terrible struggle of the artist, not the tortured angst upon which Antonia had created an entire *raison d'être.*"

When Max left after tea, Conrad was gone. She wasn't sure if he had left because of Max's interference, or because he simply had a previous engagement.

Alone, Alexandra wandered through the house, peering into the photos that lined every room, ruminating over Max's revelation. She couldn't let go of the illusions Antonia had created, and that Sebastian perpetuated. It bothered her. That and the idea of Conrad's humanness, his unwillingness to set aside his pride to get his career going. She wondered again if

Conrad had someone—a lover, as calling her a 'girlfriend' seemed absurd. Maybe that's where he went on those nights he ventured out.

He was intelligent, caring, sweet. Attractive. She let her mind skim over his body, lean and bristling with a sensuality that was very human, indeed. But emotionally, she had to admit, he appeared inordinately self-contained. Perhaps that was how Max found him inhuman. He had no apparent insecurities. No vulnerability. He didn't seem to need anything. And for Alexandra that made him safe.

When Conrad returned that night, she had fallen asleep on the couch. She glanced at her watch. It was nearly three. She heard him pass quietly into his bedroom and found her curiosity unsettling.

The next morning over coffee, Alexandra tried to shrug off the information given her the night before. So, Antonia liked to tell stories. It seemed harmless enough. But when Conrad joined her, she wondered why he hadn't set her straight.

"How was your evening?"

"Fine."

"Did you go to dinner?"

He looked up at her. "No."

She waited for him to elaborate but he was silent, so she decided to try another tack.

"I had an interesting conversation with Max after you left."

"Yes, Max is an interesting character."

"He set me straight on the family secrets."

Conrad glanced up at her sharply. "What are you talking about?"

"Antonia's gift for fable-making." She could see she had upset him. "The whole opera as myth."

"Oh, that." Conrad visibly relaxed.

"Why didn't you tell me the truth?" She couldn't entirely disguise her hurt.

Conrad shrugged his shoulders. "And what might that be?"

Again, she was hitting a wall. Maybe Conrad's loyalty to his mother was as strong as Sebastian's.

"Max is concerned about you." Alexandra decided it was best to shift the subject.

"And what is it this time?"

"He doesn't think you get out enough. He thinks your work might benefit from a little creative recreation."

"I'm game if you are." He spoke matter of factly which left her flat-footed again. In the space of her silence, he added, "He needn't worry."

"Oh really?" Alexandra found herself baiting him, still perturbed she hadn't been able to get anywhere with him. "I've often wondered myself... while your work is clearly ahead of its time and quite brilliant... where does your music attend to falling in love, desperation, obsession? Or is that only for us mere mortals?"

Conrad simply shrugged.

"I mean, to truly feel the music in the most intimate manner, wouldn't that require experiencing all those messy feelings? Or have you alone been sequestered from the annoying flaws of humanity?"

He turned to her, still not taking the bait.

"Christ, Conrad!" she snapped. "Have you never been in love?"

He looked at her without guile and Alexandra knew it was no longer a game.

"I don't think I have."

"You don't know?"

"Yes." Conrad held her gaze for a very long time as he considered. "I'm pretty sure now that I haven't been."

"What is in my heart must come out and so I write it down."

Ludwig van Beethoven

"I started seeing a doctor about six months ago. I just kept getting worse, you know?" Chandra and Alexandra walked, lazily window-shopping. Alexandra noted immediately when she met her for lunch that Chandra seemed healthier, less stiff, and that she only drank mineral water at the restaurant. "Because, of course, I was still trying to make it up to my father— or so I discovered in psychotherapy. Who knew it was actually helpful and not just some bored house—wife fad?!" Chandra chuckled weakly.

Alexandra put a hand to her friend's arm. Chandra smiled bravely and continued. "Even after he disowned me, he stayed there, you know, browbeating me endlessly until the only way I knew to erase him from any part of my consciousness was to become unconscious. Well, as unconscious as you can become while still pretending to be part of the human race."

"I knew you were having a tough time. I wasn't quite sure what to do." Alexandra squeezed her friend's arm. "I guess I should have tried—"

Chandra stopped her. "Nothing anyone could do. I'm just sorry for my behavior before Sebastian left. Jesus! Lousy evil-sore-loser!" She smiled self-effacingly. "Everyone else seemed like they were doing so well and I? I just couldn't come to terms with what to do with this gift I'd been given, that I had come to loathe."

"Ohhh, Chandra. How absolutely awful you must have felt. But you look so good. You seem… new."

"I am." Chandra lifted her chin. "You'll never believe what turned me around."

"What?"

"One of my students." Chandra scoffed sarcastically. "And you know how much I love kids!"

They both laughed. Then Chandra shook her head, still in disbelief. "This boy. Seven years old. His father's this Italian plumber, and I'm thinking this kid would be much better off with a wrench in his pudgy little fingers. But one afternoon I sit down, totally prepared for another head-ache while he tackles Bach's *Fugue in C Minor*. He just couldn't seem to grasp a thing I had taught him. Before he starts, he tells me he has been practicing extra at home. Yeah right, I think." She glanced at Alexandra with long-awaited vindication. "Damned if he doesn't get it! Plays like there's no tomorrow. At the end, he gets this shit-eating grin on his face, like—*aren't you proud?* And jumps up and hugs me in the way a kid will, so natural, spontaneous. They're not so bad, the little people. Then, bam! He's out the door. Of course, he could never know how much that single act of gratitude helped me. It turned me around, Alex." Chandra's face brightened with wistful gratitude. "I can finally give what I was never given: encouragement. Teaching is where I belong... it's what speaks to me more than any goddamn performance."

Alexandra's expression belied the tug of envy. Since sometime after Sebastian's concerti had disrupted her life, and certainly since the end of the Ketterling tour, she had felt lost, rudderless, and off course. The only times she felt steady were the hours she spent in the library with Conrad. And that wasn't furthering her career. But it was the most motivating part of her day.

"What about you?"

"Oh... I finally finished my last recording," she paused uncertainly. "I don't know if I feel so great about it, though. A lot of the pieces I had no choice over. There were two I even put up a good fight over, but they thought they filled a certain niche. I just sort of let it go. I'm under con-tract... so."

"I thought you were meeting up with Sebastian on tour."

"No. Change of plans." Alexandra's voice was clipped.

"Everything alright?"

"Yeah," Alexandra said unconvincingly. "Yes. I think so."

"His brother. Now *he's* a virtuoso."

"Conrad?"

"Oh my God, yes."

"How have you heard him play?"

"He's at *Cafe Society* on Thursday nights. I thought you knew that. Aren't you living with him?"

"I'm *living* with Sebastian." She felt a sudden anger at Conrad's deception. Why hadn't he told her he was playing there? "Conrad just happens to be there."

"Can't think of a prettier house guest."

"It is his home," Alexandra snapped defensively and then turned to face Chandra. "What is it exactly that you have against Sebastian?"

Chandra's expression darkened. "Nothing."

"No, really. Ever since the Ketterling—I don't know why you have it in for him. I mean, he beat you fair and square that night."

Chandra's jaw clenched. "It's true, Alex. I have nobody to blame but my psycho father and my inability to deal with him." She paused as if she were going to say more. "I just don't think Sebastian is good enough for you."

"And I'm such a goddamn prize?"

"You used to think so." Chandra put a hand on Alexandra's. "Look, Alex, I'm sorry. It's just, you know, Sebastian has a reputation. He likes what he wants, when he wants it. He's a 'live for the moment' kind of guy. I'm the first one to say he bowled me over with his concerti. I never knew he had that kind of talent. But talent isn't everything."

"You used to think it was."

"Yes, I did. And then I realized how lonely real talent is. And Sebastian just doesn't fit the mold. He's not a lonely kind of guy."

"How lofty it must be to sit in judgment."

"I think I have just a little bit of a right. It was me he screwed that night. Not you."

Alexandra stopped, stunned. Thinking back to Chandra quivering erratically as she clutched the piano leg.

"When he came running for you that night, out of concern for me, did he ever bother to tell you what happened?" Alexandra's raw expression told Chandra he hadn't. "I didn't think so. He took me to bed, fucked me royally, and I lost it."

Alexandra swallowed, still unable to believe what she was hearing.

"I knew he wanted it to be you, but I didn't care. At the time I was desperate to be anywhere but where I was. But it made me understand something about Sebastian. He doesn't care who he has to fuck to get what he wants. And that, my dear, includes you."

Alexandra slammed the door shut and paid the cabbie. She was still seething at Chandra's confession and angered by Conrad's lack of trust in her.

Alone, she peered at the storefronts of the Greenwich Village neighborhood. She looked around and considered her safety in the ghetto neighborhood. She saw the neon sign, *Café Society*, and walked to the door, let herself into the hole-in-the-wall kind of club that opened into a crowded, hazy mob. She could hear a piano from around the corner playing a wry and delicate blend of classical jazz.

Though she could have been listening to Bill Evans, she knew it was Conrad before she made her way through the hub of artists, writers, and students, all intensely occupying space in the thick gravy of smoke. He sat upright on a miniscule stage with the same isolated focus he used at the Bösendorfer in the living room. All that mattered was the music.

All her anger evaporated as she surveyed the room. A few people listened intently, but most of the crowd talked, drank, laughed. All her nagging irritation evaporated, replaced by a throbbing ache as she watched this man she had grown to like, more than she dared admit, pouring his heart out without anyone seeing him. She wasn't the type who would grow a hedging defense over time at the plight of so many fine musicians who performed in these kinds of places playing background music. It was as painful as bearing one's soul to a sleeping priest and every bit as empty.

A yearning pulsed through her as she heard this music, so different than what Conrad played at the house. She felt the same depth of emotion, the same artistic precision, but the question was new. And she knew it had to do with her. She watched him, no separation between the man and his instrument, so finely melded, so in concert. The impact of his haunted longing stirred in her a sensual primitivism. He hadn't exposed this sentient hunger in their melodic repartee, as if in exposing his vulnerability, they would have spoken another language entirely.

As it was, she felt as if she had trespassed on private property. She turned and walked out of the club.

Later that night, when Conrad returned home, it was so dark in the living room he was unaware Alexandra sat on the couch. He took in a deep breath and exhaled, then walked to the window and stretched his tired muscles, staring out into the night.

Alexandra walked up from behind him and stopped, unwilling to bridge the gap of space between them. The silence was deafening and then he turned.

"Let Sebastian help you get a contract."

"Why?"

"So, you can do what you were meant to do."

"Will that make you less sad?"

"What makes you think I'm sad?"

He didn't speak but took the step between them and answered her question by gently smoothing the frown from her forehead. She flinched at his touch, but he put his hand gently upon her cheek and tenderly forced her to look at him.

"What is the single most important thing to you about your music?"

"I don't know..." Alexandra was vexed by the question. She didn't want to get into any more ponderous dialogue. "I suppose that I can play."

"Exactly." He stated as if that's all there was to it.

"But one has to eat and live Conrad."

"Two things that require so little effort," Conrad answered easily.

"I don't understand you."

"Don't you?"

They stood, a breath away from one another, searching each other's eyes.

"Isn't there anything that you..." Her exasperation challenged, not him but herself, "Want?"

"Yes, Alexandra."

A soft smile graced his eyes.

His hands, those beautiful slender hands, turned themselves up to her, an invitation, a prelude to the inevitable, only she couldn't have been prepared for the impact of his intention.

As his cheek grazed hers, his arms bracing her to him, her forehead pressed into his shoulder, dizzy with the pulsing of her heart. She momentarily, but unconvincingly, fought the fierce desire, vaguely cognizant of Sebastian floating through her mind. But she was soon overcome by Conrad's scent, now so familiar to her, the fresh musk mingled with his sweat, his brand of cigarettes.

An anguished gasp freed itself as she hungrily turned to his mouth, searching, greedy, shocked by the pleasure of his tender lips, softly yielding to her own. She ached for him, had ached for him all these weeks, their mouths now devouring one another, the sure feel of his tongue, lips, and teeth.

For a long moment, he kissed her, not angrily, as she had been ravaged by Sebastian the first time, but with an adagio lingering that filled her, body and soul, uncertain whether she even remained in her skin, that somehow their connection had left the realm of the physical.

Still kissing her, Conrad led her to the couch, the incessant need of his lips upon her own, kissing her until she felt the darkness swimming over her again. She was unnerved by the utter sensation, his lips leaving no escape, her breathing now his, with no beginning and no end, this weightless plane. Now he was laying her back, with his mouth still on hers, so intensely connected to her through this new sensation, this endless embrace, fusing through her body; the deliberateness in which he owned her as her body meshed into his own, every tremor, every gasp of hers, now his. She could feel his muscles beneath the loose cotton of his shirt, knowing those muscles from having seen them so many hours, his skin, the color of arousal sinking into her own as he lay his body on top of hers. She was vaguely conscious of her hands stripping his shirt, her palms tingling against the ridges of his skin, sculpted like ancient stone worn smooth, as delicious as she had imagined, her hands drifting over his ribcage, the sleek muscles at his back.

His hands slipped beneath her neck, the hands she had watched for hours as they caressed the keyboard, slender, strong, and sure as he held her, and continued this natural possession. Exact. Precise. Knowing. The culmination of conversations, hands on keys, words that hung between them, all connected into the most powerful embrace she had ever experienced.

With one hand he slowly and carefully undressed her, his mouth trailing to the fleshiness of her breast, a circle of kisses prickling her skin, her breathing raspy and ragged until she cried out as his teeth tenderly grazed her nipple, suckling with eagerness, as if everything were about pleasing her and not himself. His mouth tortured her into ecstasy, lips branding her from her breasts down to her stomach, his hand sweetly massaging her abdomen, fingers slipping through her silky hair, now into the deep of her, inside her, so full and thick inside her as two, now three fingers thrust gently, his thumb rubbing the tip of her clitoris until she knew she would come, but he wouldn't let her. He simply kept her there, his mouth consuming her as his hand mastered her, then with a final commanding stroke, she came on and around him, shuddering as his mouth caressed her own. He then flicked the tip of his tongue to her own, bringing her to orgasm again, and arching in complete surrender and utter relinquishment, she gave him every last bit that was left in her.

When she regained her senses, Alexandra took his hand, languorously kissed his fingers, then grasped them in hers and slowly walked him to his room, so plain and bare in contrast to Sebastian's indulgent opulence. Her movements were sure and steady as she gently pushed his body back, massaging his shoulders, kneading the flesh of his chest, trailing his sides as she leaned over him, then slipping to her knees, her hands sculpting his waist, molding his buttocks, gently cupping his tender groin. Her mouth found his erection, long and hard and unyielding. He gave a strangled moan as her tongue flicked the tip of him, her lips taking him so slowly, so excruciatingly slowly that his breathing choked out in broken groans. She felt his hands in her hair urging her forward, yet she sensed a tempered resistance. Conrad's eyes questioned her own, as if his making love to her kept her from the betrayal, as if her complicity would complete it.

She shook her head free, moving back up the length of his body until she merged her skin with his, capturing his hands above his head, her body lying fully upon the length of his own. And then she found him with her hand, stroked him, each pass giving her nearly as much arousal as she was giving him. She guided him into her, gasping at his fullness, ready to take all of him as she leaned forward and kissed him, falling into a rhythm, a cadence all their own, asking and answering. She held him back, slowly, and then with a bit more urgency, as if to show him that she could cause him every bit as much pleasure as he had brought her. She heard the catch in his throat, her mouth gently gouging at the strained tendons in the arc of his neck, feeling him, knowing precisely when he could hold back no longer. Suckling his bottom lip, teasing his tongue with her own, the instant she felt his semen piercing into her, she came with him, so intensely, she couldn't separate his thudding release from her own, and in that instant their eyes found each other's, searing their unity into each other's soul.

They made love throughout the night and for much of the next week, as she had with Sebastian, endless hours that melted into each other; but with Conrad, the union wasn't marked by the aggressive, rough, and heedless desperation to consume, but rather a certainty of will, an infinite patience with their union as it was unquestionably right.

Their skin never separated. There was never a moment they weren't touching.

Never a moment he didn't have his hands on her, that she didn't lie over him, beside him, cloaking and covering him. And no sooner had they sated one hunger when the whisper of desire wound its way through the pit of their stomachs, through the lining of their skin to the ache in their human hearts.

She lay naked beneath Conrad's body, her heart heavy with an inevitable sense of deceit. And yet, had she not betrayed Sebastian, she would have been betraying herself. Denying herself would have been a greater injustice, a surer, more final form of deception. It wasn't about options or choices. Only one fate, one path could have been taken. Conrad stirred above her, and the rhythm started again, the urgent primal release of their need, lips on lips, their skin enveloped in each other.

"You make me so wet," Alexandra whispered pearly into his ear, and felt him grow thicker inside her. He lifted her, his rhythm faster, starker, as he carried her through the door that led off the side of his room and moved them both toward the pool, barely distinguishable in the pale indigo morn.

Their bodies collapsed into the water in the chill of dawn and Conrad held her close, their skin rippled together, two slick bodies entwined. Animals scurried along the cobbled paths, startled by the crash of water. Stony smiles of the gods joined in revelation as humanity's laughter broke the morning silence and echoed through Antonia's gardens.

"What are you thinking?"

"I'm not." Conrad sighed satisfied.

They lay in one another's arms on the large plush rug before the fireplace where they had made love.

"I'd love to travel." Alexandra blurted out, for she wanted nothing more than to see and experience everything with Conrad.

"People think they travel to find out about the world, but it's really a map to understanding yourself."

"That's lovely. Did you ever grow tired of it?"

"Never."

"So... do you suppose we can take a trip?"

Conrad lazily moved to fill their glasses of wine.

"Conrad?" Alexandra asked after a long moment.

"Hmmm?"

"Can we take a trip?"

"Yes... sure," he answered.

"Where?"

"Where do you want to go?"

"Is this one of those answer a question with a question because you want to get out of it?"

"I just asked you where you want to go. Does that sound like I want out of it?"

"No, but..." Alexandra felt like a foolish teenager.

"But what?" Conrad was attentive. He didn't play games; she remembered and breathed a sigh of relief.

"Do you think about the future?"

"No. Not really."

"Never?"

"What is there to think about? We only have right now."

"But how then do you plan?"

"Must one?"

"Conrad, really!" Alexandra heard the harsh tone in her voice, tried to soften it. "I know you live in the here and now, but with the current situation we're in, we are going to have to plan. I mean, Sebastian will be coming home and—"

"Let's not talk about my brother."

"But we're going to have to at some point."

"And when that point comes. we will." Conrad gently teased long slender fingers through her hair, sending shivers down her spine. He moved his leg over her body, pulling her toward him, gently nibbled the length of her neck.

"Conrad, please." Alexandra tried to concentrate. "We have to…"

His mouth covered hers. "Have to what?" His lips caressed her own again and she could feel the deep thudding need in her grow so quickly that she forgot what they were talking about. "Have to what…" His voice whispered in her ear, the heat sending a convulsive pulsing through her loins, her womb, through her thighs until she yanked him on top of her, her hand guiding him into her, driving him into her, the ache never satisfied, only wanting more, an endless amount of more until she lost all thought into orphic oblivion.

Several days later, Conrad woke Alexandra with a picnic basket loaded with fruit, cheese, bread, wine, and chocolates, or as Conrad joked, "The four food groups."

"Where are we going?" Alexandra asked as they jetted down a single-lane road.

"You'll see."

As he drove, Conrad took Alexandra's hand in his own, turned to her, and smiled. She looked long and lovingly at him. She knew she would never tire of studying his face.

The road narrowed and snaked through a darkening forest until Conrad took a sharp left down a steep ravine and then suddenly a full clearing appeared.

Conrad parked, grabbed the picnic basket, and led Alexandra to a verdant blanket of mossy greens. He spread an old quilt upon the knoll and gestured for her to join him.

"It's not quite travelling, but –"

She stood beside him. He took her hand as they peered out over the deep canyon, an isolated cavern of sheer cliff and rugged landscape.

"It's beautiful, Conrad."

"Straight across." Conrad pointed. "That was Sebastian's and my great escape."

"Of course, I can see the edge of your property."

"We called it the 'great abyss'"

"How appropriate," Alexandra stated as she peered over the edge.

"Do you like it? Being at Antonia's?"

"Honestly?" She returned to the blanket. "It's a bit much for us mere mortals."

Conrad chuckled. "Yes, dear Antonia loved its drama—perfect for the universe she created. And while I certainly appreciate the grounds, it's not meant for me."

"What does that mean?

He turned to her, kissed her. "Let's have some wine."

"Conrad."

"Darling, let's leave the worrying behind for today."

They sipped their wine both studying the craggy jagged rock formations.

"That's where I slipped." Conrad pointed to the spot he nearly fell over. "He carried me the whole way home… I don't remember most of it except hearing Sebastian's heavy breathing and then later, waking up to hear Antonia talk about sacrifice."

"Sacrifice?"

"I think she believed without sacrifice greatness was unachievable."

"Like sacrificing what one is now for what they could become?"

"Not as it concerns music. I don't believe sacrifice is at all required to play, and the notion that you're giving something up to do so is completely erroneous to me."

He pulled her close, tenderly stroked the hair about her face. "Since it doesn't suit either one of us, perhaps we should consider leaving."

She turned to him then, saw the smile in his eyes. She quickly pulled him to her in a grateful embrace.

"I'd like that," she responded. "Very much."

"I'll start looking in the city... would that do?"

"Yes, that'll do nicely."

He put her hand to his heart. "Alex..."

"Yes?"

His eyes pierced her own and she wasn't sure he said the words, or she just felt them, but it was clear to her now that he loved her as much as she loved him. She giddily thought about her perfect future.

One night after making love for hours. they lay in the living room atop blankets before a flickering fire. The TV was on low in the background so they could follow the aborted Apollo 13 mission. But now, hours later, they heard saccharine strings gently teasing *Liebestraum* and turned to see a gorgeous Merle Oberon in top hat and tails in the role of George Sand as she meets Cornell Wilde's Chopin in *A Song to Remember.*

"Oh, My Lord!" Conrad began to laugh as he pointed to the screen where an old character actor playing Chopin's professor Joseph Elsner was using the corner of his dining napkin to clean his glasses. "It's Max!"

Alexandra joined in the laughter. "Have you seen this before?"

"No. TV's have rarely been in my path. But I do like the evening news."

"Ohh, we've got to watch this," she purred, tenderly massaging blankets over their bodies. "It's sooo corny."

They snuggled together like teens as Merle Oberon adorned in male attire discovered her fascination with Frederick Chopin was more than being blown away by his talent.

"They sure have made her a beast," Alexandra complained. "I guess they had to find a villain given it's Hollywood and all. She gets to wear all this seriously great clothing. What I wouldn't do to be able to wear pants during a recital!"

"Almost homo-erotic, no?" Conrad teased.

She pushed him back, then asked seriously. "Does that bother you?"

"That she's wearing men's clothes? Not in the least."

"No… being queer…"

"Also not in the least." He reached for a cigarette. "Doesn't matter to me how many men Liberace may squire beneath his furs. He's seriously gifted."

"Ironic that he dresses in the most flowery of get-ups and here's Merle dressing down like a man as if the music isn't enough."

"Everyone's always trying to find a gimmick."

"I suppose they are." It made her thoughtful.

"Between the garish score and the fact that Wilde clearly can't play the piano, this entire film has been plotzed by Hollywood gimmicks."

"Old films not your cup of tea."

"They just have no basis in reality."

"Sometimes escaping is the only thing that will do." Alexandra's tone turned playful.

"Oh… are you wanting to escape then?" Conrad gently tugged her to him and swiftly maneuvered himself above her.

"One must not make oneself cheap here—that is a cardinal point—or else one is done. Whoever is most impertinent has the best chance."

Wolfgang Amadeus Mozart

Alexandra felt a lightness in her step as she got out of the car with a bag of groceries. She planned to cook dinner; fresh halibut from the market, with roasted vegetables and an apple tarte tatin for dessert. The moment she had seen the expensive Petit Sirah, she had known it was the perfect choice for discussions about their future. She imagined Conrad's lips at the glass as he sipped the wine she lifted into her cart, the way he held his cigarette, and the trenchant hollow at his cheek when he smoked. The mere image spread a flush through her skin that followed her for the remainder of the day.

The thought of lying in his arms was constant. To soak up everything, every sight, sound, gesture. To know the underneath of him, to know him in a way she didn't even know herself. She felt heady and intoxicated, aware she was completely at the whim and mercy of every silly cliché about love, and reveled in it. Nothing had ever made her feel as Conrad did. Not even her music.

Not thinking about Sebastian was probably the wiser of Conrad's choices because she didn't know *what* to think about him. Even if she was certain that he had been having an affair, or a series of philandering escapades, his infidelity hadn't propelled her toward Conrad. It was difficult to feel shame when she felt so completely certain about Conrad, so exacting about her feelings. It wasn't an issue she gave a second consideration. She just knew.

When she rounded the curve to the large estate, she stopped a moment gazing at the sprawling demesne and knew she would be happy to leave it. Too many memories of Sebastian lingered there. Yes, it would be messy, murky, and incestuous, even when she and Sebastian had carefully avoided any conversations that led to commitment. She wondered if they had known all along, they would inevitably grow in separate directions. He would surely see how she and Conrad felt about each other.

She shook her head. What was she thinking? As if Sebastian would bless their union, join in merriment over being cuckolded in his own house by his own brother. She was deluding herself. Conrad and Sebastian shared a unique bond as well as their history with Antonia. Conrad owed Sebastian his life. She couldn't think about all those things. She only knew that somehow it would all work itself out. Because Conrad loved her. And she loved him. And that was all that mattered.

She grappled with the groceries as she tried to open the kitchen door, wondering briefly if she could remember how to make the brandied caramel and she laughed out loud. There was a bright side to this situation. Alexandra was pondering a domestic conundrum, and how that would delight her mother.

She walked into the kitchen where Tula was prepping for dinner. Odd. She had left a note for her giving her the night off.

She didn't have to move any further to feel it. The energy in the air, the weight of the molecules against her skin. She knew before hearing the muted laughter, followed by the music.

Sebastian was home.

Alexandra dropped the groceries on the chopping block and tried to steady the contraction of her heart as she placed her trembling hands against the wood. She swallowed, fighting the dryness in her mouth. The air was too heavy. She could barely breathe.

Somehow, her legs navigated her body into the living room. As she rounded the curved hallway, she could see Sebastian's dark unruly hair as he sat at the piano grandly gesticulating and joking as if he were Victor Borge giving a comic performance, loud and boisterous.

As Alexandra entered, she glanced from Conrad, void of expression, to Sebastian, unaware at first that she stood there. He was regaling Conrad with vigor and then caught her in his peripheral vision.

"Darling! Oh, my dear—you scared me!" He ran to her and picked her up, whirling her about as he showered kisses her all over her face, her eyes, her cheeks, and finally a long protracted kiss.

They finally parted. Conrad grabbed his coat. "I'll let you have some time to yourselves."

"But you must come back for dinner. I've asked Tula to fix something extra special. I want to tell you both everything at the same time."

Conrad began to walk out of the room. His eyes caught hers briefly, but she could read nothing in them.

"Promise," Sebastian commanded.

Conrad lifted his hand in abeyance and walked out.

"Come here, you. I'm so hungry for you."

Alexandra's body felt immobilized, in shock. She was trying to catch up to reality, but she wasn't certain which reality it was.

"I'm sorry, Sebastian," Alexandra faltered. "You've taken the rug out, I'm afraid. Why didn't you call?"

"I wanted to surprise you." He frowned. "It was somewhat of a lark, I suppose, but I was growing tired of all the wonderfully hedonistic pleasures of European life. And I missed you." He kissed her again as if testing her, and she kissed him back. She wasn't ready for a confrontation quite yet.

"Please tell me you've missed me too."

"Of course I have, darling." But Alexandra's tone sounded anything but enthusiastic.

"Aren't you glad I'm home?"

But she couldn't speak.

"What's the matter, beautiful woman?" Sebastian pulled her closer. "Don't tell me someone's gone and turned your head?"

Alexandra blanched, then moved away from him so he couldn't see her eyes.

"Sweetheart, what's the matter?"

"Honestly, I've got a headache, Sebastian. I've just… just gotten over a bit of the flu. I don't want you to catch it."

"Oh, that's no fun. Come here." He walked her to the couch and sat her down like a little girl. "I'll make you some of the real English tea I've brought home, bundle you up on the couch, build you a fire… I can't wait to tell you… Oh, my Lord, it's been so unbelievable." Sebastian stood back, thrust his arms in the air like he'd witnessed the eighth wonder of the world, and as though he, himself, might just be it.

They canceled dinner for the evening due to Alexandra's "illness." When Sebastian joined her in bed, he quickly drew her to him and began kissing her neck. At first, she relented, but as his hands grew more insistent, alarm stirred within her.

It was familiar and not unpleasant, but she couldn't do this. Not after Conrad.

"Darling." She gently pushed him aside, but he was insistent. "Sebastian—"

"God I want you—"

"Sebastian!"

"Babe." He began to undress her.

"Stop!" Now she shoved him.

"What the hell?"

"I told you… I'm not feeling well."

"That's never stopped us before."

"I'm sorry. I need to go the restroom." She pushed him again, not gently, and escaped for the time being.

The next evening, there was no avoiding it. Sebastian had chosen a trendy restaurant just north of Central Park. The intimate table was cramped between the two brothers, Sebastian lit by the flicker of candlelight, as he entertained them with story after story about the tour. Waylon Jennings' *Suspicious Minds* crooned softly in the background.

Alexandra sat stiffly between the brothers as Sebastian dominated the conversation. The reception from the audiences in Europe had been overwhelming. He had been delighted at first, but in time, working that sort of schedule became highly stressful and tiring. He had started suffering headaches and fatigue, and eventually became homesick and depressed.

"I was missing you, my sweet. So, I told Monetizzare, "'That's it! We have a week's break. I must see Alexandra.'" He leaned over and kissed her playfully on the cheek.

He ordered another bottle of wine and only then did Conrad's eyes meet Alexandra's, the contact so brief, again she could not decipher its meaning. Had she dreamt the previous weeks? Had their union meant so little to him that he could sit here calmly while his brother pawed her endlessly as exclamation points to every anecdote

"So, you dashed from concert hall to mob scene, signing autographs for the masses." Conrad took a sip of his wine. "In the end, is it all that you thought it would be?"

"What the hell kind of question is that? My god, man, Europe's where it's at! Their appreciation of music, real music, Connie, makes you feel so alive, so energized. Reckoned with." A bit of madness figured into the glaze of alcohol in his eyes. "Powerful."

"So, is power important to a man of music?"

"Power is important to any man."

Alexandra couldn't believe it. More blithe conversation as she sat watching the two, their camaraderie and competition all part of their glib repartee.

"Sebastian?" Alexandra paused. "Tell me, what is the most important thing to you about your music?"

Conrad lit a cigarette, watching her carefully.

"But you know the answer, darling. To play for the people. To perform for as many of them as possible."

"And what is the most important thing in your life?" Alexandra asked.

Sebastian sat stumped. He glanced from Alexandra to Conrad and then laughed. "You, of course, Darling."

"A man who has his priorities straight," she responded looking directly at Conrad.

A long silence filled the space until Conrad lit a cigarette. "So, what's next?"

"I'll go back after this break, finish up, and then I'm home." He pecked Alexandra remotely on the cheek.

"Do you plan to start something new?"

Sebastian lit a cigarette. Before another dreaded void filled the space, he gulped his wine, and turned to his brother. "I hope you don't mind, but Alexandra told me you might be considering your own outing." He glanced piously from Alexandra to Conrad. "So, when did you decide to honor the public with your music?"

Conrad shifted his gaze from Alexandra to Sebastian. A crook of a smile formed on his lips, but he said nothing.

"Sebastian, you don't have to be so sarcastic." Alexandra defended Conrad since he seemed unwilling to do it himself.

"I have no intention of 'debuting' for a New York audience. I don't know where Alexandra got that idea—"

"But I just assumed…" Alexandra said, breathless. "All the conversations you had with Max. You've been working so hard on your pieces…"

"You assumed wrong. In any event, I have no need to reach as 'many people as possible' at this point." He tamped out his cigarette, hard.

"Then when, Conrad?" Sebastian sneered. "You must put yourself out there at some point. It doesn't just magically appear, this fame, this success."

"Doesn't it?" Conrad pegged Sebastian with a glare. "It seemed to work for you."

A long and embarrassing lull was finally broken by Sebastian's chuckling. "Hey, it's not worth fighting over. I'm only trying to help. I spoke with

Max, and he's found the perfect spot for you. It's a boutique shop to be sure. But it would be a start, Connie—"

Conrad waved a hand, clearly irritated, then picked up his drink. "That's not necessary."

"Look, Connie, I wouldn't have set this up if I didn't think the producers wouldn't let it fly. Now, trust me. You need to get your work out there. There's nothing like it. And even if it runs to a refined taste, so what? At some point, you're going to have to get out there and get wet. It would please Antonia. You did promise her."

Alexandra watched myriad emotions ripple over Conrad's face, his teeth grinding. Then, as if reconsidering he said quietly, "Sure." He raised his glass. "Why not?"

Alexandra glanced at him sharply, completely surprised, but the minute their eyes met, she averted her own. His glance conveyed a note of caution and something else she couldn't discern. At this point, she wasn't sure she wanted to anymore. She felt the threat of tears.

"Great, that's great." Sebastian clapped Conrad on the shoulder while Alexandra stood up, uncertain where she meant to go.

"Hey... what's the matter? You don't seem like your old self."

"I don't think I am," Alexandra replied numbly. "My old self."

Conrad moved out the next day, carrying boxes to a rental car as Alexandra watched in silence. When he finished, he wandered through the gardens, tracing familiar paths. She followed his steps from a distance as he passed the Hermes monument, its rose bushes long faded, and finally reached the gazebo with its statues of Apollo and Dionysus. It felt like a quiet farewell to Antonia, one last tour of the estate. When she approached, she noticed the delicate frown etched on his brow, a subtle sign of the weight he carried.

"So, you're leaving."

"Yes."

"Without…" She didn't know quite what to say. "Without even talking to me?"

"No. I was on my way to find you," Conrad answered quietly.

Alexandra wasn't sure she could breathe. "You were going to come and find me… Say, 'Been great knowing you, thanks for the roll.'"

"No." It was barely audible. "Not like that."

"I don't understand what's happening here, Conrad."

"I think it's best if I move into the city."

"What about…" Her voice raised as she put out her hands. "Us? Our plans – *Us* moving to the city. I don't understand this. You. And your complete silence since Sebastian came home."

Her hair blew in the wind, and he put a palm to the side of her face, brushing it aside. "Alex, sometimes things happen when you least expect them. When you're not prepared." He paused as if trying to figure out the best way to break it to her. "I'm not sorry it happened. God, I'm not sorry it happened, but you must understand that I'm sorry for the pain it's causing."

"Let me come with you."

"I need to go," he said with conviction.

"So do I. How can you think I could stay with Sebastian after… after us?"

"I need to go. Alone."

"Just because you walk away, it didn't happen?"

"No—"

"Makes it any less real?" She hated the desperation in her voice.

"Sebastian is my brother. I already feel like shit that I took what was his—"

"I'm not his. You made me not his."

He closed his eyes, his pain evident.

"Conrad." Her voice trembled with anger, a fury growing in her eyes. "If you are doing this as some wayward loyalty to your brother… or that you think I still want to be with him…"

But he didn't respond.

"I know he saved your life—" she escalated then began to cry in earnest.

"Don't… shhhh… shhh." Conrad tried to pull her close.

"Please." She withdrew so she could look at him, to see if there was anything in his expression to give her hope, but he pulled her closer, holding her tightly until she felt she couldn't breathe, but so grateful to be in his arms, giddy with relief until she felt him begin to release her.

"Look. I know it won't make sense to you, but I simply won't hurt Sebastian."

"And you think by letting go of me, you're even? That this is some sort of balancing of the fates?"

"It's not that. It's something else. It has to do with Antonia…" He stopped and looked into her eyes with a certainty that she knew she couldn't change. "With promises… promises I made." He exhaled loudly, releasing the anxiety they both felt, then said almost so quietly she barely heard. "It isn't our time."

"Time? Conrad! What in the hell does time have to do when you lo—" But he pressed two fingers to her lips before she could get the words out.

"Listen to me. It cannot happen now. Not now." He held her by the arms as if infusing strength and reason. "You asked Sebastian what the most important thing in his life was…" He cupped her neck the same way he had when he made love to her. "If you were to ask me—"

"Don't," she tried to divert his words, but he made her look at him

"I would answer; my music—"

She struggled against him. "Please stop—"

"I would have to say words to you like, there is no place for you where I am going. That music takes every bit of energy I possess—"

"And where was your music the days before Sebastian returned?" she demanded, pushing him away. "How can you stand there and tell me it has to be mutually exclusive? That you can't have both. You've made some goddamn pretty speeches about integrity, perfection, and purity. There are times I may feel like an imposter when I sit at the piano, but I wonder why you don't feel like an imposter as a man."

"Alexandra," Conrad replied sad and withdrawn. He looked defeated. "I will always treasure our time together. But I'm not ready to succumb to it."

"Succumb?" She felt the anger leave her body. *Succumb.* What a strange choice of words, she thought. They hadn't experienced the same thing at all.

He wrapped his arms around her, and she slumped into him. She felt every part of him which now felt like part of her being. She could feel his heart beating through his shirt and knew that to struggle against him was to lose this last bit of him. His arms tightened around her, and she tried to memorize the deepest essence of him. He pressed gentle lips to her ear and whispered, "I do love you."

Alexandra couldn't function the following days. She begged off Sebastian and his hungry eyes, his possessive hands, with the excuse of her lingering illness. She stayed in bed, sick with a heart so heavy she didn't move at all the first two days. She fell into an intractable slumber, the wonderfully inky plane hovering below consciousness where nothing disturbed, except irritating moments of waking.

Finally out of excuses, she let Sebastian make love to her. She lay there, half-engaged and numb. After, Sebastian paced by the bed with his cigarette. "Alex. What the hell is wrong?" But his anger felt half-hearted, and she was too entrenched in her cocoon of despair to hear between the lines; to hear him suffering from his own guilt, wondering if word had somehow gotten back to her that he had slept his way from country to country.

For weeks her dreams were all of Conrad. His face, hands, body, hair; sexual dreams where she came in her sleep, rushing awake when she realized it wasn't Conrad, but Sebastian, who lay beside her, his seed spilled on her stomach, his mouth on hers, his lips tainted with the dank of wine.

The linger of his cigarettes that had never bothered her before now lent an air of nausea to her already spinning depression.

One night after she had slept most of the afternoon and evening on the couch, Sebastian came in late, and she woke to find him removing her socks and kissing her toes. He glanced up at her, amorously arched a brow and began to climb onto her, the smell of liquor and cigarettes cutting into the air until she could smell nothing else.

"Sebastian, I'm sleeping."

"Yes, I've noticed. You've been doing a lot of that lately." He continued kissing her elbow, up her arm, nibbling at her neck.

"I'm really… I'm not in the mood tonight." Alexandra squirreled out from under him.

"You're never in the mood. Not since I've come home. What in the hell is going on, Alexandra?" Anger rose in his voice. "What happened after I left?"

"You know I haven't been feeling well. Can't you just let it be?"

"No. I can't let it be. Not when you used to be in heat every other god-damn minute. Are you fucking someone behind my back? What the hell is going on, Alex?"

"You tell me!"

"Okay. I give up. What's the big secret?"

"Chandra." It was the first line of defense she could think up.

The blood ran from his face. "What?! What's she got to do with anything?"

"Really, Sebastian? We'll let that pass. After all, I had no claim to you back then."

He lit a cigarette, inhaled nervously.

"Jesus, Sebastian, did you really think I wouldn't find out?" Playing poker with what she only suspected was true, but his eyes said it all.

"I don't—"

"Sebastian"

Another puff. "Who told you?"

"Who didn't?" Apparently, her fear that he had had an affair was simply the tip of the iceberg.

For the next few weeks, he apologized and lamented and allowed her to punish him, allowed her to keep her distance while he kept late hours away from the house, meeting with producers, staying in the city or at Monetizzare's apartment, leaving her to the big house and all her memories.

She mourned for Conrad and for herself. How had she let this happen? Every corner she turned, she saw both of her lovers in a photojournalistic history, a museum of canvases in the shrine that Antonia had built, their eyes following her wherever she moved. As if a curse filled the house and everyone who passed its threshold would be sucked into the vortex of deception, as she had fallen prey to the most clichéd secret of them all. At every nook and cranny, her sins were called up by Sebastian's petulant lips and intense blue eyes shining from some portrait, or Conrad's eyes smiling at her in the photo on the mantle of the fireplace.

It made her mad to live in this place, but a part of her couldn't bear to leave it. Disillusionment had seeped into her very skin, a lingering ache she couldn't shake. When she wasn't staring vacantly out at the still water of the pool, she would drift to one of the pianos, vaguely running her hand over the keys with hollowed detachment. On nights Sebastian was in the city, she lay on Conrad's bed, smelling the faint traces of him on the sheets they had slept in. There she languished for twelve, fourteen hours at a time, into that nether region that was safe, and soft and not real. She knew she was in trouble, she needed help. But she gladly capitulated to the emotional blunting, surrendering to the weight of despair as helplessness seeped through her pores.

She waited in the café for Max to appear. She hadn't slept well in days and her face was drawn. She lit a cigarette, shaken and weary as he sat opposite her. "I... I don't know why I called you. I just figured... I don't know. Maybe you would have some answers." She took a long inhale.

He adjusted his glasses self-consciously. "My dear, I was happy to hear from you." He hoped his voice didn't betray his surprise at her appearance.

"You needn't be kind. I know I look like Hell."

"You're tired, my dear. That's all." He gently patted her hand, then ordered coffee for them both. "How's the music going? I heard you're preparing for another album."

Alexandra attempted a smile but then stopped. "I... I don't understand them. Either one of them."

Max took off his glasses, cleaned them with the omnipresent untucked shirt. "I've watched them both very carefully their entire lives. Antonia nurtured every fantasy she could envision, dreaming of them both as world-renowned pianists. But she hadn't counted on their vastly different natures, nor where their paths might lead."

Alexandra sat stoically for some moments, then looked at Max defenselessly. "I didn't mean to separate them."

"I know, Meine Kleine."

"I loved Sebastian. I was mad about him. But with Conrad, I feel as if I'm whole. Do you understand?"

"Ja."

"It's like each of us is the missing link, only we're all following the wrong person. I loved Sebastian because he needed me. And he loved me because I'm the perfect imposter with whom to live out his fantasy of fame and riches. But with Conrad, I feel my real self, my true performer. I have never felt so alive about music." She shrugged cynically. "But Conrad has no need. He's self-sufficient. I give him nothing. Add nothing to his life."

"Ah, but that's where you're wrong, don't you see?"

"No. I don't see." Her voice was flat.

"You give Conrad the ability to share. Not simply be with people, but with a level of real human intimacy, something no one has ever been able to do before."

"If I gave him anything he wouldn't have left."

"My dear, you told me on the phone he said it wasn't the right time." Max lifted his brows. "Maybe take that at face value."

"I just can't seem to make any sense of it all."

"Heartbreak rarely makes sense. But if it will help you at all, I know one thing for certain. I have never seen an ounce of fear in Conrad. Until he met you."

"Afraid." She snorted. "Of me."

"Yes. He has finally met something he cannot master."

Conrad played in the recording studio while Sebastian's producers, Jake and Alan, listened from the mixing booth in frustration. A hippy engineer with long braided hair adjusted levels on the console. Jake leaned back and folded his arms, as if he had said all there was to say, while Alan chewed his bottom lip. They didn't want to piss Sebastian off.

"Tell him to try something else." Alan sniffed at the engineer. "Tell him... shit, tell him anything else."

"What the hell kinda music is this anyway?" Jake asked before the engineer could make the request.

"Shhh, for Christ's sake," Alan said.

The engineer pressed a button. "Conrad. Try another take at that last passage, okay?" He twirled a couple of knobs as Conrad started over.

"For shit's sake, just tell me, what do you call it? It's not classical. And it's not any jazz I've ever heard before."

"I don't know, something about a lost soul."

"It's giving me the creeps." Jake rubbed at his arms.

"Then maybe he's made his point." Alan kept trying to lighten the mood. Sebastian had made this deal. He'd warned them that his brother was a little left of radical, that he didn't "pretty" the music up. That it was raw and not likely to be everyone's cup of tea. Producing Sebastian's concerti had been the best gig they had ever had. It put them on the map so if Sebastian wanted to launch his flunky brother's bizarre music, who were they to get in the way? He just wanted to keep things cool with Sebastian.

"And you want to remind me why we're doin' this again?"

"You know why. I promised Sebastian," Alan said.

"And we're supposed to sit here and pretend we like it?"

The engineer cleared his throat. "No disrespect, but this guy's boss!"

"You know, Jake, I've heard this guy play before and he can haul out the Rachmaninoff. Why don't we just have him record some standard rep?"

"Yeah?" This perked Jake's interest.

"Give me sound," Alan ordered the engineer, who pressed the intercom button again.

"Hey, Conrad. That's great. Great stuff, man. You know, I was wondering if you wouldn't mind playing some Rach for Jake here. He's not familiar with your work."

Conrad glanced up from the booth. "This is my work."

"No, no. I didn't mean that. He wants to hear Rachmaninoff's 3rd. Could you play it for us?"

Conrad shrugged and began playing as if he'd spent his whole life practicing it and nothing else.

Jake jumped from his seat. "Holy shit."

Alan nodded. "See!"

Jake agreed in rapt appreciation. "This guy's unbelievable!"

"I told you," said the engineer.

Conrad continued playing and Jake and Alan listened with new respect and enjoyment.

"This guy's phenomenal." Jake nudged Alan. "People will love him on tour. He's even prettier than his brother."

"And," Alan said seriously, "he can play a lot better."

"Oh, Jesus!" the engineer whispered. He'd gotten so caught up in Conrad's performance he didn't realize the button was still depressed. Conrad had heard the entire conversation.

He calmly got up from the piano and walked from the room.

It took Alexandra weeks to get upright again. To sit at a piano again. To play notes without feeling the music she and Conrad had played. She found herself bathed in musical metaphors; appassionato, con molto agitato, diminuendo. An obsessive rondo of imperfect thinking. Could madness already be thriving, like arriving at a destination but not remembering the drive? Just when she reached some rationale, that Conrad did love her—it was the last thing he had whispered in her ear—but that he loved his brother more or owed him on a grander level, she'd start right back at the beginning.

She replayed every scene with Conrad, starting from the moment Sebastian had left for tour. Perhaps it was inevitable that while Sebastian was away and she was exposed to this man, who was equal parts talent and enigma, she had allowed herself to become more vulnerable than ever before. He demanded it of her. Or maybe she had wanted him to demand it of her. The simple truth was that she had fallen hopelessly in love with a man who wouldn't, or couldn't, return that love. Full stop.

When she was finally able to grasp the finality of the situation, Alexandra turned to the wretched task of determining her fate. Could she stay with Sebastian, who, in the end, had done her no more wrong than she had done him? Whose own intercontinental exploits were far less damaging than her own betrayal? She couldn't figure out who deserved whom more, as if she had to pay the price for the ridiculous claim to be with the man she loved, by staying with the man she didn't.

Another part of her served sentence upon Conrad by standing at Sebastian's side, sleeping with him, making love to him, playing the part of the erstwhile lover and partner. If by holding her head high, by reveling in Sebastian's glory, and sharing with him award after award for his "Second Coming" album—if her allegiance to Sebastian caused Conrad any pain, she only hoped he suffered half as much as she.

And self-flagellation never tormented anyone more. She would allow Sebastian to make love to her in his growing aggressiveness, a puppet to muscle memory, holding him as she always had, play-acting as her body went numb. She learned to remove herself until it wasn't happening to her anymore, just some inert otherling.

This distorted motivation led her down the murky path of self-loathing, where things felt heavy and the act of breathing a wearying feat. She began to dull the edges of the dark place she called home, matching Sebastian's appetites for alcohol and cigarettes.

One rare evening he came home and asked her to have dinner with him. Alexandra knew that he was trying to please her. He spoke quietly about music sales, about booking another, shorter American tour.

"I was thinking LA, San Francisco. Maybe Seattle and Chicago, and then home for the holidays. How does that sound?"

"Fine." Alexandra had taken to monosyllabic conversation.

"No. I'm asking if you'd like to join me. I think maybe if we spent more time together—"

"And if you had someone to fuck on the road, you wouldn't need to fuck strangers." Alexandra hated her words, her tone.

"Yes. That's one way of looking at it." Sebastian pushed his plate aside, lit a cigarette. "Look, Alex. I never meant to hurt you with any of that. Truth is, and I think you know this, none of it meant anything. I just... just seem to have a short leash when it comes to the corporeal and, well, I think it would help us if we stayed more connected."

She also pushed her plate to the side, Tula's culinary skills barely sampled, and refilled her wine glass. "Sebastian, let's get to the point of the matter. Do we really have anything to salvage?"

"Not if you aren't willing to put in the effort." He got up and walked to the window. His voice was almost a whisper. "I suppose you should know that Conrad left."

At the mention of his name, she felt as if she had been physically assaulted.

"Of course I know that!"

"No, I mean left town. For good. He stopped by the studio today. Said he was heading out. Didn't know where, just, you know Connie, Mr. Nomad. I tried to give him some money, but he wouldn't take it."

She could barely breathe. She got up and walked to the living room and sat at the piano. She began playing without thought. Sebastian followed her, quietly came up behind her. She continued to play until he put his hand at her elbows to stop her, then lifted her bodily from the bench and turned Alexandra to face him.

"Look, while I was gone, I know I messed up. But I wasn't the only one."

Alexandra cleared her throat. She should come clean.

"We've already established long distance is not a place we thrive. That's why I'd like you to join me."

"Sebastian—"

"I don't need a confession."

"Sebastian, please… please," her voice was a tortured whisper, "I… it was so unexpected. Believe me."

He nodded, jaw gritting.

"And I knew you had been unfaithful and of course that doesn't make it any more right or fair… I just didn't see it coming. I hope you believe that."

He cleared his throat, turned to her, and smiled tenderly as vulnerable as she had ever seen him. "I won't fight him for you. I gave up fighting him a long time ago."

She leaned her head on his shoulder and knew she couldn't fight him either. Conrad had pretty much made the decision for all their lives about what was to be done. Sebastian wrapped his arms around her, and she began to cry. He led her to their bedroom and made love to her, bringing her outside of the doom she had carried for weeks, urging her back to life, and with it the understanding that for better or worse, they somehow belonged to each other, if only because they didn't belong to Conrad.

Bound by a mutual recklessness, they began to focus on the future. Sebastian was extending his state-side tour, and he began seeking Alexandra's advice. They spent many evenings out with Monetizzare and company, and most of the time they kept things light and easy.

There was, however, the occasional hiss of damage that leaked through their finely wrapped lives from time to time. Petty arguments about a bill not getting paid. Debating which group they might join for the night, fearful of being isolated for an evening alone together. Sebastian was Alexandra's second choice, and they both knew it. She needed to stay with him to keep her only connection to Conrad, and although they accepted the twisted nature of their relationship, neither were willing to dredge beneath the surface.

Diverting intimacy was the norm, conversations were never taxing or challenging. If they did end up spending time alone and edged toward sensitive topics it wasn't long before the invectives would fly.

Inevitably, they would cover their hurt by making love, half-heartedly at first, as if they were both afraid of clinging to a ship that simply needed to sink. But then they'd discover the sore and bruised points through one another's bodies and lose themselves in surrender. They had been happy in the beginning. And it was Alexandra who had inspired Sebastian's greatness. One didn't simply walk away from such a powerful claim.

So deadened had they become that they found themselves slipping toward a sadomasochistic underpinning. Sebastian had begun to take Alexandra from behind, while he pleasured her with his hands. A punishing twist began to play itself out as he tied her up, fucking her as he circled her neck in his huge arms. Alexandra was keenly aware it would take nothing for him to snap her in two. Part of her wished he would. Sebastian's aggression knew no limits when drinking, and he pummeled into her as her arms went numb from new and ingenious methods of bondage. Alexandra would lay removed, observing their love, a ruined creature now, with a detached sense of pity. As much as their union repulsed and terrified her at times, it was also the tie that bound them together. But ultimately, in her choice to stay with him, the danger and heedlessness with which they devoured each other nearly convinced her that it was Sebastian she was meant to be with all along.

It never occurred to her that this self-penance could filter into her work because she found so little about her work that even interested her at this point. Instead, she had taken it upon herself to help manage Sebastian's tour. Knowing better than anyone the rigors and obstacles of travelling from city to city and hotel to hotel, she made sure Sebastian had everything he needed. She knew all his eccentricities and demands and finally decided to join him on tour so that there could be no room for error. Of any kind. Sebastian had a point. Extracurricular activities would be of no concern if she was constantly by his side.

Was she happy? Max had asked the question with gentle concern before they left for the tour. Happy? Alexandra couldn't afford herself the luxury to ask. She simply kept busy with Sebastian's music, the demands of his career, the demands he made of her physically and emotionally. They were exhausting, and she had no time to think about the other life she might be living. Not the one with Conrad. Or the one she might be living if she were to simply go on her own. But being alone, without either of them, wasn't a concept she could begin to fathom. She had lost her compass, and in her panic, she clung to the nearest flotsam so she wouldn't drown.

CONRAD, 1973

"Can you change the fact that you are not wholly mine,
I not wholly thine?"

Ludwig van Beethoven –
to his Immortal Beloved

He stared over the shiny green fields covering the acres west of a farm-house, dusted by the glow of a burnished sunset, while he smoked his cigarette and sat on the rocking bench. He listened to the sounds of the earth. Crickets whirring, gentle breezes rustling, crows hawking. It brought him back to the day he had arrived here, eighteen months ago now. Over two and half years since he had last seen Alexandra.

Conrad had hitched out of New York in the same way he had arrived. When the driver had asked him where he was headed, he answered sim-ply, "Wherever you're headed."

He'd stared at the passing yellow lines for long hours into the night, wondering if he had made the biggest mistake of his life, wondering, more to the point, how he would live without her.

With his single duffel bag in tow, he'd jumped from one truck to another, stopping in one small berg after another, finding itinerant work, and in the hours left he'd find a piano and continue writing his music. For months he lived that way, without paying any mind to time, world events, or geography. And then one day, he jumped from a semi and watched it trail off into the horizon. He glanced up and down the small highway, figuring he was precisely in the middle of nowhere. Exactly where he belonged.

Blistering, the sun beat down on him. As he walked, he heard the sound of heat everywhere, the sigh of quivering blacktop, the drone of the omnipresent cicadas, the crunching gravel beneath his boots. He still heard the other music too. The music the two of them had played together those many long afternoons. It lived within him. On lonely nights it had lent solace to his heart, something he'd only ever thought of as a muscle, until Alexandra.

Conrad walked for miles, his sweat-seared shirt clinging to his back, until he finally approached Casa de Karina, a bar and grill that appeared to moonlight as the only entertainment center around. A dance floor and stage with an upright piano were roped off in one corner from the rest of the tables, where lunch and dinner were served. Dollie Parton's *Jolene* warbled through an old sound system.

He sat at the counter and a slender waitress with large breasts handed him a menu. "What can I do ya for?"

"Iced tea?"

"Yep. Anythin' else?"

"Yes. I wanted to inquire about the Room for Let sign."

"*Inquire?* Well, la—di—da." The waitress cackled as she turned the corner and yelled, "Hey, Karina, some city boy's askin' about the room."

A few moments later, a woman in her mid-forties breezed out, as if in a hurry, all business. Traces of Hispanic heritage were prominent in her wide cheekbones and jet-black hair, which had been glossed into a lazy chignon. Strong slender fingers dripped long-tipped nails. Her body seemed unnaturally restrained by a form-fitting summer dress in pale pistachio cotton. She was attractive with her deep-set intelligent eyes, the dangling earrings, the cynical humor curling at the corner of her mouth. She poured him a cup of coffee and walked around to the other side of the counter.

"Thanks."

"You're interested in the room?"

He nodded.

"You're not from around here."

"No."

"You in from Albuquerque?"

He shook his head.

She eyed him curiously. "Travelin' through?"

"I suppose."

"I don't want to rent and then just have you up and leave."

"I can't guarantee anything."

She considered his candor. "How long do you think before you'll be travelin' again?"

"I don't know."

"Trouble with the law?"

"Not in the least," he responded. "Would it help to know I'm also looking for a job? Would that make me more stable?"

She pulled out fashionably long Virginia Slims and he lit it for her. "Okay. So, you're a gentleman. What else?"

"A musician."

"Play honky-tonk?"

"No, but I'm sure I can pick it up." He grinned gently.

"I need me a honky-tonk man on that keyboard over there. Gil went and broke his damn finger and now the band's screwed. Which means we have one hell of a lean Saturday night. There're only two places in town for music and this is both of them."

"I could try to help you out."

"What kind of music you play?"

"Classical."

"That won't fly 'round these parts."

Their eyes caught, and he sensed the older woman was used to acting tougher than she was. "If you can do some odd jobs around the place, that'll take care of your rent. Playing with the band will cover the rest. You any good with a hammer?"

"I've picked up a bit of carpentry here and there," he said.

"Good." The woman nodded as if they had come to an arrangement. "I'm Karina Grady. There's a large farmhouse a quarter of a mile up the road. Behind it is a cropper's shack. That's where you'll be livin'. I expect half rent up front. Can you do that?"

"Certainly." He handed her a couple of fifties.

She gave him a key and instructions and said she would be home a little later. Conrad picked up his suitcase and walked down the road to his new home, which had, indeed, barely weathered the better side of dilapidated. It was set off several yards from a rambling farmhouse. When he went to open the screen door it came off in his hands. He wasn't sure what the point of a key was. The cropper's shack was little more than a shed with a sagging twin bed and a toilet set off to one side, the latter camouflaged by a tacky piece of plywood.

For weeks, Conrad hammered and banged the place back into shape. As he rebuilt the wide porch that circled around Karina's farmhouse, he laughed, remembering Antonia leading them around the estate with a carpenter or plumber, teaching him and Sebastian to "learn to fix things because it gives a man a sense of purpose." She had added earnestly, "God may have given man a thumb, but it took Bach to tell the pianist how to use it. It's so often difficult to appreciate achievement when you have no material measure of progress. Completing these little projects will give you a sense of accomplishment."

Karina would sleep until ten from her late hours at the bar, and when she'd get up, he'd be sawing boards, building steps, or cutting weeds from the badly overgrown lot, shirtless and sweating.

"Hottest damn spring I can remember," Karina had said that first morning. "Let me make you some breakfast."

As spring melded into summer the long sweltering days took on a smooth rhythm. Karina would prepare something for his dinner before she returned to the restaurant by midday. Conrad continued to repair or retire one square foot at a time, flexing his stretched muscles beyond the limits of exhaustion. He labored until dark, showered in the main house, then returned to his shed. One night during a windstorm, Karina asked him if he'd like to stay downstairs in the front room on the roll-out couch. "Otherwise, you'll wake up with a mouth full of dirt." She glanced him over. "I think I can trust you."

He never used the shack again.

Cheaply framed paintings dangled throughout the walls of the house, all created by her seven-year-old son, Jose, who was no longer present. Karina was a woman of few words. She never spoke of Jose, nor the man in the photo with him, presumably the boy's father. "Sleeping dogs lie," she said, and Conrad could appreciate her silence.

When he moved into the front room they honored one another's privacy with a comfortable blanket of silence. They were gracefully cautious with one another, polite, neither compelled to conversation. Karina was too tired most of the time from her long shifts at the bar which, Conrad came to discover, had belonged to both her and her husband, Harlan. It wasn't difficult to fill in the pieces through the abundant local gossip that Harlan had been a rodeo cowboy who raised cattle and tried to make a go of the family farm, but never had the tenacity to stay with much of anything.

Conrad could see Karina couldn't run the restaurant, which made reasonable income, and the farm as well. He put in long hours trying to bring the ranch back to some sort of grace and did more work than Karina had ever expected of him. To thank him, Karina began to fix deliciously seasoned dinners of enchiladas, taquitos, and chalupas with all the trimmings.

They generally ate together late in the evening, discussing the day's purchases for the farm or Karina's occasional difficulties with her staff. At the end of their meals, they adjourned to the porch, smoking their cigarettes, mesmerized by the natural sounds of crisp stars, the veiled murmurs of nocturnal rustlings, and a distaff howl from a coyote.

"I love this time of night," Karina offered.

Conrad took a drag off his cigarette and exhaled gracefully. "It's beautiful."

When she turned to him, he was looking directly at her, a gentle contentment bathed his face.

"I'm glad you're here, Conrad." She turned back out to the black. "Me too."

Weeks later, as Conrad finished his coffee, his eye caught the pixilated portrait just visible under the bills Karina had plopped on top of the newspaper. Sebastian. He shifted the bills away. And by his side, Alexandra stood, smiling weakly as Sebastian shook hands with flamboyant "Stokie," Philadelphia's Orchestra conductor, Leopold Stokowski. The caption below them read, "Musical Duet Divine!!" He pulled the paper from the bills. He looked at her, his stomach plummeting. He deliberately crumbled the paper and jammed it into the waste bin.

He walked outside and climbed the ladder to work on the roofing he had started the day before. By noon, the sun honed its way into his mind as he tore the old shingles from the melted tar. Dissonant shards clamored in his head. Angry syncopations. A blistering regret at seeing Alexandra smiling by Sebastian's side. Even now, after all this time. But what had he expected?

Karina had made iced tea, trying to fight off the heat wave, and yelled to Conrad, but he didn't seem to hear her.

"Hey," she yelled again.

Conrad caught Karina's reflection in the window of her pickup.

"Thought you might like some tea."

"Pardon me?"

A loose wire whipped thru the gusting wind.

"Hey! Careful!"

"What?" he shouted.

But before she could warn him a blast of wind whisked the wire, gracefully setting it on Conrad's roofing talon. A spark flew.

"OH MY GOD!" she screamed.

An electrical shock pulsed through his body, and Conrad struggled with his footing, though he felt miles from what was happening.

When he lost his balance, he knew all he could do was accept the finality of gravity. There was nothing to hold onto, nothing to save him. As he dropped through the air, he thought that if he were to die now, he would only have one regret.

Alexandra.

Alexandra shot up in bed and looked around, trying to get her bearings. Oh, yes, the Mark Hopkins in San Francisco. Disorientation was a frequent side effect when travelling as much as they had in the past few months. But the nightmare had strangled her awake. It was about Conrad. Something about him being hurt. She got out of bed and walked into the sitting room, her heart racing. She strode to the bar and poured herself a brandy, which Sebastian always had bountifully stocked no matter where they travelled. The drink calmed her, and after a few moments, she went to the window and stared out at the glittering lights of the seaboard city, thinking how beautiful and still it was.

It had taken her months of involvement in Sebastian and his work, a devotion that bordered on compulsion, to ease away the pain of Conrad, to finally sense that he wasn't cornering every angle in her mind. She even had days where she would suddenly realize she hadn't been thinking of Conrad at all in the past hour, but of how the tour would most benefit if they squeezed in this city or that.

At the beginning of Sebastian's first tour, Alexandra had played warm-up for a couple of the concerts, and they were billed as "Classical Romance," with all the attendant interviews. But Alexandra knew with all the other work she did on Sebastian's behalf that her music suffered, and she was no longer comfortable with the performances. Neither were the critics. Sebastian had been supportive of her eventual withdrawal.

"Of course he doesn't want you to play." Max had scoffed one evening over a private dinner during one of their breaks in Sebastian's tour. "You're the one who beat him in the Ketterling."

"Oh, Max, don't be absurd, he's created his own fame now. There's no competition between us."

But Max cocked a brow. He wasn't convinced. The silent question was always asked and answered with a glance. No, he hadn't heard from Conrad. No, he didn't know where he was.

The nightmare rattled her. It felt all too tangible, a strange realness to it somehow, and she only wished she could be certain he was safe. She phoned the concierge for messages and was startled to learn that an envelope marked 'Personal and Confidential' had arrived for her earlier that day. She checked to see that Sebastian was fully asleep, then asked that it be delivered at once.

Trembling, she lit a cigarette, then opened it. "I thought you'd want to know. I've found him. He's relocated to the outskirts of Santa Fe. Be well, mein Liebling. Max."

She exhaled slowly, the smoke curling about her.

"Hey, hey there." It was Antonia's voice.

"Antonia? I knew you'd come. I knew you would be here for me. Do you know how good it is to see you?" Conrad was so happy to hear her voice again. He felt safe, knowing Antonia was there, cupping his chin, taking care of him.

It was the dream again. The one that had bracketed sleepless nights throughout the time he had been in Santa Fe. The variations on a theme were muted foggy pictures, but the end of the dream never wavered, the scenes and images precisely the same. He was a small boy wandering in the vast expanse of the Kenyan desert, searching, desperately trying to find something in the glowering heat, sweating from the fever spreading through his slender body. Suddenly he found himself in a huge circle of mad Masai warriors all leaping wildly about him as they dragged his shackled body to a fire pit where they prepared for his sacrifice.

Lars momentarily attempted to save him, until Lars transmuted into Max, his gloating eyes a wide-angled blasphemy as he pricked a spear into the center of the child's heart. Blood painted the earth as the child fell. Antonia suddenly appeared, as if she'd just made a grand entrance at one of her parties. "Don't be ridiculous. He cannot die, his gift is eternal and of God." Someone tended to his fever, brought him water, but no matter how much he took in, he could not quench his thirst, and every drop that passed through him became agony. Then it was dark. He couldn't tell who was there. But it was not Antonia. It was *her*.

A rush of warmth spread through his limbs as her lips travelled the length of his neck, her mouth reaching for his own, Alexandra's lips embracing him, teasing him, coaxing him to her. He felt every part of her, smelled her perfume. Was he awake, or still dreaming? Because as he reached for her, she moved away, farther away now, until finally she was gone as suddenly as she arrived. Why, he wondered, couldn't he keep hold of her? Why wouldn't her image stay fixed?

Flitting in and out of consciousness, he reassured himself that yes, of course, it was because of his music. "*My* music," he murmured, returning to the dream, and then remembered; yes, it is all for *my music*.

When he came to a day later and opened his eyes, he felt her presence. "Antonia?"

"Conrad?" A sweet whisper of a voice.

"I'm so glad you came again. I was waiting. Or did I come to you?"

"Conrad. It's Karina. You've had a bad fall and suffered a concussion."

"Alexandra... where is she?"

"Do you know who that is?" A man's voice. Lower, gravelly.

"I have no idea."

"Do you know anything about him?" Doctor Wells asked.

"I know enough." Karina cut him off. "I still think he would be better off in the hospital."

"That'll be a helluva bill, Karina."

"No. No hospital." Conrad moaned. He could see the vague shadow of Antonia. He didn't want to leave her. "I don't want… please. Let me stay here with you."

She glanced at the doctor.

The doctor shrugged. "Just keep a close eye on him. I'm not sure how bad the concussion is. If he stays confused for long or starts vomiting, call me. I'll be back tomorrow."

That night when he woke, he saw Karina asleep in the La-Z-Boy, a *Life* magazine spread across her chest, her mouth tense. Even in sleep, she couldn't drop her burden.

He began to sit up until he felt the pounding in his head, a shattering beneath his right eye, and his jaw clamped in pain as he cried out.

"Oh?" Karina woke and saw Conrad contorted in pain. "Hey there, Conrad, can you hear me?"

"Yes."

"Take this." She sat on the couch where he lay, lifted two pills to his mouth and handed him a glass of water. "There you go."

Conrad felt the tightness around his wrapped middle and the bandages twisted at his forehead. He turned slowly, trying to focus, the sharp pain finally ebbing. "My hands," he said, trying to wiggle them through the taped guaze.

"Your hands are fine. Just a bit of an electrical burn."

"What happened?"

"You took a swan dive right off my roof." Karina's eyes were gentle and worried.

"What else?" He tried to feel the other parts of his body, but he was only acutely aware of his head. "What else?"

"A couple of broken ribs, so you must stay very still. A broken knee and ankle. Other than that," she countered sweetly, "you're okay."

He continued to assess his hands.

"Everything's fine," she said as she took them in her own, her palms warm and dry. "Just some scratches and burns."

He continued to stare at the bandages.

"Conrad." Karina cleared her throat. "Is there anyone I can call? You've mentioned—"

He shook his head vehemently then stopped as the pain tore through him.

"Okay, just try not to worry about anything. You just need to rest. A lot of rest, and that'll make you better."

"Rest... okay... don't leave." Conrad was on the brink of unconsciousness again. "Don't leave me... don't leave, Antonia. I must talk to you about Sebastian. Maybe you can help... help Sebastian." He fell asleep and Karina sat there, still holding Conrad's hands in her own.

Karina leaned over him to refill his coffee cup, and Conrad saw the age lines gracefully engraved by her temples, as if she had done a lot of laughing in earlier years.

He smiled at her, thanked her.

She turned the TV on and brought him his cigarettes, then went into the kitchen.

"Smells good in there." She had just finished baking a cherry pie, which she topped off with a dollop of vanilla ice cream. Three weeks had passed since the accident, and he seemed to enjoy the simple pleasures she could provide.

When Karina brought out the pie Conrad turned the TV to the Carson show, because he knew she liked to relax to it on those nights when she came home in time from her earlier shifts.

She handed him the pie and fluffed up some pillows to make him more comfortable. He smoked and paid little attention until he heard the music: A third movement from one of Sebastian's concerti. Conrad stared at the screen and saw his brother performing with gusto and panache. It occurred to him that as Sebastian had grown flashier, he had become more technically lazy, finishing off the concerto with a flourishing, but flawed, crescendo.

The audience applauded, and then Johnny Carson, clapping, announced, "Sebastian D'Antonio!" Conrad was aware that Karina turned his direction and was staring at him.

"Now you know, it's pretty unusual to be this popular with classical music," Carson ribbed Sebastian, who was seated and smiling in front of the host's desk.

"It's about time that changed." Sebastian grinned encouragingly.

"Yeah, now isn't that somethin'! The second coming of Bach. Whose idea was that?"

"Well..." Sebastian demurred modestly.

"Yours or your brilliant publicist's?"

"I'm just happy for the opportunity to bring classical music back to its deserving audience."

"Spoken like a virtuoso." Carson leaned over and shook Sebastian's hand. "Your music's great. I'm even listening to it, and we all know what a boob I am." The audience laughed appreciatively. "Can't wait to hear the third coming. Let's give the one and only Sebastian D'Antonio a big hand, ladies and gentlemen."

Karina turned off the volume. She waited.

"He's my brother," Conrad said quietly. "Sort of my brother. I was adopted and we were raised together."

"Are you famous, too?"

Conrad turned to her. "Not in the least."

Over the next couple of days, Karina was quieter than usual, as if she were re-examining the man she had brought into her house, a man she had spent so much time with, and yet Conrad had given her so little information. At the week's end, Conrad was able to hobble to the kitchen table. When he sat down, Karina came to him with a skillet of scrambled eggs, full of vegetables and chopped ham.

"You're feeding me like I'm out in the fields," he protested.

When Karina didn't answer, he glanced up, and saw a sad wisdom in her dark eyes, set in a face that had lived a rough and hard life.

"Something wrong?"

"You know that piano's just sittin' there in the bar, it's emptied most afternoons, and even if there is a cowpoke or two in there, that won't make any difference."

That afternoon he rode in with her for her evening shift. He hobbled alongside her, one arm over her shoulders, her arm wrapped gently around his waist. She maneuvered Conrad between the tables and walked him over to the upright, helping him to sit. She stood a moment, then left him with a gentle pat on the shoulder.

He stared at the keys for a long moment. His hands were fine, as she'd said they would be. The tips of his fingers were still mottled by the singe marks, still somewhat painful but he was desperate to feel them beneath the brittle, faded ivories on the upright.

He gently played a scale, gnarled by an instrument terribly out of tune, so he pulled out the tuning wrench that traveled with him everywhere. He plunked about the keys for a good hour or so, calibrating it as close to pitch as possible.

Then he began to play the music as if he were at a grand piano, playing the music that came to him as it always had, from the earth, from his soul. And now, from his love. Karina was watching him, but she was a shadow in his peripheral, nothing more. Another woman occupied the space in his mind, and just as he allowed the pure pleasure of the keys to wash over him, he also let the memories of this woman fuel the music that flowed from him, and for the first time in years he began to feel hope.

> *"To stop the flow of music would be like the stopping of time itself, incredible and inconceivable."*

Aaron Copland

For the next several weeks, Conrad hobbled out to the pickup with Karina so he could play piano at the bar. At the end of the day, he would hitch a ride back to the house with one of the waitresses, or if Karina left early, he'd simply wait for her. When he was finally able to get both his ankle and knee casts removed, he bought a used motorcycle. She would often wake to find him gone and began to wonder how much longer it would be before he was gone altogether.

She didn't understand Conrad's music. Sometimes it sounded familiar, like the fancy stuff on the classical radio station, but other times it made her feel uneasy, as if the notes he labored over, which eerily reminded her of a tortured animal, had to do with his own haunted memories. She suspected it was the only thing that made sense for him in this messed-up world. Other times she would see him simply staring at the keys as if in discussion with them, unaware that she had come in, swept the floor, and taken all the chairs down from the tables.

One evening when she pulled up in her rusty red pickup, Conrad met her at the porch and led her into the kitchen where he presented the table, replete with lit candles and a bouquet of wildflowers, perched in an abandoned root beer mug. He had made Karina's favorite dinner of steak, mashed potatoes, and creamed corn.

"Conrad, you shouldn't have. Besides, you're not supposed to be standing on your feet so much."

"Weren't you the one that said fixing what's broken takes a good appetite?"

"I'm not the one that needs healin.'"

"We all need healing," he said as he pulled out a chair for her and served her as she had served him the past months during his recovery.

She took a bite and nodded appreciatively.

"Yeah, not too shabby for someone who has no business in the kitchen." He poured them both a glass of wine. When the meal was over, Conrad cleared the dishes, offered Karina a cigarette, and lit it.

"You know, Karina, I owe you quite a lot. You've been my maid, nurse, and good friend—"

"Not another word. You don't owe me a thing."

"Why'd you do all this?" he asked.

"Because you needed help, silly."

"You help every poor slob who walks into your restaurant?"

Karina took a pull off her cigarette. "Now, what do you think?" She pushed herself from the table and began filling the sink to wash the dishes.

Conrad got up and walked to the wall where a quartet of Karina's sons' paintings hung. "What happened, Karina?"

Her shoulders dropped slightly, and she stated flatly, "He died of leukemia a few years back."

"Your husband?"

"Harlan left at the first sign it wasn't just a visit to the hospital. He wasn't interested in taking the time it required to watch our son die."

"Did he send money?"

"Not a dime, and I don't gotta tell you it ran up a mountain of bills." Karina turned and looked out the kitchen window. "That's how the farm got so far behind. I had to go where the immediate money was. The bar doesn't make much, but at least it's cash. I'm still payin' off the hospital, and just barely keepin' the farm up."

"Why didn't you tell me?"

"It's not your problem." She shook her head.

"I think I might be able to help."

"I don't want your charity, Conrad." She turned around to face him but didn't look into his eyes.

"That's not what it is. Consider it a repayment. You helped me when I needed it most. Now let me return the favor."

"I'll think about it," she said tiredly.

Karina smiled every time she pulled into her long driveway. Conrad had patched and repaired everything from the stalls in the barn to the weather-beaten shack, trimmed out the windows, and put a new paint job on the farmhouse. People began to take notice, and Karina heard good things about her farm from the customers who drank in her bar, even if a few of the wags slyly claimed they had no doubt why things were lookin' so good out at the Grady place. Let them muck about in their sordid thoughts. If they only knew what a gentleman Conrad was, they would have recognized the folly of their gossip.

Not that she hadn't grown quite fond of him. But she'd had enough experience with men to know that this one was suffering a tragedy deep inside. She had been around, weathered many lovers, married twice, and buried one child. She knew when a man wanted the warm and gentle presence of a woman with no demands, and she was used to biding her time. The few times she considered using her sexuality, she suppressed the urge. It would have felt like taking advantage of a situation that, she would much prefer was mutual.

She couldn't say she had fallen in love with Conrad, but if he was of a mind to allow their deep and abiding friendship to grow into something more intimate, she wouldn't turn him away. It would have to be his decision, though. Conrad wasn't the kind to be pushed, and she knew he had to release the misery from his past just as she had needed to relearn how to breathe once her son had died.

As soon as the farm was ship-shape, Conrad began playing at the bar more often and turned his attention to the way it was run. He loved helping Karina. He had watched her so many hours, attending to his needs in her quiet, gentle manner, that it made him feel good to get her set up on new footing.

One night, bar towel slung over her shoulder, she sat beside him at the piano and lit a cigarette. He glanced at her, saw the weary lines etched into her face, and segued into a Bachian version of *I'm Gonna Wash That Man Right Outa My Hair*. She laughed and it lit up her tired face.

"Play something for me, Conrad."

With the first poignant notes of *Clair de Lune*, he felt the tension in her muscles go soft. Her body relaxed next to him as his hands coaxed the delicate melody from the battered upright, his fingers gliding over the keys. He shut his eyes, his body transported with the haunting rolling refrain, its final lilting ascent a whisper to hope. When he finished and looked up at her, tears streamed down her face.

"Are you—"

She put up a hand. "That was so lovely. So tender to come out of a man," she said, almost in a trance.

"I'm sorry—"

"Sorry?" she sniffed. "Please... it was one of the nicest moments I can remember.

Thank *you*." She squeezed his forearm, her expression a strange combination of desperate sadness and awe.

Conrad couldn't wipe the image of Karina's broken gratitude from his mind. It tailed him, the next day and the one following that. He had given her such joy with a simple piece. He considered how someone like Karina, with no exposure to classical music, would integrate the sounds. She wasn't hampered by sophistication or expectation. She was decent, salt of the earth, and her wisdom came from the brutal knocks of real life. To his surprise, he suddenly found himself wishing that his own compositions would give her the same breathless pleasure she had experienced with *Clair de Lune*.

Subconsciously, he began to soften the edges of his compositions, not bending them exactly, but when he played, the core of emotion had shifted since Alexandra. She had created a whole new paint wand of emotions to reveal within his music. And here, with Karina, he found the peace he needed to begin again.

He sat at the plinky upright, often having to unstick keys in the middle of a piece, lifting its faded grainy lid to resurrect its pitch and tune.

Starting from scratch, he let everything he had learned and picked up during his travels dissipate. Now, instead of focusing purely on the notes before him, emotion would become his guiding principle, accessibility gracing notes to balance the triumvirate; where composer, music, and audience meet in perfect communion.

He pulled out every piece he had ever written and reapplied those elements and before he knew it, he hit a stride in his work, an ease he had never experienced. Sure, composition came easily to him, and as Lars had said, anyone could figure out structure. But Lars was trying to teach him patience, to understand not just people, but the way they responded to his music as well.

After all these many years, his worldly exposure, his travels to the farthest poles, it was in a rusty café with a rundown piano that he found integration, and performed for people who didn't know Chopin from Shostakovich. He continued to rearrange and reorchestrate his pieces, and as time passed, he noticed the chatter abating in the rooms, people listening, coming up to him and thanking him for the evening. For the first time, Conrad felt a link to an audience, their appreciation of his music was humble and simple. And for the first time how they responded mattered to him.

He started playing on Sunday afternoons, and slowly the farmers and their wives began showing up too, making Sundays Karina's busiest shift. He also took to playing ramped-up boogie-woogie numbers on Saturday nights, sweet honky-tonk blues that Karina's patrons went wild for. He did it for Karina, for her business to succeed. It pleased him to expose these rural landowners and Mexican field hands to jazz and the classics, and he could see, as time went by, they developed an ear for the different composers. He realized one night after he and Karina had closed the bar, that his music was no longer motivated by the pain of leaving Alexandra. That sorrow still lived with him daily, but it lay deeper beneath the surface now. The edge of anger had finally left his music, an anger he hadn't been aware he possessed. For the first time, he yearned for community, to reach out and connect with these people whose lives were ruled by hard work, feeding their families, and cutting loose one night a week. There was a purity and purpose to their lives that made sense to him. As an outsider, he moved inside their circle with this unique language, and they warmly accepted him. He no longer felt the arrogance of superiority he had carried with him as a shield. Until he had met Alexandra, he hadn't known what it was to want, and now with Karina, he understood what it was to give.

He had begun to harbor a primal warmth toward Karina that was born of her constant grace, her kindness, her softness as a woman, and her ample breasts as they moved forcefully against the unforgiving cotton of her omnipresent tank tops. Her hands may have belonged to a woman of hard work, but the silkiness of her fingertips gently aroused him when she touched him to pass a plate or a cup of coffee. He began to study her lips as she spoke, the way they curved with her weary but beautiful smile, and he finally realized that he wanted to kiss them.

Long after the close of one of the "Sunday Soirees," as Karina had taken to calling them, Conrad asked her if she would dance with him. He picked out a tinny *Stand By Your Man* from the old jukebox and held her loosely as he led her over the jagged wooden-planked flooring, twirling her around, joining her laughter as she howled at his innovative two-stepping.

"Where'd a renaissance man like yourself learn to dance like that?"

"Music's music. I'm just *'standin' by my gal'.*"

"Is that what you think of me?" They had slowed down now.

"What do you mean?"

"You think I'm a *stand by your man* kinda gal?"

"I don't think you're any other kind of gal."

She grinned and he held her closer, dancing out the rest of the tune.

When they returned home, he bowed to her and adjourned to his front room like he always had. A long sigh followed Karina into her bedroom.

The next morning, she felt a bit rejected, perturbed even, as she made him breakfast and poured coffee. He didn't seem to notice as he read the paper.

"There's a concert I'd like to go to in Santa Fe," he said, but Karina continued washing the dishes. "What do you think?"

"I'm not your mother," she snapped. "Go if you'd like."

"Karina, I'm asking you to go with me."

"That's not what I heard you say."

"Well, that's what I'm saying: Would you like to join me?"

She didn't answer. She felt a tear slide down her cheek and hit the dishwater. What was wrong with her? She was acting like a noodle-headed teenager who didn't get a kiss last night, and now she wanted to punish him.

Within seconds she felt him come up from behind her. "Hey."

She wouldn't let him see her blubbering like a fool, so she turned her head from him and continued to furiously wash the dishes.

"Let me help." Conrad was only an inch from her, she could feel the heat from his body. His arm came up from behind her, took the dish she had in her hand, and rinsed it. Wordlessly they continued until all the dishes were done and she was able to collect herself. He handed her the dishtowel, and she dried her hands. She felt the gentle pressure of his hand at her waist and turned to face him.

"Don't play with me, Conrad." She was flustered by the sincerity in his eyes, and more tears began to well up. He leaned into her and gently kissed her forehead.

"Let me help."

Karina closed her eyes and felt Conrad's tender lips follow the tear's trail down her cheek until they reached her mouth.

"I want to help you."

He kissed her so gently it was a whisper. Then deeper, exploring her mouth. She uncertainly placed her hands at his waist, then wrapped her arms around him, clasping him to her as they embraced.

He led her into her bedroom, laid her gently upon the bed, and made love to her. Slowly, surely, and completely. It had been so long since she felt a man next to her. She was glad she had waited for Conrad. His unhurried pace and gentle tenderness made her safe. For the first time in years, the hollow aching that had lived inside her slowly began to ease into another form, a form that could be massaged and soothed and brought back to life.

1974

"The notes I handle no better than many pianists. But the
pauses between the notes—ah, that is where the art resides."

Arthur Schnabel, pianist

It was only when Alexandra watched the televised speech of Nixon resigning, his sad donkey jowls reflecting the plight of his presidency, did Alexandra realize it had been a full two years since she had performed. For in the time that she'd traveled with Sebastian while managing his career and dealing with the demands of his public persona, she all but stopped playing, even for her own personal enjoyment. It was more than just losing her inner drive. She had lost her appetite for life.

She ate only to survive. She began missing meals and dropped weight quickly, so much so that during one of Chandra's visits she asked Alexandra if she was ill, and even Sebastian muttered, "You look like Twiggy for Christ's sake, Alex. You've got to put some meat on." Most of what she consumed was in the form of coffee, cigarettes, and wine. The wine she drank with dinner often ended up replacing dinner, allowing her to succumb to a certain euphoric light-headedness which she easily misdiagnosed as joy. She might even regard Sebastian, sitting across from him at dinner as he eagerly attacked a steak, and convince herself that she loved him. That the decision to be with him was the right one.

So often during the nights of the exhausting tour, Sebastian's head would hit the pillow and he would be fast asleep, while Alexandra lay wide awake, thinking about tomorrow and the day after that, a form of insomnia perpetuated by attending to all of his needs, helping him, guiding him. One day was the same as the next. Every morning, as soon as consciousness broke its way through slumber her heart sank, and she would ask herself the same question; *Will I always feel this way? Will I never feel good again?*

At his request, she made love to him, often in the early evenings before a performance, to alleviate his nerves. She tried to allay his fears about the public and the crowds that had become the two-headed monster; one full of adulation and celebrity excessiveness, the other wanting, needing, and touching. Increased security was required to shield an increasingly edgy Sebastian from the crowds.

It didn't seem to matter where they went. The fans always found him. Even when Alexandra took every effort to camouflage the direction of their movements, he was always unearthed, covered by scores of magazines and papers. Reporters descended upon them everywhere, and Sebastian's stealth charm began to wear thin, especially when he was asked about his future.

When the American tour was finally over, they returned to Antonia's estate and holed up for several days in delicious silence. They spent their time recovering in different parts of the house. While Alexandra lay awake in one of the guest bedrooms reading terrible novels and sipping champagne, Sebastian spent most of his time prostrate by the pool, drinking gin and tonics. He had taken to nibbling the day away. He had developed a passion for cashews, couldn't get enough of them. He'd grown ravenous for cheese logs, and fondues with dipping sauces, the creamier the better. He also began drinking more, endlessly pursuing fine wines, justifying it as a quest to expand his cellar, which he proudly showcased as one of the finest collections in the Northeast.

Alexandra had also enjoyed sampling too many of the Cabernets, Merlots, and Pinots to try and keep up with Sebastian's drinking, but eventually, she grew bored with the mild inebriation that inevitably led to a headache, followed by unavoidable depression. The hangovers were fast outpacing the benefits of numbness. She was more and more put off by Sebastian's heavy drinking, so she took to spending more time upstairs.

They skirted each other for weeks on end, seeing little of each other until they had dinner. There they might discuss current affairs, or Sebastian would read a note from an adoring fan, Alexandra might share some correspondence from one of their colleagues.

After several months, when it appeared Sebastian might go on like this forever, Alexandra finally pressed the subject. "So… what now, Sebastian?"

"What do you mean, what now?"

"Eventually the phones must be answered. Bills paid. You know… life's little details. Your agents and producers have been calling every other day."

"What do they fucking want from me?" Sebastian growled irritably. "I've just made them millions."

"Yes, well, I suspect they'd like you to make them some more. According to your contract, you're scheduled for recording sometime next month."

"They can call me then. Even a genius requires rest."

"Apparently…"

"Look, am I bothering you?" Sebastian snapped. "Do I ask you when you're going to get back to work? No, I allow you to take the time you need to…" His words floated into thin air.

"To recover from my many pressing engagements?" Alexandra didn't like the sarcasm in her voice. Neither did Sebastian.

"No need to get snide, darling. I simply thought taking some time off would be… healthy. Rejuvenating."

"I think I'm in the need for some time on," Alexandra observed dryly. "I haven't touched my work in over two years."

"And what is it that you intend to do?"

"Don't treat me like one of your myopic fans," she snapped. "I had a career… or at least the start of one before all this happened, Sebastian. Or don't you remember?"

"I want you to do whatever makes you happy." Sebastian waved a hand as though swatting a fly.

"Really."

"Yes, of course. You're no good to either of us like this."

"Thank you, Herr Doctor."

"Alexandra, really, do you need to be so cynical? You're giving me a headache!"

He got up from the table and left the room. Alexandra watched him go. She had given herself a headache as well. She glanced at the piano, just visible in the living room. She rested her head on the dining room table and shut her eyes.

"....and the tour here was even more successful than in Europe. Of course, everyone is waiting for his next piece." Max had arrived quite unexpectedly earlier that afternoon. Alexandra made him his prerequisite tea. They sipped silently for some time amongst the disarray of the living room, where the piano fought for dominance over the clutter of books, sheet music, records, and ashtrays overflowing in every conceivable corner.

"I've tried to tell him to keep this area clean."

"You don't have to justify a composer's clutter," Max said kindly.

"He hasn't written a thing in... forever. I think sitting around all the paraphernalia makes him *feel* productive."

"Yes, I'm sure it's all been quite exhausting." He adjusted his tie.

"I think it's more exhausting for him now. At least when he's in front of the crowd he's energized by their adulation."

"You are the one who is tired, dear child." Max's voice was concerned.

"Yes." Alexandra lit a cigarette. "But only of myself."

Max buffed his glasses, muttered something in German then looked at her. "I'm sorry."

"I'm languishing... I guess that's the term. Either that or I've lost the ability to feel. I've watched Sebastian and myself through the lens of the great media machine. I look at him and wonder where the fine young man is that I met, eager, full of charm, cocky, but not so cocky he believed his own bullshit. And I look at myself and wonder *where did she go?*" Wistful, deflated, she repeated, "Where did she go? Along for the ride, *she cowardly answers.* Oh, Max! There's the world of music, and the world of "man-made" music. Spin. Publicity. It's... it's utter bullshit."

Max wasn't prepared for such disclosure. He didn't quite know how to respond to this side of Alexandra. He'd never seen her so sardonic, so broken, even after Conrad had first left.

"Everywhere I look," she continued, "films, books, they all share the same devastation of commerce over content. What happened to art, Max? What happened to it?"

"Alex, don't be so—"

"Cynical? I look at us sometimes—photos of all the places we've been, people we've met—and it's as if I'm looking at strangers. I doubt very much that either one of us can drum up an inkling of what it feels like to perform. Really *perform* again."

They sipped their tea both lost in their thoughts. Then quietly she continued, "I remember when I first started ruled only by my childlike fascination to make the sounds grow into something musical and beautiful. If you could just keep that purely innocent desire, knowing that you'll never be the best in the world, but you've brought your own little bit of magic to the notes with care and attention." She stopped, suddenly, remembering Chandra's premonition: *The night of the Ketterling was the beginning of our end.*

Max silently filled his pipe.

"And I? I have no idea what my function is. He doesn't need me even though he thinks he does and even if he says he never thinks of Conrad, he's always on his mind." Alexandra's bottom lip trembled. "I know he's always on mine."

"Ja." Max nodded sympathetically.

She stopped, shook it off. "You've been a lovely indulgent friend letting me ramble in self-pity. But you must tell me, Max, you must tell me whatever you know."

"He's safe."

And? her arched brows asked.

"He plays now and then."

"For whom?"

"A small honky-tonk band at a grill house called Casa de Karina. The band's become quite the draw. Really brings in the rural crowd with—" he cleared his throat "—*boogie* numbers. I'm sure you can imagine the way he would play them."

"I don't believe it." She sat in stunned silence for a moment. "So, he's playing ragtag for a bunch of cowboys and farmers?"

"He's enjoying his life, Alexandra. I just wanted you to know that he's… he's at peace."

"That's it?" her voice thin.

"In a nutshell."

"And is he…" Of course she had to know.

An awkward silence wavered between them.

"Max. Please." She gave him permission to tell her.

"The café owner. He had an accident right before I found him. She's the woman who took care of him." He didn't want to use Conrad's word, *lover.* "He lives with her."

Alexandra swallowed and nodded in a businesslike manner.

After a few moments of unsuccessfully trying to move to another subject, Max stood up and took Alexandra's hand. She walked him to the door.

"Alexandra." His voice was kind. "You think you have no direction because you have lost love."

She felt as though her throat were closing.

"But it is because you have lost yourself. There is only one way back."

It took all the courage Alexandra had to sit at the piano. It had been easily over a year since she had even placed her hands upon the keys, because the last time she had played, the sounds strangled from her beloved instrument were notes so inept and unforgiving, she couldn't bear to hear them. Every pianist knows that losing even one day of practice can be damaging to the psyche, and after several days, the threads of concentration, agility, and tightness begin to unspool. Her lack of focus and concentration degraded simple pieces. But it wasn't simply that her skill had betrayed her. It was the paucity of emotion. Nothing had motivated her to play since Conrad left. When she sat before the keys, she felt empty. Nothing could compel her to make music.

Now, long after Max went home, she lifted her hand, stretched thumb and pinky over an octave, gently willed the notes to play; the first sounds cursed the silence, unforgiving. Awkward and clumsy, she was fueled by the need to waltz over the keys but lacked the limber coordination with which to do so. Her hands simply wouldn't obey her brain.

She decided to attack basic scales before she would attempt anything else, for at least in the drilling clarity of their repetition, she could hold onto the illusion that she was accomplishing something. She willed her cloddish hands to simply put one key behind the other in fully balanced measures. She doggedly continued, laboring over scales for hours into the night, only quitting when she heard Sebastian enter into the room.

He stood swaying for a moment, then approached her with an amused expression. "Whatever are you doing, darling?"

"I was—"

"Practicing? For what?"

"I thought I'd start playing again, Sebastian. Do you have a problem with that?"

"No, my dear." He chuckled. "I suppose at least one of us should put up the appearance that we can, indeed, play."

Alexandra wouldn't allow Sebastian's resentment to get in her way. The next day she began after breakfast and didn't stop until lunch, just as Sebastian was waking. He walked in with his bathrobe half undone, his lumpish middle protruding, and for the first time, it occurred to her that Sebastian had gotten fat. Well, not fat, but he was certainly a lot beefier than she had remembered him. She was surprised at how blind she had become during the infrequent interludes when they exposed their skin to one another and wondered why she hadn't felt the weight of his sluggish heft above her.

"Have you stood on a scale any time recently?"

He scratched his stomach and yawned. "All the more to love."

She ate her lunch in silence while he pawed at his breakfast, lit a cigarette.

"Look, Alex, I know you're interested in getting back into it, but the fact is, the Bösendorfer is my writing piano."

"Fine. I'll use the library."

She walked into that room for the first time since Conrad and she had last played together. But she wasn't going to let him get in her way either. She had spent too long subverting her life for these two men, had sacrificed too much, and now, as if the proverbial light had been flicked on, the thought of those wasted years was almost unbearable; she refused to waste another moment. For the first time, she felt, if not strong, motivated and lighter. The thick blanket of fog was slowly lifting its veil.

From that point on, the library became her life. She practiced scales in the morning, attacked performance pieces in the afternoon. She returned to the basics with *The Well Tempered Klavier* and moved on to *The Art of Fugue* and Chopin *Preludes,* all of which she had accomplished quite readily her first year at the Academy. She prepared to launch into several of his larger pieces, polonaises, and nocturnes. Chopin's music was, by its nature, passionate and resolute with his expressive lyricism and poetic intimacy, two qualities she had lost along her path.

She relearned elements of her very nature as she played night and day, with determination and conviction, vaguely conscious of murmurings from the grand downstairs. The more she played in the library, the more Sebastian withdrew, surly and angry as if she was showing him up, as if they were back at the Ketterling, their rivalry reignited. Every time they passed one another in the hall he would cock an eyebrow, goading her, but she passed him by, unperturbed.

At dinner, he would stare at her sullenly, then strike up a conversation that was based on wishful fantasy, rather than reality. It might be that he'd worked very hard that day, or that she had no idea how difficult it was to create when she was "constantly flogging the same old tired piece."

"I'm sorry, am I getting in your way?" she asked incredulously

"You can't possibly understand the pressure I'm under."

"And what might that be, your bloated stomach? Sebastian, you need to stop all the drinking."

"Now that's calling the kettle black."

She stopped. Yes, she had been drinking too much, recounting their ridiculously childish arguments while inebriated. But now that she was sober, with only an occasional glass of wine at dinner, she could see that his drinking had become excessive, even for Sebastian.

Some evenings he would try a different approach. "I've begun a new masterpiece. 'sunequaled," he would slur dramatically. "It'll put the *Second Coming* t'shame."

"I'm glad you've started working again." Alexandra kept her voice even.

"Do you hear me? I've said it'll put it to shame!"

"I'd like to hear it, if you want to share it with me."

"This piece." He enunciated carefully, trying to form words that eluded him. "Is so… so complex I doubt you will even begin to understand the ramifications of what I'm doing."

"As you wish."

"Don't humor me with your superior ways, Alexandra—"

"For God's sake, Sebastian, you're stinking drunk!" She couldn't stand it any longer.

"—with your co… cold stoic ball-busting manners. You're frigid. Do you know that? You used to be a woman, but all I feel when I fuck you is a shell of flesh. You have no right to the term woman." He added barely able to enunciate something she didn't quite catch, "… ruined you."

It sickened her to hear the truth in his words. She *was* an empty vessel who could barely receive pleasure, much less give it.

An old urge to help him soon was revoked by a new desire. To get well. Strong, and to never need a man again. Perhaps Chandra had been right with all her feminist dogma. Men didn't seem to care whatsoever their impact on her life. Their lives always came first. Why didn't her own?

She would get herself back into shape. Whatever it took. She had to find a teacher who wouldn't give her any quarter and would work her to perfection.

"I would be honored," Max said as he swiped his glasses at the end of a long dinner in the city. "But you must know, I separate friends and students. While you are my student, you are not my friend. And while you are my friend, it is not healthy to be my student."

"Agreed," Alexandra said, and began her classes immediately.

She drove to Max's house three nights a week, where she stopped and started, acclimating to the boisterously loud comments in his commanding German.

"Timing. Ach… nein. Listen to the metronome. Alexandra, it's one—two—three, one—two—three, there is no fourth beat in a waltz!" She'd simply nod, grateful for the ire, for the steady challenge, for the consistent pulse of his lecturing instruction. Pacing, watching, and listening for any missed cue, for the slightest change in tempo, Max would bellow, "Focus! Forget everything else. Make your mind have only one objective."

With Max, she rediscovered the pain of humiliation, as well as the joy of accolades for, between a pianist and her teacher exists the relationship of a child to its parent, a patient to his therapist, an extraordinary bond which can supersede the agony caused by a lover.

"You can have all the intensity in the world but save it for a film score! It's not simply timing. You must listen to the pacing. Precision, Alex, precision!" Night after night, lesson after lesson. She knew he was right. He had made his discipline regarding relational boundaries very clear. He wasn't doing this as a charity case. He was helping make her better. Better than she had ever been.

After her lessons she would drive home exhausted, but with the gratitude of the hungry for a warm meal. The nourishment of hope bled through her limbs, and by the time she got home, she would hit a second wind. She couldn't wait until morning to sit and recreate the new phrasing she had learned with Max, and often stayed up until the first morning light.

After weeks of these nocturnal sessions, Sebastian returned home one night, melancholy and only mildly tipsy. "Alex?" He paused at the doorway. "Might I have a word?"

Alexandra joined him in the living room where his papers lay scattered, unusually messy and chaotic, even for Sebastian.

"I love this time of night, when it's just passing over. Don't you?" he asked her.

"Sebastian." Her tone indicated that whatever it was he wanted to talk about, she'd like to get to it.

"Okay." Sebastian lit a cigarette and pointed to the mass of papers gnarled at the floor. "I… I've been doing a lot of thinking… working on my next project. I was wondering if you…"

"Yes?" Alexandra was becoming impatient.

"Alex, you know what you're best at?" Sebastian's tone was subtle and coaxing. "You grasp what's beneath the music, more than any other pianist I've ever encountered."

"Sebastian." Alexandra faced him directly. "Are you asking for my help?"

He pursed his lips, then smiled unconvincingly. "If you wouldn't mind taking some time with me. Helping me break down and get back to the basics." His chin trembled slightly. He held out his hands like a young child who can't figure out how to make his favorite toy work. "Do you want me to say it? I can't do it. I *need* your help."

Alexandra saw in his eyes the old vulnerability, the honest exposure, and felt heartened by his words. She inhaled deeply. She would not put herself second ever again, but she could see he was trying. She walked to him, put her arms around him, and felt all his guarded resistance dissipate. "Of course I'll help you."

$$\oint$$

"So, how's it going with Max? Heard he's a real task master."

A few weeks later Alexandra and Chandra were finishing lunch. While she had maintained her practice as priority, in helping Sebastian she knew, even if she wanted to be in denial about it, that she was no longer a hundred percent.

"He's an amazing teacher. And I'm doing a lot better than I did five months ago. According to my manager, I've got another opportunity for a tour that might make its way into a recording. Seems there's a dearth, at present, of us lady performers. You know how they like to have *proof of female*."

"I'll keep my fingers crossed." Chandra twirled one of the rings she wore then asked with a curtness to her voice, "And Sebastian?"

"He's trying." Alexandra sipped her coffee. "He's really trying, Chandra."

"Why are you there?"

"Honestly, I don't know.

"You're not in love with him."

She wasn't sure what love was anymore. "He hasn't written anything in forever. He's down, and I… I wouldn't think of leaving him until he gets it back together."

"So, you do want to leave?" Chandra's eyes lit with hope.

"I…" Every time Alexandra asked herself the same question she ran from the answer. "I don't know."

"Why do you think he's so blocked?"

"You once said something a long time ago. It was so simple, yet so out of my reach. You had finally found your purpose. Art without purpose is a nomad's journey… no, what it is, is hell." She shivered. "I think I've finally found mine. And it's not some newsflash. It's quite simple, as you said." Alexandra arched her brows and sighed. "I honor the notes, the piece, what it means to me—much like Conrad tried to teach me ages ago. The rest is pure gravy. Sebastian has never played for any reason other than recognition."

"Yes, those who have no talent must have fame." Chandra lifted her hand for the bill. "But have you considered the more obvious reason why he's stuck?"

Alexandra shook her head.

"He knows he's lost you."

After Alexandra hugged Chandra goodbye, she felt jittery and decided to walk some of the caffeine out of her system. She realized she was close to Falstaff's Record Store and decided to pop in to see if there were any new Prokofiev recordings she could bring home to Sebastian as an early Christmas gift. He could use a spot of cheer. He had tried the entire week to write the prelude to his new composition, but it was off. His playing was in form, but he just couldn't develop a melody worth pursuing. Nothing sparked.

She was just crossing the street when she spotted him. What was he doing in town? And then she stopped. He wasn't alone. Entering the store with Sebastian was an adoring, and extremely young, fan. His arm cradled her waist.

She stood motionless in the gutter until she realized her feet had grown cold.

"Perhaps all music, even the newest, is not so much something discovered as something that re-emerges from where it lay buried in the memory, inaudible as a melody cut in a disc of flesh. A composer lets me hear a song that has always been shut up silent within me."

Jean Genet (1910—86)
French playwright, novelist

Karina didn't recognize him at first, then bent over in laughter.

"Conrad, do you know just how ridiculous you look in that Santa hat?" She couldn't stop laughing as he walked in, his leather jacket filled to the brim with presents, his head crowned by a goofy Santa hat. "If you don't look like the silliest thing I've ever seen."

"Silly feels damn good. Come here."

He curled her in his arms and gave her a long kiss. "That's for Yuletide."

"It is, huh?" she whispered back. "I think Santa deserves a present, don't you?"

They walked into her bedroom and fell onto the bed. They made love in between opening the presents that were hidden inside his jacket, inside the pockets of his jeans and jacket, and tucked into his sock. "Well, if Santa isn't the clever little dickens."

"Ahhhh, Karina." Conrad smiled, looking up at the ceiling. "You make me happy."

"Do I?" Her voice turned serious.

He turned to he and, kissed her in response.

"I know I'm not the cleverest. I know I don't understand all your music stuff, but I am smart about one thing."

"Yeah, what's that?"

"I'll never push you, Conrad."

He held her closer then, wanting her to feel safe, willing her to know that he cared for her in the best way that he could. He felt moved to tears, because, in her own way, Karina knew Conrad as no woman ever had. It made him wish Alexandra could have known this side of him, the side that was capable of giving. At the same time, he was saddened, because he had only so much to give Karina. He hoped it would be enough.

On a snowy New Year's Eve, Conrad had gone to the bar early to tune the piano for the "Gala—Palooza" held that evening, but when he sat at the bench, he found himself moved to play their music. *Theirs.* He had been thinking of Alexandra the past few days, random thoughts. He didn't even know what conjured her visage or made him sense her so suddenly. But he could smell her perfume, the silk of her hair against his skin, feel his hands upon her waist from the itch in his palms. When he felt her this intensely, there was only one thing for it, to play it out of his system, as he did now. Only someone stood directly behind him, startled, yet mesmerized.

He turned to see a slender older man in his mid-fifties, handsome and familiarly dashing, staring at him. He was dressed in evening attire.

"Amazing." The man's voice had the clipped English accent of British upper-class.

"Thanks." Conrad grinned, staring at the man with a shock of white hair.

"Phillip Purcell." He thrust a hand toward Conrad, still surprised. "I don't know which of us is more out of place. And you are?"

"Conrad D'Antonio."

"D'Antonio... hmmm. Related to?"

Conrad nodded.

"That music." Purcell put a hand to his chin as if determining the best way to describe it, but finally settled quite simply on, "I'd like to say, is... quite unprecedented."

Conrad nodded gratefully.

"I saw your sign out front. Are you playing tonight?"

"Yes." Conrad couldn't help but laugh. "But I'm afraid tonight's fare is a little less... eclectic."

"I see. You're a starving musician who toils for his bread and butter," Purcell suggested dramatically. "And you've been waiting to catch your big break in the city from some fat cat agent who makes his second home in Santa Fe. You scrap about and go to auditions, but no one understands your music—"

"Hold it." Conrad held his hand up, still smiling. "I fled the city. And yes, no one understands my music, but I've long gotten over the anguish and torment. Is that helpful?"

"Quite." Purcell waved his hand distractedly as if trying to figure out how best to proceed. "Listen, Conrad, I don't know what your circumstances are, but how 'bout having a bit of a chat?"

"Sure." Conrad shrugged.

"Can I buy you a beer?"

"I'll get them."

When Conrad returned, he sat with the man for some moments in silence. Both studied one another carefully.

"Bloody unbelievable," Purcell finally said. "I'm on my way to Santa Fe from Albuquerque when my limo breaks down. Bloody cold it is out there, by the by. Someone drives me here with his pickup and as the dusted white flecks play in the midnight air, I am captured by music... by an unparalleled composition I hear from inside your fine establishment. Now isn't that bloody unbelievable?"

"What, exactly?"

"Finding someone who plays like you do out in the middle of the sticks." He sipped his beer. "Do you know who I am, then?"

"I'm afraid I'm at a loss."

"I'm a fairly well-known English conductor with my own symphonic orchestra. I started with the standards, performed in what some of my more incriminating critics called 'outlandish interpretations.' I've had my successes and a good deal of notoriety. A career spotted with a fair share of 'scandal,' and I'm fairly certain that's why you good Americans will receive me on tour."

Conrad grinned. The man's vigorous charm was, by the minute, growing on him.

"So how 'bout it old man? Come by and let's explore tomorrow. I'll send a car round, say two o'clock?"

Karina joined Conrad, who made introductions.

"Well?" Purcell asked, waiting for his reply.

Conrad smiled. He chuckled then and soon he and Purcell both laughed with the kind of release of men who have met their match and mate. Karina stared at them both, wondering what the hell the joke was she had just missed.

The next afternoon Purcell's limo pulled up punctually at two. An hour later, Conrad was in the city and delivered to Purcell's studio in Santa Fe, a lush and modern affair squeezed inside a Spanish colonial mansion. They spent the afternoon and then the evening playing for each other, an excitable tension buzzing through and around them.

"Play the piece from the other night."

Conrad hesitated.

"Look, mate, I know it's intimate, but I can't get it out of my mind."

Conrad began playing his *Nocturne for Alexandra*. This was music he shared with no one. He momentarily glanced at Purcell and could see this man fully understood his music. A chill spread over his limbs and a swelling in his chest almost made him lightheaded. It was the first time that Conrad felt fully met. Purcell listened to the intensity and ferocity with which Conrad attacked this inimitable piece and as the day unfolded into evening, he played more of his unique compositions; the music he had re-written from his travels. Purcell had dinner sent in, and they continued exploring well into the night. Finally, sometime after midnight, Purcell christened a bottle of '49 Glen Elgin Whiskey.

"I've heard so many pianists in the last year, I'm up to here with prodigies and virtuosos. It must be fate that I found you like a babe in the manger. A random act of grace from the good Man above." Dawn was breaking in the eastern sky and Purcell yawned contently.

Conrad held up his glass, a little drunk.

"I've spent my entire life working within the mold so I could break out of it and attend to the reality of music." Purcell lost his bravura façade and became serious. "You, my good man, *are* the reality of music."

They had spent the last eight hours in Purcell's studio with Conrad at the piano and Purcell with his violin, playing pieces Purcell had commissioned over the years and some he had written himself. Every day for a week they explored an endless array of possibilities at their fingertips until Purcell stopped suddenly and commanded, "Right. Come on, then, let's have a drink."

They walked several blocks in the icy wind to a working man's tavern and tossed back several snifters of cheap brandy, while Purcell, excitable and enthusiastic, shared with him his vision for the future of music.

"People need education. That's all. And exposure. It doesn't hurt to have the right messenger, either." He winked at Conrad. "Did it ever occur to you that there are pieces Bach didn't write? That Chopin never felt? That Beethoven didn't get around to? But what if there was a man today who wrote music, not like them, but like what they would write if they lived in today's world, steeped in the same history, influences, and culture?" Purcell asked.

"Do you think any composer wants their shoes filled?" Conrad asked

"Give me the name of one composer today who has touched the world with his compositions on a grand scale? Who brings to the audience true enjoyment and a sense that the spirit has been touched by the experience of their work?"

"My brother," Conrad stated sardonically.

Purcell shrugged, almost distastefully. "Too bad he isn't a finer pianist. No disrespect."

"None taken."

"Join me, Conrad." Purcell bent to him and grasped his forearm. "Come and do this with me."

Conrad's stomach twisted with indecision.

"Is it the woman? What's her name, Karina? Bring her along." Purcell assessed him curiously. "Think about it. But make the right decision. Your music is too important."

"For whom?"

"Don't get all Ayn Rand on me. I'm not asking you to put your integrity on the line." Purcell filled their glasses and laughed. "Which, by the way, is precisely why you should do it."

Conrad watched Purcell. They were cut from the same cloth. He began to nod then smiled, raised his glass.

Karina confirmed the decision for him. "I'm not going to hold you back on something that's meant to be. You think it was an accident he showed up here in the middle of nowhere? No, darlin'. You need to do this."

"Karina, do you have any idea what this will mean?"

"No. I guess I don't. What I do know is that you have to make your music."

"Look. We've gotten things straightened out with the farm. I think we should hire someone to run the bar. Things are fine here, and you deserve a break."

Karina frowned. She had never been farther east than Dallas, had never really traveled in her life.

"Don't think of reasons why you can't do it." Conrad cut into her thoughts. "It'll be good for you. You'll get to see the world. It'll be fun. You'll see."

"Do you want me to go?"

"Yes. I really want you to come with me."

Karina moved uneasily into his open arms. She wasn't sure if he truly wanted her to go or not. But at this point, she wasn't ready to lose him, and if nothing else, she could make sure he was well taken care of.

"Okay. I'll come with you."

She had crawled back to Max shortly after she discovered Sebastian's infidelity. He was kind and loving, and said of course he would prepare her to tour again. She had been turned down by one conductor who admonished her technical deficiencies.

"I'll practice like hell."

"Damn straight you will!"

Then Max wiped his glasses on his shirt tail and grumbled, "I only wish Sebastian would have realized the gem he had in you, so willing to help him. But he, he is so determined to throw himself away. Verdammt Schade!"

It *was* a shame, Alexandra thought, for Sebastian had ceased writing altogether. Maybe guilt had paralyzed him with inertia. He shuttled between the kitchen and the piano, pretending to work, barely holding up through the pretense of practice. She realized that in Sebastian lay the worst kind of talent. It was ungrateful. He had created some of the most beautiful music she and most of the world had ever heard, and he had allowed it to ruin him. She couldn't stand the decay of him. The stench, not of failure, but of surrender, clung to him like a mildewed blanket.

Alexandra avoided him at all costs, but as she struggled with her new piece, she couldn't find the oak metronome, usually a sentinel at either of the pianos in the library. After searching for nearly a half hour, she realized she would have to go to him to borrow the metronome downstairs. She wanted to try a slightly different timing for Prokofiev's *Dance of the Knights* from *Romeo & Juliet*. She tiptoed downstairs, hoping he wasn't around. She would just slip in and borrow Antonia's agate metronome, usually stowed by the side table, which was littered with ashtrays and a half-filled brandy snifter.

At the foot of the bench, Alexandra saw what she thought must be the next set of concerti. She picked up a page, began humming, then frowned.

This music was nothing like his previous work. Not one bit. She began again, then sat at the piano and played several bars. She stopped, sickened by her intrusion, as if she were trespassing on the humiliation of failure. She tried to stop a tear from falling, for if this was what Sebastian had come to, it was something she couldn't bear.

She glanced at the photos on the worktable, never far from his side; the ever-present Antonia, one of herself, and one with him and Conrad linked arm in arm, some fifteen years earlier, both wearing grins of the young and innocent.

"Well, if it isn't the grand Ketterling winner come to join the little people." His voice was laced with self-pity and cognac. "It's not polite to dig up the dead."

"I'm sorry, Sebastian." And she truly was. "The metronome in the library seems to be missing."

"That's because it's … it's broken."

"Broken?"

"Let's just say in a moment of frustration I lost my temper."

Alexandra could imagine him, mad with self-disgust, sweeping it off the piano in a rage.

"May I borrow this one?" She pointed to Antonia's treasure, the agate metronome, which Alexandra now saw as a portent of Sebastian and Conrad's polarity, their contrasting personalities embodying Apollo versus Dionysus to the extreme.

"No. You may not. I'm working and I need it." Sebastian took a weaving step toward his domain, sat clumsily at the piano bench, and picked up a pencil. "In any event, there's an extra one up in the attic."

Sebastian saw that his sheet music had been moved. He picked it up protectively. "Now, if you'll excuse me."

Alexandra couldn't stand it any longer. She left without comment.

Dust plumed about her face as she made her way up the attic stairs. It took her a moment to adjust to the light and get her bearings. She walked through the stack of boxes, and couldn't help but remember the first time she'd been up here with Sebastian, when they had been so in love, when it seemed their lives were meant to yield the highest potential.

Alexandra sighed and moved toward another set of boxes when her hip grazed one overfilled with sheet music. It toppled over, scattering hundreds of pages of Antonia's old collected works.

"Damn." She breathed in the humid air, began picking up the debris, quickly trying to repack the box, barely glancing at the materials until she spotted the name at the right-hand corner, the flourish of aged script, the finely hand-painted ink notes that danced along the page.

Alexandra frowned in surprised fascination, confused as she stared at the sheet in her hand for the longest time.

Downstairs, Sebastian lit a cigarette, his eyes raw and tired, wishing he hadn't been so rude to Alexandra. He didn't mean to take it out on her. But what choice did he have? She was leaving him. Leaving him out in the cold. He flicked the ash from his cigarette, lifted his brandy snifter, and took a slow, deliberate sip. It was precisely this moment—when he saw the distorted face of his mother's portrait through the curve in his brandy glass—that a chilling realization struck him.

The glass fell to the floor, shattering, as he jumped from the bench and ran to the attic.

Something was wrong. Terribly wrong. The longer Alexandra peered at the document the more she tried to apply logic to an ever-growing sense of dread, as she gripped the sheet music and hummed the first bar. Then a bit more, and as she turned the sheet over, the melody became more familiar. Frighteningly familiar.

"No, no… this can't be," Alexandra whispered in denial.

She heard Sebastian's footsteps running down the marble hall, then up the clunky attic stairwell. He clambered to the top and looked around, trying to find her.

Their eyes met.

A long, horrible silence followed as the implications played out upon both their faces.

"Just tell me…" Alexandra's voice trembled with fear. "God, please just tell me this isn't true?"

But she could see by the haunted terror in his eyes that it was.

"How… how… could you?" The words sounded vaguely distant, as if her voice no longer belonged to her. She glanced from Sebastian back to his music. No… not *Sebastian's* music. As if to make it real an elegant finger traced the fine scripted name below the title, *For Antonia—Concerto in B Minor*. The music created by Antonia's favored myth, the fabled legend of their link to Bach through Sebastian's great-great-great grandfather: One **Franco Ricci D'Antonio**, his composition sheet dated and signed, **1842**.

> *"The man that hath no music in himself,*
> *Nor is not moved with concord of sweet sounds,*
> *Is fit for treasons, stratagems, and spoils.*
> *The motions of his spirit are dull as night,*
> *And his affections dark as Erebus.*
> *Let no such man be trusted."*

William Shakespeare

As the plane flew into the blinding, puffy clouds, Alexandra wished she could go backwards in time. Wished that she would never have to possess the knowledge of his treason, or that she would, forever after, have to live with it in silence. It was one thing to know that Sebastian was never even close to the man she thought he was. Or that his existence fleshed out a unique slant on the term 'impostor.' What choked her with bitter resentment was the knowledge that for the past several years, she had unwittingly played accomplice to the single greatest myth perpetrated in classical music. Hell, of all the arts together. Could she even think of a greater betrayal to the act of creation than this hideous subterfuge?

A trembling nausea overcame her, followed by a seething resentment at her innocent complicity. The rancor she felt towards Sebastian and the entire situation couldn't be soothed or made to go away. She asked for another brandy as the plane flew high above it all, as far away as she could get. But every minute his deception resurfaced. She couldn't erase those last moments from her mind, and they slammed back at her, cloaked her until she felt suffocated.

Above the dim roar of the plane, she could hear the hurling accusations of rage and venom as she had screamed at him to leave the attic. She had been entirely unmoved by the pall of terror she saw in Sebastian's face before he left. Even the guilt and shame that poured off him, she soon realized, had less to do with his inexcusable behavior than the anguish of being found out.

She had sat up in the attic for an indeterminable time, going over the music. This couldn't be happening; it must be a dream. No, a nightmare. It simply couldn't be true. No one could get away with a masquerade like this. No one could possibly pull this off. And yet he had. Even those closest to him had no idea, had no thought of such duplicity. Although she now understood the echoes of skepticism from those who had marveled dubiously at his accomplishment: Max's cryptic suppositions, Chandra's ugly innuendo, even Conrad's ambiguous doublespeak. But then Conrad had never seen Sebastian for the man he was, so blinded by his loyalty to Antonia and the myth he had created of his childhood savior. She had been the only one who never questioned that Sebastian had created one of the most important pieces of music composed in this century. The only one... And she'd been so utterly wrong.

She had thrown what clothes she could find and the last of her belongings helter-skelter into her suitcases, with no thought as to where she was going. All she knew was that she couldn't stay there a moment longer. When she walked downstairs, she saw him sitting at the piano bench, slumped over the keys, smoking a cigarette.

She stood rigid with her suitcases, but he simply remained where he was.

"Sebastian!" Her voice was brittle. "Look at me."

She wouldn't move until his eyes, rimmed with the tears, turned to her own.

"I know what you're thinking—"

"No, you cannot possibly know what I'm thinking." Alexandra caught her breath. "It's too despicable what I'm thinking."

"Alex, you... please hear me out. At least give me that."

She considered a moment, then slowly set her suitcases down, trying to cease her fluttering heart, trying to quell the rage rising like magma.

He stood up with his infernal cigarette and walked to the fireplace, slouched in murky shadows. "You must understand... when I first found it, I... I was going to just leave it. You must believe that. Please believe that, Alex."

He turned to her, but Alexandra's stoic face revealed nothing.

"I... I was going to tell Connie, you know, that it had been true. All along, all those times Antonia had told that goddamn story." He choked out a grunt of hollow laughter. "I always thought mother had told her little tale so many times that she began believing it. The family legend, locked up in the attic. How could I know it was true? That my great-great-great grandfather wrote music because Bach's blood *did* flow through his veins."

"And you justified it—"

"Hold on." Sebastian held up a hand defensively. "It... it wasn't as easy as you may think. I had a helluva time with it, Alex. A helluva a time. Really if you think I just glibly..." The stream of his argument was shattered as Alexandra's eyes seared through him. "Look, this music belongs to the family, it comes from the D'Antonio line, albeit indirectly. And it *has* been a gift to the world—"

"Don't you dare spout your own press to me, Sebastian."

His gaze met hers, helpless. "I had to have a hand up, Alexandra. You know better than anyone, my gifts are... well... limited."

"You had the recording contract from the Ketterling. You could have made a name for yourself with that. I just don't understand." She could no longer hide the contempt from her voice. "With your charm, your stalwart handlers would have found a way to put a spin on you, one way or another. You could have made your grandfather's music famous just in the way you have, only given credit where credit was due. Performed the music as written by your grandfather: Franco Ricci D'Antonio."

"Yes, and how long do you think it would have been before the critics destroyed the messenger?"

"How do you live with yourself? How do you feel every time you sign an autograph?" She shook her head, barely able to think through all the ways in which he had bamboozled everyone. "How did you dare bow before the roar of the almighty applause, the charming Sebastian, the handsome Sebastian, the philandering *artiste*...the consummate Imposter."

Sebastian turned at this last barb, his face as bare as she had ever seen it.

"Alex, please..."

His eyes caught hers, weak and pleading.

"Alex..." Plaintive.

Alexandra wasn't sure what Sebastian was referring to when he suddenly choked out, "Don't... please don't tell him."

His desperation made her skin crawl.

"Please." Sebastian splayed his weakness before her. "I couldn't handle it. I just... I just couldn't deal with it. Seeing Conrad's shame."

He wept. Alexandra felt ill.

She picked up her suitcases.

"Alex," he choked, running to her, "just say we'll talk when you get back."

He waited with hope in his eyes but saw none in hers.

"I'm..." Alexandra cleared her throat, the words from her mouth, an icy declaration, "I'm done."

She waited for him to move.

"You know you always come back," he said desperately. "I mean, really, do you think you can just walk out the door? No looking back? Without a shred of regret?"

Alexandra stared at him a moment, glanced around the room, and considered the memories. "Yes, that about sums it up."

Alexandra's tour was far more successful than she could have anticipated. She jumped from Chicago, Seattle, Portland, and San Francisco to LA, all blurring together in frenetic concrete images. She stayed singularly focused, wondering, during flights or the nights alone in her hotel room, if she could attribute her persistently tight concentration to all the practice and work she had done with Max; or if thinking about the alternative—Sebastian and his terrible secret—was too loathsome to acknowledge.

She played as she had in the days of the contest, untouched, unsullied, spurred by the knowledge that Sebastian had molested her artistry, her generosity, and the very notion of loving someone. It brought a purity to her performances that critics and audiences alike remarked upon. Part of her felt it was the only penance she could offer. And another part of her had finally learned that the most important thing in her life was *her* music, and she needed to honor it as such. Every night as she sat before crowds of hundreds, she pledged fealty to her audiences as she put her hands to the keys.

It was during her performance in Boston of Prokofiev's vibrant and tempestuous *Third Concerto* that a man stood in the back and listened with his eyes closed, listened to Alexandra play with complete surrender. He thought how easy it would be to go backstage and ask for admittance. He wondered if she would allow him in, and if she did, if her acute sense of hurt, possibly shame, would make her as cold and unyielding as only Alexandra could be.

Another man crushed his cigarette on the sidewalk under his boot during a brief intermission below the marquis outside Symphony Hall where Alexandra was playing. He turned to make his way back in and glanced at the eyes in the photo. The photographer hadn't done Alexandra justice.

He returned to the concert, passed the usher, and stood at the back of the concert hall. He couldn't sit, so excited was he by Alexandra, and like the audience, he responded to the power of her performance. They listened as one organism, rapt and inspired. She was as talented as Max had boasted, though he sensed a bit of the vulnerability that Max had alluded to during their dinner the previous evening. There was no doubt about it; she bent more than a few of the technical rules.

He sniffed and nodded his head. She would be perfect.

When the audience roared their appreciation and stood in ovation, Max's colleague turned to leave. When he did, he saw the other man in the lobby, escaping before the rush, who looked a lot like Sebastian D'Antonio. But it couldn't be. No, the man was hunched over, unshaven and ratty. As the man's eyes darted past his own, he was even less certain, as he raised the collar of his raincoat and immediately escaped the thronging crowds exiting from the theatre.

Across the country in a faraway town, another pianist played with utter abandon as he performed in an isolated studio late into the night. A silent piano stood across from him, but he heard the other notes answer. He closed his eyes and could conjure her vision, and that was enough.

Karina walked in with a pot of coffee, a bit diffident now compared to weeks ago, when she felt compelled to bring food or drink to Conrad because he had been sitting at the old upright for hours. Here in Purcell's studio, she felt out of place, as if she moved the wrong way, she might break something. Before, she might have kissed Conrad's forehead or made a joke, told him something amusing that happened at work. She had loved seeing the stern concentration shift when he smiled, his grey-blue eyes so vividly alive. But Conrad was doing serious work now, and she hated to bother him. Every time she visited him here in this stark room, his face was bent downward in unwavering deliberation. Last night when she set the coffee down, she wasn't sure he was aware of her presence until she said, "That was beautiful, Conrad."

He stopped playing and looked at her, but through her. "Sometimes I wonder… You know there's this brilliant pianist, Glenn Gould—a true eccentric from Canada—said something the other day that struck me."

"What was that?"

"He suggests all performance lends itself to a sort of hedonism that becomes so extreme that it degrades public exhibition to bring out the worst of man."

"Conrad, I'm no genius, and I certainly don't understand a word you just said—"

"I'm sorry. Pompous asshole, eh?!

"No." She laughed then. "Sometimes I think people in your world say things for the shock of them."

Conrad laughed and nabbed a cigarette, offering one to Karina, who continued. "But if you're asking if it's okay for you to play your beautiful music so that people may enjoy it … I think such an experience brings out the best of man."

Conrad studied Karina. As usual, the pureness of her simple expression brought him back down to earth. Now that he was getting ready to present his music, he was having second thoughts. His world would change. Dramatically. Then just as suddenly he felt drawn back. He took Karina's hand, gave it a gentle squeeze, and returned to the piano.

She poured his coffee and tip-toed back out.

When Alexandra walked out of the airport at JFK, she was greeted by several fans, a flash bulb here and there, and several reporters hounding her about Sebastian and his "mysterious absence in the music scene." There, as a beacon of certainty, stood Max.

"What a pleasant surprise," she said, leaning in to hug him. He shielded her from the onslaught of paparazzi.

"No, it is I who have the surprise."

Max drove her back to his home where he had delicious sauce simmering on the stove and poured her a glass of wine. While she filled him in on the tour, he chopped away at vegetables.

"I had no idea you were so domestic, Max."

"It relaxes me," he said as he threw the last of the carrots into his sauce. He watched as Alexandra lit a cigarette. "Then it was good, *neh?*" he asked, but he alluded to more than the question.

"Yes, Max. It was good to get away from everything."

"So, have you spoken to him?"

She touched her braid a moment, then shook her head no.

"Then it is over? *Kaput?*"

"Yes."

"And you… your heart is better now from traveling, performing and—"

"I don't want to talk about it." Alexandra silenced him and then, to soften her words, put a hand to his arm. "I just don't want to think about it anymore. It's over. That's it. As you say, *Kaput.*"

She had, in fact, heard from him several times. He had left messages at hotels. Sent telegrams congratulating her, a letter explaining that he didn't want his life devoid of her. That he could accept their split, but he couldn't accept her complete exclusion from his life. He had signed it with, "You are truly, my best friend."

She hadn't responded to any of his overtures. She simply couldn't stand to face him. She could barely keep the information she had to herself, so burdensome and loathsome, lying in the pit of her stomach like a cold stone. She wanted desperately to unload it, but no matter how angry she was with him for his unforgivable lie, she wouldn't place him in the executioner's hands of the media.

"Eh? Alexandra?" Max was asking her something, "Merlot with dinner?"

"Oh, yes, please," she answered, then frowned. "So, Max, what's with you tonight? You look like the cat that swallowed the canary."

"Well…" Max fussed with his spectacles and Alexandra sighed impatiently at this singularly familiar gesture.

"Yes," Alexandra snapped, a bit forcefully, "What is it?"

"I have a wonderful opportunity for you, *Meine Kleine.* Please, after we eat, I shall tell you about it." He pulled out her chair and served her dinner with another glass of wine. After he had cleared their plates, he poured her a generous dose of heated Hennessy Cognac. "I've been keeping this for a special occasion." Max sighed, quite pleased with himself

She wrinkled her nose in gratitude, "That hits the spot!" then laughed. "Okay, Max, out with it already."

"There is a gentleman who had the pleasure of listening to your Prokofiev in Boston and was most taken with you. Most taken."

"That's sweet, Max, but certainly no need for celebration."

"Bah, sweet. He thinks you are quite impressive. 'Uncommonly exquisite' is how he phrased it to me."

"Did he come backstage? I don't recall—"

"No. He wasn't officially there on business. He had been passing through and we had dinner the night before your performance and I invited him to join me. *Acchhh, mein Liebling*. This could be just what you need. Such a challenge. Such an opportunity!" Max's eyes were lit with excitement. "This conductor has pulled together a forty-six-piece ensemble which will be arriving here in two weeks, and they would like for you to play piano for an exhibition concert they are having in May. It's extremely good exposure, and you will be playing with the crème de la crème. Where you belong!"

Alexandra considered for a moment. "Would that mean I would be touring right away again?"

Max stalled a moment. "Yes, after a couple of weeks of rehearsal, I'm afraid so."

"Good."

He hadn't expected that. "So. It's settled, ja? I shall make all the arrangements."

"Fine." Alexandra stood and kissed the old man on his forehead. "You're like a young boy. So excited for me to play with the gang. Thank you."

"No. Thank you."

Alexandra was ushered onto a stage with three pianos, and she couldn't help but think back to the day when she had met up with Sebastian, as she tried out the selections for the contest. She hadn't thought about him successfully for days and tried to quash this memory, too. She glanced around. She was quite early, although she could hear stagehands laughing in the back.

"Hello? Is anyone there?" She checked her watch, chose a piano and sat, took off her gloves, and began warming up. She started to play the sheet music propped upon the lid of one of the pianos.

The first notes were somewhat tentative and uncertain. There was an odd timing to the piece, but it was the rhythm that made it compelling. Then the melody, a sweeping introduction, vaguely reminiscent of Rachmaninoff, suddenly spun into an eccentric but pluckish counterpoint with a hint of nationalistic flavor to it, as if she were immersing herself in some faraway country. She immediately warmed to the arrangement. Max was right. This was her kind of music.

She slid into the piece, playing with more force. Soon she let herself fully embrace the unique melody, then heard the second piano begin to answer her. She was jolted by the familiar phrasing. A rush of goose bumps slivered up her arms, a split second of joy followed by a racking shudder of emotional upheaval. She knew it couldn't be, yet no one else played tempo with those distinct accents. She glanced up.

Conrad.

His eyes gave away nothing, his face stoically expressionless. A minor tremor at her upper lip belied the train wreck inside. A third piano joined in then, played by a handsome European she recognized as Phillip Purcell, the infamous British conductor. He beamed at her and indicated for her to continue. Her hands touched keys, but she wasn't conscious of the notes they played, only of the thudding in her heart, the buzzing in her ears, the dragging weight in her stomach that threatened queasiness. Finally, Purcell stopped playing and stood.

"Well then. Here is the august Alexandra Von Triessen." He presented himself with his usual *élan*.

Alexandra's hands trembled as he approached her. Still flustered, she did her best to cover it with her familiar detachment.

"You, my dear, are perfect. As I knew you'd be." He extended his hand. "I am Phillip Purcell, conductor, and to my right is Conrad D'Antonio."

"Yes." Alexandra stood and shook Purcell's hand as Conrad approached. He, too, offered his hand, but she moved to pick up her purse as a defense.

"My lord, do you know one another?" It was obvious they did. "Oh my, of course, of course. You're with the brother, right? Sebastian."

A jolt tore through Alexandra at the mention of Sebastian's name, but she could only absorb one shock at a time. What was *he* doing here? She thought he was in New Mexico.

"Alexandra." Conrad's voice was stilted, trying to overcome his discomfort, and she knew then he hadn't engineered this bizarre coincidence.

"Conrad." Her voice barely registered.

"You two take a moment. I'm going to call in the strings and see what we have here." Purcell exited stage left.

They looked at each other for a long moment.

"I'm sorry. I had absolutely no idea you were going to be here," Conrad said. "This must be Max's handiwork."

"Yes, it is. Do you want—"

"Look, you don't have to stay—"

A long awkward silence, and then Alexandra began gathering her things. "I'll go then—"

"No…don't."

She could barely control her breathing.

"Please." Conrad could smell her hair, her perfume. "Please stay."

"Let's run through it, and then I'll decide." Alexandra's voice was clipped and businesslike.

Conrad returned to his piano. Alexandra furtively surveyed the hall filling with musicians, who began taking their seats, opening their instruments, and putting up their sheet music. She tried to concentrate through the sounds of warming up, felt the plaintive discord of violins and violas, the rumble of bass, and wheezing from the wind instruments until—

Tap. Tap. Tap.

Purcell tipped his baton at the edge of the podium and brought everyone to attention. "Okay, then. Good morning lovely humans." He took a subtle bow. "Everyone, this is Alexandra Von Triessen, celebrated Ketterling winner, who will play second piano. Are we set? Let's take it slowly so Alexandra can find her footing."

He made a final tap for silence, then raised his baton. A long moment passed as Alexandra studied the music, and then Conrad said softly, "Your cue..."

Strings slashed the silence with three swooping exclamation points that opened a vital and energetic introduction. A series of evocative chromatic notes climbed high into the sky, a bird soaring off Conrad's fingertips. Alexandra's heart raced; adrenaline pumped through her veins as she answered with a swell of rolling scales that countered the original melody. She was nervous and scattered and it showed. Auditioning by nature was the most conspicuous act, and all she craved was isolation to steady her shattered nerves. Purcell frowned as her performance grew weaker.

"Sorry," Conrad yelled, covering for her. The orchestra jumbled to a stop. "Can we take a few minutes?"

"I'm fine," Alexandra said. "If you don't mind, from the top."

Alexandra could see Purcell's hesitation and concern as he regrouped the orchestra, and they began again. She shut her eyes, forcibly calmed the maelstrom within her, and focused on the music. She knew enough of this piece from when they played it in the library, so she began to improvise. He played to her. She answered and he responded. Soon it was difficult to tell where one started and the other left off.

"Yes!" Purcell roared enthusiastically. "Bravo!"

They continued for some hours, adjusting tempo, tweaking this measure and that, rearranging accompaniment. At the end of the session, the small string orchestra applauded the two pianists with their bows tapping in unison.

"Alexandra, I think they like you."

"The music is... it's extraordinary."

"Isn't it?" Purcell winked at her and put his hand on Conrad's shoulder. "My genius here is as modest as the day is long, which makes me think he hails from somewhere near Alaska."

"Which season?"

"Touché." Purcell added impressed.

Max entered from the back of the concert hall, and Conrad joined Purcell.

Alexandra thrust the sheet music at him. "Jesus, Max!"

Max's sheepish grin couldn't cover his enthusiasm. "Please, don't be angry. I thought it would be best if you didn't know."

"Talk about gas-lighting."

"I only resorted to such tactics because, had you known, you wouldn't have come. And that wouldn't have served you, Alexandra. You would have robbed yourself of the most marvelous opportunity."

"And what might that be?" she asked, only thinking of how awkward it felt to be around Conrad, how terrifying and thrilling in the same breath.

"I couldn't help myself. When I had dinner with Purcell, he told me all about his new ensemble. When he said he was working with Conrad, why... I was *verklempt*! We both know his compositions are thrilling. Purcell told me himself, he could barely sleep from the excitement. 'But we have to find the right person to accompany him,' he said to me over dinner. 'Two pianos, they fight, they make love, they lift each other up.' How could I not respond and tell him, 'I have the perfect candidate!' Purcell stopped me and said, 'You can't possibly be thinking of his brother.' 'No,' I answered, 'I'm talking about someone who performs as well as Conrad composes.'"

"Max." Alexandra shook her head, bewildered, pained, yet, despite herself, flattered and even, yes, more than a little intrigued.

Now Max lifted his hands in surrender. "Did I do so wrong?"

"I don't know." Alexandra tugged on her braid and stared at the empty theater.

"But tell me, Alexandra, truthfully, how did you like the music?"

Alexandra snorted slightly and then stopped to consider his words. Conrad's music had changed. Or maybe she was responding to it differently, but she found it more engaging, it resonated more deeply within her. How could she be mad at Max for introducing her to the most challenging opportunity she had ever had, even if it meant working with Conrad?

"What am I to do with you?" she asked as she took his arm, and they exited the theatre together. They walked on for several paces in silence.

The brisk air felt good on her face. "Do you think this is a good idea?" Her voice cracked with the question.

"Good? I don't know from good. I think it's an exceptional opportunity for you to perform with world-class musicians, and to finally play music that best suits your style and strengths."

"But—"

"Stay focused. Like you did after Sebastian. *Die Musik kommt zuerst!* The music—always first, *ja?*"

A light rain began to fall suddenly, cleansing herself of Sebastian's betrayal. It was true, that the music spoke to her in a way no one's ever had. Just like the man who wrote it. "Thank you."

Max grinned with self-satisfaction. It had all worked out quite nicely, telling Purcell first about Conrad and where to find him. Then Alexandra. Yes, his plan had worked out quite nicely, *Ja, ausgezeichnet!*

"Music is the greatest of the arts; it is also the one which, in the present state of civilization, brings the greatest misery to those who understand it in all its facets and who respect and honor it."

Hector Berlioz (1803—69)

Several days later, Alexandra signed a contract as the symphony's second piano for the duration of the eastern seaboard tour, with additional engagements in London and Paris. She spent most of her hours practicing with Conrad at the rehearsal hall where their discussions were limited to the technical and mechanical considerations of the material in front of them. She focused, as Max had suggested, on the task at hand. But she struggled to play the new piece introduced that morning, feeling awkward and tense, her distance increasingly palpable. One afternoon, Purcell finally stopped them.

"I have heard you play enough, Alexandra, not to be taken in by your utterly charming indifference," Purcell remarked, his eyes narrowing. "You are a woman who feels much and feels deeply. But the woman who is playing right now has no heart. You must get whatever is in your way the hell out of here!" She blanched at Purcell's assessment of her. Did she appear that untouched?

"Can you give us a moment?" Conrad asked, leading Alexandra out to the bright sunlight beyond the stage door. They stood silently for a moment and then he lit a cigarette and handed it to her.

A cynical curve of her lips. "Ever chivalrous."

Conrad lit one for himself. "And I'm glad you haven't lost your sense of humor."

"I'm surprised I have one, given how 'heartless' I am," she replied, her voice brittle.

"He didn't mean that," Conrad said softly. "It's just… you're holding back and it's a little flat."

She swallowed, frowned, and felt the swift stab of rejection catch in her throat.

Conrad sighed, frustration painting his face. "I'm sorry, Alexandra. We really should have talked before now."

She didn't respond. They stood awkwardly for a long moment.

Finally, he ventured, "How... how have you been?"

She looked at him, her face inscrutable. "Just dandy."

"Max filled me in... about you and Sebastian—"

"Don't!" she cut in, her tone steely.

"Okay."

Alexandra fiddled with her cigarette. Now that his name had been spoken, she had to know. "Have you seen him?"

"We had dinner last night."

She nodded, her expression unreadable.

"He's a wreck, Alexandra."

"I don't want to talk about him." She waited, fearing he had discovered his brother's secrets.

He took a long drag off his cigarette. "What happened?"

"Conrad." Her temper flared, a bitter laugh escaping her. "I think you, of all people, know that Sebastian and I had no business being together."

"But you stayed." Conrad shrugged. "And I thought that, well, that you'd patched it back together—"

"And how could I possibly have gotten over you?" Alexandra was furious. How dare he. He had no idea what she had endured these past years. No idea about the self-loathing she had suffered only to discover it had all been a pointless, purposeless exercise.

"I didn't say that—"

"Conrad, let's get one thing straight. I left what happened behind us the day you walked away. And things between your brother and I are over. For me to continue here will mean we will not engage in conversation unless it relates to the music. Sebastian's off-limits. Understood?"

She tamped out her cigarette.

His jaw tightened. "I know how difficult this is, Alex."

"No." Her eyes narrowed, and the words slipped out raw and unguarded. "You have no idea."

He moved to touch her forearm, but she brushed by him.

"Yes, I think I have some idea. And I don't want there to be any hard feelings—"

"Hard feelings," she repeated dumbly. His calm was infuriating.

"Tell me, what I can do to make it easier for you?" he asked.

"I'll tell you what you can do," she spat, "You can stop being so god-damn sanctimonious. You can stop expecting me to have no... no feelings, Conrad. Even if they're harsh ones. You just have to live with it."

"Alex—"

"You have this neat little habit of erasing things, pretending they never happened. How polite. How absolutely calm and functional you are." Her voice broke, but her gaze remained fierce.

His demeanor gave away nothing. She couldn't stand it any longer. She didn't think, she merely saw the exit stairs and ran. When she got to the bottom, she caught her breath and massaged the skin at her temples, willing the threat of a headache away, and started walking. Walking. Escaping.

It was hot outside for early spring. Good thing, Alexandra thought, as she had stormed out without her coat. She wandered aimlessly for some moments and then stopped. This was ridiculous. She wasn't going to let him and his nonchalance, his utter indifference, get the better of her. She was going to do this. She was going to play the piano, his goddamn music, and make this work. But first, she was going to take a long walk and steady herself. She wouldn't let them see her vulnerability again.

It was late in the evening when she returned to the rehearsal hall. She was worn out, more from her overactive interior dialogues than from walking all over the city. When she entered, most of the stage lights had been turned down. It was dark and silent, her heels clicking loudly as she gathered her coat, purse, and sheet music.

She felt him behind her and when she turned, he stood, as in a movie, blown out by the glare of a remaining footlight.

"I waited for you," he said.

"That wasn't necessary."

"Yes. It was." Conrad's voice was tightly reigned, and she could see by the tremor of his jaw that he was upset. "You think this doesn't affect me? You think this isn't gnawing me from the inside out? Think again, Alexandra." A twitch at his cheek danced out of control. "You should know better than anyone about masked feelings."

Alexandra was taken aback by his outburst.

"The difference between the two of us is that I have chosen to use it," Conrad continued more calmly. "I've chosen not to let it get the best of me."

"Is that how it's done?"

"If you'd give it half a chance, it might help." He regained control.

"And what exactly should I be using?" Alexandra's voice was laced with sarcasm. "Pain? Humiliation? Or just plain anger?"

"Why don't you go for broke and use the whole goddamn lot?"

He began to walk from her, and she knew she had gotten to him. She gritted her teeth. It felt good but was immediately followed by a sinking ache in her chest. Hurting him, hurt her.

"Don't go."

He stopped, squared his shoulders.

They both waited a long moment. He turned around.

"Alex—"

"No. Stop. Please."

"Alex—"

"You couldn't possibly have expected that we would walk back into each other's life without a beat," she said. "That everything was going to just settle in, like we'd never known each other, like we'd never touched each other's lives. Or that because you have the power to channel your feelings to some lofty plane none of the rest of us get to occupy, that it's going to be easy. I'm trying my best to put you, your brother, our whole damn history behind me, and just stay in the now and focus on the music. But I'm human." She paused. "How about you?"

He smiled through a chink in his armor. "Yes, I discovered that human part some time ago."

Conrad walked back to her, and they stood facing one another.

"There's a big deep gaping hole right in the center of me, Alexandra, and there's only one way I know how to heal it. When we're playing, it's just us. Nothing else exists but us and the music." He took her hand, and this time when he touched her, she couldn't be angry. He tugged her gently toward him, until they were inches from one another, his eyes searching for the truth that lay between them. "It's just us."

Alexandra played with everything she had. And she did use it all. She had an endless well to tap into, and as rehearsals moved forward, she constantly brought fresh interpretations to the music, which challenged Conrad and, in turn, brought out the best in the orchestra.

During the preview performance for the press, a stunned audience of reporters and critics traveled an infinite spectrum via the dueling pianos; at once exhilarated by their exquisite synergy and deeply moved by their seamless union. Purcell created new superlatives, and even Max found himself stumbling for the right praise. The dressing rooms again overflowed with those who wanted to touch talent, to be in the presence of greatness, much as it had been for Sebastian only a few years ago.

Max entered with several friends, and when he came to Conrad, he enveloped him in a huge bear hug. Alexandra drifted onto the sidelines, apprehensively losing herself in these people. She wasn't particularly thrilled to find herself in that place again; where everyone adored you and nothing was real, and the music was merely a backdrop to fame.

Max snuck behind her, grabbed her hand, and blustered through the crowd to a clearing. He gently touched her forearm. *"Ja, Alexandra, mein brillianter Stern."* Then Conrad joined them, he looked at the two of them with great pride. "You two were...*Ausgezeichnet!*" He continued to press Conrad ever closer to Alexandra, who was attempting to keep her distance.

"Alexandra. It was..." Conrad's eyes shone in appreciation.

"Yes, it was." Alexandra agreed. "And I'm not going to heap on any more praise."

She glowed in the aftermath of their achievement.

"You look... you look wonderful, Alexandra," he whispered.

"I feel pretty wonderful." She did, until he shifted his gaze to a woman attired in a beautiful red dress, her black hair pulled up into a French Twist.

"It was beautiful." Karina kissed him sweetly on the cheek.

"Karina, there's someone I'd like you to meet. Alexandra Von Triessen. Karina Grady."

Alexandra could see the older woman assessing her with the camouflaged scrutiny that was only possible amongst women. Karina extended a hand with controlled nonchalance.

"Phillip's telling us we're all to go to Café des Artistes," Karina said a bit uncertainly, and Alexandra noticed a trace of her Hispanic accent. Purcell's girlfriend? Alexandra was certain he was gay. And then she saw her familiarity with Conrad, the adoration in her gaze.

"Then we'll go." Conrad placed his hand on the small of Karina's back.

So, this was the woman that Max had spoken of. This was the woman who had helped Conrad through his accident. His lover. Bile stung the back of her throat.

"Are you coming?" he asked Alexandra.

She released a long sigh. "No. I'm rather tired. I think I'll head home."

Conrad hesitated for a moment before he turned and escorted Karina out the stage door, and the room quickly emptied of the last few musicians still kissing one another's cheeks in congratulations.

Max joined Alexandra, patting her hand. "Where to?" he asked, as they walked into the cold night air.

"Somewhere I can get drunk."

> *"Art is uncompromising, and life is full of compromises."*
>
> Günther Grass

Sebastian lay on the couch, a music magazine with Conrad's face blazoned on the cover crumpled on his chest. Through the haze of smoke winding its way through the room littered with ashtrays, glasses, and bottles, Sebastian was reasonably certain three or four people were still milling about from an all-night party.

A young man, who was a great admirer of Sebastian's passed by and grabbed the magazine.

"Hey... hey, 'Bastian, old man, isn't this your brother?"

Sebastian whipped the magazine from him. "Party's over, *old man.*" He stood up and began swiping the air at the remaining stragglers. "Party's over. Everyone out. I must... I must work in a few hours and it's time for you all to leave."

As the last of them left, Sebastian shut the door and stumbled back to the couch. He picked up the magazine and before hurling it across the room, the last thing he saw was the caption below Conrad's face. "First Coming for Second D'Antonio Brother."

Sebastian shuddered with the rage he had tried to quash months ago when he first caught sight of his own photo, next to Conrad, in an obscure music magazine with a caption underneath taunting him: "Chip off Old Block, Causes New Sensation." The first tickling of envy began to rankle then and grew even more whenever he saw anything related to this "new sensation." He hated his lack of generosity as he skimmed the article "Conrad hails from the illustrious D'Antonio family, for Sebastian has a brother, and this reviewer would be hard-pressed to say the younger brother isn't every bit as talented. If not more!"

After that, it was quite beyond his control, creeping up on and all around him; an all-consuming jealousy as he compulsively amassed news clippings following his brother's career path. He tracked Conrad's tick of fame, like an unknown penny stock, blaze into a rising star. First the small venue in Santa Fe, where he had caused quite a stir on the local music scene, then on to San Francisco and Chicago. And finally, right in his own backyard: New York.

Then Alexandra joined his company. The two of them. The moment after he saw the headline "D'Antonio Brother Nabs Von Triessen for Tour" his invidious rage broiled within. He could only control his outrage by chugging half a bottle of scotch. Seething anger turned to sloppy tears. How could he? How dare he? And her?

Two nights ago, he had received a phone call from a reporter who asked if he was "speaking to Mr. Sebastian D'Antonio?"

"Yes?"

"Great! This is James Walberg of the Canadian Music Review. I was wondering if I might ask you a few questions for an article I'm writing."

Sebastian sipped his drink. "Of course. Whatever I can do to help."

"I had the great fortune to catch your brother, Conrad, in Chicago a few weeks ago, and I've been trying like hell to track him down. Do you know how I can reach him?"

Sebastian didn't respond. He slammed the phone down and drank until the stranglehold of oblivion began to loosen from his throat. Now he was hazing in and out of consciousness and realized he wasn't alone. "God damnit, I said everyone out."

As Sebastian struggled to get up, he saw the hand that picked up a fallen bottle, the hand he knew so well, and Conrad came into focus as he gently sat Sebastian upright. When he understood it wasn't a dream, that Conrad was there, he felt a surge of emotions all battling against one another. "Connie… Connie. It's you." Tears fell freely and he grasped Conrad in his arms.

"I'm here. It's okay." Conrad began to gently lift Sebastian to his feet. "Hold on there… I've got you." He stood Sebastian up, and the two brothers clasped each other in an unyielding embrace.

Conrad picked up after the debauchery from the night before, then sat poolside while he waited for Sebastian to sleep it off. He finally wandered out several hours later, barely clad in a robe, shading his eyes from the bright sunlight.

Sebastian's hands trembled as Conrad offered a cigarette.

As Sebastian inhaled, he studied his brother. He felt split in half, both sides struggling for dominance. In his heart, he wished good things for Conrad. Yes, he wanted this for him, wanted it for him completely. He just wanted it more for himself.

"I guess congratulations are in order." Sebastian exhaled.

Conrad looked at him but didn't say a word.

"Seriously, Connie. I mean it. I'm happy for you." Sebastian's words were genuine. "Hey, don't I know better than anyone how incredible it is to be on top of the world?"

Conrad watched him as he unsteadily reached for his coffee.

"Take it while you can, old boy. God knows all the tripe is true. One day you're up and the next you're down, and no one wants to even have a bite of dinner with you. Pariah."

"Why don't you try something else?"

"What do you mean 'try something else'? Like what?"

"I mean try writing something new—"

"Something new?" Sebastian spat. "That's rich. I've tried, Connie. For the past year, I've tried to write something. Write anything. It's all such dreadful rubbish, so I finally gave up." He flicked the ash from his cigarette. "Guess I'm a one-trick-pony."

"Then maybe a new track?"

Sebastian shook his head.

"You need help, Sebastian."

"Oh, and are you offering the little people a job?" Sebastian smirked.

"I am." Conrad nodded.

"Yeah." Sebastian inhaled deeply. "What could you possibly offer me?"

"I'd like you to manage my career."

"What?"

"I'm no good at it. Furthermore, I don't want to be. You, on the other hand, are quite brilliant at it."

Sebastian scrutinized his brother closely in mock disbelief. "Have you gone mad? What about my music?"

"What about it?" There was an edge to Conrad's voice, almost bitter. Sebastian's eyes darted to his brother, suddenly wondering if Alexandra had said something to him. No. She had promised and if she had, he certainly wouldn't be sitting here offering him a job.

The uncomfortable thought of Conrad and Alexandra together kick-started his hangover, causing the muscles in his stomach to tense, the bile to swell in his throat.

"Good God," Sebastian grunted disapprovingly. "Don't you remember our promise to Antonia? Didn't we give her our word?"

"Sebastian. You're in trouble. I want to help."

"Look I don't need your charity, and I certainly don't need to be around you and ..."

"I'm sure she wants what's best for you."

"Have you asked her that?"

"She has no idea I'm talking to you."

"Best let her in on this, Conrad. I don't think Alexandra cares for us manipulating her world anymore."

"Stop it, Sebastian!" Conrad's anger finally showed. "I'm trying to help you and you're acting like a perfect idiot."

"You want to help me?" Sebastian's laughter was hollow. "My kid brother, who I had to rescue from one eccentricity after another? Whose hand I had to hold through school because you were too shy and queer for people to understand you? And then when I bent over backward to get you into recording at the studio—you just walked out. Not a word of gratitude, or explanation, for that matter. Just up and disappeared when I needed you. Who in the hell do you think you are?" Sebastian sneered.

Conrad waited, watching his brother pace.

"Tastes sweet doesn't it, Con? Success. I told you it makes you feel powerful. Magnanimous. But I don't need your help. And you don't have to settle the score," he continued glibly, "I saved your sorry little life because that's what the D'Antonio's do. They lift people up, make them better than they are."

Conrad glared at him. Sebastian thought he had finally gotten him to lose his temper. To hurt him. But as much as this was the desired impact of his words, now he couldn't bear that he had said them. "Connie... come on, I... you know I didn't mean that." Sebastian's hands trembled as he lifted his cigarette to his mouth, then said under his breath, "It's just that... it's all coming down around me..."

Conrad stood. "If you change your mind, let me know."

"Jesus, Connie. You know I didn't mean it."

"You can reach me through Purcell's exchange."

"You know, you've got some unmitigated balls, coming here like this—"

"Goodbye, Sebastian."

"—unfucking believable, really, Connie." Sebastian's anger flared and he let it loose. "Considering what you've taken from me."

Conrad stopped. "She was never yours to begin with."

"Fuck you, Conrad."

Conrad merely looked at him, then walked away.

"Fuck you!"

Conrad retreated from the pool to a path through Antonia's wildly overgrown gardens.

"You can fucking go to hell!" Sebastian screamed. And then his fury spread, unrestrained, fueled by conjuring images of them. Alexandra's smooth clear body, spread apart for Conrad's taking. Together. He knew they were fucking. He could feel it in his bones.

♪

Two weeks later. Karina brought the morning papers to Conrad at the rehearsal hall. She walked up behind him and propped the paper at the perfect viewing angle so Conrad would see the two photos facing one another; one of Sebastian and Alexandra from a concert several years earlier, next to one of the most recently taken of Conrad with Alexandra. A flurry of innuendo and side-bar articles littered the music sections every time either Conrad or Alexandra was mentioned, implications that the "beautiful but somber pianist" who had always been at Sebastian's side was now playing with the other D'Antonio, the one noted for his new and innovative music. One article sniped, "It's the old spin on Apollo and Dionysus, but this time, the opposing forces aren't gods—they're two brothers, divided by the magnetic pull of the captivating Alexandra Von Triessen." The paper Karina set before him read, "Perhaps Miss Von Triessen holds a particular softness for the D'Antonio strain, both virtuoso talents who make her gifts shine *doubly* brighter. No matter. We remain her eager benefactors."

Conrad stopped playing. "Yes?"

"Are you ready, um, ready for tonight?" Karina nervously swept fingers through her hair while glancing at the paper.

He glanced up at her. "Karina, don't pay attention to this drivel." He tossed the article into the waste bin but could tell she wasn't satisfied.

"When do you leave for England?"

"I'm not sure," Conrad responded steadily. "I think we're booked for next month, after the Carnegie run."

"Look... I... you don't owe me anything, you know?"

Conrad got up from the bench and grasped the hand messing with her hair.

"Please don't let those articles rattle you. They feed off innuendo. They wouldn't know the truth if it smacked them in the head." He kissed her cheek.

Karina touched his face. "You know I have no business in this world."

"Karina, stop." He gently took her by the arm and led her away from the piano. "Come with me. Come with me to London."

"I don't know. Truthfully, Conrad, I don't even understand half of what you say. Most of what you and Phillip talk about sounds like a French menu to me."

"Is it so important that you understand it?" he asked tenderly.

"No. But darlin', what am I supposed to do? Get my hair and nails done with the girls? They're all half my age. I just don't belong on this side of the coin."

"It's never been an issue for me."

"But it is for me," Karina said sadly.

"Look, if you get homesick, come back. But at least try it. I'd love for you to see London. Maybe we can take off for Paris over a weekend."

"Only if you really want me there, Conrad. I don't want to be in the way."

"Nonsense." Conrad kissed her gently. "Now doesn't that feel like I want you there?"

Karina watched him as he returned to the piano. Within moments he evaporated into the place she couldn't begin to fathom. The place he shared with Alexandra. She left feeling just as unsettled as when she had come in.

As the preview performance had predicted, Carnegie Hall was a huge success. Audiences were overwhelmed by their rapport. Critics, fans, and musicologists had never seen any two pianists move quite as smoothly, with such empathic awareness, as though they were a single entity. The concert was booked for a further three weeks to sold-out crowds, clamoring ovations, and never less than three curtain calls. The result was even more than Purcell could have hoped for.

On the night of the final Carnegie performance, Purcell booked a back room at Le Cirque and invited the entire crew to celebrate before the London engagement.

A large table filled with Purcell and company, Conrad and Karina at one end, Alexandra, Max and Chandra at the other. Chandra took her aside, embraced her warmly, and whispered, "I am so proud of you."

The electric atmosphere devoted to the rarely accomplished permeated the room. Even Alexandra and Karina had exchanged cordial pleasantries at the start of the evening.

"You were lovely," Karina had said.

Alexandra took her hand and squeezed it. "Thank you. Thank you for everything."

Purcell stood and tapped his wine glass with a fork. "Here's to our brilliant composer."

Everyone cheered.

"And his beautiful and talented accompanist!" More cheers.

Purcell downed his glass, then became serious. "It isn't just because I had shivers galloping up and down my spine all night," Purcell insisted. "I have never seen two people play with more respect for their composition or rapport with one another. A remarkable achievement that requires four hands, yet only one heartbeat."

Karina's eyes darted to Conrad, who nodded graciously but with scant emotion. Alexandra smiled weakly.

"And here's to London!" Purcell cheered.

More praise and acclamation. Alexandra stood at this point, among many protests. "I need to get home. Finish packing."

She hugged Max and waved to the rest.

As Alexandra walked up the sidewalk to her brownstone flat she sensed, before she saw, the shadow of a man's figure nestled against the shrubbery. Startled, she began to prepare herself for the worst when Sebastian walked into the light. She hadn't seen him in over a year but, of course, his telegrams and letters, although having tapered off, still arrived with unwelcome regularity.

Even with the signs of his slide into self-destruction, Alexandra couldn't deny that Sebastian was still quite handsome, his thick brown hair now peppered with just the faintest traces of silver.

"Sebastian."

She opened the door and gestured him forward, plagued by the memories of who this man had been to her, how much she had loved and needed him. A man for whom she had been willing to completely abdicate herself.

"Would you like a drink?" She pointed to the bar. "Please help yourself. I've got to finish packing."

She heard him fix a drink as she moved into the bedroom and then felt him enter the room, leaning against the doorjamb as he watched her gather her clothes.

"You were marvelous tonight."

A slight turn of her head indicated her surprise.

"Both of you."

Alexandra pulled out a suitcase and laid it on the bed.

"Quite sensational the way you feed off one another. Or as the *Times* put it, An 'Extraordinary synthesis of talent.'"

"You could have said all that in one of your telegrams." Alexandra walked to a dresser and pulled out shirts, slacks.

"I wanted to see you in person."

"Why is that?" She carefully folded her garments. "I've told you—"

"It's not about that."

Because she continued with her chore, quite untouched by him, he moved closer, took a shirt from her, and held both of her hands in his.

"Please, I need you to look at me as we talk."

"But *we're* not talking, Sebastian. You are."

"Then listen to me, Alex." Sebastian's voice caught and she looked into his faded blue eyes, those eyes she had once wept at the beauty of. "I need to ask you something."

A momentary panic, a tensing of muscles, made her want to pull away.
"I want... I want you..."

He leaned to her then. Paralyzed she allowed his full beautiful lips to touch hers, as if having done it for so long, she had no other option but to comply. But the moment his tongue, sour with the taste of tobacco and whiskey, touched her own, she pushed him away.

"Sebastian—don't."

"Damn it, Alexandra. Don't be like that."

She didn't mean to eviscerate him, but she simply couldn't fathom what he was asking.

"Please, Alexandra. Don't just toss this aside without giving us even a moment's consideration—"

"You can't be serious."

"Look at us, Alex. We belong together. I took you with me when I was on top. Now we should be back together. Now that you're on top."

"Seriously cannot talk about this with you."

"Okay, you want me to say it? I'll say it. Yes, I took my grandfather's music. No, it wasn't the most noble move on earth. Okay? I confess, but Alexandra —" he grasped her hand "—it belongs to me. Me. It's mine by inheritance."

"And just how many other concerti do you have stockpiled in the attic? Or weren't there enough to sustain a career?"

He looked away as he took a deep breath. "I know, I know. I deserved that. I've told you I'm sorry. But don't you see?" His eyes were filled with pain and anguish, intensified by the burden of his inescapable sins. "I'm not that kind of performer. I'm... I'm like you. I play other people's music. We don't create. We present. Don't you remember? We're impostors."

Alexandra's eyes softened in the face of the shameful co-conspiracy. "Yes. We were impostors, weren't we? Pretending. Masquerading. That you were a gifted and brilliant artist, and I was the woman who would forsake my music for your needs. Quite a pair, weren't we?"

Sebastian read this as acquiescence, grabbed her by the shoulders, and tried to kiss her again, but this time Alexandra's lips were unyielding, her body intractable. He held her away and looked for some sign of reprieve in her unforgiving eyes.

"We're the same, you and me. We don't belong with the Conrads and Maxes and their patronizing idealism. We're like my mother, who never had any talent of her own, so she made herself out of nothing... out of stories, and legend, and myth... but we're what the people want. They don't want the truth: Acne-scarred savants who bathe but every three days. *We* are what they want to believe. *We* are what makes music accessible to the masses. And that is what my mother wanted us to give, Connie and I."

"Then you've fulfilled your destiny."

"But we're the same—"

"No. Sebastian. I used to be like you, throwing away what gifts I had because I didn't know how to use them."

"And I suppose you've had a spiritual epiphany—"

"Nothing so cinematic, I'm afraid. Merely a case of missing identity. Lost purpose. But I found it, Sebastian. Do you have any idea what that means? To have a purpose beyond your own selfish needs? To know that your function is merely to be an instrument, and serve nothing but the music? How could you know? You're nothing but a leech. You use people, you suck people dry for your own twisted needs. Just like you used me. You sucked me dry with your need—"

"And you don't think Conrad's using you?"

"No!" she hurled back. "I'm using *him. His* music. I'm using it to stay alive."

Sebastian felt kicked in the gut, sickened by the inevitable.

"You're... you're still in love with him."

Alexandra's eyes bore into his own, confirming his worst suspicions, and she finally stated what had never been voiced. "I've never *stopped* loving him. Not for one minute."

"I knew it." Sebastian deflated. "I knew it all along," he repeated dumbly, the charm and arrogance gouged out of him. He stood motionless. He had lost.

He began moving slowly to the door as if he no longer had sight, then he turned, his voice pleading, breaking. "Alexandra?"

She hesitated, moved as always by his vulnerability, knowing that she was the only one with whom he could be entirely honest. She walked over to him.

"There's only one way, Sebastian." She placed a cool palm on his cheek. "You've got to make it clean."

He shuddered, choking out tears he couldn't cry.

"Please. Sebastian. Make yourself clean." She kissed his forehead and gently pushed him out the door.

"It is cruel, you know, that music should be so beautiful.
It has the beauty of loneliness & of pain:
of strength & freedom. The beauty of disappointment &
never-satisfied love."

Benjamin Britten

When they arrived in London they were driven by limo to the Beaufort, where Purcell had arranged rooms. On their drive from Heathrow, Conrad pointed out famed tourist spots he had visited, just after he had parted company with Lars. Karina's awe pleased him; she was like a child finding surprises at every turn. As he watched her soak in this new culture, he only wished she'd had more influence in her life, that she'd had the gift of travel, because Karina's mind was fine and alert, and she was one of the wisest people he knew. It gave him a sense of satisfaction that he could enrich her world with this experience. Yet, something continued to nag at him.

At the front desk, Conrad checked his messages but didn't find what he was looking for. "Has everyone from the Purcell party checked in?" he asked.

As the clerk studied the register, Karina watched Conrad carefully.

"Yes...oh, forgive me. No. Miss Von Triessen is not here yet."

Conrad thanked him and took their key.

Later, he took Karina for a stroll through Covent Gardens and then to a pub, where they dined on bangers and mash, washed down with rich, dark ale. After dinner they cabbed through different areas of town, Conrad again idly pointing out areas of interest until they stopped at Blackfriar's Bridge and walked along the Thames. But all during this precious time she was finally able to spend with him, time where he wasn't at the piano or on the phone to Purcell, he kept glancing at his watch, scratching the edge of his jaw, grinding his cigarette into the ground, agitated and preoccupied.

"Conrad, what is it?" she finally asked.

"What is what?" He glanced at her sharply.

"What's wrong?"

"Nothing. Why do you ask?" Conrad put his arm around her as they continued to walk.

She let it drop, unwilling to draw him into a conversation she wasn't ready to have.

As soon as they were back at the hotel room, though, Conrad wandered restlessly, smoking one cigarette after another while he flipped through magazines, studied his music, and stood by the large window that overlooked the disappearing lights in the fogged cityscape. Intermittently he walked to the phone. "Yes, any word from Miss Von Triessen?" His fingers beat a quick rhythm against the wall while he waited. "Yes, please call when she checks in."

Karina cocked her head, chewed at her bottom lip and when she could stand his listless apprehension no longer, she asked softly, "Why are you so damned concerned with where Alexandra is?"

"She was supposed to have arrived hours ago. I'm..."

"Worried?" Karina asked. "You haven't thought of anything else since we arrived."

He grabbed his music but didn't answer her. "Conrad, I've never asked you for anything, have I?"

He shook his head.

"You're not the kind of guy you ask a lot of pesky questions. I knew that getting in. But I've just left my home and everything I know. I need to know if I've made a big mistake." He cocked his head, clearly not following her lead. "Should I be headin' back?"

"Karina." Conrad shook his head. "Don't be ridiculous."

"I'd appreciate a little honesty here."

"I've never been anything but." Conrad held her glance. "Why don't you tell me what's going on?"

"That's what I'd like to know. What *is* going on?" she demanded.

"I'm just concerned."

"No, I mean with her."

"Nothing is going on between us, Karina."

"I may not know anything about your work, Conrad, and I may not understand a blasted piece of music, but I've been around enough to know why two people avoid one another like you do."

"Karina..." His voice trailed off uneasily.

"Isn't that what's happenin' here?"

His eyes closed with the weariness of defeat. "It's not like that."

"You think I can't *feel* it. It's just like all those fancy articles say. There's no ending and no beginning. And it isn't just the playing. You're tied into her every move. You're not *worried* about her. You can't breathe right now. Not knowin' where the other half of you is. Have I about got this right?"

Conrad's jaw clamped as he listened to Karina's summation.

"I thought so," she said and walked out the door. Conrad closed his eyes. A piercing objection twisted in his gut. He hated hurting Karina, hated seeing the pain in her eyes, the raw need, but he couldn't deny her accusations. Alexandra was like breathing.

Hours later, Karina returned, and from the look of her wet hair, she had taken a long walk in the drizzling rain.

"She's at a hotel called Claridge's. She checked in three hours ago," Karina stated flatly.

"No, Max. I'm fine. Why?" Alexandra glanced around the room. No champagne on ice. No flowers. No notes. It was exactly what she wanted.

"Conrad's called here twice," Max said.

"Conrad?"

"Yes. Is there anything wrong?"

"No, Max. I've told you."

"Then why all the secrecy? Why aren't you staying at the Beaufort?"

"I just wanted to be anonymous." What she didn't say was that she needed space. She needed time. She needed to breathe her own air, not share it with people who might take it from her.

Karina took off the last of her makeup off in front of the bathroom mirror. She could see Conrad's reflection as he walked up behind her. He placed his hands on her shoulders.

"I never meant to shut you out." His eyes were tender and giving. It reminded her of the first time he'd come up behind her while she had been washing the dishes.

Karina patted his hand, then completed her regime and replied wearily, "Some places can only be filled by one woman."

"You know how much I care for you."

"Yes. I do know."

He bent to kiss her, and she wrapped her arms around him, trying desperately not to cling.

During the first day of rehearsals, it was clear they were having a problem with the new piece, and Purcell insisted on utter privacy. It was the music Conrad had written after he left Alexandra. Both Purcell and Conrad understood that the music was Conrad's attempt at finding resolution but to Alexandra, it was a new composition that Purcell wanted to premiere in London.

Purcell rented a plush, beautiful manor just outside the city, and had a car shuttle Conrad and Alexandra from their hotels to the house each day until they were finished. Food was sent in. New coffee was prepared every few hours by an assistant, but other than that there were no interruptions. This was the first leg of the European concert, and Purcell had no intention of having it blown because his performers were having interpretation problems.

"I don't understand. You two see eye to eye on almost every piece of music Conrad's written. Why is this one different?" he asked them both, but neither of them had answers. Alexandra had tried to move into the music as Conrad instructed but each time they played it, it felt wrong. By the end of the second day, Alexandra sighed as dusk approached. "I think we need to scrap this. Go back to the music we played in the States."

"You want to tell Phillip?"

"No… but really, Con—" She flinched. Her guard had wavered, and she had called him by the nickname reserved for Max and Sebastian, and on occasion, even Purcell. It felt entirely too chummy. Especially in the current surroundings. The assistant, who came in every three hours, had just left, but not before building an intimate fire.

"Look, Alexandra, maybe we need to try something else for a while, get back into our rhythm."

She glanced at him, and then diverted his gaze by attacking an extremely difficult set of scales. Conrad answered with his own scales, brusque and technical. Their eyes met again. "Fine," she said. "We'll do it your way."

An hour later, Purcell appeared. "Darlings. The cavalry's arrived with some delightful nibblies to replenish your strength." But even Purcell's humor couldn't lighten the mood as he whisked into the room. Alexandra poked at the food while Conrad drank coffee and Purcell chattered excitedly about ticket sales and press.

"Right. I see I have a captive audience here. When should I send the driver back for you?"

"Give us a couple more hours," Conrad said.

"How's it going then?"

Icy silence answered him. "Look, I'm popping over to Royal Albert. Why don't we hang it up for the evening and go to dinner?"

"I'll have dinner in my room, thanks," Alexandra said, rising to put on her coat. "But I wouldn't mind catching a ride back with you."

The next day they started in again, neither of them speaking other than to ask a question about whether this phrasing felt right, did the clustered harmony have the effect they intended, or did it still sound as if they were going in opposite directions? Morning bled into afternoon and the assistant brought them tea and scones at five. On and on like this it went until one evening Purcell arrived to hear their progress.

"Okay, then. Let's hear what you've got for me," he suggested.

They rose wearily and returned to the pianos. Alexandra's tempo was off, and Conrad sounded flat.

"Well..." Purcell muttered as if trying to convince himself.

"What do you think?" Alexandra asked.

"It's... better... yet a certain..." Purcell began, then shook his head. "Rubbish! You're not in sync. It still sounds forced."

"We can work it out," Conrad said quietly.

"You sure, Connie?" Purcell asked. "Because if not, I think we should just go back to what we know works. We can't afford a learning curve in London. I'll have my secretary bring around some food if you want to keep trying?"

"Sure."

"Is that okay with you, Alexandra?" Purcell asked.

"I think we should stay here until we get it," she agreed.

"Right. Then might I offer a suggestion?" Purcell positioned himself between the two pianos. "Your pianos sound like unhappy lovers who've just had a bloody squabble and tried to make up, but with very little success. Now you're being polite, and the performance sounds just that. Polite. I've never pried into your personal lives, and I don't mean to now. But we have a helluva lot riding on this leg of the tour. So, fix it. Or be done."

He glanced from Conrad to Alexandra. "I'm off. Please, no dead bodies when I return." He walked out as he had entered, with great flourish. His departure created a heightened awareness of each other.

They sat alone, with the embers highlighting Alexandra's stark cheekbones as she sipped a café au lait. A long silence followed in which both attempted conversation.

"Looks like our knuckles have been rapped," Alexandra finally said.

"I don't think he means it as chastisement. I just think it's worrying him."

"How about you? You worried?"

"I think…" Conrad attempted, then merely put up his hands in a gesture of helplessness. "I think we approach this in different ways because we feel differently about the core of the music."

"I don't think it's the music. It's the interpretation."

"Maybe…."

"You said this piece was about redemption. Can you explain what you mean by that?"

Conrad paced a moment. "Like the cliché, 'learning from your mistakes,' only finding deeper meaning. A way to exonerate it."

"You mean one-up the error."

"Something like that."

"And these mistakes that we're talking about," she began, "were they of the common garden variety mishap, or the kind of blunder that sinks its teeth into you?"

"The latter."

"And were they the product of an error in judgment, or something more eviscerating, like cowardice?" When she pegged him directly in the eye, she was thinking of Sebastian, but he couldn't know that.

"Nothing so dramatic." He paused a moment. "Thinking one set of circumstances to be true, and then discovering later it wasn't the case." Then more quietly, "Thinking one thing to be true of your nature but finding out otherwise."

"Conrad, quite frankly, I'm not getting anywhere talking in vague metaphoric circles."

"I'm sorry. I didn't mean to be obscure."

"Maybe that's what's wrong. Maybe you have no idea what you mean."

"Then I'll be direct." A muscle twitched at Conrad's cheekbone. He took a long moment, then cleared his throat. When he looked up at her, she could see he was struggling. "Alexandra… this music was written for… for you. Please try and meet it halfway."

She couldn't hide her surprise. The heat from the fireplace flushed her cheeks as she thought of the music. Of course, it made sense. No wonder she had been so conflicted with the piece. This was how he felt her, the underneath of her. The notes slid into place now; an aching melancholy, a desecrated opium den, a taste of what was, what could have been, and the haunting search to return.

She felt her heart skip a beat, a yearning flush.

She returned to her piano and leaned back to stretch her weary muscles. As she did so he silently moved behind her, and she felt his hands gently massage the stiffness at her shoulders.

The instant he touched her she froze.

"Redemption is also about forgiveness," his hands dropped and he walked to his own piano.

They began playing. A new tension permeated the music. She heard the subtle plea for mercy in his plaintive interpretation, and in her response, a delicate thread of clemency opened up the music. When his eyes met hers, honest and resolute, her defenses melted away and she let him see into her for the first time since they had come back into each other's lives, a startling moment of disclosure. She then closed her eyes and began to let the music take her over, swaying, unaware of the world, only the music *and his hands at her shoulders.*

His broad beautiful hands scaled the keys without effort

Just the simple touch of them teasing the muscles that ached from hours of repetition, those elegant torturous hands easing the stress, suffusing her with energy,

Deftly climbing the difficult scale, a teasing decrescendo as he parsed the music with gentle strokes

his fingers, now gently stroking her neck, trailing exquisite waves of rapture upon her skin,

his agile fingers insinuating his dominance over the keys, delicately owning them

owning her as she felt his breath at the curl of her ear, chilling down the ridge of her spine,

staccato racing of her heart as her fingers trembled over the pizzicato seduction.

He answered her yearning, questioning desire with the sultry mystery of the lower octaves, beckoning to her,

his hands parallel executioners as he reached from behind, slowly kneading the taut skin of her stomach, a rhythmic possession of her aching skin, contouring her breasts, a sculptor's hands, inching down her ribcage. Her blouse deftly swept from her skirt, she could feel the heat of him as he pushed gently forward into her, his hands now circling her waist, wrenching her to face him, his mouth hot upon her own as—

He stopped.

It took Alexandra a full moment to break herself from the searing intimacy of the music. She looked up and saw Conrad bent over the piano, a lock of ash wood hair grazing the keys.

Slowly, he stood and walked to her, then dropped to his knees in front of her and burrowed his head in her lap. A strangled, muffled sound emitted from him that might have been her name.

Everything came back in an instant. The intense yearning, the unparalleled joy, and the pain. The devastating agony that had taken her years to defy now crept up her throat until she was paralyzed.

Conrad's arms slid around her body, until he finally glanced up at her, his eyes as unveiled as she had ever seen them. She hesitated only a moment before lowering her hand to his head, smoothing his hair with tender absolution, holding him to her, and for the first time suffusing him with the strength to bear their love.

They lay in one another's arms, caressed by the flickering candescence of firelight. Alexandra tried to speak the words she'd waited so long to say, but barely a whisper escaped her lips as she felt Conrad's skin melting into her own.

"Conrad, I…" But he put fingers to her lips, and then replaced them with his mouth, kissing her so thoroughly she began to feel the weightlessness she only felt with him where the world disappeared and only the two of them, existed.

She explored his face, touching his cheeks, her hands sweeping through his hair, kneading the tight muscles in his shoulders, traveling down the length of his torso to the swell of his hunger for her. She began to tease him gently with delicate fingertips, then more forcefully began to stroke him, his desire for her mounting, growing harder, until he closed his eyes, and let himself be taken by her hands, mastering him in a way no other woman had or could. He heard Karina's voice echo in his ears, gentle accusation—*you breathe for each other*—as Alexandra forcefully commanded him to a place where consciousness fled. He became aware only of her hand upon him, gentle thrusts urging him to climax, until at the last moment he gently pushed her aside, held her down at the shoulders, and entered her so gently she couldn't breathe, gasping as his elegant thrusts became their syncopation, each effort fueling her endless hunger.

His lips tenderly travelled over her body, prickling her skin, his mouth so deliberate, certain… as if they had been making love for years without the aching span of time between them.

His hands, those artful beautiful hands, cradled her face, as he held his lips just a breath from her own. His gaze seared into her revealing himself, fully, completely, sharing her pain, showing her that he had suffered as deeply as she had these past years. His eyes laid everything bare, and she could scarcely breathe from seeing him so utterly raw and exposed. She wanted him deeper, ever deeper, so that no separation could be possible between the two of them again.

As his bottom lip touched hers, a swelling warmth that began at the base of her womb shot up through her stomach until a tumult of pleasure began to cascade upward, growing ever wider, stronger. His lips upon hers, kissing her so deeply it created an almost unbearable intensity of feeling, swelling now, heavier in her chest. An unbridled intoxicant began to sweep through her entire body as she began to come, an agonizing climax, pulling her under until she had to have him come inside her. Grasping his buttocks, she brought him to the same ecstasy he had given her, vaguely aware as she began to come again, that he choked out her name in rasping shudders. Their bodies continued to tremble in waves, slowly weaving into a gentle, lulling melody, breathing in concert until sleep caressed their joyous finale.

Later, with little time left before they had to re-enter the real world, Alexandra traced the lines of his face, his eyes, his nose, and the delicate curve of his ear, precisely capturing this moment in time.

"Sebastian came to see me the night before I left."

"He came to see me as well." She shifted, surprised. "What did he say?"

"He had a confession to make."

Alexandra sat up afraid and hopeful. "Yes?"

"He said I was a fool not to tell you I love you."

She frowned. That was the last thing she expected to hear. "That was a confession?"

"No. He confessed that he knew all along how we felt about one another, and he was sorry if he ever stood in the way. He knew that I would never take what wasn't mine."

"How noble." Alexandra laughed derisively at his choice of words.

"Alexandra..." He pulled her close. "You must always remember it doesn't matter what Sebastian has done. He lives in hell. I only hope he finds a way to make peace."

And she wondered for a moment whether he did know Sebastian's terrible truth, but he silenced her question with his lips.

"In the intricate dance of a love triangle, Descending Thirds mirror the cascading descent of hearts, each note a step away from harmony, echoing the bittersweet symphony of longing and betrayal. As emotions shift like falling notes, alliances form and dissolve, creating a melody of passion and jealousy. Each descent pulls one closer to another, yet further from resolution, crafting a haunting tune of love's relentless pursuit and inevitable discord."

Byron Harrington, Poet

Sebastian's execution was sloppy and melodramatic as he ravaged the piano, botching the fine melody of his concerti. He had been drinking steadily for three days in Antonia's lonely, decaying manor. An empty bottle of Dewar's Scotch sat next to him as he methodically destroyed the lines of his music like an abusive parent, punishing the demon he had brought into the world so that his sins might be forgiven.

He had speculated endlessly over the last three days what might have happened if he hadn't done it. What if he had taken a different track? What if he had gone by it honorably? Honor, the endless task set before man to continually prove his worthiness. He ran every scenario he could think of. Spiraling into a sort of madness, he could only draw one conclusion. He would have dried up after the Ketterling tour. He was a second-rate hacker with first-rate charm, who possessed a flair for feigning virtuosity. People wanted to believe he was that good. Conrad had it right. He would have been perfect at managing his career. He would have found the angle. He always found the angle.

The question remained: how could he live with himself? After drunken days of hazy soul-searching, he deciphered an elaborate solution. As Alexandra had requested, he would make himself clean. He would make amends for his despicable past. Yes, he thought in that concise moment of intoxicated clarity, he would help other musicians as his retribution. Maybe he would start producing. Find talent and expose it to its best potential. If he helped fledgling artists as his mother had done, maybe if he devoted the rest of his days to it, he would be able to look at himself in the mirror again. It was a good plan.

Yes. It was an excellent plan. He lumbered to the attic, with its secrets, memories, and Antonia's myths. This too he would make clean. Get rid of it. Stock and barrel.

It was an onerous job, lifting all the piles of sheet music. Sweat streamed from his face as he heaved the boxes laden with musty pages, his mother's operas, all the pages of composition from their favorite composers; a retrospective of Bach, Mozart, Beethoven, Schubert, Prokofiev, Liszt—his beloved Liszt. All these he and Conrad had mastered. Of course, Conrad had cut a far wider swath than had Sebastian, but that was irrelevant now. All of it flew into the boxes. Music that belonged in the past, that never should have made it into the present. He began hefting the lumpish boxes down the attic and lugging them to the statue of Hermes where he planned to torch the lot, a purging sacrifice to the gods.

Back in the attic, he gulped the remains of a scotch bottle, then tossed it aside as he made his way back to the haphazard boxes at the other end of the attic.

And then he stopped. He saw the mahogany chest with the bronze CJD monogram embossed above the hinge. Conrad had packed his belongings in this trunk before he left on his grand nomadic adventure. It had never occurred to Sebastian, until this moment, to look in it.

He only momentarily struggled with the morality of breaking into what wasn't his.

Taking another swig, he fumbled with the catch, then lifted the lid. He pulled out sections of music, more obscure composers, pages of a cryptic language Sebastian couldn't understand. He tried to fathom the complex hieroglyphics in the dim and dusty chamber, the blur of his intoxication rearranging the keys and chords. More notes spooled off the pages. He tried to grasp the musical message hidden within, when suddenly...

No... what was this? Something wasn't right here. Why hadn't he noticed this before? No, it simply didn't figure. He stared at it seemingly forever, as if by doing so, it would finally make sense. He stared at the pages so long he nearly passed out.

Abruptly he bolted upright.

He grabbed the chest, toppling it over, the pages cascading around him, covering the floor. He tore through sheet after sheet, strangled sounds coming from him as if he were a tortured animal, as if his rage would never stop. If only he had looked here. First.

He fell to his knees, scrambling like a child, catching his breath as his eyes widened. No… no it couldn't be. He ripped through the rest of Conrad's belongings without a shred of respect, brutishly destructive.

He wiped at his face, blinking rapidly, doubting his vision, trying to understand what he was seeing. He frantically searched for another page and saw it was torn in his frenzy. He began to gather all the sections and carefully began piecing them together, sweat, tears, and snot mingling together.

Bundling the music to his chest he jumped up and dashed down the attic stairwell. He rampaged through the house, his fury building, pulsing thickly through his veins, a fever spreading as he careened against pictures, ripping them from the walls, smashing Antonia's trinkets to the ground.

Lumbering to the piano he crashed against it, dropping half the music in his hand, and in a drunken choreography, he stumbled over his own feet and bashed through the French doors out into Antonia's gardens.

He kicked the patio furniture, staggered past Hermes's statue, past Antonia's favorite alcove. Sepia-toned memories flashed through his mind—all the many moments in her garden of evil. That's what it was… a garden of evil, where man was tempted to his lesser self. Not his lesser self, the only self he came into the world possessing. For it was altogether possible he had no choice in the matter, ruined not because of his nimble machinations of fate, but because fate had dealt him the only hand he could play.

Running as fast as he could, blinded by the darkening forest, he escaped the taunting glares from the Gods who knew of his imperfections.

It didn't matter. He knew if he followed this direction he would find it. He floundered, tearing through craggy branches, overgrown foliage. And as he ran, his boyhood steps dogged his heels.

A branch gashed into his cheek, pain searing like a flash of bright light. He saw Connie's young face coming out of his coma, his pale cheeks and eyes so huge. Conrad, weaving in the garden, listening to the earth.

Sebastian's veins pummeled against his skin, his chest heaving as he continued to run. He could hear his ragged breathing, a distorted choral refrain as the vision of Alexandra suddenly came to him. Her neck. He thought of her long, beautiful neck framed by the caress of her braid, how his hands had spread across her flat stomach, how he could break her body in two had he wanted to, she was so slender, so fragile. He wondered what she would think when she found out.

Was that his own raspy quest for air, or the breathing of the forest pounding in his head? He saw the clearing, faint in the dim light. Gasping for breath, he made one last dash, one last long-distance effort. How proud Conrad would be of him to pull it out like this. How amazed Antonia would be in this moment. She would finally understand what her son was made of. What she had made of him.

Sebastian reached the clearing, huffing before the deep crevasse that spanned eternity, and stared out at the vast beyond. His muscles burned, blood surging, alcohol and adrenaline infusing him with a strength and vigor he hadn't felt in years.

What was that?

Suddenly he could hear it. Through all the noises in his head—the forest sounds, the thick percussion of his veins. Yes, he began to hear it. The strain of his concerti—his grandfather's music—inside him, all around him, as the music sprang from the ground and shot through him.

Sebastian laughed out loud, his gleeful surrender resonating with the music swirling around him. Infused with the sounds of the earth, Sebastian suddenly knew his brother's secret. He finally understood. One had to be mad to hear the music. And now he, too, could hear it, this delicious symphony for salvation. In a state of grace, he surrendered to it, humbled by the force of his self-destruction, and fully accepted that which many cannot: his own, preciously flawed, humanity.

He held the concerti high above him, then assumed the position of the cross. He tipped forward and saw the ground far, far below, the sheet music twisting gently in the wind as he released it.

The trailing echo of his brother's name shattered the lonely silent forest, a diminuendo of his plea, as Sebastian plunged to his death.

"Lesser artists borrow. Great artists steal."

Igor Stravinsky

The graveyard was filled with hundreds of mourning fans. Conrad and Karina stood to one side, Alexandra and Max to another. She stared at all their images, a surreal tableau as she listened to the reporter's somber tones on the evening news, repeating what she'd already experienced first-hand.

"The world of classical music played tribute to arguably one of the greatest composers of our era, Sebastian D'Antonio, heralded as the second Bach, who became internationally famous for his "Immortal Romance Concerti." The picture cut from the cemetery, where the masses had gathered in record numbers, to a biographical sequence of Sebastian's life.

The night she'd heard the news haunted her, obsessed her. She couldn't erase the image of the red blinking light the night she returned to her London hotel. Flinging herself on the bed, wearily excited, her muscles weak with exhaustion from Conrad's lovemaking, she'd nearly ignored the voicemail indicator on her phone. But the small, pulsing signal was relentless, so she had gotten up to retrieve her messages.

She listened dumbly to the recording of Max's distraught voice. When she placed the receiver back onto the cradle, she heard the scream from somewhere outside her, as if through a long tunnel.

The tour, of course, had been canceled. After the call, Purcell had made arrangements to fly everyone back to the States, and Alexandra, scheduled on a different flight, didn't see Conrad until the funeral.

It was held on one of those bleakly ominous days when clouds burrow close to the ground, as if Heaven knew it had occasion to scoop up fading spirits. At first, Alexandra couldn't find Conrad through the mass of people, the musical literati, press, women she knew to be Sebastian's old flames, and those who were titillated by the gossip, many of whom believed his hedonism had finally got the better of him.

There he was. In one of the many clusters of black dotting the plush grounds of the cemetery. She began to walk to him. A choked whisper of disbelief escaped her lips as he turned, and she saw him full on. Dark shadows highlighted his sunken cheeks. He was ashen and mechanical. Alexandra's heart trammeled in her chest, her senses tuned to him, absorbing his pain, wanting to own it, clutch him from it, knowing it wasn't possible.

She walked to him and slipped her hand into his, but his fingers remained still and frozen.

"Conrad..." Her voice was lost in the crowd.

He moved his head to the side, but his eyes wouldn't meet hers.

"Oh, God, Conrad." Alexandra's voice broke with the pretense of being strong. "Please let me—"

She stopped when he suddenly turned to face her.

She couldn't speak because his eyes, those beautiful blue-gray eyes, had lost every bit of light.

"I... I can't. I can't talk with you right now." Conrad's voice was hoarse.

"Of course not. After the service. We'll go—"

"No. No..." His words spun out into the void. "I can't, Alex. I just can't bear... I can't do it."

Alexandra was immune to the grand words of the priest, lamenting the "terrible tragedy of a shining light, taken from us before his time." All she could hear was Conrad's cutting refrain. His unforgiving eyes.

She couldn't tolerate both their losses. She had suffered, endured, and waited. Only to have it all taken away. She wondered now if she possessed the strength to endure losing Conrad. Again.

It was difficult enough to make peace with Sebastian's death, for even after his betrayal, a part of her still loved him. But without Conrad, life seemed extraordinarily pointless.

The music was an anguish Karina only knew too well. She felt awful for Conrad and sad for herself, but after learning what had happened to Conrad's brother, she promised Purcell she would stay with Conrad until he asked her to leave. Now, she shifted uncomfortably in the cold and austere manor, as Conrad sat at the grand piano and played with absolutely no expression on his face. He had been completely inscrutable since they had arrived days earlier, where he had focused primarily on the arrangements for his brother's funeral. In all her life, Karina had never seen such an eerie and bizarre place. And, of course, Sebastian's despair and destruction seeped from every corner.

Conrad could no longer tolerate being at the estate and, almost without words, it was decided Karina would return to Santa Fe. He drove her to the airport in silence. Wordlessly, they waited at the gate until she couldn't stand it any longer.

"What will you do?" she whispered softly.

She wasn't sure he heard her as he waited a long moment and then turned to look at her. He attempted a smile, but it was almost more heartbreaking than when he was stoic.

"Will you," Karina started, not sure she wanted to really know, "stay in New York?"

He shrugged.

"Will you be coming back?"

He looked at her then.

Suddenly he took her in his arms and held her close. Then slowly they parted.

He took Karina's face in both hands and tenderly kissed her lips. "Thank you, Karina. Thank you for everything."

Max set the large magnifying glass to the side. He let out a long sigh, then put a gnarled hand to his glasses, pulled them from his face, and began to rub the lenses in consternation.

"Mein Gott." He packed his briefcase up and headed out the door.

When he arrived at Alexandra's he was taken aback by how pale she was. She seemed to have lost weight, and the dark circles underscored tears and sleepless nights.

"Alexandra, dear child."

She embraced him, but her movements lacked energy. She seemed rote and impersonal as she led him into the living room. He paced while she fixed him a drink as the snippets about Sebastian's brilliant career echoed in the background.

He was clearly agitated and trying to find the best way to approach Alexandra.

"Alexandra..." Max stumbled. "While I was at the estate, helping Conrad, I discovered something..."

She handed him a drink.

He took a huge swallow to brace his nerves. "Mein Liebchen, I don't know how... how to tell you this."

Alexandra barely had the energy to speak. "I know."

His eyes met hers and he saw the bleak resignation in her eyes.

Days later, she called. There was no answer. Then suddenly the phone was disconnected. It was only through Max, assisting Conrad with the remains of the D'Antonio estate, that Alexandra discovered Conrad had closed the house, unable to touch a thing, and had sent Karina back to Santa Fe.

Alexandra choked on the words she needed to get out. "Is he going to join her?"

"No." Sadness filled the old man's voice. "*Ahhch, Verdamdt.* All Conrad's fine strength seems to have evaporated. He's lost, Alexandra. Lost."

"What... what can I do?"

"Do?" Max repeated. "I don't know. All these years his music has been his life support and those close to him, merely accents. But Conrad's absolutely crushed by Sebastian's death. Far more, even, than I would have expected."

Sadly, she watched him clean glasses with his shirt for the umpteenth time. When he placed them back on his face, he turned to Alexandra, nodding his head as if he had just figured something out. "You know my dear, perhaps there just might be a silver lining in all this misery. Perhaps the only way Conrad may heal and become one of us is by being torn in half."

But in the weeks to come, Alexandra didn't see any signs that he was capable of reaching out. Only silence. His dissipation, in turn, destroyed the moments they had shared before the world changed. It didn't matter if Purcell and Max rationalized that he needed time. All Alexandra knew was that he had finally come back to her, only to be wrenched away, again. And in doing so he had destroyed the only other thing that had ever mattered to her. Music.

Purcell set a single miniature crimson rose beside her as he bent to kiss her cheek, then sat opposite Alexandra at the Garden Café.

Over the course of lunch, Alexandra barely touched her food as Purcell kept up the conversation for them both. When they were finished, they walked around the grounds, Alexandra twisting the stem of the rose in her hand.

"Look, darling, I can't tell you how sorry I am for you both. I know it's the devil of a time for you, but you must put it behind you. You must get your strength back, return to the world, your music. In the end, it's always about the music."

"Yes." Alexandra was unconvinced. "That's what Max always says."

"It's where you will get your strength."

"Strength?" A pained irony filled her voice. "How might that happen? I can't stand to even look at a piano, much less play it."

"Give it time, Alexandra."

"That's all I have now."

He walked her to the parking lot and handed the valet his ticket.

"I'm sorry, Phillip. About the tour. Did you lose a lot of money?"

"Nothing compared to what the world's lost in your talents." Purcell kissed her forehead as if she were a little girl. "But I'm a firm believer in remaining optimistic. And I find it hard to believe that God placed the two halves of you in this world without intending for you to eventually come back together again, restored to your natural state as a whole."

Alexandra shrugged and Purcell continued. "I don't know if that means anything, I don't know if it's meant to be personal or professional. But it will sort itself out. In the meantime, let me know if there is anything I can do. Anything at all."

She paused, knowing he had made a promise she was going to ask him to break.

"Where is he?"

"I can't say as I know." Purcell's performance was unconvincing. "You know he blames himself, Alexandra. He won't give himself an ounce of space around this whole sordid mess."

"They were so close... strangely so... bound by their mother and something else. Something I couldn't ever figure out." Alexandra stared at the rose in her hand. "Why is it that those things you find passion for, things that start so fine... so true and beautiful, end up like this?"

She handed him back the wilted rose, browning at the edges, already showing signs of decay.

The valet pulled up her car. She clung to him momentarily, then backed away.

"Damn."

She turned to him, and he put a key into her hand.

He smiled grimly. "He's at my Soho studio."

For the next few days, Alexandra spent most of her time merely sitting in a chair, lying on the bed, tossing through sleepless nights knowing where he was and knowing she couldn't go to him. Sometimes she read, mostly she couldn't concentrate. Later, when she could no longer sit alone with herself or her thoughts, she took long walks. In a city of millions, how could one be so isolated, she wondered, as her feet traced miles of sidewalks.

She stared at the crestfallen arc drooping from her cigarette and suddenly extracted the irony she had been searching for. It is music that has destroyed me, that has destroyed us all, she thought as she sat in the vacuum of her lifeless apartment. She wondered if there were others, like herself, living in their bodies without hope of connection, suffering various states of catatonia. Numb and broken, fragile pieces scooped up off the sidewalk as if a life could shatter and blow away like unnoticed debris.

Would music ever again be about passion that compelled her every moment, when playing was an exalting triumph, not a bitter, twisted form of breathing?

They said genius gave birth to insanity, but she believed it was the other way around. Not having the gift drove the most accomplished artist mad. Sebastian's end was proof. And how many others suffered in the name of music, tortured from the illusion they had talent? How many had strangled the joy of life from every minute of their daily existence in the name of their art? How many awaited a lifetime for a few mere tense moments to determine whether, they in fact, could claim a career? Or felt the cloying tug of resentment as they chilled at another's success, wanting desperately to be in their shoes because they were just as good, just as fine, just as presentable. Where did persistence end and luck begin? Fame, as indiscriminate as a lottery, handed to the random chosen few while the rest, the mass of quarantined poets, writers, musicians, and sculptors, ached in obscurity and self-pity.

Suffocating. She was suffocating from her morbid thoughts, her memories of them. She grabbed her coat. She walked through the past, under an overcast sky resurrecting memories to try and make it somehow be worthy of having lived it.

God, how she was drained from the last ten years. Of knowing them. Both of them. She couldn't sleep at night without dreaming of Sebastian, and she spent her waking moments with their images playing like movies in her mind. Damn them. Damn them both. When had they not touched her life? When had she had a moment's reprieve? She tried to remember the last time she was happy. Really happy. The first year after the Ketterling. Before Sebastian. Before Conrad. Before men had become a third party to the only piece of her she could claim. She had never really been in love with Sebastian. She knew that now. And Conrad, she had loved too much.

No. No, damnit. She wasn't going to let them do this to her.

Her pace quickened. A sense of purpose forged within her. She accepted the inevitable. She had to go back. She had to return to the estate. If she saw it one last time, she could exorcise the demons, put an end to it all. She called a cab and gave the driver the address.

She gazed at Antonia's manor for some time before she walked up the rounded graveled entrance beyond the leafless trees. She studied the storybook mansion, now sagging in decay, as if the massive structure knew that it had lost its life's blood, and there was nothing left to sustain it. No straggling artists, no laughter, drinking, chattering of dinner guests, no Sebastian. No Antonia to keep the allure of the apocryphal artist alive.

Alexandra still had a key and let herself in. The front entrance, always filled with sunlight, was now cold and uninviting, as was the rest of the house as she wandered from room to room. Everything felt mid-stream; some half-filled boxes cluttered about, sheets covering some of the furniture, half the paintings were still up, and the others were leaning against walls nearby. She lingered at the many portraits she had passed by all those years, took note of Antonia's sculptures and exotic artifacts, then wandered to the French doors and looked out to the pool, now covered by leaves, the water a murky brown.

She followed the final steps of Sebastian's path of destruction, then headed up to the library, filled with echoes of yesteryear. She shut her eyes, and heard the slivery strains of *their* music, but it gave her no comfort, the chords now twisting into an aria of resentment and unresolved anguish. She couldn't stand it any longer, quickly turned, and closed the door. The music stopped.

When she wound her way from the library, she couldn't help herself. She entered Conrad's room, stripped bare, save his bed. The numbing exhaustion that lived inside her skin swept over her, and she thought maybe she had made a mistake. God, why was she tormenting herself? She had to leave.

She quickly ran down the stairs and through the hallway directly to the living room where the Bösendorfer gleamed in a sudden ray of sun, the only living matter standing out in the cavernous room. She slowly walked to the behemoth, brushed a finger against the burnished wood, and sat. A long sigh escaped her lips as she let her hands trail the keys on the piano, thinking this was where it had all begun, and she flashed to the night Sebastian first played his concerti, so arrogantly proud as he claimed his grandfather's music.

Ruins now. Everything had been destroyed in this place, this estate Antonia was so proud of. Antonia's grand illusions had spread like a cancer, Sebastian's malignancy had contaminated every part of this home, blighting everything he touched, right to the last moments of his life.

She gazed at the side table by the piano that still held Sebastian's drinks, and two ashtrays filled with stubbled butts to the distaff sheets of music, still scattered on the floor. She bent, picked them up, and absently placed them at Sebastian's table, next to the photo of him and Conrad.

Something registered, like a peripheral flash.

She was drawn back to the sheets, staring at the hand-scored page that faced her. This was unlike any of the sketch paper she had seen Sebastian use. She picked it up. A fascinating array of notes painted a melody... a very familiar motif, not unlike those of his concerti. She turned the page, scarcely giving it another thought, then stopped.

Confused, she leaned closer to the sheet music in her hand.

For a moment it didn't register, but as she continued integrating the notes on the page, her mind began to battle this startling reality, for she refused to believe what was staring her in the face.

"No... no..." She felt faint, closed her eyes, then opened them again, feeling as if she were reliving a nightmare—only one couldn't possibly relive this nightmare. Yet, every detail enhanced the impending terror she was beginning to feel. "No. No... no. This can't be!"

Her heart began to pulse rapidly, her breathing quickening. She stared at the page for the longest time trying to make sense of what lay before her, then grabbed the papers and stuffed them in her purse.

It was too late to go to Armory's Music Supplies that night, so Alexandra had to wait until the next morning. She paced half the night away, smoking cigarettes, trying to piece together broken clues to a larger picture, creating one vivid scenario after another, each improbable and preposterous.

"I don't think Sebastian killed himself over his... his grand deceit," Alexandra called Max at three in the morning. "Not after so much time had lapsed."

"But Alexandra, why else would he have done it?" Max replied groggily.

"Look, I want more than anything to give him the benefit of the doubt, but..." Alexandra didn't want to be rude to the dead. "I just find it a little difficult to think Sebastian suddenly gained a conscience and could no longer live with his deeds. No." Alexandra inhaled from her umpteenth cigarette. "Something happened that night. Something drove Sebastian to that cliff."

"Alex, I know how difficult this is for you. All of us." Max sighed. "But, in the end, it's quite simple. He couldn't live with the guilt. And my dear," Max concluded, "unfortunately for him, I'm sure the future looked very bleak."

But Alexandra knew Sebastian loved himself too much to get rid of his own company.

She called a cab at 9:00 am and drove straight to the music supply store. She rushed in, looking disheveled and frantic. A slender youth in his late teens came to assist her.

"May I see your manager?"

"Sure. He's here in the back." The gangly youth led her to a back office, where a shrunken and aging gentleman with stooped shoulders sat eating a donut and drinking coffee.

"Can I help you?" he asked.

"Yes." Alexandra stammered, flustered. "How long have you... I mean has Armory's, been selling sheet music?"

"Since 1910." The old man looked as if he might have been there since then.

"I'm sorry, I don't mean just this store. I mean since they began printing sheet music altogether."

"That would be 1910."

Alexandra closed her eyes, trying to calm herself. "Thank you." She tried to steady her legs as she walked from the store.

Outside she drew in huge gulps of air as she hailed another cab. "Broadway and Mercer."

She surveyed her reflection in the elevator up to the loft. Her French braid was unruly, her skin, more pale than usual. She wondered if she'd simply gone crazy.

She leaned against the studio door for a long time, listening to the tenor of notes coming from inside, sad and slow, filled with a tortured pathos and regret she was only beginning to understand. She shut her eyes, bathed in helpless desire, longing to see him again but terrified to do so.

She opened the door with the key Purcell had given her and saw Conrad leaning over the keys, his normally erect posture bent in pain, lost in the music. She studied his unshaven face, almost swallowed by overgrown silky blonde hair, a halo to his suffering. She moved in his general direction, but it seemed to take forever to get there. Only when she was right before him did he become aware of her presence.

"Alexandra?" his voice was thin, as if it came from far away, yet he continued to play.

She impatiently put a hand to his to stop him playing.

"Conrad."

He grinned weakly and raised eyebrows in an uncharacteristically cynical gesture. "What are you doing here?"

She swallowed. Hands trembling, she pulled out the pages from her purse and laid them before him, so he could clearly see the sheet music, the sheet music upon which **Armory's Music Supplies** was embossed in the faintest and smallest of Helvetica fonts at the backside right-hand corner.

"Why...?" Her voice was a whisper.

He sat there a moment and then looked at her. He was about to say something but instead shrugged in a gesture of resignation.

"Please, Conrad, you have to tell me why."

A long moment passed. He put his hand to his forehead as if trying to remember, frowned, and said quite simply. "Because he needed me."

"I needed you. The world needed you. How could you..." She felt tears welling and wanted to stay calm. She tried to quell her aching for him, the old need in her for him that now battled with something new, frustration and impatience.

"You have to make this make sense." She heard her voice escalating. "You have to justify ruining three lives, Conrad, and a helluva lot more than that!"

Conrad slowly lifted his face and saw her suffering. He moved a hand toward her, but she backed up.

"I'm waiting." Her eyes unveiled, painted the most tangible form of pain he had ever witnessed.

"It's strange how something so innocent, with such pure intent, can end up so distorted."

She saw how badly scarred he was and now fully understood the inestimable toll Sebastian's suicide would take on him. He was reed thin, his richly vital eyes, cloudy mirrors. She thought she saw an involuntary quiver to his hands as he reached for a cigarette, his strong hands always so sure.

"Tell me."

He lit his cigarette, and he let out a long sigh with the smoke. "It all started during one of Antonia's parties."

She watched him as he journeyed back in time.

"All the usual suspects were there. All the stragglers, Antonia's pets, her protégés... projects. And, of course, Sebastian eating it all up." Conrad paused, a twitch at his left eye. "He loved it—all the entertaining—the nightly parties, loved playing host to Antonia's worldly hostess, and no matter how tedious those nights became, they reveled in it. Especially Sebastian. He got such a kick out of it all."

Conrad remembered Sebastian's sensual grin and dark wild hair now and how Antonia used to run her hands through his dense mane back in those years when he was just starting to change; Sebastian maturing, becoming more of a man and less of a boy.

"'Of course he exists, doesn't he?' Antonia had winked at me. 'Conrad, explain to these good people why I call him Sebastian?' and later, after the telling of this unruly legend that had long lost hope of ever being tamed, she would denounce any skeptics with 'Proof! Proof is the genius that beats in Sebastian's veins. Anyway, if you want proof, it's up in the attic.'"

Conrad paused a long moment

"A few days later, I was up in the library working on some new music, my music, when, on a whim, I began to play around with what Antonia's illustrious great-great-great grandfather's music would have sounded like." Conrad recalled the day as if it were yesterday, a blazing sharp image, the way the sun angled in the library, how the stiff parchment of the paper before him absorbed the ink, notes blossoming into melody.

"What if he *were* a descendant of Bach's and what if Franco Ricci had written these fabled concerti? What would have motivated him? What body? What textures? It fascinated me."

He'd started with the single motif, a melody he had heard in his head while he watched Antonia's graceful carriage moving through the world she had created, a goddess in her revelatory stance, picking a rose here, musing through her mythical gardens there. "Of all the old masters, I adored Bach. It was fun playing around with it, dissecting pieces, creating a pseudo-Baroque-inspired counterpoint, and then assimilating it to a more romantic sensibility. It was just the kind of thing Antonia would love, I thought. Add some Rachmaninoff extravagance, throw in some Chopin for angst. Hell, it was just a gift. For Antonia."

The notes built upon themselves, twirling about as he gave them life, and later they appeared upon the page as fast as he could script them, hearing the beauty of Antonia so richly in his head, mingling with Sebastian's laughter floating up from the pool. He had stopped a moment and walked to the window, watching Sebastian performing swan dives for Antonia, aping for her. He had her in stitches, the best of who Sebastian was, making his mother happy. Making everyone around him happy.

"I wrote all of the concerti that summer."

Even as Alexandra heard the words her mind continued to reject them. "But… the authentication."

"I spent hours copying the music the way it was written in the old days, making notations precisely as they would have been, and orchestrating it all for the instruments of the day. I then went to copious efforts to age it with various sources of stains and heat." He remembered how intent he had been. The deliberate operations, the crinkling of the pages and re-ironing them, scuffing them about to deteriorate the paper as authentically as he could.

"I made two copies of everything I wrote, my originals on the Armory sheet music I kept in my trunk, and the second copy on the parchment.

When I was finished, I searched for the perfect spot to hide the music. In the attic, I came upon a box that held Antonia's sheet music, from the days she toyed with opera, and stuffed them in so that they might be found. Then I was going to lure them up." He shook his head. "If Sebastian had really looked closely, really examined the pages, he would have seen in a minute…" His voice trailed off.

"He didn't want to see. He wanted to believe."

"He had been taught to believe," Conrad set the record straight, waited a moment, and continued. "It was a prank. It was nothing more than a childish prank."

Alexandra closed her eyes, rapidly trying to sort out the past years with this new reality imposed over the old.

"I was going to let Sebastian in on it. Then show them to Antonia. I knew it was the sort of thing that would cause her no end of joy, that she'd parade the music around to those unbelievers, that she'd retell the story again and again. I planned to give them to her as a gift afterward." He slumped as he ran a shaking hand over his face. "It was all for Antonia."

Alexandra shook her head, barely able to believe what she was hearing. "But… why? Why *didn't* you tell Sebastian?"

"It was the same summer Antonia had the first of her seizures. We never knew when they were going to strike, or how long they might last." Conrad's cheek twitched involuntarily. "We spent the rest of the summer at the hospital, then back home with nurses. By the time we returned to school, I thought better of it. I was going to show the music to Antonia, but her health was never quite reliable after that, and then time passed, and I suppose I forgot about it. That is until I heard Sebastian playing the music the night I returned home."

Conrad got up and walked to the window to look out at the skyline of the city.

"And what was the truth?" Alexandra asked.

"The truth?" Conrad thought back to Antonia that day, so weary, but in her there remained the spirit of one who would always bend life to her terms. He remembered her frail hands squeezing his own. *Promise me that you will help him make beautiful music, and that he will never know the truth about himself.* The promise that had changed all their lives.

"Conrad?" Antonia had cocked a fragile eyebrow, her voice dry with resignation. *"You know... my great-great-great grandfather... he wouldn't have known Bach from the Beach Boys. He was nothing more than an olive farmer."*

"Conrad?" Alexandra's voice brought him back.

"Who can ever tell what the truth is? Truth is as unforgiving as myth. And ever-changing. Like the myth Antonia built around herself, her protégés, all of us. As if she steeped Sebastian in a hotbed of creativity, a Garden of Eden, filled with the struggling artists she picked up along the way, he'd somehow take seed, begin to ripen, and develop into the prodigy she always wanted him to be."

"Even if he had no talent."

"But he did have a talent."

Alexandra's eyes turned sharply to his.

"He had a talent to be human." And in Conrad's voice was all the regret of his own limitations.

"Are you going to—"

"No." His tone was resolute. "Sebastian will be remembered as a brilliant composer whose light shone on us all too briefly."

"And what about you? You never wanted credit for the... music? *Your* music."

"I never put much thought to fame. What bothered me was that Sebastian needed it at all costs. Yes, I'm sure I thought about it. But, quite frankly, it didn't matter."

She thought how like Conrad to be so untouched by his own masterpiece.

His eyes found hers, a spark of warmth flaring. "It's never been about that for me."

"Yes. I know," Alexandra said quietly.

For a moment they sat in peaceful silence before Alexandra picked up her purse to leave. His eyes met hers, gentle and unwavering, a sad smile filled with lost potential.

"Alexandra..." Conrad's voice caught in a chasm of uncertainty. A question hovered between them, but they both knew answers weren't possible in that moment. Tentative, she placed her palm against his jaw, needing once more to touch him.

"You're not at all the man I fell in love with." Her lips brushed his, a dry, fragile kiss. "You are so much more. Goodbye, Conrad."

She lowered her eyes, not trusting herself to look at him again, then turned and walked from the studio. Once outside, she took a deep breath as she glanced up and down the street, then slowly descended the stairs. She walked as quickly as she could away from the loft so that she wouldn't turn back.

And as Alexandra walked, Max's words echoed in her mind. Maybe Conrad needed to be torn in half to heal. Maybe Max was right. Maybe only through great pain would Conrad become more human. Or maybe, Alexandra thought, Conrad would always be a genius savant, who would live every bit as much a rich and textured life as mere mortals—rendering the most savage lows and exalted highs—only the way he would live it was through his music. And when people heard his music, they would hear God.

A rush of adrenalin surged through her and she felt the itch in her fingertips that made her need to feel ivory under them. A tease of excitement surged through her chest because this time she was going to reclaim her music, knowing she would never allow anything to compromise her talent ever again.

Alexandra would play for *her* purpose and her purpose only, and that meant using her unique gift to make people feel the glorious notes and melodies from the brilliant and flawed composers that came before her. She no longer questioned who she was, or who she was performing for. She smiled. It was time for Alexandra—her music, unattached to anyone else's desires, or genius.

Embracing the cold wind, she walked down the darkening road, alone, but full of hope and determination as she disappeared into the night.

The End